A qualified parachutist, Harvey Black
Intelligence for over ten years. His expe
surveillance in Northern Ireland to ope
Berlin during the Cold War where he fe:
dragged from his car by KGB soldiers.
a more sedate life in the private sector as a director for an international
company and now enjoys the pleasures of writing. Harvey is married
with four children. For more from Harvey, visit his website at
www.harveyblackauthor.org.

Also by Harvey Black:

DEVILS WITH WINGS

Devils with Wings
Silk Drop
Frozen Sun

THE COLD WAR

The Red Effect
The Black Effect
The Blue Effect

FORCE MAJEURE

Paralysis

PRAISE FOR HARVEY BLACK

"Harvey Black's geopolitical survey is beautifully intertwined with personal stories of his characters. He builds tension relentlessly… looking forward to the next book!" – Author Alison Morton

"…tension, suspense, action, intrigue and moments of tenderness too which are a nice touch. I recommend the book entirely." – Steven Bird

"Factual along with gripping, takes me back to the days of the BAOR and what we all trained for… look forward to the next instalments." – Jon Wallace

"This book needs another one to follow on and complete the story. A similar story to Tom Clancy and his *Red Storm Rising*." – A Jones

"This is the best read I have had in ages very techno and extremely fast moving. It could have happened." – TPK Alvis

"This is a thriller in the style of Robert Ludlum or Tom Clancy. Credible characters and fast pace… thoroughly enjoyed the roller coaster ride!" – Author David Ebsworth

"The build-up is gripping and enthralling." – Author Sue Fortin

"If you have enjoyed *Chieftans, Red Gambit, Red Storm Rising, Team Yankee* etc, then don't miss this. Well written, realistic, unputdownable."
– R Hampshire

PURGATORY | HARVEY BLACK

FORCE MAJEURE 1

SilverWood

Published in 2015 by SilverWood Books

SilverWood Books
30 Queen Charlotte Street, Bristol, BS1 4HJ
www.silverwoodbooks.co.uk

ISBN 978-1-78132-341-0 (paperback)
ISBN 978-1-78132-342-7 (ebook)

British Library Cataloguing in Publication Data
A CIP catalogue record for this book is available
from the British Library

Set in Bembo by SilverWood Books
Printed in the UK on responsibly sourced paper.

To my sister and brother-in-law, Shirley and Paul

CHAPTER 1

The squadron of British Challenger 2 tanks were lined up on the eastern edge of the forest, hull down in berms recently prepared by the Royal Engineers. Out to their front, they had a pretty clear view out to some three or four kilometres, a perfect killing ground for when the enemy tanks eventually turned up. The border in this area was over fifty kilometres away, but the Soviets had crossed that three days previously, and had already been seen passing Sums'ka oblast, using the T1705 as one of their main axes.

Major Warren reacquainted himself with the key landmarks, not that there were many, the flat open fields providing very few points that could be used. But, on the other hand, it made it ideal tank country: both for fast movement across the open ground and for the tanks with their 120mm guns, waiting to take them out. It was 0330, and the entire regiment was on stand-to, not just as a matter of routine, but because they knew that today they would have to fight.

Although negotiations were frantically being progressed, it hadn't stopped the Russians from crossing the Ukrainian border in force. The southern stretch of the eastern Ukrainian border, from Velyka Pysarivka in the north to Novoazovs'k in the south, bordering the Sea of Azov, jutted out, like a bulge, into the western border of Russia. The Russian Army commander had decided to pinch out the bulge by thrusting southwest through the area of Velyka Pysarivka and northwest through Novoazovs'k with a further attack from the Crimean Peninsular. The continuing escalation between Russia and NATO, allied with Ukraine, had instigated the movement of Western troops to secure Ukraine's neutrality. In the south, US forces bolstered the Ukrainian army. A British, German, Dutch and Polish force strengthened the north. One British brigade was lined up with the Russian main northern axis of attack. Although the Russian Army was pushing against the entire Ukrainian front, pinching out the bulge was a major objective.

The Major's radio crackled.

"Zero-Bravo, this is One-One-Bravo. Incoming. Out."

Major Warren dropped down into the tank, sealing the hatch in the process.

"All call signs, this is Zero-Bravo. Incoming. Batten down. Good luck. Out."

Seconds later, the first artillery shells hit the British lines. Along the two-kilometre brigade front, 152mm shells exploded, the Russian 2S19s keeping up a rate of fire of eight rounds per minute. The bombardment increased as the 203mm shells from the 2S7s added to the barrage. Within a matter of minutes, hundreds of Russian artillery pieces were delivering a devastating barrage against the British defenders.

The side of Zero-Bravo's Challenger lifted fifteen-centimetres into the air as a projectile exploded close by, the squadron commander's tank reverberating from the force of the blast. After thirty minutes, the bombardment suddenly stopped, the silence almost as disconcerting as the barrage itself – almost.

"All call signs, this is Zero-Bravo. Report. Over."

"Zero-Bravo, this is One-Zero. One-Two intact, lost contact with One-One. Over."

"Roger that. Out to you."

"Zero-Bravo, Two-Zero—"

Before 2nd Troop could continue to report, Regimental Headquarters interrupted. *"All call signs. One-One-Bravo. Incoming aircraft. One minute. Out."*

"All call signs, Zero-Bravo. Air to ground attack imminent. Out."

Before Warren had finished putting the handset down, the air around them became violent again as, first, Sukhoi Pak FA aircraft released precision-guided bombs which were followed by the older Frogfoot ground-attack aircraft. Again, the British lines were battered. The Russians didn't have it all their own way as the gunners pounded the Soviet artillery with counter-battery fire and surface-to-air missiles swept some of the attacking aircraft out of the sky. High up in the air, British Typhoons clashed with Soviet air superiority fighters, there to protect the vulnerable ground-attack aircraft below them. Silence fell over the squadron again, and Major Warren thrust his shoulders out of the turret, calling to his tank troops to stand by. His binoculars soon showed him the mass of Russian T-90 tanks powering across the open ground. Columns of earth shot up amongst the fifty-ton tanks as British artillery zoned in on the advancing tank regiment. The T-90s' 125mm smoothbore guns moved from side to side as the tank commanders and gunners searched for targets, knowing that British Challengers would be waiting for them. Out of his squadron of twelve tanks, Major Warren knew that at least two were lost, or unable to communicate, but he could still pack a punch with those that were left. Mechanised Infantry Combat Vehicles could be seen dispersed amongst the advancing Russian force, and he dropped back down inside his tank and gave orders for his squadron to open fire as targets presented themselves. His gunner fired, the Charm 3, with its depleted uranium, armoured piercing round, left the barrel at over 1,500 metres per second, striking the Russian tank just over one second later, bringing the armoured vehicle to a halt, killing the crew, smoke billowing around it as the vehicle caught fire, fuelled by the exploding ammunition within the fighting compartment. Finding a second target, he ordered his gunner to fire again. Although a direct hit, the T-90 kept coming. They shifted to a second berm before the Russian tank commanders zoned in on their location, from where they took out two more tanks, the squadron accounting for thirteen T-90s and twelve Russian BMP3s. The Russian commander ordered his attacking forces to withdraw. The British clearly needed more softening up before he had another bash at punching through their lines.

The British squadron shifted again, keeping the Soviets guessing as to their locations, knowing it would start all over again once the Russian commanders issued the appropriate orders.

CHAPTER 2

Three generations of a family died today. Charlie and his wife, Elsie, hurried as best they could as the warning sirens wailed throughout the city of Birmingham. A brilliant white light blocked their view of any objects or colour around them. Charlie's cataract-covered eyes blinked out, as if a switch had been flicked turning his world, and his wife's, into darkness. Even before his thoughts turned to how he and his wife were to get home, blinded, the rapidly inflating fireball, expanding out to a thousand metres in a matter of seconds, engulfed them, vaporising clothing, flesh and bone. The lives of the two lone-surviving grandparents of the Watson family had just been snuffed out.

Two kilometres further out from Ground Zero, Charlie's son, Craig, laden down with bags of food and other essential supplies, part of the stocks he was reluctantly building up to survive the Armageddon he was sceptical would ever happen, pushed his way through the shop doorway of the Tanning Studio, clashing with others fighting to get under cover as they were all bathed in the blinding white light of the detonation 500 metres above their heads. He crashed down onto the floor in a tangle of arms and legs, his shopping bags spewing their contents, which were crushed by pounding feet as others followed him in. It mattered not as the blast wave and searing heat struck the three-storey building on Church Street. The glass frontage erupted, showering the occupants with bullet-like shards of strengthened glass, piercing their bodies with hundreds of splinters. They had little time to register the shock, or the pain, as the concrete and brick structure above and around them was blasted into oblivion, disintegrating around them, the larger surviving chunks crashing down onto their fragile bodies, smashing skulls and limbs, killing all.

Two and a half kilometres away, Mrs Annie Watson, with Peter and Josh in the back of the Ford Focus, slammed on the brakes as the car in front came to a sudden stop, the driver blinded by the flash of the nuclear explosion. Looking over her shoulder to chastise the two children for fighting had saved her from being blinded herself, but not from careering into the back of the now stationary car in front – the car's crumpled front, cracked windscreen and exploding airbags testament to the violence of the collision. Shocked, her body thrown forward into the tightened seat belt and air bags as a car hurtled into the rear of her car, her first thoughts were for Josh and Peter in the back. As she twisted round, free of the now deflating airbags, to check on their safety, their eyes wide open in panic, the shockwave struck. Sudden and violent, a hurricane force blast flipped the car over in front, its upside down chassis flying over the car as her Ford Focus was thrown up into its flight path, locking the bonnet with the upturned Vauxhall, a second, third and fourth vehicle piled into the coupled cars forming an entangled mass that was in turn engulfed by the collapsing buildings around them. Annie managed to reach out to her two children for a mere few seconds before the buckled roof, deformed by the weight of the cars on top, mixed in with chunks of masonry and other debris, pressed down, compressing their fragile bodies, literally squeezing the life out of them. All along the road, hundreds of cars had been similarly destroyed. A few of the many drivers and passengers, although trapped and badly injured, initially survived. But none would make it out alive. Not because of the second and third nuclear bombs that struck the city, or the fallout that would slowly irradiate them, but simply because there would be no one able to help or in a position to initiate a rescue. In fact, any rescue attempt anywhere in the city was unlikely to appear for weeks, if at all. The last of the Watson family, along with 400,000 others, had just ceased to exist. Of the remaining population of over two million that lived in the Birmingham, West Bromwich and Dudley area, three quarters of a million had received injuries ranging from crushing injuries, third-degree burns and high doses of radiation to minor injuries. Any injury was unlikely to receive treatment, unless administered by friends or family.

GROUND ZERO | ZERO HOUR
ILFORD-ROMFORD-DAGENHAM TRIANGLE, LONDON

The nuclear ball of flame detonated a kilometre above northeast London, over a million degrees of heat at its centre, vaporised all it touched. Expanding out to a radius of one kilometre in the first second, reaching two kilometres in less than ten seconds, the now 6,000 degrees centigrade fireball ignited anything flammable in its path, consuming everything on route, eating into flesh and bone, hungrily engulfing all that lay before it in a deluge of hot, fiery gases, laying waste to all it touched. The searing heat stripped away clothing and flesh, leaving blackened, broken corpses.

Lawrence brought his hands up to his face, seeing and smelling the roasted skin as his fingers melded with the bubbling flesh on his face. But he felt no pain: there were no nerves alive to signal the agony that lay beneath the surface. However, as his clothing smouldered and his flesh melted, shock and then unconsciousness took over. A woman close by screamed again and again, barely audible above the noise of crashing buildings and the roaring rush of air as the raging fires in the centre of the city sucked in more and more oxygen. Her screams were not from pain. Like Lawrence, Meihui felt no pain. Her screams were brought on by the spectacle of her flesh melting before her eyes, before she too lapsed into silence as her body succumbed to shock, then oblivion. Neither would survive that day, but would be consumed by the ever-growing firestorm.

Further afield, running towards his home, overtaking other panicking pedestrians, Mike saw the route ahead of him light up as if he was under the beam of an extremely powerful searchlight. Resisting the temptation to slow down and look back, he pumped his arms up and down even harder, picking up speed, a sense of dread driving him forward, but to no avail. The hurricane-force wind, levelling buildings in its path, picked him up by his legs and carried him in its destructive grip, smashing his body into the side of a multi-storey car park, fracturing every bone in his body. Beneath him, another pedestrian was pinned to the concrete facing, his body peppered with shards of glass and debris. The man died almost instantly. Any person not under cover was thrown around like a rag doll. The tempest continued on, tearing asunder every building blocking its way, wreaking havoc.

GROUND ZERO | ZERO HOUR
ILFORD-ROMFORD-DAGENHAM TRIANGLE, LONDON

Oliver Price was proud of his fallout shelter, following some of the advice and plans provided in every daily newspaper for a full week. The pamphlet he and his family had been provided with by the Government, *Protect & Survive II*, was a carbon copy, with a few minor amendments, of the older Cold War booklet issued in the sixties. When the peace talks over Ukraine had broken down, it had been hurriedly issued by the Government a mere two weeks before the bombs struck. It had been his bible. The closet under the stairs of his family's four-bedroom detached house had been recommended as the ideal location for a shelter. Inner doors from two of the bedrooms had been placed up across the entrance of the small room, padded out with two single mattresses, and a wall of sandbags stacked up against those. Oliver Price had even sandbagged the treads and risers and placed props inside the closet to shore up the wooden stairs and the additional weight above their heads. He felt his family couldn't have been more secure. The minute the sirens had wailed, he and his family, pre-warned by a BBC emergency broadcast, had fled to their temporary abode, tuning their battery-powered radio to the emergency station. They sat in their cramped space amongst their contingency food supplies, cans of beans, tins of chopped ham with pork, soup, sausages, peas, along with a bottle of their favourite Reggae Reggae sauce to give some added spice, and other items they considered essential to their survival should the unlikely nuclear event occur. Large plastic containers of water lined the walls. First-aid items, consisting of various medicines and bandages, and placed there by his wife should they be needed, were stowed on shelves. Oliver was confident they had enough provisions to last them for twenty-one days, the time recommended by the Government before you exposed yourselves to the contaminated outdoors. They laughed and joked in the dark, treating it as a game with their two teenage daughters, confident that no one would be insane enough to release nuclear weapons. Their older daughter, Alexandria, complained about not having a signal on her iPhone whilst Sophie tapped away on the family iPad, ready to test them all with a recent quiz game she had downloaded earlier. They saw nothing of the light that blinded many in the city, lasting only a few seconds but taking away the eyesight of many of the citizens caught out in the open.

The thermal pulse and blast wave quickly followed; first engulfing their detached home in a heat storm that defied anything they had ever seen or experienced before, smoke pooling under the ceiling as the door and window frames fed the flames. More was to come as the blast wave followed, shattering any remaining windows, pulverising walls, collapsing the roof, timber, masonry and tiles crushing down on the Price family's meagre defences. Although the blast extinguished the fire, once it had passed, smouldering flames reignited and a firestorm raged through that part of the city. Heat, dust and radiation penetrated the partially breached shelter, the family coughing and spluttering as they fought for breath, looking up as the stairs creaked and trembled above their heads, debris from the upper floor and roof struts bearing down on it. But it mattered not. The firestorm that followed engulfed their house, and many other homes in the area, consuming the oxygen at a phenomenal rate, feeding the flames, raising the temperature and replacing the life-giving air with carbon monoxide and carbon dioxide. Oliver, along with his wife and two teenage girls, gagged for breath. However, sucking in a vacuum, their eyes bulging in the dark, their hands clawing at the walls, scrabbling to get out of what was to become their tomb. They were slowly asphyxiated. But they were not on their own: tens of thousands had just been killed in the local area. Across the length and breadth of the country, 47 million people had either been killed outright, were in the process of dying, or would be dead before a month passed by. The majority of the remaining population, some 20 million people, had been, or would very soon be, exposed to radiation sickness, starvation and a future that could only be described as grim.

GROUND ZERO | ZERO HOUR
SALFORD-MANCHESTER-STRETFORD TRIANGLE

Shaheen staggered out of the jagged cavern that was all that was left of the office block that had been his place of work for the last ten years. Although it was daylight outside, the sky was now a deep dull grey as clouds of nuclear fallout rose up in a canopy of deadly nuclides and debris. A red glow flickered on the underside of the clouds, making a myriad of changing patterns, the mushroom cloud a modern-day skyward piece of art. Looking to his left down Lloyd Street, he could see plumes of thick black smoke spiralling aloft to join the rapidly expanding mass of filth and poison. He staggered slightly as he brushed dust and particles of masonry off his torn suit jacket and spat out the grit that ground between his teeth. His head spun as he dropped to his knees in between the ragged chunks of concrete, remnants of the building he had just left, his stomach heaving. Champagne and canapés splattered the dust-covered pavement as his body ejected the remains of last night's office celebration of the managing director's birthday. He had drunk more than planned after being informed that, once the dust settled on the European standoff between NATO and Russia, promotion was in the offing. He heaved again and again, emptying the contents of his gut until all he could retch up was the burning taste of bile. Through watery eyes, his head swimming, he couldn't mistake the bright red flecks of blood decorating last night's food. He retched until his sides ached and then became even more painful. A sudden trembling in his gut was followed by a putrid smell as he evacuated his bowels. A foul-smelling, blood-streaked stream of diarrhoea ran down his legs as he staggered to his feet, only to collapse, his legs could no longer support him. On his knees again as more foul-smelling liquid left his body at both ends, he scratched at his head, a sudden irritation that was in competition with the rest of the warning signals his body was emitting. The relief was momentary as he rubbed his scalp hard, mixing flakes of skin with bomb debris. A strange texture confused him as he brought his hand down to investigate, the clumps of matted hair causing his eyes to open wide, the discovery adding to the fear that was now racing through his mind. He was an intelligent man, a degree from Oxford University testament to that. Although a Masters in Maths and Politics, he didn't need a science qualification to inform him of what was occurring inside his wrecked body. As he lay down, the flickering lights of the burning city reflected in his dull eyes, his thoughts were of his parents and the woman who worked in the company office, who he hoped to take for dinner one day. Instinctively, as he closed his eyes, he knew it unlikely they would open again, or he would ever leave the spot he now occupied.

Purgatory – Hell on Earth…

CHAPTER 3

The soldiers lined up along the fence in front of the only entrance to the Regional Government Centre, their weapons at the ready. They looked intimidating and ominous behind their black respirators, eyes peering through the large single visor of their army issue General Purpose Respirators, at the mob in front of them. The camouflaged NBC suits, designed to protect the soldiers from the nuclear fallout, added to the aggressive stance being shown by the regional controller for this area. Plumes of frozen breath were exhaled from the black masks, baleful, menacing. The mob was screaming insults and demands, moving ever closer to the thin line of Regular and Territorial Army soldiers. The crowd's eyes were wide with fear, pain and a strong hint of madness. Beneath their thick coats, they shivered. Blankets draped across their shoulders, and scarves and headscarves wrapped around head and ears for additional warmth hid the horrific burns many were suffering from. Countless numbers of the civilians had raw, open sores, their hair shrivelled and burnt, skin melted into a sickly sheen. These were the survivors, ordinary members of the public that had found the strength to make it here. Many couldn't come. Many that had survived the exposure to super-lethal radiation and related thermal injuries, the consequences of a nuclear blast, were too sick to make the journey, suffering from severe radiation sickness, coughing and heaving up blood. They remained behind at the encampment, dependent on family members or friends to bring them food and water. Attempts had been made to set up tents closer to the Regional Government Centre, but that had been discouraged very quickly, the army and police forcing them away. Rows of large military ridge tents had been erected further away. The encampment had been set up on two wide open spaces, close to the banks of the River Nadder, to house the homeless.

"We're starving out here."

"Let us in. We need water, for God's sake."

"I bet you lot are living like kings."

Also with a scarf wrapped around his neck for additional warmth, the captain in command of the small force present looked behind as more soldiers joined him, lining up on the far side of the four-metre, razor wire-topped mesh fence. It made a good boundary line, identifying no-go areas, but certainly wouldn't stop a determined assault. He called the men forward, through the gate, to line up either side of him. He watched the ever-growing crowd, dust being kicked up from the layer of ash and fine powder that covered the once grassed area in front of the entrance to the site. The ash, although only mildly contaminated now, was still potent enough to exacerbate the illnesses already suffered by many. Continuing exposure would eventually affect the others. Generated by a small nuclear device detonated on top of RAF Chilmark, the wind had driven the heavily contaminated particles north-west, away from the RGC, but unfortunately drove the cloud across the village of Chilmark itself and other populated areas. Above the captain, the skies were dark, a layer of particles caused by the 300 million tons of dust thrown up into the atmosphere as a consequence of the detonations. Occasionally, a shaft of light from the sun would pierce the barrier, bathing the selected spot in a warm, yellow glow. But it would be many years before the Earth experienced the full benefits from its solar benefactor. In the meantime, the United Kingdom would slip ever deeper into a period of desolation as the temperature steadily declined, and the bitter cold made surviving an even greater challenge.

The mob moved closer, pushed from behind by the ever-growing additions to the crowd. The captain looked sideways at his sergeant, concern showing in his eyes as the front edge of the crowd moved to within three-metres of his soldiers and the gate. He nodded.

The sergeant lifted the megaphone close to his mask. "*Stay back. You must stay back.*"

"We need food and water," wailed the crowd.

"*We are not currently authorised to distribute food. You will be notified when the time comes.*"

"We must have water."

"*You must use your own rations until the food can be released.*"

"My children need food," screamed a mother.

The crowd surged forward another metre, those at the front pushing back, conscious it was they who were getting ever closer to the soldiers.

"Fix bayonets!" ordered the captain.

There was a clatter of steel against steel as the soldiers locked their eleven-inch bayonets into place on the end of their SA80 assault rifles. One bayonet clattered to the concrete slab at the entrance, testament to the nervousness of the men, many of them young, faced with such a hostile crowd. Some of whom may well have family somewhere out there.

"*Stay back! Stay back!*" reiterated the sergeant, adding to the message the now bayonet-wielding soldiers were giving.

The captain turned back towards his men. Clouds of white, frosty breath emanated from the line of masks as the tempo of their adrenalin-primed hearts increased, their lungs now demanding more air. "Now, follow orders, lads. If this gets out of hand, they'll be all over us, and the food reserves we have will be ravaged. Any hope those people have out there will be lost. Listen to my commands and be ready. If it plays out right, we can disperse them quickly." He turned to face the crowd again. "Bravo-Company. Ready!"

The soldiers to a man raised their weapons to the ready position.

"Let us in," bellowed the crowd.

"Above their heads, take aim."

The line of assault weapons lifted, pointing at an angle just above the mass in front of them. The protesters at the front pushed back again, finding the strength to move the crowd a few centimetres, before it surged angrily forward again.

"*Please move back,*" pleaded the sergeant. "*We will be forced to open fire.*"

"Bravo-Company, stand by."

The crowd had moved to within two-metres again.

"Fire!"

Crack! Crack, crack, crack!

An uneven volley of shots left the soldiers' rifles, rounds zipping above the heads of the crowd as some ducked while others panicked, pushing back against the mob, trying to weave their way through the throng, keen to escape, someone else's turn to be in the limelight. The baying crowd, now in the region of a thousand desperate refugees, regained their confidence and soon threatened the nine soldiers lined up against them. They came back angrier, more determined than ever to have their own way.

"Sergeant." The captain indicated that Sergeant Saunders should hand him the megaphone. At the same time, he withdrew his 9mm Browning pistol from its canvas holder. He moved back as did his sergeant until they were both in line with the soldiers.

"Food will be distributed when authorised. If you do not disperse, I will order my men to open fire."

The noise from the baying horde grew louder, and they inched their way closer and closer.

"Bravo-Company! At the crowd, aim!"

The rifles were locked into their owners' shoulders, and this time they were aimed directly at the crowd. The throng held for a few moments before those at the rear pressed forward again.

The captain turned to his men. "Do not, I repeat, do not open fire without my command." He turned back to face the crowd, lifted his pistol until it was pointed at a particularly verbose individual, and squeezed the trigger. The crack of the shot made his troops flinch, the 9mm slug taking the man in the chest, knocking him back into the arms of the crowd behind him. He fell to the ground, lifeless. Blood blackened his blue waterproof jacket, the rabble screaming around him.

"They've shot someone."

"They bloody killed him."

"The bastards have murdered someone."

Captain Redfern hissed back to his men, "Bravo-Company, over their heads." He turned back to face the crowd. "Fire!"

Crack, crack! Crack, crack!

It was enough: the crowd broke into a panic and ran, those at the front trampling over those behind them desperate to escape death. Within minutes, the mob had left the area, returning to the government-supplied tents or their own makeshift accommodation made up of plastic sheeting and blankets.

"That was a close one, sir. You did the right thing."

"I had no choice, Sergeant Saunders," whispered Captain Redfern. "There was no guarantee that the men would have obeyed my order to fire into the crowd. It was a gamble."

Sergeant Saunders nodded in agreement.

"Right. Everyone back, secure the gate, and I'll report to the controller."

The men dispersed, going back to their normal duties of guarding the complex from within the fence line. Captain Redfern headed towards the bunker entrance, passing between the high concrete walls that led him through the blast doors. He clattered down two sets of concrete steps until he arrived at the lower level, the hum of the generator to his left, next to the control gear, oil and water tanks. At the bottom of the steps, straight ahead, he entered a small room where he removed his helmet and peeled off his respirator. Next came his NBC suit. It wasn't ideal, but at least the majority of any contamination wasn't spread around the complex. When anyone came back in from patrolling the wider area, returning with their protective clothing heavily contaminated, they would change in a room on the upper floor where their outer clothing could be bagged up and showers were available. Once finished, he left the room. Turning left, he made his way down the narrow corridor, popping his head into the main control room that had been set aside for the army and police.

"Still getting rowdy, Alan?" the senior officer, a Colonel, asked.

"Yes, sir. They're getting pluckier each time. It won't be long before they become unstoppable. We've had our first civilian casualty."

"It's only thanks to your perseverance and crowd control that it hasn't happened sooner."

Alan ran his hands through his mop of black hair, a sadness in his eyes. "I'd hoped people would see sense."

"The police have handed out notices, and we've both explained to them that food will be distributed in a few days' time."

"I know, I know. Doesn't make it any easier."

"The men OK?"

"They're fine, sir, but I have my doubts that they will open fire if ordered."

"Only time will tell."

"Is the warehouse still secure?"

"For the moment. Like you, they've had to resort to shooting."

"Anyone killed?"

"No, not this time."

"Principal officer still adamant we wait?"

"Yes, Alan, there's no shifting him. It makes sense though. We know that a good percentage of the community stockpiled food and supplies prior to the strikes. We have to force the public to use those up first."

"Next week, then?"

"Yes, more than likely."

"We need more men for the next time they have a go."

A corporal, sitting at one of the four desks in the four by three metre room, a large map board with a chart of the area of Chilmark pinned to it behind him, held up a sheet of paper. "Looking at the latest sick list, sir, that's something we won't have."

"How many?" asked the captain.

"Two more down."

"Permanent?"

"They'll recover in a couple of days, but then…"

The corporal didn't need to say any more. Many of the soldiers suffering from radiation sickness would have a period of calm before the effects of the dose bit deep and their health deteriorated further until death finally overcame their fight to live. The majority had received some exposure as a ramification of the radioactive fallout. But, ensconced in the bunker, many were initially protected as a consequence of the ventilation towers covering the entire U-shaped block, filtering out the contaminants in the air. But, at some point, the occupants of the Regional Government Centre, as an upshot of their assigned duties, had to venture outside. Each carried a dosimeter, recording their exposure. The scientists, part of the local governmental team, would then check, record and monitor each individual's exposure readings.

"I'll take a drive to the hospital later and check on them."

"Take Sergeant Saunders and a second Land Rover with you. It's getting pretty hairy out there."

"What do the boffins next door say, sir?"

"There will be an update tomorrow. Not just on the status of the fallout, but also on their interpretation of what it all means for us. In the meantime, let's grab the principal officer and update him on this morning's events."

The captain looked at his watch. "If I'm not mistaken, there'll be a fresh urn of tea on upstairs."

The colonel laughed. "You read my mind, Alan. I'll get the PO. You and Sergeant Saunders meet us in the canteen."

"Sir."

Captain Redfern rotated on his heel, turned left, then left again, and headed back up the steps. At the top, he turned back on himself, then turned right, the common room, sickbay and male and female washrooms on his left. Opposite the sickroom, he pushed the door to the L-shaped canteen open and joined the half a dozen already in there. He acknowledged most of them: two from the communications centre on the lower level, three from the Department of Transport,

21

Energy and Environment. Round the corner sat a member of the fire service along with a uniformed policeman. The civilian members of the Regional Government Centre looked at him suspiciously, recognising where, perhaps, the true power of the new post-apocalyptic organisation might lie – although Captain Redfern and Colonel Bannister had never given them cause to feel threatened.

Captain Redfern dragged one of the tubular steel chairs out and sat at a table of the same ilk just as one of the housekeeping staff wheeled a trolley across with a large tea urn perched on top, surrounded by a stacked array of white china cups.

"Morning, Alison."

"Morning, Captain," responded the head of housekeeping. At twenty-nine years old, she was three years younger than the army officer and responsible for a team of five who cooked, cleaned and dealt with the laundry for the sixty-two occupants of this seat of government for the region of Gloucestershire. She smiled. "I guessed you'd be in."

"Apart from you, Alison, it's the attraction of the biscuits that always come with a sound cup of tea."

"Flattery always works, Captain Redfern, " she answered with a beaming smile, brushing her honey-blond hair behind her left ear.

Before he could respond, the door opened behind him and, followed by other members of the RGC, the PO, led by Colonel Bannister, accompanied by Sergeant Saunders, entered, the three of them joining Captain Redfern at the table.

"Morning, Alison," boomed the PO. "Treats today?"

"Of course, Mr Elliot."

The sergeant dragged over two additional chairs, one a bright blue plastic bucket seat, the other a tubular steel chair with a thin padded seat.

"Thank you," responded the PO, sitting himself down at the square Formica-topped table, unbuttoning his jacket, then gently smoothing into place his wispy grey hair.

They passed pleasantries with Alison as she served them a cup of tea each, two Hobnob biscuits tucked onto the saucer.

"Thank you," they all chimed, and she wheeled the trolley to serve the next group in the rapidly filling canteen.

Captain Redfern savoured his tea and crunched on a biscuit, not without a small amount of guilt thinking on the incident he had left only moments before.

"Getting ugly outside, Captain Redfern?" asked Elliot, the principal officer, dunking one of his biscuits.

"Yes, and they're getting braver each time. It won't be long before they make a concerted effort to try and overrun the site."

"They'll be sorely disappointed," added Colonel Bannister. "There's very little food here."

"Have they been targeting the warehouse, Colonel?"

"Yes, PO, but only in small numbers. With no transport, it's difficult for the crowd to make the journey."

"Somebody will stir them up. Then we'll see them in much larger numbers. What's the latest count?" Sergeant Saunders asked.

The PO pulled a folded sheet of paper from his now grubby suit jacket and studied its content. "The latest count is in the region of three to four thousand. But most are in a sorry state. Superintendent Collins has increased the frequency of patrols, but with only eleven constables they have to tread warily. It's only possible when they're accompanied by one of your patrols, Colonel. What are your current numbers?"

Captain Redfern answered on the colonel's behalf. "Twenty-eight, sir. I have assigned eight to the warehouse, which allows four on duty at all times. They also have a Scimitar reconnaissance tank, but it won't help very much if they're mobbed. But it's a good visible deterrent. I have ten men here, four more supporting the police, and six patrolling the general area, directing refugees to the camp and ready to respond to an incident wherever. They have a Land Rover and a Fox scout car. And, of course, Sergeant Saunders and myself."

"But two of the soldiers based here have just gone down with the sickness," added the sergeant.

"And the hospital has been swamped," the PO reminded them.

"When will a feeding programme begin?" the colonel asked.

The PO waited while Alison topped up their drinks, a special smile for the captain as she refilled his cup.

"Three days."

"Why so long, sir?" asked Sergeant Saunders.

"The straightforward answer, Sergeant, is that they should have their own stockpiles of food. It's imperative that we force them to use those up first. Also, we will have to use food as payment for any work parties that need to be assembled. And there's another factor we have to consider." He dunked his second biscuit. "Many will die of radiation sickness. If we feed those people, who will no doubt be dead within the week, we will have wasted valuable resources."

"That's a bit harsh," Saunders responded.

"The PO is correct, Sergeant Saunders," Colonel Bannister said in support. "We have limited resources which have to be husbanded carefully."

"When will MAFF start their operations?" enquired Captain Redfern.

The PO pushed his empty cup aside and kept silent as Alison gathered up the crockery. "Thank you, Alison. What delights have we got for dinner tonight?"

"Corned beef hash again I'm afraid, Mr Elliot."

"Ah, but the last one you did was superb. I shall look forward to it."

Alison beamed at the compliment and pushed her trolley away. They continued their conversation in their huddle.

"Thank God she's an excellent cook," added the colonel. "We must have thousands of tins of the stuff."

"To answer your question, Colonel, the Ministry of Agriculture, Fisheries and Food will start their survey in about a week. The radiation levels are still too high to send people out unprotected for extended periods of time. And," he continued, turning towards Captain Redfern, "they'll require some protection, which your men will have to provide. So, until we are assured of the security of this Regional Government Centre and our food warehouse, they will have to stay put."

"Any contact with the other regions, sir?"

"Only Berkshire and Exeter so far. And they're both in a mess and requesting support from us. Berkshire's RGC is buried under ten feet of rubble."

"What problems, sir?" asked the colonel.

Chairs scraped as other occupants started to leave, slowly filing past on their way back to their places of work.

The PO leant forward and spoke quietly. "Easier to say what problems they don't have. Exeter has no military, and the Regional Government Centre has been overrun. Their food supplies have been ransacked, and the officials are no longer in control. A member of the public has taken command and has forced the Assistant PO to contact us for help. The PO was killed during the takeover."

"Anything from Pindar or the Permanent Joint Headquarters at Northwood?"

"Nothing, Captain, nothing." The PO pushed back his chair. "I need to get on."

He turned towards Colonel Bannister, who also stood up. "I need a report on the warehouse security and the hospital as soon as possible."

"I'll get Captain Redfern on it immediately."

"Thank you, gentlemen. Good day to you all."

The PO exited the canteen, leaving the three soldiers alone, apart from Alison and two of her staff cleaning up behind the long stainless steel counter at the rear of the canteen.

"Take a patrol out to the hospital, Alan. Then check in on the encampment as well while you're out."

"Will do, sir."

"Take a sizeable force with you. We can't afford to lose any more men."

"We could take a couple of constables, sir," suggested Sergeant Saunders.

"Good idea. I'll speak to the superintendent. They can meet you up top. Right, let's get on with it, shall we?"

CHAPTER 4

*Tap, tap, tap…tap, tap, tap, tap. [O] Tap, tap, tap…tap, tap, tap. [N]
Tap, tap, tap, tap, tap…tap, tap, tap. [W] Tap…tap. [A] Tap, tap, tap,
tap, tap…tap, tap, tap, tap. [Y]*

Stan Keelan tapped back a response on the cold water pipe
that was connected to all the sinks in the Close Supervision Centre
(CSC) of F-Wing, HMP Wakefield. It was a single tap, followed by
three more: the letter 'K' confirming he had received the message.
He moved from the area of the sink and toilet and quietly approached
the steel door of his stark, cage-like cell. The only natural light was
from a small slit-like window, high up on the back wall. The light
bulb in the cell suddenly flickered into life, and he could hear the
doors of the other CSC cells being slowly unlocked and opened.
He stood in front of the hatch as it clanked open. The sallow face of
a prison officer stared back at him.

"Step back, Keelan," ordered Kennedy, a Senior Prison Officer.

"Certainly, Mr Kennedy."

Keelan took three steps back. Once the officer was satisfied the
door was clear, he shut the viewing hatch and unlocked the door.
Pulling the heavy steel door out and open, he stepped inside and
found himself stood face to face with Keelan's large shaved head.
Keelan wasted no time. Wrapping his huge arm and muscled bicep
around the back of the head of the sickly, underweight guard, he
pulled him into the cell. At the same time, the home-made shiv,
a sharpened piece of metal with fabric wrapped around the one end to
form a handle, was thrust deep into the man's stomach. He pulled the
prison officer's head tight into his chest, muffling the man's screams
as he withdrew the blade and slammed it into his abdomen again and
again. The officer found one last vestige of strength and reared his
head back, spluttering his last breath, spraying blood over the smiling
face of the giant who held him in his clutches. His attempts to break
Keelan's grip were futile as the blade dug deep for the last time.

Keelan allowed the lifeless body to drop to the floor. The officer's eyes, deep in his gaunt face, stared back. Keelan wiped the blade on the leg of his grey prison trousers and peered through the doorway, seeing two other guards lying on the floor of the CSC, without doubt dead like their senior officer. He took one last look at his cell and stepped out. He walked past the pool table in the centre and headed for the gated entrance where another prisoner was unlocking the barred gate from the other side.

Keelan was shocked by what he saw. Although he had always kept his head closely shaven, as did many on the wing, the prisoner on the other side of the bars looked very different. His skull was hairless apart from a few tufts hanging lank across his forehead. His grey-looking skin hung in loose folds on his face, red and brown blotches adorning his head and stick-like arms.

"Christ, Isaac, what the hell's happened to you?"

Isaac forced a smile, a black space where two of his teeth were missing. "You should see some of the others. I'm one of the lucky ones."

"Shit. Let me through."

Isaac stood aside as Keelan walked through the now open steel gate.

"Hey, Doug. Are we on?"

"Hey, bro." Douglas Salt, a tall twenty-four-year-old, shambled across to his fellow CSC cellmate, swinging an iron bar in his right hand.

"We in control?"

The young man took off his silver-framed spectacles and wiped his forehead with the back of his hand. "Completely. But you gotta see the main wing."

"Yeah, I've just seen Isaac."

"He's one of the lucky ones. Some have got their skin dropping off. Makes us feel sick."

"They've kept that quiet."

"Now we know why we've had limited access to the rest of the wing."

"We need to get moving before the authorities get their act together and we have the filth on us."

"There's only about twenty guards here, and half of them are in the prison hospital. Looking at the CCTV, I can't see any sign of the police responding. I doubt the guards had time to sound any alarm. The takeover was pretty smooth."

27

"Keelan buddy, it's time we got out of here," suggested Withers who had just joined them.

"Yes. Round the boys up. Just our lot. I don't want any of the other fuckers tagging along. Me and Doug will meet you at the end of the wing."

They parted. Keelan and Salt made their way down the centre of F-Wing. Either side, the cell doors were wide open, and they could see prisoners lying on their beds. Coming too close to one of the cells, Keelan's senses were assailed by the odour of sour vomit, urine and faeces making him gag. The faces that stared back from their beds were in as poor a state as Isaac. Above, on the upper level, the odd prisoner peered over the balcony, one of them calling down asking what was happening. Salt and Keelan ignored them, remaining focused.

They made their way to the reception area where two more guards were sitting in the corner of the control room, handcuffed and under supervision. They too, along with the prisoners supervising them, looked unwell. In fact, it appeared as if the high-risk prisoners from the CSC were the only ones that had come through the events of the last three weeks with any semblance of health, their isolation working to their advantage for once. They had seen the build-up to the war on the TV, and couldn't miss the sound or reverberation of the explosions that had rocked the prison.

Salt shuffled through some papers on one of the desks, then a lunch bag, pilfering two cans of Coke, one of which he tossed in the direction of Keelan. Half a dozen prisoners made a noisy entrance into the control room, wanting to exit the prison before the authorities arrived.

"You lot can fuck off. We're busy," Keelan called back over his shoulder.

The heavyset ringleader of the group, a chair leg swinging in his right hand, stepped forward and placed his left hand on Keelan's shoulder. Keelan, his back to the group who had just entered, swung round to his left, and his huge right fist connected with the prisoner who had the audacity to lay a hand on him. The crunch of gristle was clearly audible as the man's nose collapsed under the force of the blow. Blood and snot sprayed the area. The convict staggered back, arms cartwheeling as he tried to maintain his balance, failing, and crashing into the men he had arrived with. Three additional prisoners came in behind the intruders and quickly laid into them with home-made clubs, chair legs and a broken pool cue. The Intruders, severely battered, withdrew, dragging their bleeding bodies to safety back inside one of the wings.

"Dickheads," scowled Doug.

Keelan cast his eyes over the three that had just beaten up the intruders: Todd Withers, Milo Gill and Mickey Wicks. Doug Salt moved to Keelan's left, a big smile on his face. "That's them told."

"Let's get out of here," ordered Keelan.

After spending a few minutes gathering anything that could be of use, particularly any food and water, all five exited the main entrance of the prison. The generators, still operational, provided enough power for some of the key functions, the security doors for one. For the first time in years, the convicts now found themselves on the other side of the reflective windows that lined the control room. The reinforced prison windows had survived the ferocity of the tail end of the blast wave that had struck Wakefield.

All took a deep breath, savouring the outside air rather than the smell of sweaty bodies, disinfectant and stale cooking. But there was a taint in the air, their overpowered nostrils unable to immediately discern the smell of ash, dust and lingering death.

Keelan crouched down next to a wall on the left, peering over at scattered beer barrels in the backyard of a brewery next to the arches of the railway viaduct that ran alongside it. "What the hell's that smell?" he uttered.

Salt crouched down next to him. "Smoke. Smells like someone's had a bloody big bonfire."

Milo Gill joined them. "Christ, there must have been a hell of a fire after the bombs."

Salt rubbed his foot in the layer of grey ash and dust on the concrete path that ran down towards the shuttered vehicle entrance of the prison behind them. "Look at this shit. Been more than a bonfire."

"Hey, a brewery." Gill pointed in the direction of the large brewery sign on the building opposite.

"Never mind that," scowled Keelan. "We'll find some more salubrious surroundings later. Let's just get away from here for now."

"We need to change out of these," suggested Salt, pointing at his grey prison clothes.

"Good point. I always said you were a smart fucker, Salt," Gill complimented him.

"Let's do it." Keelan waved them forward. "Watch out for the Filth," he warned.

They all ran across the road and headed down Parliament Street, red-brick brewery buildings, streaked with black soot, either side of them.

"Here's a pub," called Mickey Wicks, the fourth member of the group, pointing to a small pub on their right, peering through a broken window.

"Yeah, somewhere to sit and wait for the Filth," growled Salt.

"Keep moving," snapped Keelan. He beckoned them forward, the sound of glass crunching beneath their boots and trainers.

"It looks like it's been looted," observed Todd as they moved past it.

The five men reached a T-junction. Keelan quickly scanned each way, also glancing back over his shoulder ensuring they weren't being followed. "This way." No one questioned him.

The group headed down Westgate, passing beneath the steel span of the rail bridge above. On either side of the street were abandoned cars, either left for lack of fuel, electrics burnt out from the effects of Electro Magnetic Pulse, a by-product of the nuclear bombs, or just burnt out along with the blackened line of shops.

"Where is everybody?" wailed Todd.

"It's like a bloody ghost town," joined in Mickey.

They stopped at a crossroads allowing Keelan to get his bearings. Drury Lane was to their left, the darkened Theatre Royal opposite. Ahead, they could see a church spire.

"Keep going. We'll head for the church." Keelan had decided.

"Going to wash away your sins, Stan?"

"Shut it, Todd!"

"Hey, only kidding, Stan."

They passed more shops, either burnt out, looted or both. Still no people. They looked hungrily at the fast-food cafés, disappointment coming quickly as they discovered the state of those differed little from the rest of the shops on the grey, dust-covered street. Just as they arrived at fork in the road, Marygate forking left while to the right there was an open-plan shopping precinct, Salt, hearing a noise, brought them to a halt before shoving them towards the shopping centre. "Get out of sight," he yelled.

"It has to be the cops," panicked Milo.

They had no sooner run for cover when they heard the roar

of vehicles coming from the direction of Marygate and the Bull Ring. Salt urged them to take cover inside one of the shops, the glass fronts and doors blown or burnt out. Just as Milo was dragged in cursing, a green army Land Rover, followed by a Saxon armoured troop carrier, came into view turning right onto Westgate, heading away from the concealed escapees. Perched in the back of the open-topped Land Rover, two masked and helmeted soldiers looked out, scanning either side of the road, their assault rifles pointed where the soldiers perceived there to be a potential threat. Clouds of dust swirled behind the vehicles as they sped away, hiding them from view as they continued with their patrol of the city.

"Fuck, that was close," whined Milo.

"Move your ass a bit quicker next time," snarled Keelan.

"It's not just the Fuzz we have to worry about," suggested Salt.

"Do you think they're headed for the Nick?" asked Mickey.

Keelan nodded. "We need to find some cover where we can lay up and get our bearings. Plan what we do next."

"And food," added Milo.

"Alcohol for me."

"You can fucking wait, Todd. Priority is cover, food and water. In case you haven't noticed, the place is in a world of shit," Salt retorted.

Salt led them deeper into the shopping complex. Most of the buildings were without roofs, and most of their contents were covered in black ash. All of the shops had been rifled and picked clean of anything edible. Primark had also been ransacked, but the five escapees managed to find enough smoke-blackened clothing, but unburnt, to replace their prison garb. It was also a relief to acquire some warm clothes: the cold was starting to bite. After a brief discussion, the decision was made, by Keelan and Salt, to head further out of the city, find a location where they could hold up in relative safety, and, more importantly, secure some food and water. They headed north, looking for the wealthier districts, choosing the streets where the houses appeared larger and more presentable.

"There's someone in that house." Withers pointed as he watched a figure dart through the front door of the double-fronted Victorian house at the end of the road.

"Did they see us?"

"I doubt it, Doug. They weren't looking in our direction."

"As good a place as any to lie up for the night, Stan," suggested Doug Salt.

"Agreed. Let's get a bit closer." Keelan led the group forward, the five men keeping close to the mix of hedges, fences and walls that bordered the affluent residences that ran along one side of the road. The dwellings opposite mirrored those. All of the houses, some with large bay windows, had their panes shattered, but at least they weren't like the blackened carcasses that occupied the greater part of the inner city.

Ground Zero, south-west of the river, the site of the 500-kiloton detonation, had obliterated the area out to a radius of three kilometres. Further out to the west of the city, where a second bomb had struck, various levels of degradation had occurred relative to the distance from Ground Zero. In the area of Ossett and Lupset, a firestorm had swept through the city. Although the fire brigade, who had placed their tenders in a place of relative safety prior to the strike, had attempted to tackle a few of the fires, the conflagration was such that they had little impact, and after four firemen were killed, the teams were withdrawn. The high levels of radiation were also a concern, so it was agreed the firestorm would be left to burn itself out. Now, a twenty-five square kilometre area of the city consisted of blackened structures with no windows and the roofs open to the elements. The local authority in charge had no idea of the number of deaths, but had calculated that it would be in the region of 30,000 dead and over 40,000 injured. Many who had initially survived had since died of their wounds, from radiation sickness and/or starvation. Bombs had also been dropped on Leeds, Bradford, Dewsbury, Huddersfield, Barnsley and Castleford.

Once the group were within a few metres of the one and a half metre high brick wall that fronted the Victorian property that was of interest, Keelan called a halt. "Milo, Withers. You go to the front door. Let them know you're there as a distraction, but keep calm and try not to frighten them too much. Salt, Mickey and me will enter from the back. Got it?"

They nodded their understanding, and Milo and Withers headed for the front door. The other three men followed them through a second small gate, next to the drive. The larger gate that secured the drive was closed, wired up to prevent vehicle entry. The side gate, controlling access to the rear of the house, was accessible, and the remaining convicts, after cutting away the wire that secured it, passed through it. With weapons, picked up on the way, hidden behind their backs, they walked down the path that led to the back door. The wall of the house was on their left and the brick-built garage on their right.

The other two men had now arrived at the front door. Milo rapped the gargoyle-faced knocker on the dark blue painted door and listened for an answer. As expected, there was no response, and the boarded-up windows prevented the two men from peering inside. Withers cursed as broken glass crunched underfoot as he attempted to push the chipboard away from the window so he could look inside.

Keelan, Wicks and Salt passed the garage and continued to make their way in between the wall of the house and the now six-foot high privet hedge on their right, peeping round the corner before making their way to the half-pane back door. The glass was missing, replaced by a solid piece of chipboard. The lower part of the door appeared undamaged. The window to probably the kitchen, along with the window to the room next door, was similarly protected.

"They're switched on, Stan. Should we try somewhere else?"

The big man adjusted the bobble hat and shook his shaven head. "No, if the people living here seem pretty switched on, it means they have something to protect other than themselves."

"Food?"

"That's what I'm thinking."

They were interrupted by Milo as he suddenly appeared from the front of the house.

"Fuck, Milo, you made me jump," admonished Salt.

"Sorry, just trying to be quiet, is all."

"Quiet round the front?" asked Keelan.

"Yeah, Stan. What d'ya want us to do?"

"Go back to the front and wait with Withers. We'll go in through here."

"Right." With that, the man left to join the other convict covering the front door.

"How do you want to play it?"

"Crowbar on the hinges first, Doug. Weaken it. Then I'll shoulder charge it."

"Stand back then." Salt pushed the wedge of the crowbar he had picked up earlier from more scavenging into the slight crack of the door jamb, applying pressure before steadily levering it from side to side. Wood started to splinter, and he continued the motion until a large chunk split off from the door frame. He crouched down and did the same to the lower hinge until that too split.

"Behind me, Mickey. Once I'm through, you pile in and clout anyone you come across. Salt, you behind him."

The big man moved back, lowering his shoulder, preparing his eighteen-stone mass to throw it at the door in front of him. For a large man, he moved forward so quickly that it startled both his fellow escapees. His shoulder connected with the chipboard and he grunted as his full weight pressed against the door, which held for a moment before giving way. The hinge at the top of the door parted as did the bolt top left and the mortice lock in the middle. But the bottom hinge held. The consequence for Keelan was twofold. First, the door swung round to the left, the lower hinge still gripping the door, then causing him to trip over the door and fall flat on his face on top of the door itself. Then an explosion deafened Keelan, and Mickey was flung back by the force of the buckshot from the two barrels of the breach-loaded shotgun, his face and chest a mass of blood and shredded flesh.

The occupant of the house fumbled with the break-action shotgun, and broke it to reload, fumbling with the extra cartridges in his pocket, cursing that he had mistakenly fired both barrels leaving him exposed. Salt responded in a flash, bypassing Mickey, leaping over the sprawled body of Keelan, stamping on the man's shoulder in his haste to get through the doorway. He smashed into the shape he could pick out in the dark interior, forcing the person back into a worktop and kitchen cupboard. The man yelled in agony, his back bent over the work surface. Salt's powerful hands gripped the man's neck, squeezing his throat for all he was worth. The gun clattered to the floor as the occupant struggled to hold Salt at bay, but to no avail. Doug Salt was tall, lean and fit, and the forty-two year old banker quickly succumbed as Salt squeezed harder and harder, at the same time pummelling the man in the groin and stomach with one of his knees until the banker passed out, collapsing to the floor.

Keelan got to his feet, rubbing the shoulder that had connected with the door and subsequently stood on by Salt.

"Check his pockets for cartridges and get the gun loaded," he urged Salt.

"What about Wicks?"

Keelan looked back at the blood-soaked body sprawled just outside the doorway. "He's fucked. Get the gun loaded. Cover me while I check out the punter."

Salt rifled the man's pockets, found half a dozen shells, and reloaded the shotgun, taking a stance by the door that led out of

34

the kitchen into the other rooms of the house. He covered Keelan as he searched the banker, who was still unconscious, for any other weapons. Then, rummaging through the drawers and cupboards in the kitchen, Keelan came across a ball of twine, which he used, cut into strips, to bind the man's hands and feet.

"Let's go. You lead, Doug. We'll go through the house and make for the front door and let the other two know what's happening."

Salt moved through the open door, the barrels of the shotgun probing ahead of him. In the hall, there was a room adjacent to the kitchen, a study, but it was empty. Both moved cautiously towards the front door, the luxurious carpet softening their footsteps. The doors to the rooms either side of the corridor were shut. Keelan, on seeing the front was heavily barred, instructed the two outside to come in through the back door while he and Salt searched the rest of the house.

"What was the shooting all about?" queried Milo anxiously.

"Mickey's had it, but its safe to come in now."

Keelan and Salt continued their search of the house. The two front rooms were empty apart from a dining room suite in one and a luxurious lounge setting in the other. There was a fireplace with a Victorian mantelpiece, a leather three-piece suite, Victorian yew side tables, and a 50-inch LED TV mounted on the wall. Before they went upstairs, Keelan called to other two who were now behind them, their faces white after having passed Wicks's dead body.

"Wait here. Give us the gun, Doug. I'll go first."

Keelan took each step carefully, the stair carpet muffling his footsteps, the occasional creak of old stair boards causing him to pause momentarily. On reaching the top landing, he stopped to listen, but all he could pick up was the heavy breathing of Salt behind him. They checked all four of the bedrooms and the bathroom, and found them empty. The two men went back down and congregated with the other two in the hallway.

"Where the hell are they?" exclaimed Milo.

"We can ask the bloke," Todd recommended.

"I bet there's a cellar. It's an old house," spoke up Salt.

"We didn't look in the utility room. Todd, Milo, check it out," Keelan instructed. "Doug and I will have a little chat with our captive."

The two, as instructed, headed for the utility room next to the kitchen while Salt and Keelan pulled the now recovered banker up into a standing position, pushing him up against one of the tall cupboards.

Keelan's six foot three bulk towered over the middle-aged man, his large shaved head blocking the banker's view from anything but the convict's grimy, scowling face.

"Where are the others?" Through his grip on the man's shoulders, Keelan could feel the banker's body trembling.

Before the victim could respond, a shout was heard from Milo. "Found it! There's a bloody cellar!"

"Check it out," shouted Keelan. "Go with them, Doug."

He stared into the man's face. "Your family?"

The man nodded. "P-please d-don't h-hurt us," he stuttered.

"Have you got food down there?"

"Yes." He nodded, a slight smile playing across his face in an attempt to ingratiate himself with his captor.

"I'm going to loosen your ties. You fucking make a move and I'll kill you. Understand?"

The banker nodded rapidly as Keelan cut the twine that secured the man's feet and hands.

Just as he had finished, Salt returned and whispered in his ear, "Bloody goldmine down there. Food, water, beer and whisky. And the best bit: women."

The banker started as he picked up the gist of the last part of the sentence.

"Please, not my family. They've been through enough already." He pulled himself up to his full height of five foot eight. "I won't let you harm them."

The air shot out of the man's lungs as Keelan put his full weight behind the blow that struck the man in his plump stomach, forcing him to bend and drop to his knees, gasping for breath and retching.

Milo joined them in the kitchen and received further orders from Keelan.

"Get the women into the lounge, and bring some food, water and drink up. Doug, take this piece of shit down to the cellar, and make sure he won't bother us."

"What about the boy?" asked Milo.

"How old?"

"Fifteen, I'd say, and the girl is about seventeen."

"Tie him up with Daddy here. She goes in the lounge."

"Gotcha."

Salt hauled the banker towards the utility room, heading for the cellar, while Milo went to carry out his orders. Keelan made his way to the spacious lounge, slumping down into the large leather armchair. He suddenly felt weary. They had been on the go for over twelve hours since the breakout, on the alert at all times. He was thirsty, hungry, and was sick of the taste of dust and grit in his mouth. He slid down deeper into the chair, tempted to close his eyes, but he needed food and drink, and to secure their location first. Then some entertainment.

The door was pushed open, and a skinny teenager collapsed in a heap in the middle of the floor, whimpering. Her mother was moments behind, and the daughter immediately shuffled across the carpet and clung onto her, the mother reciprocating. Withers and Salt were close behind.

"The other two secure?"

"Yeah, Stan," responded Salt, ogling at the two brunettes cowering on the floor. "We've also patched up the back door as best we can. We can move some furniture later and prop it up against the door."

Keelan nodded, his eyes wandering over the two women lying at his feet. The daughter looked to be around seventeen, maybe a year older. Her skirt was fashionably short; her long legs ran down into a pair of pink trainers. Although she wore a white blouse with a shapeless blue jumper over the top, it did little to hide the contour of her small but well-shaped heaving breasts. The mother, late thirties or even early forties, looked in good shape. Although she'd had at least two children, it was obvious from her figure that she had maintained a good level of fitness, unlike the husband, he thought. She was dressed in a knee-length skirt with thick dark denier tights, a blouse and jumper not too dissimilar to her daughter's. Both had shoulder-length, dark brown hair and were definitely on the right side of attractiveness.

Keelan lurched up from the chair, "Me and Salt first. You two keep watch."

He reached out and grabbed the mother's hand, wrenching it away from her daughter's grip, pulling her up and clamping his large hand around her mouth before she could utter a squeal. Salt responded equally as quickly, second guessing Keelan's action, and grabbed the young girl who started kicking and thrashing about. Any attempt at protesting or screaming was stifled rapidly as Salt ruthlessly crushed all resistance. Keelan, one hand around the mother's mouth and one around her chest beneath her armpits, dragged his captive through the lounge doorway, along the hall and up the stairs, the speed and

Keelan's embrace preventing any form of resistance. Both of her heeled shoes were lost as her feet bounced on each step, and by the time she was thrown onto the king-size bed in what was her and her husband's bedroom, the fight was almost out of her.

A single short cry from her daughter, now being hauled into the room opposite, emboldened her with the strength to make one last effort to escape and run to the aid of her daughter. She kicked out with both legs, catching Keelan on one of his muscular thighs. Although slightly deadened, it was not enough to prevent the thickset Keelan from responding. She sat up and pushed her feet off the bed, connecting them with the bedroom floor. But that was as far as she got as a powerful backhander struck the side of her face, knocking her back down onto the bed. Stars sped away from her as her skull reverberated from the blow, a trickle of blood running from the corner of her mouth.

Keelan moved quickly before she could recover. Throwing her legs back onto the duvet, he climbed onto the bed, his knees astride her legs as he reached round behind her, finding the zip of her skirt. There was no pretence about easing it off as he prized the zip apart, ripping the skirt down over her hips, knees and legs, almost tearing it apart such was the violence of the action. She tried to sit up, desperate to go and help her daughter but, before a scream could pass her lips, he slapped the mother hard across the face again, stunning her. He tore at her tights, pleasure etched on his face. His last sexual experience, a blowjob from a woman, a male sex slave, in the shower, was well over six months ago.

As thick as they were, holes soon appeared in the opaque tights as he dragged them down her legs, leaving red weals as he did so. Once over her feet, he threw them across the room, thrusting a knee between her legs as she attempted to draw them up towards her chest. His second knee slammed into an olive brown thigh, a hand across her mouth stifling her cries. He forced his knees apart, in turn pushing her legs wider. His free hand gripped her knickers, pale blue, matching her brassiere beneath her upper clothing, ripping them away, the dark bush exposed as the fragile material snapped. They joined her tights on the floor of the bedroom.

His hand now free again, he groped at her breasts, her eyes wide as he painfully squeezed and kneaded them, pulling her jumper up over her face, tearing at her silk blouse, the buttons popping as the delicate top disintegrated. He reached back, pulled a knife from his pocket, and severed her bra straps, the bra clip unable to prevent the final disrobing of her breasts. His face wild, his chest heaving as his breathing accelerated, his pulse rate soaring, Keelan fumbled with the belt of his pants and quickly forced his jeans down exposing his throbbing manhood.

He wished she could see it, see what was coming, but the jumper was held over her face. Later, she would both see it and taste it, but for now pure release was at the forefront of his thoughts. He dropped on top of her spread-eagled body, his heavy weight forcing the breath from her. He jabbed at her unsuccessfully, forcing her legs further apart, thrusting at her painfully two or three times until he found the opening he was looking for. He groaned as his swollen cock pushed deep inside her. The woman's body tensing, she bit into the jumper that covered her face. Two shallow strokes were followed by long deep ones, his body tensing as he ejaculated into her after only a few seconds, his head held back, and a manic grin on his face. He slumped down, spent, sucking on her dark nipple as he felt himself getting hard again. He smiled. Life was good.

CHAPTER 5

The driver rocked gently in the seat of the David Brown tractor as it trundled down the country lane towards Little Farringdon. The Range Rover would have been a better option, but it only had a half-tank of petrol whereas the 2,000-litre tank of diesel on the farm was still three quarters full. He slowed down as he approached the A361, checked for traffic to his left, although he wasn't expecting to see any, and then swung right heading south towards the two lakes. He picked up speed; a plume of smoke, lifting the weather flap, shot up from the vertical exhaust mounted at the front of the engine. In a couple of minutes, he had crossed the River Leach and passed between Roughgrounds and Horseshoe Lakes. The large roundabout that led to the small village of Lechlade-on-Thames was visible ahead. He checked that his shotgun lying on the floor of the cab was easily accessible, and adjusted his face mask and the hood of his sweatshirt. He patted the dog's head at his side as the animal's eyes locked onto his, looking for reassurance. On reaching the roundabout, he turned right, ignoring road protocol that required you to circuit the roundabout clockwise: traffic was almost non-existent these days. Even before the nuclear strikes, fuel was in very short supply, limiting the movement of vehicles. Petrol and diesel stocks had been reserved for the forces and essential services although, as a farmer, he had received a reasonable allocation of diesel fuel. The battle for the protection of Ukraine, Poland and West Germany had quickly assumed priority, with supplies being diverted to feed the ever hungry tanks and armoured vehicles of the British Army allocated to the NATO forces rapidly despatched to the Continent. What fuel was left in the UK had been only enough to last a few days, but then Armageddon struck. With over 300 megatons of nuclear detonations shaking the British Isles to the core, the need to fuel their family cars was the last thing on people's minds. By then, it was too late to run.

The road took him past a housing estate on his left, and he observed the houses, looking for any signs of a threat. Most of the surviving occupants had left, moving to one of the large encampments set up by a Regional Government Centre. There they sought food, water and shelter. The blast wave from the 500-kiloton nuclear warhead that had devastated the RAF base at Brize Norton, which surged across the village, had shattered all of the windows, lifted many of the roofs, leaving their homes open to the elements. Although the wind had been blowing in a north-westerly direction, taking most of the contaminated fallout away from the village, changes in weather conditions and shifts in wind direction meant that some contaminated particles had still dropped onto the village and surrounding areas.

At the end of the road, Tom continued north-west, along a narrow lane that led to an allotment area belonging to a garden centre. The tractor bounced across the cultivated strips of land. Tom kept the wooded area to his south, skirting the village until he was able to approach it from the north-west. On arrival at his chosen position, he parked up. The tractor was pretty well hidden from the small village, and it was less than a 200-metre walk to his final destination. The wind had been blowing towards him, driving the sound of his approach away from the built-up area, helping to conceal his arrival. All being well, he hadn't been heard. Although he would have preferred to have used the Range-Rover, even if fuel had been plentiful, he doubted it would have made it across the churned up fields. Completing the entire journey on foot would have been even better, but he would have been exposed to the contaminated air for too long. And, anyway, he wouldn't be able to carry enough supplies in one go on foot. Although three weeks had passed since the dropping of the bombs and missiles, the polluted ground and radioactive particles in the air would still expose him to danger if he stayed out for too long.

He climbed down from the tractor. "Here, boy."

The collie jumped down from the cab, sniffed the air, and took a turn around Tom's legs before sitting to his master's left.

"What can you hear, eh, boy? What's that?" Tom's voice was muffled through the surgical mask and scarf wrapped around his face, his eyes peering through the goggles that were better suited to scuba diving.

The dog's ears pricked up, twitching like miniature radars searching for sound. But Sam remained where he was, panting steadily, his pink tongue flicking out occasionally over his black nose.

Tom patted him. "Good lad."

Tom moved through a sparse copse and headed for the large building he could see through the gaps in the trees, the spire of the parish church visible in the distance. Tom and his dog followed the hedge line, Sam sniffing the hedgerow, leaving his scent when he smelt the conflicting odour of another animal. He scooted out in front, checking the ground ahead but never more than a few metres, before circling back.

"Good boy."

He adjusted the double-barrelled shotgun in the crook of his right arm as they walked the last ten metres.

"Wait."

Sam stopped immediately and was instantly on the alert.

"Seek."

Sam ran forward, sniffing the air, while Tom waited. Sam toured the area, checking an outhouse and the other side of a low wall that crossed their path, breached by a small but open gate. The dog gave out no danger signals, his black tail wagging freely, pleased to be out of the confines of the farmhouse.

The two made their way around the back of what was once a hotel, passing between the rear of the building and one of two tennis courts. Tom doubted guests would use them again for many years to come. The owner was a good friend of his, and was now holed up in the farm with his and Tom's wives. They took it in turns to rummage for supplies, one of them always remaining behind to ensure the farm's and their families' security. The hotel was far from safe, having been ransacked on numerous occasions. But the looters had never discovered the hidden cellar which held a small supply of dried and tinned food that would have been used to feed the twenty or so guests when the premises had been open for business. The village housed roughly 2,000-plus people, but most of the inhabitants had fled further north during the latter part of the war, conscious that the military airfield would be a likely target if the UK was attacked. Those that remained, no more than a dozen, were ensconced in their own properties, eking out their remaining meagre provisions. The small village shop, hotel and post office had been stripped bare. This unknown food source was all that was left. It had remained undiscovered, so far. He'd had little contact with the locals since the missiles struck, bar one family. The parents, along with their four sons, one a teenager, the other three in their early to late twenties, were seen as the village bullies. They also had a daughter and two cousins living with them. They had confronted Tom only two days previously as they scoured the houses searching for food and water. Fortunately, he had been away from the hotel at the time, and a blast of pellets over their heads caused the cowardly group to run. Deep down though, he suspected their paths would cross again as the family were forced to widen their search radius as starvation started to take hold.

Tom made his way through the open door, the crunch of broken glass seeming disproportionately loud as he entered. He stood still and listened for a few minutes. Nothing. Moving back to the doorway, he called Sam over. "Here, boy. Good lad. Stay, stay. I won't be long."

The dog lay down across the entrance, doing his master's bidding: not waiting for the command to round up sheep on this occasion, but acting as sentry. The days of chasing sheep were over. The small flock Tom had on the farm had been found dead: three weeks in the open, exposed to high levels of radiation, and finally killed by the poisonous fodder. But Sam was getting used to this new role. Tom made his way inside, comfortable that Sam would warn him of any intruders. He flicked on his torch. Although there was sufficient light to move around, with parts of the roof missing and chunks out of the walls, the deeper inside he went the less light there would be available. Tom found the large kitchen in the centre of the hotel and moved the square table, positioned at the far end, to one side, pushing it up against the kitchen range. He then rolled up the large piece of lino, lifting the kitchen table legs up, using them to hold the coiled covering back in place. A hatchway, leading down to the hotel's only cellar, was now revealed.

Tom wasted no time. Lifting it up, he made his way down the stone steps that led to this inner sanctuary where Andrew, the owner, had stashed various stocks of food. They had both agreed at the outset that, should the war escalate and there was a breakdown in control, they would join forces and hide out at the farm. When the bombs and missiles struck, they had left what stores there were at the hotel as a reserve or in case looters overran the farm and a fallback position was needed. He placed the shotgun on a shelf off to the side, peeled back his hood and positioned the elasticated straps of a head torch around his forehead and across the back of his head. His arms were now free, and he immediately got to work. Tinned goods were the target for today. His plan was to carry two dozen boxes up to the back door, then bring the tractor up, and stack them quickly onto the rear loader, limiting the time he stayed in the area. He got to work.

Tom eventually dropped the last box but one, this one full of catering packs of tinned baked beans, and was about to turn and get the last when he heard a low growl from Sam. Tom ran back to the cellar, making his way down into the cellar quickly where he retrieved his shotgun before making his way out and back to where Sam was still growling.

"What is it, lad?"

The dog's hackles were up, teeth slightly bared, and the throat rumbling continued. Tom stood alongside the collie. The dog was now in a low crouch, poised to defend his master against a potential assailant. Tom stroked Sam's black and white coat. The six-year-old looked up at him, reassured by his master's presence.

"Good lad. Steady now."

Tom crept from the room, peering around the door frame. It was clear. He edged his way south-east along the outer wall, clutching his shotgun, until he reached the corner where he took a peek to the left. The sound of a crash emanated from a building across the way, followed by the sound of a splintering door. Sam, who had been following close behind, bared his teeth again, the throaty growl increasing in intensity.

"Steady, lad, steady."

Tom brushed the dog's hackles down. He saw movement as two young men exited the building, probably one of the few houses not yet looted by the Reynolds family. Sam must have heard their scavenging activity. Tom watched as the two moved north, deeper into the housing estate to continue their scavenging.

Tom sighed with relief: the last thing he wanted was a confrontation with those two. "Let's go then, Sam. Get our stuff and bugger off home. What do you say, eh?"

The dog's ears pricked up at the sound of 'home' and he trotted after Tom, returning to where the boxes had been stacked, and then back inside the hotel. Securing the hatch and returning the linoleum and table to their original position, Tom left the hotel. He cut across to where he'd left the tractor, knowing that speed was now of the essence. Sam leapt into the cab, and Tom followed him. The engine started first time, and he manoeuvred the farm vehicle towards the hotel, reaching it in only a couple of minutes. He spun the tractor round and reversed up to the door until the hydraulic hitch, supporting a loading platform, was in the right position. Tom jumped down, commanding Sam to stay in the cab, and proceeded to stack the boxes of tinned food onto the platform. He was near completion when a sharp bark from Sam alerted him, but looking up from his task he saw nothing. About to place the last box onto the tractor's loader, he saw one of the two men he had seen earlier running towards him. He recognised him immediately as Ryan. At six two, although quite skinny, the young man had a reputation for meanness and had recently served three years in prison for GBH.

"Hey, old man, what you up to?" Ryan called out. "Hey, bro, we've caught ourselves a looter," he hollered back over his shoulder to his brother Brian who had also appeared on the scene.

Tom dropped the box, and the contents, tins of tomatoes, spewed out as the cardboard container caught on the tractor's mechanism at the rear.

"Shit," he said to himself, suddenly realising the shotgun was back in the cab.

Ryan was within metres now, picking up speed, intending to charge the middle-aged farmer, take him down, and steal the contraband. Brian, slightly weightier than his brother and suffering from a minor learning difficulty, lumbered after him, wanting to join in the sport that he felt sure would ensue. Tom prepared himself for the onslaught, cursing his stupidity. Ryan launched himself at Tom, the six-footer dominating Tom's shorter stature. Tom, catching a hint of red from the corner of his eye, picked up a tomato can that had caught up on the loader, and swung his right arm, the tin clutched in his hand, with every ounce of force he could summon up behind it. The can connected with Ryan's eyebrow, splitting the skin, blood flowing freely, causing the young man to stagger to Tom's left, collapsing onto the ground, reaching out and taking Tom down with him. They landed in a heap, Tom winded, Ryan dazed.

Tom saw Brian pounding towards them, knowing he needed to act quickly if he was going to come out of this alive. As Brian lined up with the tractor cab, Sam launched his agile body, his front paws colliding with the brother, knocking him sideways and down. Brian quickly scrambled to his feet, Sam's powerful jaws grinding the man's arm between his sharp teeth. Brian, screaming in agony, tried to yank his arm free of Sam's grip, dragging the dog away from the tractor. Tom wasted no more time as he heard Ryan groaning, and saw him clutching his bleeding head, slowly regaining his senses.

Using the now dented tin, he struck at Ryan again and again, pounding the man's skull until the tin was shapeless and had split at the seam, tomatoes and tomato juice mixing in with the congealing blood. He got to his feet just as he heard a yelp and saw Sam flying through the air after being booted by Brian who was now rubbing his mangled arm. Brian looked up and caught Tom's eye, a mixture of pain, fear and hatred etched on his face as he got ready to charge. Tom kicked off first, sprinting for the cab, and heading around the side opposite to where Brian had also made his move. Tom got there first, grabbing the shotgun, spinning left as Brian made his way around from the front of the bonnet.

Boomf…boomf.

Both barrels erupted, and Brian, his face and chest a mangled mass of flesh, blood and bone, was flung backward, flat on his back, his staring, lifeless eyes unable to see the cloudy, dust laden skies. Tom wasted no time in reloading the gun. After checking that Sam wasn't seriously hurt, he ran back to where he had left Ryan and stood over him. The man was clutching at his head, an accumulation of blood clouding his vision.

"You could have killed me, you nasty fucker. Wait till Brian gets hold of you. Brian, where the fuck are you?"

Tom lowered the barrels of the shotgun. Many thoughts raced through his mind: survival, his family, food, resources, and a hate for people like Ryan, Brian and his obnoxious family. His final thought before he pulled the trigger, the shot punching a hole in Ryan's chest, was: *The world has changed. There are no rules now.*

CHAPTER 6

"See anything?" Commander Parry asked the armed Marine scanning the shoreline.

Corporal Davey lowered his binoculars. "Not a dicky bird, sir. Saw a glint of light, probably reflecting off a piece of broken glass. Looking pretty bleak across there, sir."

"Let me know the minute you see anything."

"Sir."

"Victor-Two, come round to starboard five degrees," Parry ordered via the hand-held radio.

"*Aye, aye, sir,*" responded the lieutenant commanding the RIB, a rigid inflatable boat, that was ahead of the ship with a line linking the two.

The captain of the British SSN HMS *Ambush*, one of the UK's latest nuclear attack submarines, watched as the RIB, with a towline attached forward of the submarine, moved further right. Such was the damage to the submarine's controls, and without the harbour master's boat and the usual heavy-duty tugs that would have been despatched to help bring them into harbour, he'd had to resort to using their on-board RIB to provide additional steerage.

They were returning from operations in the area of the Norwegian Sea, where their assignment had been to seek out and attack any Russian naval forces spotted heading for Northern Europe, with the intention of disrupting supply lines between the continent and the UK. NATO command had been successful, causing so much damage to the Russian Northern Fleet that the Russian ships were forced to withdraw. *Ambush*, harassing the Soviet navy as it fled east, suffered a near catastrophic attack from a Udaloy Destroyer, rendering the submarine immobile and in danger of sinking in the bitter depths of the Norwegian Sea. It was only the timely arrival of a US carrier-borne Hornet, firing a Harpoon anti-ship missile, that prevented the Soviet destroyer from finishing off its prey. But the damage had been done, and what was left of the crew fought for three days to keep the submarine afloat. Out of the crew of 130, only seven survived. Many died in flooded chambers; others, although in dry, watertight compartments, were trapped and soon ran out of precious oxygen, slowly suffocating until the air finally gave out. Out of contact with Fleet Command, and the Admiralty back in the United Kingdom for that matter, Parry coaxed a barely serviceable submarine through the Greenland-Iceland-United-Kingdom-Gap (GIUKGap), passing through the North Sea, his aim to steer the stricken submarine to Portsmouth's harbour. And here they were now.

Parry picked up the handset and communicated with the Helm. "Right rudder, ten degrees."

"*Ten degrees, right rudder, aye, sir,*" came the response from the helm.

Parry waited for a few moments as the sleek black hull slid round through the water. "All stop."

"*All stop, aye, sir,*" responded the helmsman below.

He must have felt lonely down inside the boat, with only a petty officer for company. Commander Parry and Marine Corporal Davey were on the bridge fin while the other three survivors were in the RIB.

The submarine drifted – only the RIB out front controlling its headway. Parry picked up his binoculars, zooming in on the boat acting as their steerage. Lieutenant Wood's face filled the lens, his lips moving as he instructed the sailor controlling the RIB. He swung the binos right and scanned the area of his approach. They had successfully negotiated the narrow gap, with Old Portsmouth on the right and Gosport on the left. Now, he needed to get alongside. The Mary Rose Museum was on his starboard side. He intended placing the submarine alongside Western Way, not far from the shattered remains of HMS *Victory*. His radio crackled.

"*Victor One. Taking line across now. Over.*"

"Understood. Tide's strong. We'll be stationary soon. Make it quick."

"*Aye, aye.*"

The inflatable sped for the wharf, the crew trailing out more rope as it moved further away from *Ambush*. Parry just hoped there would be enough. They'd had to splice two lengths together as it was. He checked the water, looked across at the wharf. They were stationary. The submarine would soon be drifting back the way they came, pushed by the tide that was heading out.

"Helm. As discussed, turn her over gently."

"*Aye, sir.*"

The pump-jet propulsion kicked in, just enough to hold the vessel in position. It would be on and off for the next ten to twenty minutes as the helmsman jockeyed the vessel into position. Parry looked across at the wharf, no more than a hundred metres away now. The RIB was alongside the wharf wall, and he saw two figures shimmy up one of the steel rung ladders pinned to the wharf wall, leading down into the sea itself. The rope was dragged around one of the large bollards and secured.

"*Victor One. Secured. Over.*"

"Acknowledged. Wait my command."

"*Aye, sir.*"

"Helm. Five knots."

"*Helm, aye.*"

The submarine trembled slightly as it fought against the tide, picking up speed, the bow turning slightly towards the wharf. The men on the harbour started to take up the slack, ready to let it out again once *Ambush* passed the point they were at.

Parry watched the harbour wall get closer. He waited and waited.

"Helm, standby."

"*Standby, aye.*"

The submarine powered forward. He waited.

"All stop."

"*All stop, aye.*"

The vessel was now no more than fifty metres from the wharf, but its bow was slightly past the top corner of the wharf where the harbour wall continued east along the northern way. The tide eventually stopped the submarine's forward movement, and the landing party pulled quickly on the line, tying it off as the bow was directly opposite their position. As the submarine drifted south, the hawse yanked on the bow, pulling the submarine into the side.

"Helm. Harbour party ready."

"Harbour party, aye."

What it really meant was that the helmsman would stay in position while the petty officer sprinted outside towards the stern, ready to toss the line so the stern of the vessel could also be tied up.

Parry looked back as *Ambush*'s stern got closer and closer, picking up speed.

"Helm. Standby collision."

"*Standby collision, aye.*"

The 7,000-ton submarine, with no power or tugs to control its direction or speed, collided with the wharf wall, crushing the fenders, nearly throwing the petty officer onto the wharf as he heaved the line ashore. The two men waiting grabbed it, pulling it in rapidly, until they held the thicker hawse just as the submarine pushed itself away, the force of coming alongside making the harbour wall shudder. A gap started to appear between the wall and the submarine.

"Bloody quick," yelled the PO, knowing time was running out.

The hawse was spun around the bollard just as the submarine's 7,000 tons tugged hard, reversing its direction to again come up against the wall. This time the shore party was ready, the slack was taken up, and the submarine brought under full control. They would worry about setting up a spring, which would stop the submarine moving backwards and forwards along the wharf, sometime later.

Parry turned to the Marine. "You stay here and keep watch."

"Sir."

"Helm. We are alongside."

"*Aye, sir.*"

"Victor-Two. Seen anybody?"

"*Negative, sir. No sign of life. It looks desolate out there. Over.*"

"Leave Taylor onshore, but he needs to keep his respirator on. The rest back on board."

"*The RIB, sir?*"

"Leave it where it is for the moment."

"*Aye, sir.*"

Parry climbed down the inside of the fin, dropping down inside to join the helmsman, peeling off his respirator as he did so.

"God, sir, that sounded a bit hairy."

The captain smiled. "It was, Page, but you did a great job, and we're alongside safely."

The remainder of the crew came back on board and, after removing their respirators, entered the submarine to join their captain.

Commander Parry, captain of the submarine, congratulated the men. "Well done, Lieutenant Wood, Harper, Petty Officer."

"It was a bit hairy when we came alongside, sir," responded Petty Officer Bell.

"What did you see on the wharf, Chris?"

"Nothing more than we saw from the fin as we came in, sir,"

responded Lieutenant Wood. "The buildings, those that are standing that is, are blackened hulks. No glass in windows, and some of the buildings have collapsed. UK's definitely been nuked."

"Any sign of life?"

"No, sir, nothing."

"Not surprising, though," added Petty Officer Bell. "All of our naval bases would have been high on the Soviets' target list."

"Yes, yes." Parry stroked his dark but grey-flecked beard, something he did subconsciously when options were running through his mind. It was a habit he had picked up during his officer's 'Perisher' course as a lieutenant commander. The commanding officer's qualifying course still gave him nightmares. "What was the last reading?"

"In the immediate vicinity, the radiation levels are tolerable. Providing we're not exposed for more than four or five hours in twenty-four, we should be OK. That doesn't mean there won't be hot spots though."

"But the readings will improve over time. Well, we've had enough exposure for today. As your duties as helmsman are over for now, Page, I want you to take responsibility for the dosimeter recordings. I want them checked and a record made last thing at night. So long as we're on board, that is."

"Sir."

"What are your plans then, sir?"

"Well, Chris, we get everyone on board and batten down for the night. Then, at first light tomorrow, I'll take Corporal Davey, Petty Officer Bell, and Harper and complete a patrol of what's left of the base. You stay with Taylor and Page and keep our home secure."

The PO ran his hand across the top of his shaved head. "You're looking at an hour each way, sir. We'll not see much. We'll need to get back under cover within a few hours."

"I appreciate that, Petty Officer Bell, but I'll feel a lot happier knowing what's in our immediate vicinity. We can't stay on board *Ambush* forever. We have to make contact with higher command as soon as possible and establish the situation. We may not be able to fight, but they could maybe use us on other ships."

"What about our families?" asked Page who had left a young wife behind at the base.

"They would have moved the families away from here, Page. But the best way of gathering information is to start at the top, get the bigger picture, and take it from there. We're still a military unit and may well be needed to continue the fight."

"Don't you worry, lad," counselled Bell. "The captain knows what he's doing. We all have families out there. So, one step at a time."

"Well said, PO," added Wood approvingly.

"Comms would be good."

"We've tried, PO, but you've seen the masts."

"Unfortunately, yes. They'll never transmit again."

"I suggest we get the RIB tied up port side, then get Taylor in, batten down, and get some food. There won't be too much of that. Another reason we need to explore the immediate vicinity. Then we can make plans to go further afield."

"Agreed, sir," said Lieutenant Wood.

"Let's get moving then. PO, you take Harper with you, pick up Taylor and bring the RIB around. Corporal Davey will cover you from the fin. Page, sort out a brew, and, Chris, you and I can pore over some maps of the local area."

"Aye, aye, sir," they all responded and went about their duties.

CHAPTER 7

"Push the crowbar in a bit deeper."

"It won't budge, Bill."

"For fuck's sake, get out of the way, Vincent. Give it to me."

Vincent handed the crowbar over as instructed, brushing bits of brick and concrete dust out of his eyes as he did so.

Bill grabbed it. "Get the beam of the torch on the gap then, Aleck. Can't see bugger all."

The third member of the group, coughing as pieces of dust and fine particles invaded his mouth and lungs, crouched down alongside Bill. The powerful torch beam lit up a narrow gap between a horizontal layer of concrete that supported a wall of brick.

"Is that better, boss?"

"Yeah, now keep it steady."

Bill pushed the hefty crowbar between the gap, pressing down hard, attempting to lever one of the bricks free. If he could just get one to move, it would be easier to chip away at the rest. There was a sudden crack as a red brick split in two, half of it crumbling free.

"Gotcha." Bill called over his shoulder, "Have those supports ready, Vincent."

"They're here, Bill."

Bill continued to hack away at the mortar that cemented the bricks together, releasing the other half of the broken one. He pulled the mask further up over his nose and mouth as swirls of brick dust irritated his nose and mouth. Another hour was spent in the confined space of the collapsed building, removing more brickwork, and supporting the exposed gap with steel props until it was wide enough to admit a person.

"Pass us one of the torches."

Vincent passed a second torch forward.

Bill was now able to light up the cavern he had revealed. He pushed his head through, closely followed by his shoulders, and then rolled onto his right shoulder into the darkened room. He picked himself up off the floor, moved forward at a crouch, the torch held out in front of him, the beam flickering left and right as he quickly got his bearings.

The room was a mess, and he had to step over a collapsed RSJ, a lintel, and clumps of rubble to make any progress. He soon found what he was looking for. Shards of glass crackled beneath his boots as he approached the smashed cabinets, bending down to peer at them. The building above him groaned, and pieces of plaster and other debris decorated his shoulders. He looked up, the beam of light from his torch reflecting off the cloud of particles swirling about the air. He was ready to make a run for it if there was the slightest sign of movement above him. The three-storey parade of shops, on the outskirts of Croydon, had caved in as a consequence of the blast created by the nuclear missile that had struck the Biggin Hill Airport, east of London. Bill had thought it unlikely they would be able to access this particular shop, such was the devastation in the area. But, after three days of hard digging, his group had come up against the wall of the shop he particularly wanted.

The structure above him seemed to have settled, and he relaxed slightly, but always ready to sprint for the opening should the mangled mass above him show signs of collapsing. *I'll be out of here like a shot,* he thought. He managed to gain access to one cabinet, the others crushed by the sheer weight of the remains lying on top of them. Bill played the beam of light across the shattered cabinet, a smile spreading across his face when he saw the five shotguns lying on their sides amongst the splintered wood and jutting shards of glass. He grabbed the first one, pulling it out, and dusting it down. It looked in good nick. On checking the other four, three seemed OK, but the fourth had a badly bent barrel. He smiled to himself. It was a great find. "Got them," he called back to Vincent. "Pass the bags through."

Bill made his way back through the debris and took the two bags that Vincent was stuffing through the hole.

"Both of you come through, you can help me load. But be careful. It's a bit dodgy in here."

"Are you sure it's safe, Bill?"

"Get in."

Vincent, followed by Aleck, climbed through the gap that Bill had made earlier and scrambled their way to where Bill was waiting.

"Here, hold the bags open."

Vincent held the first of the zip-up sports bags open, and Bill loaded two of the shotguns followed by boxes of cartridges, cleaning kits and anything else he thought might be useful. Then he filled the second one. With two bags full and a satisfied smile on Bill's face, they clambered out through the hole. The three men then made their way back out, scrabbling down the route that led them through the tunnel, supported by blocks of masonry and other large chunks of debris, they had come through earlier. All three were relieved when they reached the exit.

It was late evening, and they stepped out under darkened skies. Bill shivered. Now outside again, the sweat, a consequence of the exertion in the tunnel, dried on his skin, chilling his body. Extinguishing their torches, Bill led them away from the collapsed building, crossing the road to pick up the three concealed bicycles, still there where they had left them.

During the cycle back to their destination, they stopped every few minutes to listen and watch for signs of any other inhabitants of the city on the move. They were in foreign territory, and Bill would be much happier once he was ensconced back in his tower block, amongst his own people. Twenty minutes of cycling later not only warmed them up again but found them approaching their base, their home. They were close now, and Bill could see the shadows of two of his men patrolling the outside of the building: one with a pickaxe handle, the second with a vicious-looking carving knife taped to the end of a broom stale. Each would also be carrying a clasp or cook's knife as additional protection. Bill continued to watch as they turned the corner, walking away from the three men. He would wait until they completed their circuit. He had no intention of taking them by surprise.

Bill scanned the twenty-four-storey block, the odd flicker of light where elements of the eighty-two souls inside had probably grouped together to socialise, wrapped in scarves and thick jackets to keep out the cold. It was their home, their sanctuary, and their fortress. With these shotguns, he had a real chance of maintaining the security of those inside, protecting them from the marauding gangs that were intent on rape and pillage.

"We moving, Bill?" asked Vincent.

"No, we wait," he snapped in response. "The guards will be back round soon."

A further five minutes saw the two men saunter around the

opposite corner and head for the covered porch that led to the main entrance of the building. Inside were two more of his guards, waiting to take their turn in protecting the building and its occupants from attack.

"Let's go," he hissed and sprinted from behind the building, wheeling his bike alongside, heading for the entrance to the tower block.

"Jake, Malcolm," he called out to the two men, not wanting to startle them and risk getting a cook's knife in his gut.

"That you, Bill?"

"Who did you think it was? All quiet?"

"Not a peep. Had a few kids scavenging around, but we soon fucked them off. Got them then?"

Bill held up the bag that had been hanging from the handlebars of his bike. "Yes."

"Sound. We can better defend ourselves next time that mob try it again," Jake responded.

"We'll leave you and get these inside."

Vincent and Aleck followed Bill as he headed deeper into the covered main entrance, the once glass-filled doors now boarded up with just a small slot in the wood to allow the men inside to see who wanted to gain entrance.

Bill hammered on the door with the butt of one of the guns and was responded to with a "Who's that?"

"Bill and the boys returning."

A light shone in his face as the man inside checked him out. Then there was a clatter on the other side as the braces and barriers were removed allowing the single door to be opened. A small gas lamp flickered in the entrance hall, and two men hovered either side of the door, on the alert for any tricks.

"Boys. We have a bit more security now." Bill indicated the shotgun he was carrying.

"That's a relief, Bill. Well done, you guys. Do we get them tonight?"

"We need to clean them up and sort out shells and the like first. First thing tomorrow, I promise."

The two men smiled. Although they knew it was necessary to keep watch over the block both day and night, it was a scary experience keeping out some of the mobs that roamed the streets. The shotguns would be a welcome addition to their armoury.

"Right, lads, we'll leave you to it."

Leaving the bikes in the reception area, Bill, Vincent and Aleck made their way up the stairs, tiring quickly. It was a long climb to the twelfth floor, the six passenger lifts no longer operable. On reaching the level they sought, Bill pushed the door, to what was now his control room, open. Two females, a thirty-year-old single mother of two and a teenager, were in the process of brewing tea using a small gas camping stove off to the one side. In the centre, a large conference table was strewn with maps and papers, and, along one wall, a further array of maps depicting the streets of Croydon and the surrounding area. The tower block, which they currently occupied, was marked on the map and ringed in green. A second circle, out to 200 metres, and two hatched areas, marked in red, also adorned the map. The hatched areas of New Addington and Fieldway were considered no-go areas and housed one of the gangs that had attacked them two days previously. The first green circle was the area they deemed a no-go area to others, their territory, an area they protected as best they could. The second ringed area, in red, they would patrol and keep an eye on, but wouldn't put up a fight to hold. Bill saw it as no-man's-land. There were also numerous yellow and orange hatched areas: yellow for heavily contaminated, and orange for areas they wanted to investigate to scavenge for food and other essential supplies.

Bill dropped the shotgun onto the table followed by the bag he had been carrying. Vincent placed his on the table as well.

"That for the boys downstairs?" asked Vincent.

"Yes," she responded.

"Any tea for us, Sally?"

"Yes, Bill, on its way."

"Us too, Sally," piped up Aleck.

"Of course, boys, you've earned it. Kelly, sort some tea for the boys."

"Sure, Sal," responded the blonde-haired, pimply-faced teenager.

Vincent and Aleck started to take out the contraband and lay it out on the table. The total haul was four shotguns and about 400 cartridges, along with cleaning kits.

"Start a war with that lot," suggested Kelly, the seventeen-year-old.

"It'll help keep us safe," Bill informed her as he slumped down into an office chair.

The NLA office block in the centre of Croydon had been

a good option. Once the bombs had struck, tens of thousands of houses were destroyed, flattened or burnt to the ground throughout London and the peripheries. Food and water supplies had become scarcer by the day. Bill Watson then made for the NLA tower block, gathering a few other families whom he knew and trusted along the way. Anticipating anarchy, he believed that they would be more secure hiding out in an office block rather than in the centre of a residential area, particularly as so few of the surviving blocks of flats had remained standing. There had only been half a dozen windows left in the NLA building, but they had been on the opposite side of the building, partially protected, facing away from the blast wave. The rest of the windows had been completely shattered, leaving the aluminium frames open to the elements. This room had all its windows; hence the reason he had chosen it as his operations centre.

In the early days, Bill had organised the families zealously, gathering other groups to join them. Initially, they had survived with only what they had brought with them from their homes, not wanting to go out into the contaminated environment during the first few weeks after the strikes. In the meantime, office furniture had been pushed aside, open windows boarded up, or at least at the rate of a dozen a day. Then scavenging parties were organised, looking for food, water and badly needed supplies, particularly food and medicines. A list had been drawn up which also included mattresses, bedding, bicycles, camping equipment, such as stoves and utensils, and any weapons they could lay their hands on. There had been a few confrontations with other groups as they also came out into the dust-ridden gloom looking for food and water. Some groups had a more ominous purpose, preferring to steal off others and partake in gang rape. But his colony had eventually reached a total of eighty-two people, providing him with the manpower to protect the families and build up an ever-increasing level of resources to help them through whatever was thrown at them in the coming months and years.

He had chosen this particular tower block not only because of its size but also because of its use as business premises. There were no occupying families to contend with, which would have made it more difficult to secure full occupation. The rooms were significantly larger and open plan, as opposed to the rabbit warrens of individual flats in a residential block. This, along with only two entrances, he surmised, would make their home easier to defend.

In the first few days, at least two families had challenged his authority, questioning his right to lead, stating that they would not follow his orders but go their own way. Bill had been a fireman before the world changed, and was stocky and fit to go with it. A few blows from Bill's ham-like fists had restored order, and the families in question had been evicted subsequently. The majority of the new occupants were satisfied with Bill's leadership, comforted by the fact that someone at least knew what they were doing. A few resented his control, but they accepted they were in the minority and certainly didn't relish the prospect of being ejected from what was proving to be a relatively safe environment.

After the bombs had struck and the many fires had burnt themselves out, anarchy ruled the city and surrounding areas. Competition for food and water was on, and the strong preyed on the weak. A small local government centre had started off well, trying to restore order, but was eventually overwhelmed by the sheer number of people. The police officers and soldiers, many of them ill with radiation sickness, had slowly dispersed, returning to protect their own families from the ever-increasing levels of violence. Two Territorial Army soldiers, along with their families, had actually joined Bill's group. His only regret had been their inability to bring their assault weapons with them.

The government centre was eventually overrun, even before they could initiate the distribution of food. So, law and order, little that there had been, was now non-existent. But now Bill had these new weapons, and with the knowledge where more modern firearms could be obtained, he could use them to further strengthen the group's position.

Just as his eyes started to close and he was drifting off to sleep, he was brought back up by Sally bringing him a drink.

"Here you go, Bill, have this. Then go get some sleep, eh?"

Bill smiled and took the proffered cup of black tea, wondering how long tea would be available to them as he sipped at it.

"Thanks, Sal. Yeah, I will soon. Need to chat with Trevor and Robbie first."

Sally flicked a piece of her shoulder-length, dark brown hair out of her green eyes. "I'll send Kelly to get them?"

"That'd be great." He smiled, and she reciprocated. She was a good-looking woman, he thought. Maybe one day…

By the time he'd finished his tea and had his cup topped up,

Trevor and Robbie had arrived. Bill dismissed the two women for the night, and the three men gathered around the conference table.

Trevor, a wide grin across his face, admired the shotguns laid out on the table. "Bloody good job, Bill. Now we can take better care of ourselves."

"Too right," added Robbie, a mechanic in a past life. Although not officially, Robbie was Bill's number two. The man, a solid six feet in height, was incredibly fit, a triathlete, and as sharp as a knife. Bill had allotted him the responsibility for controlling their non-food supplies. Trevor, on the other hand, was a skinny as a rake, with white hair and matching coloured beard. But he too was as bright as a button and could handle himself when the situation required it. As an ex-chef, he had been given responsibility for the group's food and water supplies.

Bill nodded. "I'll get the TA lads to check them out, clean them up, and give us some instruction on how best to use them."

"Shouldn't be difficult to fire. Just point and shoot."

"I'm sure it is, Trevor, but I just want to be on the safe side."

The two men nodded, accepting Bill's judgement. Bill pulled one of the maps towards the centre of the table, closer to where Trevor and Robbie stood. Both recognised the area immediately.

Bill tapped the map around Coulsdon. "According to the ex-TA lads, there's a TA drill hall based here on Marlpit Lane. They reckon it's probably been stripped of weapons before it was destroyed, but I reckon it's worth a look."

"It's about five miles away, Bill, and we don't really know what the score is around there," pointed out Robbie.

"We got these now," Trevor said, pointing at the shotguns.

"I know," responded Bill, "but there are bound to be some automatic weapons out there, and unless we can get some of the same, we'll be outgunned every time."

"The boys said that just before they left, the TA units were running out of ammo."

"I still think it's worth a try, Robbie."

The man nodded and they both looked at Trevor, who then also nodded his agreement.

"Right, we need to pull together a plan."

"When are you thinking, Bill?"

"Give it a week. We know where we can find a gas-powered forklift. We can use that to lug stuff out of the way."

"Another tunnelling job, eh?" laughed Robbie.

"You sure you weren't a miner rather than a fireman, Bill?"

Bill smiled. "We have problems lighting fires now, never mind putting them out. Anyway, I have a new trade now: scavenging."

"Who do we take? We still need to defend this place and keep our foraging teams on the go, and protected."

"I'm leaving you here, Robbie, to sort all that."

"OK. So, who are you taking?"

"Trevor, the two TA lads, Ken, Reece and Kenny."

"That twat Kenny? Are you sure?" exclaimed Robbie.

"Better I can see him," countered Bill.

"If he gives any more trouble, we'll sort him," added Trevor.

"Need to watch his two boys though. Under twenty, but still seem nasty pieces of work."

"I know. Right, we can go through the plans tomorrow, Trevor. I'm fucked. Join me for a nightcap though, eh?"

"Yes," they both responded.

"On the way up to my place, Trevor, grab the TA lads. I want these weapons ready soonest. They're no use to us like this."

"Sure, Bill."

"Let's go then."

Bill picked up one of the gas lamps, blew out the second, and led the way out, followed by his two key supporters. A quick drink, then he would get some sleep. There was so much to do if they were going to survive the next few days, let alone years.

CHAPTER 8

Glen could hear his breathing resonating in his ears as he moved along the concrete-lined corridor. It always made him smile when he wore his army respirator. It reminded him of his son saying he looked at sounded like Darth Vader when he had worn it for his son Jack, over a year ago. He very much doubted his son, along with his wife Jackie and daughter Louise were alive. They were in married quarters in Hereford, the location of the Special Air Service's Regimental Headquarters, which had taken a direct hit from a 100-kiloton nuclear missile. The headquarters was now nothing but a giant crater. The houses around the town, out to a radius of at least three kilometres, had been destroyed and heavily contaminated. At five kilometres, most people exposed would have suffered third-degree burns at least, and many would have died of their injuries. Treatment would be almost non-existent. Even if his family had survived the blast, it was more than likely that the effects of a 500-rem burst of radiation would have finished them off. He had come to terms with it, but would investigate the area before he could put his mind at rest and start planning his future.

He arrived at the first of the steel doors, sensing Greg close behind him. He sucked in deeply through the filters of his mask as he prepared to open the steel, blast proof doors. The old and no longer used Regional Government Centre had provided them with the protection they needed to survive the nuclear onslaught, but the internal support facilities were all but non-existent. The generator had enough fuel to last a mere three days. After that, they had spent eighteen days in near darkness.

Using his torch, Glen located the lever he would need to pump in order to operate the hydraulically-controlled armoured door. Checking the lever was set for open, he pulled and pushed on the handle, pumping pressure into the system. After only twenty seconds, he heard the welcome groan as the heavyweight door shifted, a small gap slowly showing between its edge and the concrete-lined opening. A sigh of relief hissed through his mask, thankful that the door frames hadn't been knocked out of alignment. He said a silent prayer for the engineers who had designed and built the bunker. He continued the action for another two minutes, changing with Greg behind him, swapping again later. Eventually, the door was fully open. He shone the torch through the gap, and then followed the corridor left, then right, the dogleg acting as a buffer should the main outer door be breached. At the outer door, Glen went through the same motions as before, but stopping when the gap was only half a metre wide. It was dark outside. The group had deliberately timed the opening of the door during hours of darkness. They had no idea what could be waiting outside for them.

Once the SAS troop had ensconced themselves within the depths of the RGC bunker, it was agreed that they would wait a full twenty-one days before they surfaced, allowing the heavily radiated ground and atmosphere to lose some of its lethality. The reduction in radiation levels would be at a relatively safe level after twenty-one days, but contaminated dust, animals and foodstuffs would still remain an issue for a long time to come. During their wait, they had discussed the options open to them.

"We need to check on your family, Glen."

"Thanks, guys, but I can't expect you to detour from your own plans."

"What fucking plans," Greg's face broke into a smile. "A few beers, a good woman, and then a nightclub? I don't think."

The others laughed.

"Anyway, you're not to be trusted on your own," added Greg.

"What are their chances, do you reckon?" asked Roland.

With just a single lamp providing light, they couldn't see the hurt in Glen's eyes but could sense a slight tremble in his voice as he answered. "To be honest…nil. But I have to look all the same."

"Why the bloody hell didn't she move away then?" exclaimed Greg.

"Her damn mother," scowled Glen. "Wouldn't leave Hereford, so Jackie chose to stay with her, along with the kids. Anyway, we never ever believed it would come to this. What do we do after we've taken a look? That's the million dollar question."

"Everything could be OK out there," suggested Roland, the youngest member of the troop.

"Don't be a wanker. You heard it! And the last of the reports from the head shed warned us of multiple incoming."

"Yeah, his last encouraging words were 'wipe out'," moaned Glen.

Plato, who had been relatively quiet until now, spoke up. He was deemed to be the brightest individual of the troop, forever reading about a range of differing subject matter, from the mating rituals of the sperm whale to the readings of the philosopher Aristotle – hence his nickname, the name of another well known philosopher. Plato, or Tyler, his real name, was considered to be the analyst within the troop, taking the lead in the planning of any operation they were involved in. The troop had been brought back from the Ukraine once hostilities had ceased, and the NATO and Soviet armies watched each other warily across no-man's-land. As the politicians negotiated, while eating salmon and cucumber sandwiches and sipping on Pouilly-Fuissé wine, the troop had been tasked with rooting out some of the Spetsnaz sleeper cells that MI5 believed were still operating in the United Kingdom, waiting for orders to strike again at the country's leaders and infrastructure.

Plato had meticulously planned the assault on one particular cell, hidden in a bunker deep in the heart of the Dovedale National Nature Reserve. It had resulted in six dead Spetsnaz operatives with no casualties within the troop. They had discovered food, communications equipment, maps and an arms cache, including one of the deadly nuclear suitcase bombs. Not that a half-kiloton device would have made much difference considering the UK had since been hit with at least 300 megatons. After that, and a quick celebration, the troop of eight men, the mountain troop of Two-Squadron, 22 SAS Regiment, had been split. Sergeant Glen Lewis and his three men were diverted to Wolverhampton while the rest went on to provide close protection for the Defence Secretary who was meeting with other NATO leaders. The peace talks with the Russians were going badly, and they were digging their heels in over any possibility of withdrawing their troops from eastern Ukraine.

It was while the four men were heading for Wolverhampton that they got the first warning of an impending nuclear strike. Diverting to Swynnerton, they had only been at that location for an hour when they received the 'Black' warning. Sealed up in the bunker, they had lost all contact with the outside world, but could hear, and feel, the rumbles of numerous powerful explosions. On one occasion, the bunker was shaken so violently they had expected it to collapse in on top of them. Fortunately, it held, and all were in agreement to hold out for a full twenty-one days.

"The way I see it, we have three options, providing, that is, we aren't able to make contact with headquarters." Plato listed them. "Head south-east, make our way to London, and suss out if the Pindar Bunker is occupied and operational. If the Joint Operations Centre is online then we can seek further orders. Number two: we find one of the larger Regional Government Centres, latch on to it, and see how it pans out. Finally, we find a base of our own. Come up with a plan for the future. God knows what that is likely to be. By the way, each one of those options is preceded by a trip to pick up Glen's family."

"Thanks, Plato. Right, guys, Chinese Parliament time. Which of those rocks your boat?" asked Glen.

Greg, always the most outspoken of the four men, was the first to respond. "I agree with Plato's list, but they're all shite options. Number one and three for me. Get to Pindar, suss out what command and control is like and, if it's fucked, move on to plan three and look after ourselves. Suss out any nightclubs still up and running on the way," he added with a laugh.

"I'm for joining an RGC, see if we can make ourselves useful," opted Rolly, the youngest of the team. "They'll probably need our help. Sorting out the communities has to be the priority. Get the country back on its feet."

Greg leant forward in the dim light of the bunker, and he shuffled his padded seat closer to the group. "Don't be a twat, Rolly. They'll be in shit state. You remember the briefings we've had about nuclear warfare? Three quarters of the fucking population is going to be sick or dying, and the rest will be homeless and starving. Come under the command of some jumped-up local council official and work with some twatting reservists who've had a couple of bloody days' training? Bollocks."

"We now know where you stand," responded Glen with a chuckle. "Still opt for an RGC, Rolly?"

A red tinge coloured Rolly's cheeks. "Well, I…uh…see where Greg's coming from. But shouldn't we…help…?" His voice tailed off in the darkness.

Greg patted his shoulder. "Stick with us, mate, we'll see you right. What about you, Glen?"

"Option one and three makes sense. Sorry, Rolly, but if we get sucked into working with one of the RGCs, it'll be controlling a labour workforce, burying or burning the dead, or riot control. Some may survive, but you know people. When the food runs out, it'll fall apart. Plato?"

"That's the one that makes the most sense. Sorry, Rolly."

"Nah, that's fine. Troop decision, and I'm happy to go with it." Inside, Rolly was relieved. He hadn't been comfortable with what he thought was the right thing to do versus what he wanted to do.

"So, when twenty-one days are up, we head for the smoke. I'm for grub. What we got for tonight?"

Glen pulled down his night vision goggles, a green mist showing the corridor outside the outer steel blast door open to the sky that led to the perimeter of the site. It was unoccupied. Turning round, he tapped Greg's arm, indicating the soldier could continue with the pumping, opening the door even further while he and the third man back, Plato, moved outside.

Glen unslung his HK G36 and, on getting a tap on his shoulder from Plato, moved down the corridor. The walls either side became lower as they moved further away from the door, the concrete bund being replaced by sloping banks of earth either side. On reaching the end of the access point, Glen went left, Plato went right, and Rolly, the fourth member of the team, stayed in the centre, with Greg keeping watch. Glen covered the left arc, scanning left and right, searching for any signs of life. Looking half-right, he could see an oblong building, showing up as a shimmering green shadow. There were no signs of life, nor any movement for that matter. About fifty metres away, alongside the building, he could see the shape of their Land Rover, still in situ, appearing unharmed and in one piece. They waited ten minutes before expanding their search radius. The cold started to ease its way through his clothing, and Glen shivered. The four men continued their search of the immediate area up as far as the two-metre-high fence line, and then regrouped.

Glen kicked off a quick O-group. "First signs looking good. Greg, I want you and Rolly to do a full circuit. Immediate area, then out to 150 metres."

"Make sure you do a test for radiation while you're out there."

Plato dropped his pack, removed the man-portable device and handed it over to Rolly.

"Meet back here in sixty. Got it?" added Glen.

"Yes, boss," they all concurred.

The two men tasked with the patrol went out through the gate they had driven through twenty-one days earlier and completed their patrol, reporting back that all was clear. Radiation was detected, but the radiation readings were at a satisfactory level. While on patrol, their packs and other kit had been brought to the Land Rover, which was covered in a film of fine dust, by Glen and Plato, and once it was confirmed the vehicle would start, one of the few EMP protected vehicles in the army, the equipment was loaded on board. The majority of their kit was piled into the quarter-ton two-wheeled trailer. A tarp over the top, secured to the sides, ensured the items would stay in position should they encounter any rough terrain.

It was 0410. Dawn would be with them in less than an hour. They had agreed to stay in situ until full daylight, concerned about driving and stumbling around in the dark, not knowing the full outcome of the nuclear exchange.

When the time came, NVG goggles were removed, but respirators were pulled back on. Until they could assess the levels of dust in the air beyond the bunker complex, which would have to be done visually, they preferred the full protection afforded by their respirators and camouflaged NBC suits. Glen was also worried about dust being kicked up by the vehicle and finding its way inside. Better safe than sorry had been his mantra. Glen and Plato climbed into the front two seats, Plato driving, while Greg and Rolly positioned themselves in the very cramped rear of the long wheel-based vehicle. Even more supplies had been piled into the back of the canvas-topped Land Rover. They estimated they had at least two months' worth of supplies, and plenty of ammunition, provided they used them sparingly. They left the RGC, heading south-west on a minor road, more of a lane to start with, avoiding the M6 motorway to the east, suspecting it would be clogged with abandoned vehicles as panic set in, people racing away from the major centres of population, or major military bases, seeking the relative safety of the countryside. Within twenty minutes, they had crossed Meece Brook, which ran north to south, and soon found themselves on the A519. Apart from the occasional abandoned car, smoke from a fire outside a roofless house, they came across no other signs of life.

"Just seen a sign for Newport," Plato pointed out as he slowed down a little, the two nodding soldiers in the back stirring slightly, recognising the change in the engine's rhythm. However, they kept their eyes closed and continued to doze.

Glen turned the map on his lap slightly and responded. "We need to avoid the towns. There's a minor road or track coming up on the left. Swing south there. Then it'll take us towards Shifnal. We can continue down the A442 and cross the River Severn south of Bridgnorth. Once there, we can take a breather, and the two sleeping beauties in the back can take a stint."

"Wanker," piped up Greg before adjusting his position and closing his eyes again. Sleep while you can was very much his motto: you never knew when the next opportunity would arise.

It took them nearly an hour to get to the northern outskirts of Bridgnorth. Before they drove into Bridgnorth, Glen directed Plato off to the left, taking the A454, passing the Stanmore Country Park on the left before swinging west along the A548. Although Bridgnorth had been spared a direct hit, Wolverhampton and Coventry to the east had each received a one-megaton ground bursts and two 500KT air bursts over the cities. Birmingham was struck by two one-megaton strikes and three 500KT airbursts, and Kidderminster to the south, the location of a major Regional Government Headquarters, had suffered from a one-megaton missile strike and two one-megaton ground bursts dropped by Soviet bombers. With other strikes in the area, Bridgnorth would have suffered from an element of the hurricane-like blast wave. Thermal radiation could also have reached the town, causing major burn trauma, and igniting combustible materials and burning down many of the houses. On top of that, the fallout cloud would have undoubtedly deposited contaminated particles in the area kicking out between ten and 100 rads per hour.

"Greg, Rolly. Stand to. We're coming to a built-up area. Be ready," warned Glen.

The two men were immediately alert, weapons checked, and at the ready.

Plato maintained a steady sixty kilometres per hour, the Land Rover's tyres thrumming on the tarmac surface of the road as they passed an industrial complex on the south-eastern edge of Bridgnorth. They cut around a large roundabout, heading west between an avenue of burnt trees. They couldn't see many houses, but the ones they did see were blackened and interspersed with the wreckage of other buildings, cars, and even someone's power boat, still attached to its trailer.

"Another roundabout coming up," informed Glen.

"Gotcha."

Plato picked up speed, and the Land Rover tilted over as he took the roundabout quickly, the trailer bouncing on one wheel before settling back down. Trees continued to line the road either side.

"Coming up to the bridge. Be ready, lads." Glen knew, as did the rest of the troop, that bridges were always a good choke point, an ideal ambush location. He was far from wrong as Plato pressed hard on the brakes, the wheels locking, the front tilting slightly left, the back end sliding right, the trailer swinging round in an arc behind them, barely maintaining its balance, pulling the back end further around as the vehicle finally ground to a halt, kicking up a cloud of dust as a Saxon armoured troop carrier careered across in front of them. Within a matter of seconds, they were surrounded by armed men in various states of military dress.

"Get ready," Greg warned. "We're not fucking about with these muppets."

A captain walked towards the cab of the Land Rover, and Glen pulled back the hood of his NBC suit and peeled off his respirator and slid back the door window. The captain looked to be a regular but, as Glen scanned the rest, it was clear they were a mixture of Territorial Army soldiers, police officers and some form of militia.

"Sir," responded Glen as the captain came up to the side of the vehicle, pulling the scarf down that had been wrapped around his mouth. "Gave me and the boys quite a fright back there."

"And you are?" asked the captain sternly.

"Bravo-Two-Two."

"And they are?"

"We're on an operation tasked directly by Joint Ops Command."

Greg and Rolly looked at each other in the back, both thinking the same. *Bullshit.*

"And that mission is?"

"I'm not at liberty to divulge that, sir. Why the sudden road block? Why not just flag us down?"

"There's a large group terrorising the local area. Some of them are deserters. We can't afford to expose ourselves. They need to be hunted down and brought into line if we're to get this region back on its feet." The captain peered at the rear seats of the Land Rover.

"Your men will be a valuable additional resource."

"We have received independent tasking, sir. We don't come under RGC orders."

"And where have you got your orders from?"

"Joint Ops at Pindar," lied Glen.

"But our headquarters have received no communication from London."

"We're on a different frequency, sir."

The captain rubbed his chin, uncertain what to do next. "It would be good to be in touch with London. We're operating on our own out here."

"Have you been in touch with other RGCs?"

"One, briefly. But we think they were overpowered by the local population who appear to have taken control. You will have to come with me...and your rank?"

"Glen Lewis, sir."

The captain huffed. "Prima donnas, eh. Well, for the moment I'm in control. I need you to step out of your vehicle. We'll take care of it, and then you're to come with me."

"With all due respect, sir, we don't come under your control or your orders." Glen sensed the two in the back shift position and Plato stiffen next to him. He looked out of the corner of his right eye: the GPMG machine gun atop the Saxon lined up on him and his men. Other soldiers were watching warily either side.

"You come under regional government control now, soldier."

"You lead the way, sir, and we'll follow in our vehicle."

The captain thought for a moment, recognising that he could have a potential bloodbath on his hands. He suspected he could win the firefight but, in the current circumstances, he couldn't afford to lose any more men. There were casualties daily, through death, desertion and sickness. He made his mind up. "You follow my vehicle." He pointed towards a short-wheel-based Land Rover. "The Saxon will be right behind you. I'll give them orders to take you out at the first sign of trouble, you understand?"

"Yes, sir. We can then confirm our task with your regional controller, and then we can get on with our mission."

The captain nodded, indicated for the men close by to mount up, and signalled for the Saxon to come in behind the SAS troop.

"When I move, you move."

"Sir."

The captain walked over to his vehicle, and the roar of the Saxon engine could be heard as it manoeuvred behind them. Two land Rovers manoeuvred into position in front of them.

"As soon as we cross the water, head south, Plato. Greg, Rolly, I want two smoke, two HE grenades, then two more smoke out the sides."

All three acknowledged.

"We'll go cross country, follow the riverbank, and head west as soon as we see the right spot. They're just begging to open fire. But, with that Saxon bouncing all over the place, they'll be lucky to hit a barn door. If we can lose it, then we'll take out any of the soft-skinned vehicles left on our tail."

"And if we don't lose the Saxon then this baby will discourage them." Greg smiled as he fondled the MBT LAW anti-tank missile he had pulled from out of the back.

"Yeah, but only if we have to, Greg. They're soldiers like us after all."

"Not all," added Plato. "A right motley crew, if you ask me."

"He's signalling," informed Rolly as he peered in between the heads of Glen and Plato.

"Let's go," ordered Glen. "Keep a bit of distance between us and them, and not too fast. Floor it as soon as we're across the bridge."

Plato put the vehicle into four-wheel drive, then applied power to the Land Rover, and it picked up speed, catching up with the two open-topped Land Rovers in front. What appeared to be two Territorial Army soldiers were in the back of the nearest one. The vehicle leading had an armed policeman and an individual in jeans and a combat jacket. The civilian was also armed with an SA-80. Within minutes, they were off the bridge, passing beneath an old iron bridge carrying a road and railway east.

"Crash barrier either side, observed Plato."

"Wooden, but looks solid enough. Keep going." Glen looked in the wing mirror, caught a glimpse of the Saxon about thirty metres back, a Regular soldier holding onto the pintle-mounted GPMG, ready to act if needed. The vehicles ahead slowed down as they approached a bend. A second flyover could be seen as Plato reduced his speed to ensure they maintained a reasonable distance from those in front. But, they would inevitably bunch up.

"Fucking fence has gone, but the trees are too dense," warned Plato.

"Keep moving. Get ready in the back. Smoke first."

"Roger that," responded Greg as he lay side by side with Rolly on top of the paraphernalia of stores they carried in the back. Once they received the order, they would dip their heads beneath the rear canvas flap and prepare for a fire fight if needed. They passed beneath the flyover and the road straightened up.

"Barriers gone," informed Plato. "We're in a dip, banks either side of us."

"Just be ready."

"It's flattening out."

"Stand by," warned Glen.

"Roger," came the response from the back.

"Gap coming up," informed Plato. "Ready, ready, ready..."

"Now," yelled Glen as Plato spun the wheel left, the body of the vehicle tipping right as they sped through the knee-high grass.

Whoompf...whoompf. Two smoke grenades exploded behind the Land Rover just as it came off the road, small clouds of smoke growing steadily bigger and denser, the breeze taking it across the road as they heard the chatter of machine-gun fire from the Saxon. But the gunner was firing blind, and the driver, swerved into the bank on the right, his vision impaired by the rapidly blooming smokescreen.

Crump...crump. Two grenades exploded, thrown by Greg and Rolly as the Land Rover smashed through the overgrown, little used gate that protected a field of crops. The gate was shattered, splinters smacking at the windscreen as Plato tried to maintain control of the careering vehicle, the trailer going haywire behind them.

"Smoke," called Glen as Plato turned left again, forcing a trail through the crops as he steered in an arc, back towards the edge of the field. More smoke billowed up, engulfing the area behind them, acting as a shield, hiding them from view. They needn't have worried. The Saxon was up against the bank on two wheels, and by the time the lead vehicles had cottoned on to what had happened and spun round to come back and investigate, the troop were well on their way. Guided by Glen with the map, and an element of common sense, the Land Rover clawed its way across field after field until they eventually made it to the B4363, continuing their journey south.

"Well, Rolly," chided Greg, "that answers the question about joining one of the ragtag outfits."

"What now, Glen?"

"Stay on this road, Plato. Cross the A456, then across the A44, and come at Hereford from the east. Give it half an hour. Then we'll swap drivers."

It took the troop six hours to complete the 100-kilometre journey, passing through Kinlet, Cleobury Mortimer, crossing the A456, then through Stanford Bridge. Once across the A44, it was a straight run down the A465 until they were able to turn eastward. They approached the town of Hereford from the east, along the A438. The sight that met them shook even these sturdy soldiers. The 500-kiloton burst had done its job well. The fireball had radiated out to nearly a kilometre, incinerating all in its path, generating a firestorm that raged through the town. The air blast that quickly followed, the overpressure expanding out to nearly two-kilometres, demolished most houses, blasting roofs off others, shattering windows, killing thousands. Those that were lucky enough to have escaped the devastation that struck had been radiated with a 500-rem radiation dose. Without speedy medical treatment, ninety per cent of the population would be dead within a matter of hours, or at the most a matter of weeks. Even those that, by some miracle, had survived in those first few moments in what was clearly hell on earth, thermal radiation, out to over ten-kilometres, inflicted third-degree burns on any survivors exposed to it. Some experienced fourth-degree burns: burns that went deep, extending through the fragile layers of skin and flesh, into the underlying fat, muscle and bone, harrowing but painless as the nerves were destroyed before they could register the horrific torture that should have been. All of the fourth-degree burn victims were dead.

In total, the town of Hereford, and the surrounding area out to a radius of some ten to twelve kilometres, had suffered over 35,000 deaths and 8,000 casualties, the fallout affecting even more people, reaching as far as Liverpool that, in turn, received two one-megaton bombs themselves. The houses either side of the road were houses no longer, but begrimed, roofless, windowless shells. A woman, her face covered with severe leather-like scarring as were her arms, shivered in the cold while clutching a small blackened form, partially wrapped in a grubby shawl, to her chest. Her dirty, hairless head turned to follow them, the missing ear on her left side replaced by a seared blob of shrivelled flesh.

"Shall we stop?" asked Plato.

"No, keep moving. There's nothing we can do. And we risk

getting caught up with the local administration again."

"That's if there is any in this godforsaken mess," added Greg.

Greg, who was now driving, with Rolly in the front passenger seat, steered the Land Rover around the chunks of debris and avoided the abandoned and blackened cars sitting on their wheel hubs, tyres burnt off and the paintwork non-existent. The closer they got to the centre of the town, the worse it got. The debris turned into rubble, and the abandoned cars were often on their side or angled across the road, blown there by the force of the blast.

"Hang next right," instructed Glen. "Let's do a CTR of the hospital."

The rail bridge ahead had collapsed, and Greg put the vehicle into four-wheel drive. It bounced across the rubble as Greg manoeuvred the Rover through the clearest sections, almost getting stuck at one point and tipping over the trailer the next. Eventually, they got across. Although the road was clearer, rubble still slowed their journey as they turned down Central Avenue, across the big roundabout, straight along St Guthlac Street before turning right onto Union Walk to complete their recce. The hospital was off to the right – what was left of it. Like most of the buildings, it had been burnt out and, being higher than the surrounding buildings, had taken the brunt of the blast wave. It was unlikely that it could ever be used as a hospital again.

Plato waved the radiation detector around. "Getting some pretty high readings around here. I suggest we don't stop here too long, boss."

"I have no intentions of staying any longer."

"Shall we go for the married quarters?"

"No, there's no point. We're moving closer and closer towards Ground Zero, so by the time we get the married quarters…" Glen didn't need to continue. They all knew what he meant. "Turn her around, Greg. Let's head south."

CHAPTER 9

Ten men and two women patrolled up and down the line. Metre-long solid ash pick helves, to be used as batons if needed, swung from their hands, a white band with the letters CPS (Civilian Police Support) around their upper arm.

Captain Redfern watched them as they walked the line, scowling at some of the hungry refugees, using force of will to keep them in line. It reminded him of some of the films he had seen, about the Second World War and the Holocaust. *Yes, Kapos*, he thought: used by the German authorities to police the Jews as they were rounded up to be shipped to the concentration camps sprouting up all over Eastern Europe. Alan had protested about the use of civilians, but the PO and the colonel had overruled him. He could understand their reasons behind the decision, lack of manpower within the police force, but it still felt distasteful. Even though his unit had been joined by a further five soldiers and two police constables from the outlying districts, they only had thirty-two soldiers and thirteen civilian police officers to control a crowd of over 4,000 now. This was the survivor's first meal that had been doled out by the RGC. It wasn't much: a tin of luncheon meat, tin of soup, and a packet of dried biscuits. But, for some, it would be the first thing they would have eaten for perhaps up to a week. At the end of the line, a water tanker provided water, the survivors filling up tin cans, plastic bottles, jugs, bowls, basically anything they could lay their hands on. A small woman, clutching what looked to be a two-year-old child to her body, tripped over the blanket flapping around her feet, and a CPS officer standing close by grabbed her arm to prevent her crashing to the ground. She thanked the man, and he returned the thanks with a smile.

Alan relaxed a little, annoyed at himself for letting his imagination run away with him. He walked over to the Land Rover. Sergeant Saunders was in the driver's seat, his gloved fingers drumming on the steering wheel, waiting. His helmet was off and the NBC hood pulled back, his short mousey brown hair matted to his head.

"We going back for the brief now, sir?"

"Yes. What's your thoughts on this new CPS unit?"

"Bunch of misfits, but the best of the bunch. Health wise, that is. Not sure about anything else. So long as we don't give them anything more than a pickaxe handle, they shouldn't be a problem."

"I suppose."

"I'll tell the boys to keep an eye on them."

"Good call. Right, back to the RGC."

"Let's find out what's going on then eh?"

"I hope so. It's about time. I know we need to plan, but we also need some action as well."

Sergeant Saunders started the engine, put the vehicle into gear, and headed north slowly but still kicking up a small amount of partially contaminated dust, that trailed behind them.

"We need some rain, sir."

"Or a miracle."

Although the L-shaped room was one of the biggest in the bunker, it was still crowded as the key members of the Regional Government Centre gathered for a major briefing. There was standing room only as the group, pushing steel-tubed desks and chairs back as far as the communication wires would allow to make room, gathered around a large map on the main wall. At the centre of the semi-circle were the top six men, given governmental authority prior to the nuclear strikes to take responsibility for the region. The senior man was Douglas Elliot, the principal officer. Then there was his deputy, Edward Cox, assistant PO, Chief Scientist Rupert Lowe, Superintendent Derek Collins, in charge of the police, Colonel Bannister, looking resplendent in his No. 2 dress, preferring it to combats, in command of the armed services, and finally Dylan Wright, the individual responsible for the Department of Employment, in baggy trousers sporting a dark blue blazer.

Elliot, a large barrel-chested man, his suit now hanging slightly loose on him after three weeks of rationed food, dominated the room. He scratched his balding head and cleared his throat. "Gentlemen, perch on a chair or desk if you're able. Get as comfortable as possible," the PO suggested. "This may take a while."

The attendees shuffled and made themselves as comfortable as possible. They were a mixed bunch, a representative from each of the main departments that were deemed necessary to put the region back on its feet. Both the colonel and the captain wondered what input some of them could possibly provide. There were representatives from the Departments of Transport, Energy, Employment, the Social Security Agency, Ministry of Agriculture, Fisheries and Food, the Environment, army, police, scientists, finance, and the Office for Information. Other departments, not represented at the meeting but still within the building, consisted of British Telecom, housekeeping, communications and the Department of Trade and Industry.

"Colonel, an update on the security situation please?"

"Of course. I'll provide an overview. Then I'll hand over to Captain Redfern who can provide a more detailed update of our current position."

Captain Redfern nodded his head, and the colonel continued. "There are four elements really. First, the control of the feeding station recently set up. It's got off to a good start, just a few minor disruptions. The captain will fill you in on his thoughts and any concerns he may have. Secondly, the warehouse. As some of you know, days before the food station was set up, there was a major assault on the warehouse. The QRF, the quick reaction force, was able to respond in time, and they were beaten off. The most disturbing element of the attack was that some of the perpetrators were armed with automatic weapons."

"Where could they have got them from?" asked the PO.

"Any number of sources. Perhaps they managed to find a military armoury somewhere. We know there are army deserters out there, or they may have taken the weapons off a soldier after killing him or her."

"God help us," groaned the PO. "Carry on, Colonel."

"Our patrols are operating effectively enough and, with the additional manpower, including the CPS officers, I'm confident we can secure this compound, the warehouse, the feeding station, and out to a twenty-kilometre radius. Finally, we are ready to support Dylan as soon as the go-ahead is given for the labour force to be recruited."

"Dylan will update us on that shortly," informed the PO.

"Anything to add, Captain Redfern?" the colonel asked.

"Only regarding the recruitment of CPSs. I'm concerned that we're pulling together an unofficial group that could potentially get out of control if not watched closely."

"I disagree with the captain, by the way. But understand his concerns," advised the colonel.

"I'm with the captain on this," added Superintendent Collins, smartly dressed in his blue police uniform, despite the circumstances and the cramped conditions of the bunker. His cap tucked under his arm along with his brown leather gloves.

"If we're to gather a big enough labour force, and control it, to start work on clearing the mess out there, we must have additional supervision." Dylan Wright, head of the Department of Employment, jumped in.

"They will be your responsibility then?" responded Captain Redfern.

"I…ah…well…I suppose they will be."

The PO interrupted. "Gentlemen, please. We will monitor the situation, Captain. But we do need a labour force, and once people realise that they will only get top rations when they work, and reduced rations for those that don't, we could well have our hands full. And they are an official force sanctioned by the Government. Thank you, Colonel, Captain. Rupert, a science update, if you please."

The chief scientist, with his matted but thinning hair sticking out above his ears, was almost the epitome of a mad professor. He was even wearing a white lab-coat, although not so white after spending three weeks in the bunker.

"Harrumph." He cleared his throat and shuffled the papers he was holding until he came to the one he was looking for.

"The local area," he began, "has a contamination level that will allow an individual to stay out for five or six hours. But the two hot spots are north of Chilmark, around Hindon and the RAF base. These should be avoided at all costs. As you have been informed before, the levels of radiation in the town of Chilmark are dropping slowly, but I would advise that the labour force is only out in the open for a few hours a day to start with, increasing the time as and when I get more positive updates. One of our key tasks is to find any livestock and corral them close to our chosen site, particularly any potential milk herds."

"Will we be able to drink the milk?" asked Edward Cox, the deputy PO.

"There is no doubt that the cattle, or goats for that matter, will have eaten contaminated fodder, whether in a barn or grass in the fields. Those that have survived, that is. Many will have died from the initial high levels of radiation. But it has been decided that we should use the milk rather than discard it."

"Won't it affect us?" asked an astounded representative from the Department of Transport.

"Undoubtedly, but food is going to be so scarce we have little option. It will be many years before the levels drop back to anywhere near pre-strike levels."

"What about the animals themselves?" queried Kate Worth, the head of MAFF.

"Yes, they will have suffered injuries, and tens of thousands will have been killed. Those that have survived can still die, and there will be an increase in malignant skin tumours, particularly in white-coated and piebald animals."

"Crops?"

"Well, with an anticipated tenfold increase in ultraviolet B, soya beans and wheat have been and will continue to be affected marginally, whereas others, peas and onions for example, have probably all been scorched and likely killed."

Rupert held up a sheet of paper. "I have a list of what can possibly be harvested now if available, and a list of those crops that should be planted if we are to see out another year."

Somebody in the group groaned.

"We must not despair," the PO encouraged. "Those people out there are depending on us. We have the knowledge, the resources and the means to get through this, providing we strive for that same purpose and work together. Rupert, continue please."

"You need to understand the bigger picture. It's estimated that 3,000 megatons of nuclear weapons will have been released across the world, and the UK will have received over 300 megatons of that. There have probably been huge forest fires in some parts of the world, and there is the potential for thousands of oil wells burning away furiously. This will…is having a major impact on our weather, in the northern hemisphere at least. Our industrial network, power stations, hospitals, water provision and other centrally provided services will have been decimated. Very little will have survived, including our homes. Three quarters of the housing stock in the UK will have been within the strike zones, and will now be roofless and windowless. In some of the larger towns, there would have been a raging inferno, fuelled by the plentiful material available and high winds, destroying everything in its path. We—"

"I think we get the message, Rupert. Cliff, what's the status of our current food stocks?"

Cliff, the Food officer, pulled a notebook from his pocket, running his tongue across his crooked teeth as he consulted it. "Well, based on our present food programme of a bowl of soup in the morning and one main hot meal in the evening, and assuming numbers will remain at the 4,000 mark, we have three days at the camp, less than one day here, as an emergency that is, and three to four months at the two warehouses – notwithstanding the fact that feeding a workforce will require an increase in rations though."

"Yes, but that will be countered by a reduction in rations for those not working," interjected Dylan Wright.

"And there will be many more deaths yet," added the chief scientist. "Many with wounds or injuries may yet succumb, and we could all potentially be exposed to disease and other infections."

"I understand that. Nevertheless, we do need to restock our supplies soon though. Three to four months will go by pretty quickly."

"Thank you, Cliff. We do intend to implement a major scavenging operation along with starting to clear up the mess out there."

"You mean Chilmark, PO?" asked Colonel Bannister.

"Yes, Colonel," responded Elliot. "We need to clear the streets so we have access, dispose of the bodies, then repair the houses and make them habitable again. We can't live in this dungeon forever, and neither can the population live in tents like some Third World country."

"That's pretty much what we are currently," cautioned Alan.

"That's as maybe, Captain. But I have no intention of letting it remain so. Right, last briefing before we finish the meeting. Dylan, your employment and workforce plan please."

"Thank you, PO." Dylan adjusted one of the sheets attached to his clipboard and peered at the information through his half-moon reading glasses. "I'll start off with a breakdown of the population that is under our protection. We have managed some form of census, but with the population shifting around all the time, it's not completely accurate."

"That will be resolved when meal chits are issued to the labour force," suggested the Colonel.

"So–so That will certainly help. The count I have is 3,909. They have been subcategorised into adult males over the age of fifteen, adult females over the age of fifteen, and those below that age. We have 1,701 males, of which 685 are sick or dying, 1,910 females, 409 sick or dying, 112 female children and 186 male children. When I refer to the sick, I mean those that will not survive. But many of those that have been categorised as available for work are far from fit."

"Malnutrition?" asked the PO.

"In some cases, yes. But many of the fit, and I use that term lightly, have wounds and injuries that have shown improvement, but are far from healing properly. There are not enough medicines to treat them, and they'll always be susceptible to infection, relapses and possibly death. Recruiting them for our labour force will just speed that up."

There was a moment of silence, those present recognising the cold truth of the position the country was in, eventually broken by Elliot, the principal officer.

"Listen." Hands, palms up, held out in front of him, and his voice a mix of pleading and determination, he made eye contact with as many of those present as he possibly could. "Civilisation, as we have become used to for the duration of our lives to date, has gone. Prior to this post, I was a senior administrator, a public servant, who had access to funds, electricity, a workforce, rules, both primary support and leisure facilities, a wife and two sons. My wife is dead, my two sons were killed in the Ukraine fighting the Russians, and I am now the leader of some 4,000 people. I have been on courses run by the Government, but none of them have even come close to preparing me or any of you here to survive the devastation that has struck our nation and many others around the world."

His tone changed, and his demeanour stiffened. "If you think things are bad now then you're in for a shock. Because if we don't gear up, to use one of the terms I've heard you use, Captain Redfern…" Alan smiled and the tension in the room eased slightly, "…if we don't gear up to provide the population food, shelter and medical facilities, they will die. And if they die, it's likely that we will slip into that same void with them. We are the fortunate few in that we have our health, are fortunate that we have good food, and an environment that is far better than some are living in out there." He flung an arm in the direction of the roof of the bunker. "I am absolutely sure though that none of us want to spend the rest of our lives in this smelly box, especially as the luxuries of tea and biscuits and soap run out. We have to lead those people out there, and I will not accept half-hearted efforts. Everyone is either with me or I will replace them with someone else. Is that clear?"

Most immediately responded with positive tones and nods, but with the odd grumble. But Elliot knew he had the core on his side, and he felt confident that his chiefs of police and army command were very much a part of and in support of his regional government.

"Good. Make it quick, Dylan. I think we've been crammed into this room long enough."

"Tomorrow, we start the recruitment process for our labour force. For the evening meal, everyone, except children, at this point in time anyway, will need to be in possession of a meal chit. Those agreeing to work will receive a blue chit, and those not will have a red chit."

"And the difference between them?" asked Edward Cox, the deputy PO.

"A blue chit will equate to roughly 1,400 calories per day whereas the red chit will only be 1,000."

"And the sick, the children?"

"Children will receive 600 and the sick…well, it has been agreed to give them the same as the children, and families will be responsible for their care."

"There's going to be some unrest over this," warned Superintendent Collins.

"If we give out any more, we'll run out before we can replace the stocks we have," defended Cliff.

"You'll both need to be prepared," jumped in Elliot. "We have to have a labour force if we're to survive the months and years ahead."

"Have we had any contact yet with a more senior organisation?" asked Mathew Gray, part of the finance set-up. The only person present, apart from Colonel Bannister, wearing a tie. "Surely, central government must have surfaced by now and will want to take control of the reins."

"I understand your frustrations, Mathew," responded Elliot, mild impatience showing through. "I'm sure we'll hear from them when they're ready. In the meantime, we need to prepare for the worst."

"Can't we send some of the soldiers to the city, to London? Make contact? They can establish communications with some of the other counties maybe."

Elliot chose not answer immediately, gathering his thoughts, wanting to choose his words carefully. He recognised that many of the members of the RGC wondered why they were planning to make the effort of clearing the towns and villages, preparing farms for use again. They genuinely believed that they would get a call from some Downing Street official who would tell them all was well again and they could go back to their nine-to-five jobs. But he thought differently. The world was never going to be the same again, not in his lifetime anyway. In fact, he felt sure it was going to get worse before it got better.

"Mathew, Mathew, please. We've had this conversation before. If central government rises from the ashes, I will be the first one to raise a cheer, believe me. I'd like nothing better than the country to return to its former glory. But, until then, we carry on as if we are on our own, because at the moment that is exactly what we are. We have nearly 4,000 people out there who are depending on us. The safety of this centre rests on a knife edge, and I'm certainly not sending our soldiers on a wild goose chase. We need them here to protect us. Any last questions before we bring this meeting to a close?"

Alan indicated he had a question.

"Yes, Captain Redfern."

"Just about the feeding centre – when is the opening planned?"

"Apart from issuing some cold rations presently, I want the centre in full swing the day after tomorrow. I want to have a hot meal waiting for the labour force when they return from their first day's work. Is something worrying you, Captain?"

"No, sir. Just thinking ahead. Security of the food being transported from the warehouse and the feeding centre itself."

"I have every faith in you and your men, Captain. Right, gentlemen, I've taken up enough of your time as I'm sure we all have lots to do."

As the meeting dispersed, Colonel Bannister caught Alan's arm and pulled him aside while the occupants of the room slowly made their way out. "How do you plan on having the food regularly moved to the site?"

"We'll use the civvy trucks and move the supplies across at about four."

"Why so early?"

"Most of the population will be asleep and we'll need the trucks at six to start moving the labour force."

"Escort?"

"Just two Land Rovers, sir. We'll have speed on our side."

"Good. The last thing we need is an incident that holds up their meal when they get back from the fields."

"I need to go through the shift rota with Sergeant Saunders. The food centre and the work parties will put a lot of extra pressure on my lads."

"Liaise with Superintendent Collins. We need to make better use of the police constables. I want to keep our unit free as much as possible."

"Something coming up, sir?"

"The feeding centre and workforce are a start, but we need to start looking further afield."

"Fuel, vehicles, spares, food?"

"Yes, Alan, we need to cast our net wider. Resources will get scarcer by the day, and we need to start and replace as much of them as we can. Survival isn't going to be as straightforward as some people imagine."

"And the PO knows that."

"He does. We're lucky to have him in charge. It will need someone strong to lead us through this mess. Our support is key to that."

"The army is behind him, Colonel."

"I didn't doubt you'd be behind him, but it's good to hear it all the same."

"When does the wider search start?"

"We want to give the feeding station time to bed in, and allow the workforce to get used to a daily routine. But no more than a week. We can't afford to wait any longer."

"I'll start the planning with Sergeant Saunders first thing."

"I've got a meeting with the PO now so I'll catch up with you later."

"Sir." Alan saluted and the colonel returned it. Bannister went to meet with Elliot, and Alan went in search of his number two, Sergeant Saunders.

CHAPTER 10

Keelan left the woman whimpering face down on the bed and dragged on his clothes. He slapped her arse, thanking her for sharing his first experience of anal sex. His body was soaked in sweat, and he was in need of a drink, and not just water. Checking his watch again, it showed 1130pm. It would be dark outside, not that there was much light in daylight hours, but he wanted them to have the full cover of darkness for their next move. They had eaten a good proportion of the food that had been stocked in the house, packing the rest in any bags they could find. Water, a life-saving commodity, was also running low. The four men had repeatedly raped the two women, the mother and daughter, during the last forty-eight hours. But Keelan had kept the mother to himself these last eight hours, the daughter having been suffocated by Todd in a frenzied attack. His black and swollen right eye was testament to Keelan's rage on discovery of the event – not because he valued the girl's life, or even felt sorry for her, but for the waste, preventing the group pleasuring themselves with her body for a little while longer. The rest of the group were pretty pissed off with Todd as well, depriving them of their entertainment.

Keelan tightened his belt, grabbed his jacket, and made his way down the stairs, calling back to the woman as he went through the bedroom door. "Don't fucking move!"

The other three men greeted him as he entered the lounge, and Salt handed him a half-full mug of coffee.

"Cheers, Doug. We all ready?"

"Yes," responded Todd. "We've left nothing."

"What about the woman?" asked Milo.

"She can fend for herself," answered Keelan.

"The soldier boys'll look after her," added Salt.

"Plan still the same?" asked Todd.

Keelan looked at Withers slumped in one of the armchairs, the black eye visible in the flickering candlelight, then ignored him.

85

"Milo."

"Yes, Stan."

"Did you find any tools?"

"Yeah. Got me some pliers and a couple of screwdrivers. Not that I need them."

"Just in case, mate. As soon as we're out of this dump, the first thing we need is some wheels. A van, if possible."

"Could be a long search. I doubt there's much fuel about, and that EMP shit will have fried some of the vehicles."

"I know, Doug, but we've got to try. We ain't going to walk to the Smoke."

"When we leaving?" asked Milo.

"Soon. Doug, will you check we got everything? Milo, have a sniff around outside. See if we're in the clear."

"Will do. Back in ten."

Milo, his rat-like face already sniffing, got up from the sofa, his hands held up in front of his body mimicking a rodent, and headed for the back door. An expert car thief, specialising in high-value cars, he had come a cropper when he knifed a punter who had caught him helping himself to the man's Range Rover Vogue. Although he had stabbed the man seven times, and believing he'd left him for dead, the car owner had dragged himself back into his house and alerted the police before lapsing into unconsciousness. On coming round in hospital, the detective inspector recognised the man he had described instantly, and the hunt was on. The viciousness of the attack ensured a long jail sentence for Milo, and knifing a fellow prisoner two years later ensured he ended up in the CSC Wing at HMP Wakefield.

As the four men left the house, they heard the screams of the mother on discovering the battered body of her daughter. Keelan cursed himself for leaving her alive, or at least unrestrained. It was too late now. He had no intention of going back.

They traipsed in the cold through the outskirts of Wakefield for over three hours, avoiding an army patrol on one occasion and a marauding gang of men on another. It wasn't from fear that they hid. Keelan just didn't want the complication of answering the military's questions or getting into a wasted fight with people who meant nothing to him. The group must have checked over a hundred vehicles, before they eventually found one that Milo could work his magic on. It was just in time as another five minutes of Todd whinging about his feet and the weight of the load he was carrying and Keelan would have happily killed him on the spot.

Now, they were ensconced in an old Commer van, Milo amazed that it still worked regardless of the bombs striking the country. They circled Wakefield to the east before heading south. The further south they went, the greater the devastation. They spent the first few hours of darkness getting out of Wakefield, dodging the wreckage of buildings and cars, before heading south along the A638. They avoided the M1 and the M62. All lanes appeared clogged with abandoned vehicles, and along with that a low profile was preferred. The group eventually found themselves on the B6422, Salt taking a turn with the driving, giving Keelan a breather. Keelan was in the passenger seat, and the other two were asleep in the back. The four men had kept east of Barnsley, and also wanted to avoid Doncaster to their south-east. Whenever they had detoured from their route, taking them closer to larger towns and cities, the more obvious it became that they were moving closer to a Ground Zero, the point at which the nearest nuclear missile or bomb had struck. There was also the distinctive stench of rotting bodies, those killed in the early days, or those having recently died from their wounds or radiation poisoning.

"I reckon we'll be getting close to the A1 soon, Doug."

"We don't want to cross it, not just yet. Need to avoid Doncaster though. Bound to have been hit by something. Be a pile of shit now, I shouldn't wonder."

"Pile of shit beforehand," laughed Keelan. "Anyway, everywhere seems to be in a mess. What the hell happened here? Where are the authorities?"

"Remember the build-up on the news?" Salt reminded him. "Bloody Russians ended up not only making a play for the Ukraine but were obviously keen to have a bash at Poland and Germany as well. All hell broke loose."

"Didn't do them no good, though."

"Nor us." The lights of the van picked out a roundabout ahead. "I reckon we go right here," suggested Salt.

"Yeah," responded Keelan. "The sign for the A1 shows straight ahead. Why don't we just use the bloody A1? Be a darn sight faster."

"It'll be chock-a-block with vehicles, Stan. We'll end up getting bogged down. There would have been a mass panic before the bombs hit. The minute the authorities started their announcements and emergency preparations, the country would have gone crazy. Stocking up with food, packing their cars, and heading out of the cities."

Salt steered the Commer to the right, not bothering to go the full circle that normal traffic protocol required.

"Watch out for the blue lights," laughed Keelan.

Salt responded with a chuckle and continued the drive south.

"What's so funny?" asked Todd.

"Go back to fucking sleep," snapped Keelan, still pissed with the man for killing the girl. Keelan had considered dumping him but, for the moment at least, they needed the numbers. The road took them slightly west before coming back on track to the south. Salt negotiated the roads, passing between Warmsworth, west of Doncaster, and Conisbrough, crossing the M18 which, like the other main roads, was jammed up with abandoned vehicles, as Salt had predicted. Continuing on, passing between Maltby and Tickhill, more destruction was visible.

Keelan decided it was time for them to make a stop: get some food down them, and then rest up. "Let's skirt around Worksop. See if we can find somewhere to hold up."

"We'll need fuel for tomorrow as well," added Salt. "This baby," he said, tapping the dashboard, "has less than sixty miles in the tank."

Keelan started scanning for somewhere they could pull over. Although dawn was rapidly approaching, the continuously overcast, dust-laden clouds yielded very little light.

"There's fuck all here, Doug," cursed Keelan as the vehicle passed house after house on the roadside that were missing windows and with their roofs open to the elements.

"Doncaster, mate, and Sheffield bound to have taken a hit."

"Contaminated?"

"More than likely. We have to keep away from the big stuff for now."

"Do you reckon most of the country is like that?"

"What bits I picked up from the screws in Wakefield, prior to it all kicking off, was that if it went nuclear, we'd cop it for 300 megatons."

"I take it that's a lot."

"Shit-hit-the-fan time, mate."

Keelan thumped the dashboard. "Fuck, we need to find somewhere. I need some food and a decent kip." He shuffled in his seat in an attempt to get more comfortable. "There's a dip in the road coming up. Maybe that will have sheltered some of the houses from the worst of it."

"I'll keep my eyes peeled."

They weren't disappointed: two semi-detached cottages had escaped with little damage, the folds in the land providing them with some form of a shield, the blast wave having travelled overhead. The suction had dislodged a few tiles but, all in all, they had fared pretty well. A couple of the upstairs windows had been shattered and one or two tiles had been knocked out of position but, apart from that, most of the windows and the rest of the roof were intact.

Salt pulled over onto the side of the road in front of the houses.

"Why are we stopping?" asked a sleepy Milo from the back of the vehicle.

"You lazy bastards might have got some kip, but me and Salt are knackered and hungry. Make yourself useful. Wake that lazy twat in the back with you, and go and collect some firewood. It'll be bloody freezing out there."

Keelan opened the passenger door and shivered, his prediction proving to be correct.

Salt rubbed his hands together. "There's no doubt it's getting colder, Stan. We'll need to find somewhere to hold up over winter. I reckon it's only going to get worse." He clambered down from the driving seat. It was bitterly cold outside. While Todd and Milo gathered some firewood, he and Keelan went to investigate the cottages. It didn't take long to establish that the properties were unoccupied. Getting in wasn't a problem: the two front doors were unlocked, their occupants not expecting to return. Salt shuddered. The anticipation of the benefits of being free from prison, although starting off well, appeared to be heading in the wrong direction now. After a thorough search, no food was discovered, but they did manage to gather blankets and bedding from both cottages, dumping them in the lounge of the first one where they could all benefit from the warmth. The group soon had a fire blazing and, wrapped in blankets, squatting on mattresses laid across the floor, the four men settled in to their temporary abode. Food from their supplies stolen from the other house, were passed around, followed by a bottle of wine. Once that was finished, Salt brought out a half-bottle of whisky he had discovered in the house next door. After taking a good slug, he handed it to Keelan. Milo and Todd accepted the pecking order that was. Neither of them would ever think of challenging Keelan, or Salt for that matter.

Keelan, his heavily tattooed hands and arms showing beneath his rolled-up sleeves, was very much a killer. The hulking fanatical bodybuilder was obsessed with lifting weights, pushing his body harder and harder, often seen showing off his bulging biceps. His first taste of prison had been at the age of seventeen. Used as a courier, he would move drugs for the older drug dealers. He quickly earned their trust, and was soon active in actually selling drugs on the street himself. Caught with a large stash of methamphetamine, also known as ice or crystal, and related drug money when he crashed a stolen car, he was put away for three years. Released after one and a half years, he was soon back inside for grievous bodily harm, after beating to a pulp a man who looked at him the wrong way in a pub. He found himself back behind bars for four more years.

Back out again, and after a major fallout with his girlfriend, he literally crushed her windpipe with his bare hands, choking her to death. What happened next horrified even the most hardened of policemen: Keelan then went into the bedrooms of the woman's three daughters, Nicola, Bridget and Samantha, throttling the two youngest, one after the other, before moving to Samantha's room where he raped the nine-year-old before strangling her too. Keelan then laid his girlfriend on the bed and propped her three daughters up against the headboard with their feet resting on her body. He received a life sentence. Then, after stabbing a prisoner, he ended up in HMP Wakefield's Close Supervision Centre in F-Wing.

Salt's background was not dissimilar from Keelan's, although he was much smarter than the big man. His immature fifteen-year-old girlfriend Lorraine also came from a dysfunctional family. Salt was twenty-one at the time, Right from the start, they both lived in a world where science fiction and fantasy movies became their lifeblood. They were both infatuated with each other, planning their future together – where they were going to live; the type of home they would have; even the number of children: three boys and a girl. A virgin when they met, Lorraine thought he was the only one for her. On becoming pregnant, and after a huge row with her parents who in the heat of the moment threw her out, she spent the next two nights sleeping rough in Salt's car. During that time, they plotted the murder of her parents. Sneaking back into the house – she was still in possession of her own key – they crept up the stairs, Salt carrying an eight-inch cook's knife. They hovered outside the main bedroom where Lorraine's mother and father were sound asleep. Knowing that her mother was on tranquillisers and her father's penchant for half a dozen whiskeys before he went to bed, she told Salt that they would be dead to world. That state was soon to turn into reality.

On easing the door open, Salt hovered over the sleeping parents of Lorraine and then stabbed the couple repeatedly. At least thirty wounds were inflicted on the two bodies, with severe knife wounds to the hands and face as they tried desperately to defend themselves. The father, in a state of stupor due to the alcohol in his blood, was the first to go, an early knife wound to his jugular. He surrendered to his fate almost silently and was unconscious in a matter of minutes, dead soon after. The mother though screamed relentlessly, forcing Salt to focus his hate, via the stabbing knife, on her until she too passed into unconsciousness and eventually death. The next-door neighbours heard the screams, but it was nothing new, so they turned over and attempted to recapture their sleep, assuming it was just another row between the mother and her dysfunctional daughter.

Lorraine and Salt left the house, Salt covered in the blood of the two he had just killed. They headed for Salt's car. A lone policeman came across the couple and, initially thinking the blood soaked man had been injured, went to assist him. The cook's knife struck again and again, and the police constable, too shocked to fight back, unable to call for help, fell to the ground where Lorraine joined in with Salt. Having picked up a large stone nearby, she helped to beat the policeman until he blacked out. He later died of his wounds, and the couple were caught, curled up asleep in Salt's car, when a second policeman on patrol casually shone his torch through the window. The two lovers didn't stir and, seeing the blood on Salt's clothes, he called for backup before he woke them up. Arrested and tried, Salt received a prison sentence of twenty-five years and, after stabbing a fellow prisoner, ended up in a cell next to Keelan. His girlfriend Lorraine received a more lenient sentence of ten years, the courts believing her to have been under Salt's influence.

The bottle of whisky now down to a quarter, Milo piped up, "Where do we go from here, Stan? We need to get some more supplies and somewhere decent to hold up."

"Yeah," whinged Todd. "There's no comfort here and no bloody entertainment. We need to get some woman to play with." A sly grin spread across his face.

Salt looked at Keelan, and both raised their eyebrows.

"You'll just do as you're fucking told, Todd," snapped Keelan. "We need to head south, towards the Smoke," he added, turning his gaze towards Salt and Milo.

"The Home Counties, Stan," suggested Salt. "The city will have been pulverised if what we've seen so far is anything to go by."

"Yeah, but we can dip into the city to stock up. Bound to be some skirt there."

"How many people are left, do you reckon?" asked Milo.

"God knows," responded Salt. "It must have been pretty bad judging by the number of people we've come across."

"Radiation sickness?" suggested Keelan.

"Probably," Salt answered. "And major burns, I would have thought."

"Wouldn't people have hidden in bunkers and cellars?" blurted Todd.

"What bunkers?" challenged Keelan.

"We weren't prepared for anything like this," added Salt as he threw another piece of wood on the fire, the sparks jumping out causing Keelan to curse.

"Fucking watch it Doug, you'll set fire to us."

"Sorry Stan. Anyway, the Cold War was supposed to be over."

"You're too smart for your own good, mate."

"Yeah, and what I ain't got here," Salt flexed his bicep, nowhere near as powerful as Keelan's but still quite pronounced, "I make up in here." He pointed to his head.

"Sorry, I meant to say smart arse," laughed Keelan. He accepted the bottle that was handed to him and finished off the last mouthful. Rubbing sleepy eyes, he lowered his head to the pillow at the end of his mattress. "I need some kip. We can worry about tomorrow in the morning. Chuck some more wood on the fire, Milo mate. But no bloody sparks."

Milo obeyed, placing two bits of wood carefully, which had been picked up from the grounds of the two cottages, spitting a few sparks, onto the red glowing fire.

"Yeah, I'm busted as well." Salt kicked off his trainers, tucked his stocking feet beneath a blanket, and also settled down on the double mattress dragged down from an upstairs bedroom.

"Sounds good to me," assented Milo. "I need a piss first."

"Go round the back of the house," asserted Keelan. "Toilets don't work, and the last thing we want is the prison stink in the house."

Milo got up to go out. Todd just rolled onto his side on his single mattress and was, like Keelan and Salt, snoring in a contented sleep within a matter of minutes. On his return, Milo took a swig of water from one of the canteens and stepped over Todd to get to his own bed space. Like the other three, he was asleep in moments.

CHAPTER 11

Tom shot up in bed, his wife quickly following. He checked his watch: it was two fifty in the morning.

"What is it, Tom?"

"It's Sam. Something has disturbed him."

She too could now hear the deep growl coming from the throat of their collie downstairs. Tom threw his legs out of bed and hurriedly pulled on a pair of jeans, followed by a sweatshirt dragged over his head and shoulders. His wife was also in the process of getting dressed, recognising the potential threat and needing to be ready for whatever might occur.

Tom picked up his shotgun that lay on the floor next to the bed, checked that the two shells were in their respective chambers, and closed the side-by-side double barrels with a soft clunk, applying the safety immediately. He headed out of the bedroom and was met by Andrew on the long landing. He too was armed and ready. The candle on the landing, always left alight, flickered as Tom moved past it.

"You heard it too then?"

"Yes," responded Tom. "We live on a farm, and it's not like Sam to get spooked easily."

Sam's growl picked up and his snarl grew stronger as they made their way down the curving stairs. Tom looked over the rail to the right and down into the hall below. The dog was not visible.

"You take the front of the house, Andy. I'll take the back."

"What about us?" asked Tom's wife.

Tom looked back up the stairs to see the dark shadow of his wife, backlit by the candle, with Andrew's wife, the broader shape of Madeline, looking over her shoulder.

"Arm yourselves. Then wait at the top of the stairs. You know what to do."

They had planned for a possible intrusion, knowing that there was a good chance that someone would want what they had. The two wives, Lucy and Madeline, knew what was expected of them. Tom and Andrew continued their way down the stairs. Once at the bottom, Andrew headed for the front door which was visible before they hit the bottom step, and Tom headed for the kitchen and the back door. Keeping the beam low, Tom flashed the torch across the door to the kitchen, which was half open. As he made his way through the gap, Sam ran over to him, and a quick stroke revealed the dog's hackles were stiff. Tom crouched down next to the dog, stroking his coat, calming him down, listening. The collie licked his lips, and then peeled his mouth back over his teeth as something brushed against the outside of the back door.

"Steady, lad, steady," Tom whispered, straining his own ears to pick out any identifiable sounds coming from outside.

He turned around sharply as a head torch flashed around the room, and his friend crouched down next to him. "There's movement outside the front door."

"Same here. You'd best get back."

Andrew returned to his position at the front of the house, and Tom moved round the large kitchen table, avoiding the chairs, sidling along the still warm Aga until he was crouched at the base of the back door of the kitchen. He reassured Sam with a gentle pat on his coat to stem the grumble that slowly rose in the dog's throat again. A thump next to the solitary kitchen window caught his attention. Glassless, but boarded up for security, it was still a weak point in the farmhouse's defences. Tom stood up, moved and waited silently next to the window, but it went quiet again. He then heard a scuffle next to the door and changed position, moving to the door, placing his ear up against the thick oak, straining to pick out individual sounds. Whispers could be heard outside and another strange noise he couldn't quite make out. He was sure he had heard the sound of water splashing. Someone must have knocked over a bucket.

He reflected for a moment, and then turned to his dog. "Stay, boy, stay."

Sam wagged his tail, and then sat, tongue flicking as he went to lick his master's hand. Tom left his dog and, keeping his torch low, moved as quickly as possible to the front door where he found Andrew with his ear up against the door, and dropped down next to him.

Andy turned towards him. "Clumsy bastards, whoever they are, just knocked over a container of water. Did we have some stocks outside?"

Tom jumped up. "Get Lucy and Madeline down here now. Get all the supplies you can gather and start moving it to the side room."

"What is it?"

"I'm not sure. I need to do one last check. Now go, Andy."

Tom sped back to the rear door of the house to find Sam still growling and sniffing at the door. He placed his ear up against the wood again: there was a slight thump on the door and the sound of dripping water. The dog stopped sniffing and suddenly scooted backwards, wrinkling his nose as another splash of liquid hit the door, followed by a similar sound up against the boarded up window. Tom checked the window, then moved back to the door, sniffing around the gaps at the edges. Now it was his nostrils that wrinkled: a distinctive smell burnt into the receptors of his nose.

"Petrol," he hissed to himself. *Or something similar*, he thought. His mind raced. *The bastards are going to burn us out!*

"Stay, boy."

The dog sat down obediently, and Tom raced out of the kitchen and across the main hall to the front door just as his wife came downstairs.

"Get the children to the snug now. And move the supplies for a quick exit."

"What is it?"

"Just do it, Lucy, please."

She ran back upstairs, meeting Madeline halfway. "Grab Patrick. We need to get the kids to the back room now."

"What's happening?"

Lucy couldn't see the fear in Madeline's eyes, the head torch her friend was wearing blinding her slightly. But she could sense it in her friend's voice.

"I don't know, but Tom's instructions were explicit. We need to move the emergency supplies to the room as well."

"Oh, Lucy, are we running?" Madeline, the weaker of the two women, whimpered.

"Perhaps. Just get Patrick, and we'll find out when we get down there."

They didn't have to go far. The two children, Mary, seven, and Patrick, thirteen, were outside their respective bedroom doors, the shuffling and disturbance outside waking them both.

"Mum," moaned Mary sleepily. "Why are you up?"

"You need to get dressed now. You too, Patrick."

"But, Mum, I'm tired."

"Me too," piped up Patrick.

"Just do it. Get dressed now. Quickly!" snapped Lucy. "Madeline, you see to the kids and I'll start on the provisions."

Her friend just stared at her, holding her dressing gown close to her chest for comfort.

"Maddie, now!"

Madeline snapped out of it and turned to follow the two children to ensure they dressed quickly, and then she too would need to get her own clothes sorted. Lucy, who had dressed earlier, ran back down the stairs and headed for the room next to the lounge, a room they referred to as the snug. She met her husband again on her way through the hall. Tom's torch flashed in her eyes.

"What's happening, Tom?"

"They're dousing the house with fuel."

"Oh Tom, what do we do?"

"Get out of here, that's what."

Andrew joined them. "I can smell it by the front door as well. They're not hiding the fact now. They're slopping it on."

"We'll watch the two doors while you and Maddie get everything ready. Some of the emergency bags are in the snug, as you know, but we need to shift as much food and water as we can carry. The kids will have to load up as well."

"How long?"

"I don't know, honey. The doors are oak, but once the fire takes hold we'll be choking on smoke in a matter of minutes."

"It'll be an inferno with the amount of fuel they're sloshing on the doors," added Andrew.

They heard a thump on the front door.

"Move now," commanded Tom.

While Andrew ran to the front door, Lucy headed for the snug, and Tom ran back towards the kitchen and the rear door. He got a whiff of burnt fuel as soon as he entered the kitchen. A thin film of smoke was filtering beneath the edge of the door, a tinge of burning fuel added to the mix. Sam began barking.

"Shush, lad. Shush."

Tom shone his torch around the edges of the door. The trickle of smoke was steadily increasing in volume as the petrol-fuelled fire caught hold. The crackle of flames could be heard eating into the solid wooden door. Tom was confident the door would hold for at least ten minutes. But the boarded up windows were another matter. He turned left, the beam of light tracking his movement, confirming that the window frame and chipboard that had replaced the shattered windowpane were also alight. White wisps of smoke, visible in the beam, filtered through any gap it could find. Tom moved closer to the window, placing the palm of his hand parallel to the board. He could feel the heat. Soon it would burn through and smoke wouldn't be their only enemy. The crackling of flames grew louder, and Sam began growling again. Tom patted the dog between his ears. "Come on, boy, let's go."

Tom weaved around the table, the dog close at his heels, and both entered the hallway, his torch lighting up the bulky form of his friend crouched next to the front door. "It's started," he called.

"Here as well, Tom. How long do you reckon we have?"

"Ten minutes tops. Probably nearer five for the windows."

Andrew coughed slightly, a layer of smoke starting to weave its way around his legs, gaining height as the heated tendrils made their way towards the ceiling.

"Wait here." Tom ran back into the kitchen, the dog sticking to him like glue. Flames were licking around the edge of the window frame now, and there was a glowing blackened hole forming in the centre of the door. He yanked open the drawer in the side of the large kitchen table, and grabbed six tea towels.

Returning to the hall, picking up a plastic container of water on the way, he handed a tea towel to Andrew. "Douse this with water and wrap it around your face and neck. It's not much, but it'll help a little."

"Thanks."

Andrew dropped his tea towel on the floor, Tom doing the same. The container of water was opened, and Andrew soaked both pieces of cloth which they then quickly wrapped around their mouths and noses, tying the ends into a knot at the back of their heads.

"The window in the kitchen will burn through any time soon. We need to make our way out. Go and chase Lucy, Maddie and the kids. I'll wait here and cover. Let me know when you're ready to leave."

"You sure you'll be OK, Tom?"

Tom held up the gun and then pointed at the collie. "They'll not find it easy."

"Heading for the Land Rover as planned?"

"Yes. Have everything we're taking put next to the door. We'll go out together. They shouldn't see us, but strength in numbers, eh. Anyway, they'll be coming through there or the kitchen." He pointed at the front door and then indicated in the direction of the kitchen.

Andrew left and went to help the two wives who could be heard shuffling between rooms, moving the items that would be needed once they made their escape. Tom moved closer to the kitchen where he could keep an eye on the back door as well as watch the front. The kitchen was the weak point, with both the door and window now well alight. The window in particular was burning well, flames flaring on both sides now, with glowing red lines forming along the edges where the wood was breaking down. The door too was weakening, with all sides of the frame ablaze. It wouldn't be long before the men outside lost patience and kicked their way through a door or window, or both.

He instinctively knew who it was. He'd hoped that the Reynolds family would think their brothers and cousins had come across some looters like themselves and come off worse. But, clearly, they believed that Tom, and the rest of the group at the farm, were responsible for killing Brian and his brother Ryan. Unless, of course, it was hopelessness. Losing two members of the family would put pressure on the rest to hunt for food. Maybe it was starvation and desperation that was urging them to go to these extremes. *Why don't they just ask for help?* he thought. He knew the answer before he'd finished the question. If they had asked, he would have responded with a resounding 'no'.

Tom moved away from the kitchen, closely followed by Sam, and headed for the snug, their route of escape to the outside. Andrew waited by the door for Tom's appearance. The front door, and the entrance to the kitchen, was out of sight now, but the crackle of flames coming from both was clearly audible and getting louder. Smoke was billowing into the hall and steadily scaling the stairs, seeking out higher ground.

"Are we ready, Andy?"

"Nearly. Lucy is fetching the last of the medical kits from the lounge." His voice was muffled by the damp tea towel.

Thump…crack…thump…crack. There was a loud crashing sound as an axe wielded by Ryan's enraged father smashed through the weakened kitchen door. A shower of sparks billowed around the cooking area as the giant of a man shouldered his way through, oblivious to the clouds of sparks singeing his hair and beard, alcohol-fuelled rage closing off all thoughts but one: revenge – to kill the man who took his two sons from him. He wasn't certain it was the farmer, but there weren't many other families still in the area. Bernard, head of the Reynolds family, had been in and out of institutions and prison since he was nine, and the rest of his family, his four sons, one daughter and two cousins, who lived with him and his wife, followed in his footsteps. Even his wife, Charlene, originally from North London, had been convicted many times for prostitution and drug handling. Her birth certificate had her down as Barbara, but that didn't quite have the right ring for the punters in Ponders End. Many blamed the family's deprived education and limited intelligence for their poor start in life. Tom, on the other hand, knew they were just lazy and plain mean. Ready to commit whatever crime or atrocity was necessary to impose their will on others and enhance their way of life. The youngest son, Brian, killed by Tom two days previously, was believed to have been responsible for the deaths of seven cats in the area over a ten-day period. At least two had been found hanging outside their owners' front doors. As usual, the police were unable to prove his guilt. But everyone in the area, including the police, knew the culprit was Brian.

Then, in the house, three things happened almost simultaneously. With a flare of yellow and red light from the flames that were in the process of engulfing the kitchen, Bernard Reynolds charged through the inner kitchen door, shotgun brandished in front of him. Lucy, rushing out of the room opposite, medical kits clutched in her arms, crashed straight into him. Both ended up entangled on the floor as Sam barked and growled at the intruder. In the meantime, the two remaining sons had followed their father, and the two cousins were minutes away from hacking their way through the front door.

Tom reacted quickly, firing a single barrel at one of the sons, Barry, but missing him, peppering the ceiling instead. Ever thickening clouds of smoke and a torch that was becoming increasingly ineffective in the swirling smoke, it was hardly surprising Tom missed. Andrew joined him and also fired, his shot catching the other son, Frank, in his right shoulder and the lower side of his jaw. The man screamed as he dropped to his knees clutching his face.

Tom snapped into action and charged at the father, placing a boot in the man's gut, giving Lucy a chance to extract herself as Sam joined in and wrenched the father's arm to and fro, a timely distraction. The man squealed as the collie tore at his bloodied arm. Barry, in the meantime, had raced around the mêlée and, seeing Mary poking her head through the door of the snug desperately seeking her mother, headed straight for her. The roar of the flames intensified, and clouds of grey smoke billowed around the ground floor area of the farm. Tom choked, the tea towel, his makeshift face mask having dried out, allowing the toxic fumes to penetrate his throat and lungs. The only plus side was that the intruders, were equally debilitated, if not more so.

Bernard Reynolds, finding his arm free as Sam succumbed to the ever thickening smoke, lashed out and grabbed Lucy's leg as she tried to run away. Tom stamped on Bernard's hand and grabbed for Lucy's arm as he did. The man howled and flung a meaty fist in Tom's direction, missing, the effort causing him to suck in a deep lungful of smoke, forcing him up on his hands and knees, coughing and spluttering as he fought for breath. Lucy also choked on the fumes as Tom dragged her unceremoniously away from her assailant. In the thickening blanket of smoke, Tom had no idea where the rest of his group were. He hadn't heard the front door splinter as a sledgehammer finally knocked it off its hinges, giving the cousins, a short, rotund teenager, eighteen last month, and his more athletic brother, an opportunity to blunder through, blinded as soon as they entered the hall, their watery eyes rubbed sore trying to clear their vision.

"Go," yelled Andrew who reappeared at Tom's side, helping to pull Lucy, who was now struggling for air, up off the floor.

Tom groped his way through the smoke, nearly tripping over the figure of Barry sprawled on the floor, a bloody gash across his head where Madeline, in a rare show of courage, protecting the two children, had struck him with a heavyweight, marble table lamp. He turned, keeping his back to the door, and saw Andy and Lucy stumbling towards him through the smog, coughing and retching. He pushed the door open with his backside, knocking Patrick, who was guarding the door with his mother, back.

"Sam! Sam!" he called. The dog responded to his voice and shot past him into the snug, pleased to escape the thick poisonous air. Lucy and Andrew stumbled through the open door, crashing to the floor in a flurry, quickly followed by Tom who banged the door shut behind him. Then he slammed the heavy bolts across, top and bottom, securing the room. He bent at the waist, hands on hips, his chest heaving as he tried to catch his breath and draw air into his lungs. The room was smoke-filled, but not as dense as the other side of the door.

He raised his head. The flickering light of the gas lamps lit by Madeline revealed the smoke-blackened faces of Lucy and Andrew scrabbling up from the floor. Maddie had one arm around Patrick and Mary, and a lamp blighted by blood in her other hand.

The outer door was open, unlocked earlier by Lucy, and it was time to move. They would have to leave what had been Tom and Lucy's home for over twenty years. Andrew and Maddie were the only ones with a head torch, so Andrew led them out into the darkness of the lean-to that stood alongside the rear of the house. In daylight, anyone peering inside the lean-to from the outside, would see a small workshop. Shelves lined the outside wall of the house with a three-metre workbench in the middle. This is where they exited from the snug, through a small lower stable door just over a metre high. The upper part of the stable door had been sealed many years ago. The egress was by way of passing through the short doorway, then crawling beneath the workbench, dragging their additional emergency supplies with them, until they were able to stand. When Tom, the last person through, stood up, Andrew knelt down, reached under the bench and pulled the door shut, locked it, then slid two large bolts across to secure the heavy door. Once the Reynolds family finally battered their way into the snug, they would eventually come across what could possibly be a small door low down, but with no handle and just a small mortice lock to show it could be used as an exit point. By then, it would be too late. Tom, Andrew, and their respective families, would be long gone. Once satisfied their escape route was secure, Tom pulled on a coat, part of their emergency clothing, checked all were ready and equally dressed for warmth, then put on a head torch.

"We've rehearsed this. So, me first, Lucy, the children, Maddie, and then Andy. Ready?"

"Yes," they responded collectively.

"Let's go then."

They picked up the supplies they would take with them and Tom eased the outside door of the lean-to open, and peered left and right. Flickers of light provided by the increasingly violent flames devouring the kitchen around the corner could be seen reflecting off the trees and the yard in front of him. He moved left, walking slowly, feeling Lucy's hand under his coat and holding on to the belt loop of his jeans. Everyone else should be following suit, keeping physical contact with the person in front of them. He took them to the left, along the side of the house, away from the source of the fire and any members of the Reynolds clan that might be outside. After ten metres, he turned ninety degrees to the right and led the group across the open yard. Now, they were at their greatest risk, out in the open, completely exposed, even though it was a dark, moonless night. They passed through a gate, the hinges well oiled and silent, Tom taking them across a second yard, empty stables on the left. At the end, he turned left, keeping close to the wall, a set of pigpens at the back. Skirting round the side of them to access the rear of the pigpens, the two families arrived at the location of their escape vehicle. The Land Rover, a trailer hitched ready and partially loaded with jerrycans of diesel, was draped in a large tarpaulin.

"Get round the other side, Andy. Grab the end, and we'll drag it out of the way."

Lucy, Maddie and the children moved to the side while Tom and Andy, dropping the supplies they had carried with them, peeled back the tarpaulin, exposing the dark shape of their transport.

"Everybody on board," hissed Tom. "I'll not start her until we're all in."

Tom and Andy kept watch while the two mothers loaded what they were carrying into the trailer. Then they hustled the two children into the back, seating them opposite each other on the bench seats near the front. They followed after, securing the back door. This left the two men to complete one last scan of the area, leap into the vehicle, followed by Sam, and, once started, the two families headed to where they hoped they would find safety.

CHAPTER 12

Captain Parry led the way through the streets, a steady wheeze from his respirator as he sucked in filtered air and blew it back out. He'd kept his 9mm Browning holstered. Corporal Davey, a Marine, walked parallel with him on the other side of the street – if you could call them streets. Davey was armed with an SA80, as was Able Seaman Harper behind him. Every step he took involved manoeuvring around chunks of rubble as they made their way down Charles Dickens Street. Further back, the group had passed the shattered Portsmouth City Council building. It had seemed pointless in hanging around the submarine any longer and after two days Commander Parry had decided that they should take a risk a delve deeper into Portsmouth. They had been on the move for at least two hours, and the devastation became more apparent the deeper they moved towards the centre of the city. What cars there were on the streets were either on their sides, crushed, or even flipped over on their tops by the force of the blast. After that, the firestorm had blistered the paint and burnt out the upholstery. Most of the vehicles and their contents smelt rank: the dead bodies of the drivers or passengers trapped in the confines of their metal coffins had lain there rotting since the strike.

Clearly, rescue has not been an option, thought Captain Parry. It didn't bode well for their search to find a functioning administration, but now he doubted they would even find survivors. Many of the taller buildings looked like blackened, jagged teeth, where the upper storeys had been torn asunder, the debris carried by the hurricane-force wind into anything that stood in its way. What had happened after the blast wave was apparent: not only evidenced by the darkened, gutted buildings but also the layer of dirtied ash that covered everything in their path. The blast wave, having shattered the upper storeys of the buildings in the city, was followed by a firestorm of unimaginable intensity that engulfed anything and anyone that would feed it.

Parry wriggled his shoulders, feeling uncomfortable in his

NBC suit and mask. It wasn't something he had worn very often. In fact, the last time he had put it on was during a training course, and that was probably two and a half years ago. Although tempted to avoid wearing the cumbersome gear, his petty officer, PO Bell, had been insistent they left the submarine fully protected from whatever contaminants were out there. Now he could see the state of the city, and the dust clouds kicked up as they traipsed down street after street, he was glad he had capitulated. He was also glad of the warmth the extra layer of clothing provided. Parry was amazed at how cold it was once they had left the confines of the submarine. They moved further in, observing worsening signs of destruction. He suspected they were getting closer to Ground Zero, where the single nuclear missile, launched from a Soviet submarine, had struck. Parry had expected to find more extensive damage to the harbour itself, and suspected that the missile or bomb had missed its designated target point.

He glanced up at the buildings ahead, and knew the group would need to change direction. He signalled a halt and checked his street map, not that it was proving easy to negotiate their way through the streets with no signs and very few recognisable landmarks. And the devastation seemed to be getting worse. He beckoned the PO and Lieutenant Chris Wood forward and signalled the rest to keep watch. Watching for what, though, he was unsure.

The three crouched in a circle facing each other, and Parry held the map out in front of him. "I believe we're here," is voice muffled by the mask, pointing at Charles Dickens Street. "This curves round to the right towards Alec Rose Lane, then left to Isambard Brunel Road."

"It all looks the bloody same off the map, sir. Wherever we are, I suggest we change direction. Looking at the level of damage, we have to be moving towards the centre of the blast," suggested Lieutenant Wood.

"I agree, Chris, that's what it looks like. Best if we start going north, skirt the city, and head towards the hospital."

"Why the hospital?" asked Chris.

"If there are survivors, the hospital would make a sensible rallying point."

"Makes sense. Is there a government bunker in this area?"

"If my memory serves me right, Crowborough covers the east, apart from London, and Chilmark to the west, so unlikely. So the hospital would make sense."

"That's one hell of a trek though, sir, if you don't mind me saying."

"Speak your mind, Petty Officer Bell. We need to cover all options."

"We'll never make that in one go." Bell tapped the map. "We could hold up somewhere to the west, maybe check out the marina, see if there are any boats afloat. Cut through Victoria Park and follow the A3, M27 north. Much faster than negotiating our way through this mess. Take us about three hours. We don't want to be out here in the dark. No telling what we might come across."

"I like the sound of that. What do you think, Chris?"

"I can see the value in that. Let's go with it sir. See if we can find some supplies or even transport on the way. Maybe we should go via Mountbatten Way. I doubt we'll find any of our ships, but it would be good to check out for any survivors."

"I agree. Let's do it then."

Captain Parry briefed his small command, and they turned back and walked the way they had just come, cutting through Victoria Park. The park's trees had been stripped of their foliage, ravaged by the blast wave and the firestorm that followed it. The group moved down Queen Street, the scene no different from what they had just left: abandoned vehicles, most burnt out or crushed, buildings blackened and shattered. They turned right and headed north, taking a cut through between two blocks of flats, or at least the skeletal structures, windowless and roofless, which remained.

The sailors were midway through the gap when there was a crackling sound, followed by the sound of tortured metal and concrete as a weakened section of the structure suddenly gave way and toppled over. Tons of reinforced concrete crashed down less than fifty metres from their position. As they threw themselves to the floor, a cloud of dust blossomed around them, driven by the debris hitting the ground. The jagged lumps deflected upwards, eventually landing amongst the seven men, showering them with pieces of masonry and steel. Larger chunks rained down on them as they tucked in every extremity as close as possible to their bodies. The pounding continued as a second building, much closer to the men, lost its upper levels, set off by the collapse of the adjacent building. Huge blocks smashed into vehicles, tarmac and the pavements, shattering the paving slabs, the blocks themselves shattering into smaller pieces, sending slithers of concrete to slice into the sailors close by. A final display of violence saw two more buildings surrender their defiance of the bomb that had torn them apart a matter of weeks ago, crashing down around the men cowering beneath, smashing Lieutenant Wood's back in, practically severing his body in two. Corporal Davey was completely buried under a three-ton piece of masonry, his breath crushed from his body, his flesh and bones pulverised beneath the weight, killing him within seconds. Taylor panicked, jumped up, and ran away from the madness and confusion that surrounded him, only to be pummelled by a rain of concrete. Then a steel girder stopped him in his tracks, slicing off a leg at the knee, a second striking him across his shoulders, breaking all the bones it touched, his life quickly ebbing away.

Parry found it harder and harder to breathe. His respirator wasn't coping with his desperate need for oxygen. He sucked harder and harder, pulling the sides of the mask in with the effort until he felt light-headed. He knew the mask had to come off. He yanked it up over his face and screamed as he twisted his body into a jagged piece of concrete lying next to him. He sucked in the air, but then coughed violently as the dust layer he had disturbed was pulled into his lungs. He panicked: unable to breathe properly, feeling a heavy weight on his legs. With visibility at zero, the tension still tangible from the last days of the battle with the Russian navy, his body gave in and he sagged, his head resting on the remnants of the building that had just collapsed around them.

Eventually, his coughing fit subsided, his breathing settled, and he started to take stock of his surroundings. A layer of dust was forming on his upper body. The remaining buildings in the area seemed to be maintaining their integrity. Parry tried to sit up but a searing pain shot down his side. He raised his body up on his elbows, the visibility improving as he could now see his legs caught beneath a jumble of large chunks of masonry. He tried to pull them out but, apart from more pain lancing down the left side of his body, nothing moved. More dust was settling, and he could now see his dust-encrusted respirator. *No wonder I couldn't breathe*, he thought.

He looked about him as best he could, the shapes of more rubble coming into view. The jagged walls of the building they had been alongside were now visible. He saw a outline of something familiar about ten metres away but couldn't quite make it out. Rubbing the dust out of his eyes, causing them to water and forcing him to squint, the picture cleared. It was a pair of legs, at least from the knee down – except one was shorter than the other, severed off just above the shin. They appeared immobile. The rest of the body that he didn't recognise was hidden in the rubble.

He tugged his own legs again, the pain returning but not as bad. But he still couldn't shift his legs from beneath the weight that pinned them down. Could he feel them both? He thought so. An attempt at moving his feet failed, and there was a moment of panic. He prayed it was just the pressure of the objects on top of his feet and legs that were responsible and not because, like the body he could see to his left, they had been crushed or even severed.

Parry heard the crunch of gravel behind him, and strained his head back and then to the left and right in order to see the cause of the noise. "Who's that? Is someone there?"

A shadow descended over him before a recognisable figure crouched by his side. The full beard of his PO coming into view.

"Petty Officer Bell, thank God. Where is everyone?"

PO Bell was also without a mask. "It's not good, sir. I've seen Lieutenant Wood and Page, both dead. Page's head has been caved in and the lieutenant must have had every bone in his body broken. I reckon that's Corporal Davey to your left, but it doesn't look good from here. I'll check him out in a minute, but no doubt he's dead as well. How about you, sir? You OK?"

"My legs are trapped. What about the rest of the group?"

"Not a dicky bird, sir. They've got to be under that mess back there. We were lucky it fell slightly behind us. Otherwise, we wouldn't be having this conversation now."

Bell leant in closer to his captain. "I'll check out your legs, sir. Then check out the poor bugger over there."

PO Bell ran his hand down Parry's legs, testing them slightly, searching for breaks or gashes that would indicate a crucial injury. He could only check to just above the knee, the rest was buried beneath the rubble. The dust had settled so he had a pretty good view of the situation.

"Not looking too bad, sir. Your legs seem to be pinned from the knee down."

Captain Parry raised his body on his elbows again. "Can you move it?"

"They're heavy chunks, but no real big ones. I'll just try and shift them one at a time."

The biggest was right on the top, but precariously balanced. One shove with his shoulder, and it tumbled down away from them with a crash and a shower of dust.

"Aaaagh."

"You OK, sir?"

"Yes, yes. Just hurts like hell. That took some of the pressure off, and some of the feeling has come back."

"Just a couple more should do it." The next one was not so easy, and Bell had to rock it back and forth until eventually it gave way, crashing down to join the first one.

"I can move one of my feet."

"I'm not going to be able to shift this last one so easily."

"Find something to lever it with. Must be something amongst the debris."

Bell left his captain and went in search of a length of wood or something similar. He was soon back, grinning and holding up a length of steel. "Have you out in a jiffy now, sir. Get ready to pull your legs away."

He was true to his word. The last piece was soon levered off, and the captain was free at last.

"Let me help." Bell lifted one of the captain's arms and heaved him up, placing an arm around the man's waist and pulling the captain's right arm around his neck and shoulder. Parry was now standing on a pair of very shaky legs. The sharp pains had gone, his right foot was weak and throbbing. But his left foot was not so good.

"Perch your backside on there, sir." Bell pointed to a steel RSJ that could be used as a seat. "Then let me have a look at it."

Once the captain had sat down, Bell examined Parry's legs for a second time.

"Your left foot looks badly swollen, and I can see a piece of bone sticking out above your sock. Looks like it's busted, sir."

"It feels numb, but there's no pain."

"That'll come. I need to cut that shoe off. Otherwise the swelling will have nowhere to go, and you could have the blood to it cut off."

"You have a check on the others first. We need to find some cover and batten down for the night."

"Shoe first, sir, eh? You'll be going nowhere otherwise."

Parry capitulated, and Bell cut into the offending shoe, the occasional groan from his captain as he jarred the man's ankle. After about five minutes, the shoe had been pulled off and the swollen foot and ankle lowered onto the ground. Parry lay back, gritting his teeth as the swelling foot regained some blood flow and the nerves came to life.

"I'll go and look for the others now, sir. You hang fire."

Parry nodded.

Petty Officer Bell went from man to man. Lieutenant Wood was dead, his body all but severed in two. Bell could see bits of the camouflaged uniform of Corporal Davey. The Marine was buried under a three-ton piece of masonry, and there was no sign of life. Taylor lay face down, a steel RJS pinning him down. A second girder lay in between the man's body and a lower limb which it had hacked off when it struck. Taylor too was dead. Page and Harper had suffered similar fates but appeared to have been killed almost instantly, Page with a crushed skull.

As Bell made his way back through the debris, he checked his watch and looked up at the slate grey clouds. Three twenty. It would get even darker in the next couple of hours. He picked up a length of distorted wood on his way back to Parry.

"No go, sir, they've all bought it."

"Damn, damn. It's my bloody fault. We should never have left the safety of the sub."

"We couldn't have stayed there, sir. Supplies of fresh water and food wouldn't have lasted past two weeks. There was no option but to explore further afield."

"Yes, you're right. But it doesn't make it any easier."

"I've got a pressy for you, sir," Bell said, holding aloft a makeshift crutch. "If we can get you on your feet, using this, we should be able to make some headway."

He sawed at Parry's NBC suit and trouser leg with a clasp knife, cutting two slits as far up as the man's knee. The more he could see of the task that lay ahead of him, the better. He pulled the two bits of trouser leg back up and tucked them out of the way, then peeled the black sock off and over the piece of white bone, Parry's leg trembling beneath his hands. His captain's face said it all: the pale face, glassy eyes and furrowed brow communicated the pain the man was experiencing. They both knew what needed to be done.

"Still OK with this, sir?"

"Have no choice. I can't move as it is, and we can't stay here. So, catch-22 really."

"OK, I'll bind your legs at the ankle and again just below the knee."

"I'm as ready as I'll ever be."

Bell played his torch over the wound, the thick piece of jagged bone white against Parry's grime-covered skin. The muscle didn't appear to have been torn, damaged probably, but no major trauma. The bleeding seemed to have stopped, the flow congealed and black around the wound.

"Going to give you a jab of morphine. It'll dull some of the pain, but not all of it."

"Hope I don't get addicted to the stuff." Parry forced a laugh but, inside, he was terrified. He, like many people, had come across pain, but he knew this would be like nothing he had ever experienced before.

"I'll keep it under lock and key," responded Bell as he made his final preparations. He watched the captain's face, a sheen of sweat had formed on his forehead, even in the bitter cold, but seeing it visibly relax as the drug started to take effect.

"I could get used to this. Can't even feel the lumps I'm lying on."

"How about your leg?"

"It's stopped hurting. Feels like I'm floating. Can't even feel the cold now."

"Let's get it done."

Bell knelt on Parry's lower body in an attempt to keep the man still. But to no avail. Once he'd grabbed the lower part of Parry's leg and pulled it away from the upper piece of broken bone, twisting it back and up so the two pieces met, the captain practically lifted the petty officer up off the ground. Then he screamed, a scream that caused the hairs on the back of Bell's neck to stand on end, before the officer passed out. Bell took the opportunity to push the two jagged pieces of bone together and quickly bind them with a first-aid field dressing. Tight, but not too tight. Secure enough that it would keep the two pieces connected. Bell wrapped one of the trouser belts he had acquired from the crew, they no longer had a use for them, around the top of Parry's leg, just below the knee, along with two lengths of wood, and pulled it tight, adding a second belt just above the ankle. Next, one went around just above the fracture, the captain's body wincing as Bell jarred his broken leg. Parry's lower leg was now completely immobilised. The left leg, should the splints hold, would hopefully mend, and eventually the captain would recover, although he might be left with a limp.

Bell rummaged inside the medical kit, extracting a plastic bottle of antibiotics. He would start the captain on a course of these as soon as the officer came round. *What we do next is anybody's guess,* he thought.

CHAPTER 13

The occupants of the building were gathered in what used to be a conference room, that was when the office block was a going business concern. Some of the community were not present at the meeting, either on guard duty or considered too young to attend the meeting. The glow from two camping gas lights providing a reasonable amount of light. Now, the carpeted surface was free of desks and conference tables, moved to other floors or rooms to be used as barriers, temporary beds, and even as emergency stocks of firewood. The group of sixty-four people were huddled together for warmth, blankets wrapped round their shoulders and pulled tight to trap in as much heat as possible. There was a wood burner in the room, a network of pipes taking the smoke and fumes through a hole cut in one of the boarded up windows. The burner was merely ticking over, taking the real chill off the room. It had only been lit thirty minutes prior to the start of the meeting, a concession to use a valuable resource, a desire to foster a feeling of fellowship and mutual support. Bill knew that, if the community was to survive, they needed to work hard and stick together. If it fell apart, they would be exposed to the few marauding gangs that occupied the city, bent on rape and pillage. He reflected as the thought passed through his mind, such an old-fashioned term yet, in these modern days, when they had practically been blown back into the Middle Ages, it seemed a apt description.

Bill was stocky, his muscled body giving shape to the dark blue sweatshirt over a pair of grey hiking trousers covering equally muscled legs. He wasn't a particularly attractive man, but his angular features; broad shoulders and full head of dark brown hair often drew attention from women of a similar age. Stone grey eyes from either side of a straight nose scanned their faces as they sat in front of him in a U-shape, facing him and the other four key leaders of the group who were sitting on four of the old conference room chairs. No children were present, just the adults over eighteen. There was a wide range of ages in the group. From the newly weds, Curtis and Elizabeth, both twenty-one, married two weeks before the attack, to Martha and Bill, in their late seventies, but still a bundle of energy. They would need to be. All members of the community had to contribute if they were to maintain their place and be fed and protected from the elements, and scavengers and marauders roaming through the battered city.

Bill stood up and started the meeting, his booming voice grabbing their attention. "Thank you for all attending, and I apologise for dragging you away from anything important. However, due to the disparate way we are spread throughout our new home," his right hand swept upwards indicating the office building they were in, "it's important that we all understand what is happening in our new world and that we are in no doubt of what is expected of us if we are to survive this new hell that has been dumped on us."

He walked the full width of the room, from one side of the threepenny-bit shaped room to the other, before turning towards the group and walking to the centre of the on looking assembly. He looked around at the questioning faces peering up at him, turned round and walked back to his original position. Then he faced them again.

"Before I run through some changes, I first need to reiterate that we all have duties to perform. No matter how hard, important or trivial they are, all are necessary for the survival of the community as a whole. You don't need to be reminded that I won't tolerate any individuals, or families for that matter, who don't subscribe to and provide the support that is required of them. There is so much we still need to do so I will also be assigning duties to the younger members of our group, at least from the age of eleven. The rest of the kids can contribute wherever we find an opportunity for them to do so." He walked over to his left until he was opposite a section of the group leaning up against the outside wall, a line of boarded up windows behind them. Bill searched the faces until he found the one he was looking for.

"Howard," he said, looking at a man in his fifties sitting next to his wife, Ellie, his knees drawn up and encircled by his blanketed arms, "I know you're an ex-policeman, and I'd like you to take on a very significant role for the group. I need you to ensure that we live and work together in peace. There are no hard and fast rules, just common sense. You'll very quickly come up with some simple rules that can be followed, I'm sure. Do you accept?"

The man scratched his salt and pepper beard and thought for a moment before responding. "Gladly. Anything that makes our survival easier and more certain."

Bill smiled, bent down, and shook the man's hand. "But that doesn't mean you're reinstated and can chase me for non-payment of parking fines."

The group laughed at the joke, shuffled in their places, getting more comfortable, relaxing slightly.

Bill looked at the group as a whole again. "Howard has my full authority to deal with day to day minor issues or disputes. Go to him first rather than me or any of the other leaders."

In spite of the fact that they generally liked Bill and were thankful for his foresight and that he had taken the lead to form this small community, providing them with a roof over their heads, food, water and protection, they were in awe of the man. Some actually feared him. Although he always appeared to be fair, there was no doubt in anyone's mind that, equally, he could be unswerving and ruthless.

Bill continued his pacing. "We've pretty much been holed up in this building, our new home, for four weeks now. Currently, we have a decent level of supplies, but with over eighty mouths to feed they'll be consumed pretty quickly so need to be replaced. Some of us, for differing reasons, have been outside, into the city streets. It's still dangerous. Areas remain contaminated, many of the buildings are unsafe, and there are gangs out there who are keen to take what we have. But now it's time for us to go into the outside world in greater numbers and with a definite purpose."

He turned to the second man sitting on the seats at the front. Robbie, an ex-mechanic in his early forties and Bill's number two, stood up. At six foot two, a triathlete, and as sharp as a knife, he was a man to be reckoned with if you ever got on the wrong side of him.

"First, we need to top up our supplies. Robbie will post a notice on the board after this meeting detailing the supply teams. These teams will be looking for non-food items: fuel, batteries, medical supplies, clothing, bedding, anything that we think we'll need to equip us to survive these coming winter months and probably years. He will then discuss your modus operandi with you. Thanks, Robbie."

Robbie nodded his acceptance of the role and sat back down.

Bill turned to his right, looking at the man sitting at the end of the row of seats. Trevor had a shock of white hair with a beard to match. In his forties, a chef for one of the city's major hotels up until the bombs struck, Bill felt he was the ideal candidate to take charge of this critical operation. "Trevor here will take responsibility for provisions. Some of you will be assigned to scavenging teams and will be expected to search for and bring back any food, water or other sustenance that will be of use to the community. Trevor has already started to draw up a list and will provide a marked map for the teams of the likely areas where foodstuffs may be found. I will also take a team out myself. Questions?"

A young man in his late twenties, his wife's blonde head resting on his lap, spoke up. "What about the soldier boys and other authorities that could still be in control out there?"

"A good question. Mathew, isn't it?"

The man nodded.

"He can lead one of the teams tomorrow, eh, Trevor?"

"Already on my list, Bill."

Bill walked towards the assembled group.

"Nice one. So, Mathew, you'll be taking a team out on a foraging run tomorrow. You OK with that?"

Mathew nodded, comfortable with the decision made and secretly pleased that he had been given that responsibility.

"Now, to answer your question. We're not really sure what the situation is like out there. We know from our brief forays that there are gangs roaming the streets and they are the real threat. A threat to our home as well. But I'll come on to that later. As to the Government, we've not seen any real evidence of their presence. We suspect there is a regional centre, or a sub-division of it at least, to the south-east, around Crowborough. One mixed patrol, army and police, was spotted about a week ago. But, like us, they will have kept a low profile while radiation levels were high. Again, like us, I'm sure they'll be more active in the future. No doubt the gangs out there and the military will clash. But, Mathew, you and the other team leaders when nominated are to avoid contact with any local authority and certainly the gangs in the area. We must keep a low profile until we can establish ourselves. I'm sure all are aware of our presence, but so far they haven't been inquisitive enough to come and pay us a serious visit. But, in due course, they will. And we'll need to be ready."

"What about protection?" asked Mathew.

"Each group will have someone assigned for that purpose. Which brings me on to the next point: security."

Bill walked back to the last of the men sitting out at the front. Trevor sat down, and Simon stood up. "Simon will be responsible for the security of the tower block along with the security of the teams operating outside the building. I've given him a team of twelve, and those of you assigned to his security detail will be notified later. They will be given some training in the use of the shotguns we've acquired and in the makeshift weapons that are in the process of being made. Simon and his team will take responsibility for the twenty-four-hour protection of this." His arm swept around the room. "This tower block is all we have. If we lose its protection, we'll be on the streets and at the mercy of the environment and the thugs. Worst of all, we'll be without shelter, food and water. Even though Simon and his boys will watch over us day and night, should we be attacked or under serious threat, all will be expected to participate in the defence of our home."

He scanned the faces, making eye contact with some. "Clear?"

"Yes," responded half a dozen quietly.

"Clear?!" Bill asked again, raising his voice.

"Yes," the entire group replied this time, making a more concerted effort to show their commitment.

"Good, we can't survive in isolation. We need to work together in order to get through whatever will be thrown at us. And, believe me, a lot of shit will come our way. Thanks, Simon, I'll leave it at that for now. Simon will update us when he's ready."

Simon sat back down. Bill looked at the faces staring back at him and felt sure they looked more upbeat, more confident, secure in the knowledge that there was direction from him in how the group would manage the uncertainties of the future.

"One last thing, and then you can go about your business. Sally has promised us all a mug of hot chocolate after the meeting. Powdered milk I'm afraid, but something to look forward to. Is that right, Sally?"

"Yes, Bill," she confirmed, beaming, pleased to get some recognition.

"Last but not least, Owen."

The man stood up. Although barely above five foot five in height, Owen was far from slight. His chest and arms bulged inside his shirt and jumper, and muscled legs strained at his jeans. Even his face and neck muscles looked and probably felt like iron. As well as being fitness fanatic before the country's demise, his job as a drayman, delivering barrels of beer and crates of bottled drinks to the pubs in the area, had ensured his muscles had been regularly exercised and tested.

"Owen will control our internal operations: finalising where people will be housed, our eating arrangements, which will remain collective for a while longer, rubbish disposal, heating, fitting out and so on. Whatever is required to ensure we have an efficient and clean habitat to live in. We're not completely on top of each other, but it won't take long for the quality of our new abode to deteriorate and become dirty and unhygienic. That could well lead to disease, illness and death. Rats could also become a serious problem. It's up to us to work together, OK?"

Most of the gathering nodded their heads. What Bill was saying made sense.

"Are there any questions before I close the meeting?"

A woman in her mid-thirties raised a hand.

"Martha, how are the children settling in?"

Martha had only been with the community for about a week, found wandering the streets with her three children. After being gang raped, she escaped with her three sons while the thugs that had abused her slept in a drunken stupor. Unable to find sufficient water supplies, the five men had resorted to alcohol to satisfy their needs. They had also satisfied a more basic need by holding Martha a prisoner and satisfying their lust. Owen, leading an exploratory team into the city, had come across Martha and her three boys huddled against the skeleton walls of a house, shivering with the cold, dehydrated and hungry. Had she been able to she would have screamed but, such was the shock at seeing the three men and the thoughts of what might be done to her again, nothing left her throat. Philip, her eldest, blocked their way, defending his mother as best he could, a black eye visible where his last efforts to protect his mother had failed and he had paid the price with a beating. However, talking to her softly, plying the family with water and food, demonstrating that they were safe, she eventually came round and returned with them to the tower.

"Very well, Mr...Bill."

"Martha, just call me Bill please. Your question?"

"I just wanted to thank you for taking me and my family in off the streets. It's hell out there. We feel safe here, and me and my boys will do whatever to ensure you don't regret that decision."

"You're welcome, Martha." Bill looked at the larger group. "If we see others in need, and they're the right fit for us, we will offer them sanctuary here. We don't want to overdo it and put too much pressure on our supplies, but the bigger we are, the stronger we'll be. Right, enough of me talking. Let's head off to the common room and sample Sally's hot chocolate."

The group started to rise to their feet and head towards the door, chatting as they did. There was a lot to talk about. Although there was an element of fear about what the future held for them, there was also the semblance of optimism knowing that Bill seemed to have their future security in his capable hands.

CHAPTER 14

Once the troop had left the devastation and gloom of Hereford, the troop had driven east for about fifteen klicks, keeping to minor roads as much as possible until they arrived at Jones's Wood, where they hid themselves and their vehicle in amongst the trees for a couple of days. Once the Land Rover and trailer were camouflaged, they felt sure they would be hidden from any prying eyes. It gave the soldiers a chance to grab some food, reflect on the day, then get some sack time, but with someone always on stag. But soon they would be on the move again.

"Ready, guys," called Rolly as the water came to the boil. He poured the boiling water into four black plastic mugs, the smell of coffee filling the air, displacing the dank smell of rotting vegetation strewn across the forest floor. A sprinkling of powdered milk in two of them, Glen and Greg drank their coffee black.

The fallen tree trunk, used as a bench, rocked as Greg sat down heavily next to Rolly. "Pass it here, mate, bloody gagging for a brew."

Rolly handed him a mug, and Greg savoured the aroma: Nescafe Gold, his favourite. Taking too big a sip, Greg burnt his tongue and cursed, then spilt some on his knee as Glen sitting next to him nudged him slightly.

"Shit, boss!"

"Don't tell me Rolly's made hot coffee again?"

"Wankers."

Plato joined them, having been the last one to put away his gear and stow it in the Land Rover. Rolly passed the last mug to him.

"I hope to God we don't run out of this stuff."

"Plato mate, next time we do a supply run, coffee will be at the top of the list, believe me."

"Glad you're watching my back for me, Greg," he replied with a grin. "What's the plan then, boss?"

"No change. As we discussed last night, we head south," responded Glen.

"You OK with that still?"

Glen turned and looked at Plato, his expression blank. "Not sunk in yet. But I was expecting it. I suppose that's helped."

"What about your parents?"

"Birmingham."

"Buggered then," joined in Greg.

"What about you guys? Any family you want to track down before the move south?"

Greg placed his empty mug on the dew-damp ground and held up a hand and looked at Glen. "Let me see." Holding his little finger: "Parents are dead." Holding two fingers: "Only child." Three fingers: "My ex? Well, I doubt there'll be a need for divorce papers now, or solicitors for that matter." Four fingers: "Girlfriend? I've moved on."

"Was that the stripper from Saxones?" asked Plato.

"Exotic dancer. I don't do strippers."

"I thought you'd have a go at anything," chimed in Rolly.

"Bloody hell, if I was as fussy as you, Rolly, I'd still be a virgin," responded Greg.

All four burst into laughter. Plato also had a wife but, like a number of the regiment, he was estranged from her. Rolly was single, born in Harlow, where his parents still lived. But he knew, as did the rest of the troop, that Harlow, like the majority of the London area, would be a ghost town.

"This is surreal. The entire world is in the grip of a nuclear holocaust, and all we can talk about are Greg's tarts," said Plato.

This time, the four men were in stitches, and it was only Rolly passing small packets of biscuits down the line, one pack for each of them, that broke the moment.

"Breakfast is served," groaned Glen. "Plato, take us through today's route while we enjoy the luxurious breakfast that Rolly has so kindly provided for us."

The group became serious as Plato ran through what had been agreed the previous day.

"Our biggest worry today is the River Severn. We don't know what's out there and what efforts will be made to gain control of any crossing points."

"That's if they're up to it. It could be they're in too weak a condition to do anything," suggested Rolly.

"There will always be someone strong enough and who wants to be top dog," countered Plato.

"We've already come across one lot of wankers playing at being God," piped up Greg, grimacing as he scratched at the heavy stubble covering his face.

"We certainly have. Hence, we pass around the major conurbations. We head south-east, keeping to minor roads until we come to the M50. We'll cross that, using an underpass. A link for farmers, it allows them access to their fields either side. After that, we can cross the river just west of Deerhurst."

"The river will be the trickiest," suggested Rolly. "How far to the motorway?"

"That's about fifteen Ks," continued Plato. "A further sixteen takes us to the River Severn, then ten to Bishop's Cleve, passing over the M5 beforehand. Still want to recce Cheltenham, Glen?"

"Yes, just from a distance. You never know if we have to come back this way in a hurry. We've got fuel and rations, but they won't last forever. We have to restock whenever possible."

"Yeah," added Greg. "If we want to stay mobile then fuel will be one of our greatest needs."

"I doubt there'll be any of the distribution terminals left, but we can try local garages to start with."

"Nearest terminal from here is probably Bristol way – Avonmouth," Rolly informed them.

"There's always the privately owned pipelines. The terminals may be destroyed, but fuel could be trapped in between pumping stations."

"Private pipelines, Plato?"

"Yeah, Glen, private pipelines. There's one owned by Esso, for example, that runs from Fawley to Birmingham. And this," he slapped a map down on the foldaway table in front of them, "is a map of where they all are."

"How the hell did you get a hold of that?" asked Greg.

"Do you remember that detachment I was on, testing Government anti-terrorist measures?"

"Yeah, a two-week holiday more like," mocked Greg.

"I never said it wasn't." Plato smiled. "But I pretty much know the ins and outs of the private and Government pipelines in the UK."

"Sorry to bring you guys back down to earth, but we'll have to settle for any petrol station we can find in the short term." Glen looked at his watch which read 0530. "Time we moved out."

The troop packed up and were on their way by 0600. Taking

the smaller country roads, they followed the route outlined by Plato, passing through the M50 underpass without incident. They discovered a route across the River Severn. No effort had been made to control the crossing. In fact, they saw no other signs of life, and the houses on the roadside they did pass looked to have all their windows shattered, were covered in thick layers of dust, and appeared unoccupied. By 0825, the troop was in the vicinity of the next motorway, the M5. Three hundred metres before they came up against the M5, before the road climbed up and over the motorway, they turned off into the undergrowth alongside the carriageway, making sure the vehicle and trailer were well hidden and couldn't be seen from the road.

"You two, stay and watch the vehicle. Rolly and I will do a recce."

"I'll get a brew on then," suggested Plato.

"How long?" asked Greg.

"Give us an hour," replied Glen. "That way, if there's anything of interest, we'll have time to take a look. No comms, lets keep it low-key."

"Roger that."

"Ready, Rolly?"

"Yeah, ready for a leg stretch." Rolly, lean and rangy, found the confines of the Land Rover constricting for his legs and always welcomed the opportunity to give them a stretch. He grabbed his C8 carbine and exited through the rear door. Glen left the front passenger seat and joined him outside. Like Rolly, Plato also used a C8 carbine, but with Elcan optics and an L17A1 grenade launcher slung beneath it. Glen, on the other hand, preferred his HK G36. Greg's weapon of choice was the LMG36, a light machine gun with a heavy barrel, bipod and high capacity magazines.

"We'd better mask up. No telling what's around here."

"Sound idea, boss."

Both pulled on their respirators and then dragged their camouflaged hoods around them, ensuring their faces were well protected. Their camouflaged NBC jackets were zipped up tight. They were glad of the extra warmth: there was a biting chill in the air. Glen looked up at the slate grey skies. The cloud looked low, dull and menacing, and not a single shaft of sunlight could be seen. In fact, no glow from the sun was visible at all. He shivered.

"Getting colder, boss."

"Seems like it, Rolly. Let's go."

They left Greg and Plato to guard the Land Rover and all of their gear, and headed east through the undergrowth, climbing the bank that led up to the road. Within a matter of minutes, they were at the edge of the motorway, a steel crash barrier across their front protecting the northbound carriageway. The two soldiers crouched down in the bushes and listened, the only sound their laboured breathing as they sucked air through the filters of their respirators. With the carriageway slightly above them, they could see very little of the road, but the tops of the nearest vehicles were in their line of sight.

Glen nodded, got up from the crouch, and moved forward, climbing the side of the shallow embankment, Rolly watching his back. To his right, Glen could make out the flyover they would eventually cross that supported the minor road over the six lanes of the M5 below it. In front of him, on the hard shoulder, on the other side of the crash barrier, a line of dust-encrusted cars came into view. Immediately in front of him was a people carrier, black privacy glass in the rear side windows. There was no sign of a driver or front passenger. Not that he expected there would be: the car and the thousands of others strewn along the motorway had been abandoned for weeks. He looked over his shoulder, checked Rolly's position, then indicated he was crossing over and Rolly was to follow. Glen pulled his HK into his shoulder and lifted his right leg, stepping over the crash barrier but not taking his eyes off the vehicles in front. He walked in between the people carrier and an old VW Passat to his right. Both were pushed hard up against the crash barrier.

Rolly joined him, and they scanned the area around them, the reason for the crush of vehicles obvious. It was as if the entire three lanes of traffic had been violently bulldozed across the motorway. The majority of the vehicles, particularly those that must have originally been in the fast lane of the northbound carriageway, had been overturned and thrown up against the other two lanes of traffic. Both of the men moved towards the central reservation, having to weave through the tight gaps, occasionally having to climb over a crashed car's bonnet before reaching the central reservation and turning left, peering into the empty cars, vans, trucks, and even a bus. On closer inspection, some of the paint on the cars was burnt and blistered. Glen signalled to Rolly, then crossed to the other side of the central reservation, weaving his way across the southbound lanes, where the cars travelling south had also been shoved across the motorway, crushed up against the central barrier. Along the stretch, a large number of vehicles had been flipped over and now straddled the centre of the motorway.

Glen pulled out his binoculars, sensing Rolly alongside him, watching over both of them whilst Glen was distracted by his current task. He lifted the binos to the front of his mask and scanned the city of Cheltenham to the south-east. The devastation in the northern part of the Cheltenham, the Kingsditch Trading Estate, was plain to see, and, as he scanned to the right, the blackened remains of the housing estates stood out like saw-toothed basalt. Even further to the right, very little could be determined. The site of the Government Communication Headquarters (GCHQ) had received a direct hit from a one-megaton nuclear warhead. It confirmed the reason for the state the cars were in. To their south, he was sure that Gloucester, along with its airport, would have also been a target of Russian anger.

"How's it looking?"

Glen handed him the binos and took up a watch position while Rolly did a sweep of the devastation of what was once a spa town, the home of the flagship horse race, the Gold Cup steeplechase.

"See where GCHQ used to be? That would have been high up on the Soviet's target list."

"That's why we have all the traffic," responded Rolly. "Poor buggers were trying to get away, knowing Cheltenham was fucked. Didn't do them any good though. Couldn't have been much of a warning."

"Same for them all, mate. Motorway is chock-a-block in both directions. Poor bastards from the north have been running south, and this other lot trying to get as far north as possible."

Rolly lowered the binos and pointed at the wrecks. "By the look of these, they were hit by both the blast and thermal wave."

"Probably a one-meg, half a meg at least."

"What next, boss?"

"I just want to have a further look along the line of the vehicles. Then we'll head back for that brew."

"And get this bloody mask off."

They walked further north, along the hard shoulder, the cars shunted up against the central reservation blocking all other routes. Some vehicles had been compressed hard up against the next car in line. Many were overturned lying on their sides; others had been flipped upside down, their shells mangled. The two soldiers walked past an upside down Mini Cooper and a Luton van on its side, rear doors split open with the contents – mattresses, bedding, chairs, suitcases, much of it burnt – strewn over the other transport nearby. Some the suitcases had been torn open. Not from the blast, surmised Glen, but later, by some other means.

"We may not be on our own, so keep your eyes peeled," Glen's muffled voice warned Rolly.

"Yeah, looks like the dust has been disturbed. Maybe in the last couple of days?"

"Or less. See the fuel caps?"

"I do now. Someone's been bleeding the tanks."

At least a dozen vehicles could be seen in the immediate vicinity without their petrol tank caps on. They had been left dangling from the filler tube of the car or van, or torn off and dropped nearby.

"Cover me." Glen dropped down next to a Ford Focus, sniffing at the petrol cap opening, but, apart from a whiff of stale fuel, he sensed the tank was empty, sucked dry by its owners or by looters to satisfy their own demands for petrol. As he rose up from his crouching position, he got another smell, less pleasant than that of fuel: the smell of death. Looking through the window of the car, the driver, or what was left of his decomposing body, was slumped over the gearstick, no doubt knocked unconscious when the hurricane-like blast wave struck. It wasn't the first time he'd seen death by a long shot, but this was different somehow, more ominous. He was sure that there were many millions of dead bodies out there, across the country, rotting as this one was in the car. Glen moved away, raising his left arm and signalling Rolly to go left, which he did, finding a gap between a Ford Transit and a 3 Series Saab. He stepped back over the central reservation barriers, a ten-metre gap in between them, and turned right, tracking Glen on the opposite side, but keeping ten metres back. In places, the gap between the cars on the southbound carriageway narrowed considerably, where larger vehicles such as HGVs had been hammered by the blast wave, forcing them to strike other vehicles, like balls on a pool table. It wasn't easy keeping track of Glen as he often vanished from sight, disappearing behind stacked vehicles or something large like a coach. Glen came into view again, signalling with his arm before dropping down, triggering Rolly to respond likewise.

Something had caught Glen's peripheral vision. Something fleeting, but enough for his trained eye and subconscious mind, sifting the data, for Glen to react, signalling with his arm, then dropping down, halting them both. He had just saved his friend's life.

A chain of events was set off: Rolly dropping down to a crouch behind a Vauxhall, wary of what Glen might have observed; the woman over anticipating the kickback from the shotgun and pulling the weapon up a fraction of a second before she fired; and the soldier's quick movements putting her off her aim, ensuring that the pellets flew harmlessly over Rolly's head. Glen responded in an instant, firing towards the gun flashes. Two bullets struck the individual. Her body, swaddled in a thick coat and layer upon layer of clothing beneath, was thrown back over the bonnet of an Audi A6. She was dying as she slid down onto the tarmac. One bullet had shattered her shoulder, but the fatal first bullet had punched a hole straight through her chest.

Then all hell broke loose. A high-velocity round punched a hole straight through the door of a flipped-over Vauxhall and through the opposite door, passing less than a metre from Rolly. A second shotgun opened up. Glen felt the pellets peppering his small rucksack as they ricocheted off the bonnet of a Volvo lying on its side. However, they caused no injury: the range was too great, and the vehicle absorbed most of the pellets' velocity. Another high-velocity round, this time aimed at Glen, dug its way into the engine block of the Volvo.

"Damn," Glen cursed to himself. "We should have had comms."

But they didn't. That meant he couldn't communicate with Rolly, not easily without warning their ambushers, and he couldn't guide Plato and Greg in, who he knew would be hotfooting it to their location by now. But what he did know, and so would Rolly, was that their two comrades would not come onto the motorway, and risk getting caught up in the crossfire. They would try and position themselves alongside the enemy, and would make sure they didn't place themselves in Glen's and Rolly's lines of fire.

Glen quickly raised his body, and fired a double tap in the direction of the incoming fire before dropping down again. Time to move forward, he thought, knowing the exact same thoughts would be running through Rolly's mind. He heard two rounds fired to his left, and immediately did the same. Rolly then fired four shots, giving Glen a message that he was in a bad position and would be best providing cover. Glen fired a further two shots confirming he understood. Five seconds, and he would need to move. They had wasted enough time as it was, and whoever was firing at them would have them tagged by now.

Four shots in quick succession from Rolly, and Glen was up. He put two shots into a location where he had seen movement earlier, then darted forward about ten metres before finding cover and taking stock at the same time. He pumped a further four rounds towards the enemy, eyes would be on him now. He heard a satisfied squeal as Rolly skirmished forward, firing and hitting one of their ambushers. Glen was up again, but quickly hit the deck as a hail of gunfire ensued, rounds zipping past him. He made a quick assessment of the firepower they were up against: two automatic pistols, pretty useless at the range they were firing at, two shotguns, a hunting rifle, and something more sinister – a semi-automatic weapon, a British Army SA80 by the sound of it.

Recognising Glen's situation, Rolly was up again, moving forward, peppering the likely area of the enemy with half a dozen well-placed rounds. Glen didn't waste any time either, and also scrambled up, weaving around an old Suzuki pickup truck and a Clio before firing four shots in the general direction of the enemy force. Then, spotting a figure on the move, he pumped two more rounds, the first taking a middle-aged man in the shoulder, spinning him around so that the second shot bore into his back, exiting the other side. The man tumbled forwards as two more rounds struck the area around him.

Rolly had set the momentum now, and Glen had no intention of letting him down. A fresh magazine and he was up and racing forward. Two more shots fired, and a long burst from Rolly, enabled Glen to keep moving forward. The dull clang of bullets punching holes in the car bodies followed by the sharp cracks of the automatic weapons as their rate of fire increased as the two SAS soldiers upped the pressure. Their attackers suddenly broke. At least half a dozen figures were up on their feet, blankets flapping around their shoulders as they raced to escape the now incessant rate of fire as the two SAS men's bullets sliced through them. Fire came from the left as Greg and Plato added to the rain of lead peppering the escaping group.

There was a sudden shout: "Stop, please stop."

Another voice joined in as a man threw down his hunting rifle. "We give in, we give in."

Within minutes, the four SAS troopers had disarmed the assailants, covered their arcs, and waited until satisfied that the immediate threat was over. Greg was the first to rise and move inward, the other three shifting position to fill the gap. There were eleven people in total. You couldn't distinguish male from female such was the bulk of clothing worn. All were in a huddle, in a semi-circle, up against an overturned HGV trailer unit. Glen sucked in air, needing to fill his lungs, the sides of his mask concave as he tried to pull in more air than the filter would allow. The masks would eventually clog up with dust, and the few filters they had left wouldn't last forever.

Glen moved forward to join Rolly. He could see numerous pairs of eyes looking up at him, peering out of their own home-made masks. Some had surgical masks tied on with string; others had what looked like a piece of gauze sandwiched between thin layers of material. They could breathe through it, and it would provide them with some protection from the contaminated dust, although for many the damage had already been done. He recognised their fear, fear of the imposing figure he must have represented in his camouflaged uniform, with his black respirator cowled with a hood.

He pulled back his hood and peeled off his mask, seeing the figures visibly relaxing, though only slightly. Looking at the ragtag group sitting in a semi-circle around him, he asked, "Who's in charge here?"

All of them turned and looked at a middle-aged woman, probably in her late thirties, dressed in what can only be described as a pair of ski pants with a matching jacket, a coat wrapped around her shoulders for additional warmth. Her blonde hair was straggly and lay about her shoulders, a one-inch line of mousey hair along the roots indicative of it not being her natural colour. Even with a long narrow burn scar down the side of her face, she was still a relatively attractive woman and exuded a strong character.

"Am I allowed to stand, soldier boy? Or will you shoot me too?"

"Yes, ma'am you can stand. Don't forget, you fired on us first. What's your name?"

"Ma'am is fine. You did come into our camp with weapons. But to show you how friendly we all are, you can call me Judy."

"Thank you, ma'am, Judy. I'm Glen. This man with me is Rolly, and covering our backs is Greg and Plato." Glen turned and called over to Plato. "Bring the Land Rover a bit closer in so we can keep an eye on it."

Plato left, equally concerned that their vehicle and the valuable supplies on board were at risk.

"You have food?"

"Some," responded Glen warily. "What do you and your friends

127

do for food, and why are you up here and not down in one of the towns or villages?"

"So many questions, soldier boy."

"Glen, please."

"Glen it is then." A small smile showed through the thin layer of grime. "We have some food, but not much. Any you can give us will be very welcome. As for the towns? Full of miscreants who just want to steal our food and take anything else they want, if you know what I mean."

It was Glen's turn to smile. "Is that why you fired at us?"

"That was a mistake. Someone let fly, and everyone followed suit. I'll speak to that individual later. So, my apologies for that. Saying that, we came off far worse. You have killed a number of our group."

She turned as a figure on the ground behind Greg groaned. "What about the injured? Are we allowed to help them?"

"Off course. And we'll help you with your wounded."

"Much obliged."

Greg moved and crouched down next to the groaning man shrouded in thick clothing, the red patches showing he had been hit at least three times. Glen looked across and Greg shook his head.

"He won't make it?" she asked.

"Unlikely. Greg, check out the others. But keep your eyes peeled."

"Will do, boss."

"You their boss?"

"Only by agreement. So, what do you do for food and water?"

"Water we get from streams and rivers. As for food?" She waved her arm in the direction of the line of abandoned vehicles. "When the people fled from the towns and cities, they stocked up with all sorts of goodies. One car had about 200 gold sovereigns in it." She laughed. "Gold. Some good it'll do anyone now."

Rolly sauntered over and Glen asked, "Everything OK?"

"Yes, boss. The wounded have been patched up."

"He speaks. Now, who might you be, soldier? Kind of cute, if you don't mind me saying."

Glen turned and glanced at his friend. The glow of crimson showing between the SAS soldier's helmet, and the scarf wrapped around his neck.

"Rolly, my friends call me Rolly."

"Mmmm, rolls off the tongue."

Rolly scowled at him as Glen let out a chuckle. Rolly hissed, "Not a word, not a bloody word."

She became more serious. "Will they survive?"

Glen looked over at Greg and raised his eyebrows.

Greg responded. "Best if they had some antibiotics. But keeping the wounds clean and changing dressings regularly will contribute to their chances of pulling through."

"Thank you both."

"It's the least we could do."

"How many...dead?"

Rolly answered this time, lowering his head before responding, conscious that he was responsible for at least two of the deaths, "three."

Judy didn't respond immediately. "It's the world we now live in."

"So where do you get your food from?" Glen asked again.

"From these," she pointed to the vehicles again. "We reckon the line of traffic stretches for fifty miles or more. We have up to the horse box," she pointed north, "back down to the overturned caravan." This time she indicated south. "We think a few thousand vehicles in our patch, maybe as many as ten."

"Why the limit," asked Rolly.

"We have the Brummies down thataways and the cockney sparras up there."

"Cockney sparrows? Londoners, I take it," suggested Glen.

"Yeah, bloody pain they are. But we defend our territory and they defend theirs."

"What happens when the food runs out?"

Her shoulders slumped for the first time. "Then the fighting gets worse."

"How many are you?"

"We were forty-five, but you soldier boys have reduced that some."

"Where are the rest?"

"Hiding. We don't have many weapons."

"You have an automatic."

"Yeah, we found it in a Range Rover, along with about 200 bullets. The one thing that's kept the buggers around us at bay. Until you lot came along, that is."

They heard the growl of the Land Rover being manoeuvred closer to the embankment on the west side of the motorway.

Glen turned to Rolly. "Get Plato up here, and bring up any

medical supplies Greg might need. But stay with the Rover, let's keep it secure."

Rolly walked towards the edge of the motorway.

"We'll help you get your wounded comfortable."

"That would be appreciated, Glen. We have some first-aid kits we found in some of the cars, but the nurse we have with us could do with some guidance on treating gunshot wounds."

"Let's go and take a look then." Glen waved at Greg, indicating they were coming over.

A crowd, now some thirty-plus, were slowly gathering around the wrecks that had become their homes, and they moved aside as Judy led the way. She instructed four or five to gather any wounded and take them to the hospital. Both Glen and Judy weaved in between various cars, passing two Ford Transits lying on their side, a Leyland Daf, a people carrier and even a Bentley, although it had seen better days. The two of them, trailed by the group, Greg keeping his distance watching over Glen, eventually arrived at a coach that had managed to stay on all of its four wheels.

"Our medical centre, hospital and maternity ward," his guide informed Glen.

Plato was making his way through the crowd. "Where do you want me?"

"They're being brought to the coach."

"I'd like to see them."

"Can you and I have a chat first while Plato and Greg continue to work their magic?" suggested Glen.

"Sure. Does he know his stuff?"

"Greg and Plato have saved my life more than once."

She seemed satisfied with that answer and led Glen further along the motorway, arriving at a camper van. Glen followed Judy into a Fiat camper van, more like a small motorhome, in pretty good condition despite the fact that it was covered in dents and gashes and the paintwork was badly blistered. Once inside, Glen took off his small rucksack and sat opposite her on a bench seat, that also doubled as a bed, at a small table at the far end.

"Just excuse me for a minute." Judy went down towards the cab where there was a cooker and small sink. He heard the splash of water, and she soon returned. Her scarf had been removed, and he noticed she had wiped some of the grime off her face. He was sure he could see a hint of make-up on her pale face. He looked around the inside of the motorhome and could see she had added a feminine touch wherever possible. Sure that the bench seat he was sitting on, once the table was collapsed, would become part of a small double bed, he estimated the home could probably sleep six.

"My manners are terrible." She smiled. "I haven't even offered you a drink."

She slid along the bench and walked to a camping gas stove sitting on a hinged shelf and lit it, placing a dented aluminium kettle of water on top of it.

Glen twisted round so he could see and talk to her.

"The water's safe," she informed him. "We have a geek in the group that has some sort of kit he can use to filter it and check it. Coffee?"

"Would love one. Your group OK for coffee then?" he smiled.

"We have some. Not all of the vehicles in our area have been fully searched yet."

"It won't last forever, you know."

The hiss of the gas stove filled the silence while she thought about his last statement. "I know. It plays on my mind. The group look to me for answers."

"That's a lot of responsibility on a pair of small shoulders."

"Tell me about it."

The kettle came to the boil and she poured the water over some coffee granules in two matching coffee mugs. She brought the steaming mugs over and placed one of them in front of him. "Sorry, but no milk. We have a couple of youngsters, so we save the powdered milk for them."

"Your group get on well together? Fairly placid? Apart from opening fire on my team, that is."

"Yeah, I'm really sorry about that. It was an accident. We came off far worse, remember?" she snapped.

"I know, but you need to make sure they keep their fingers off the trigger in future."

"I'll speak to them. And thank you for helping with our wounded."

"We did the damage. I'm sorry some of them were killed."

She sat down opposite him again and both took a sip of their already cooling coffee. The camper van was slightly warmer than the outside, partly driven by the gas stove that shared its heat, but there was still a chill in the air.

"So, what are your plans when your supplies run out?" Glen asked again.

She lowered her head, her blonde hair covering part of her face. Glen felt a twinge in his stomach, not quite sure what it was or why.

She looked up again, taking in his rugged, but trusting face. His dark hair, short, but not a crew cut, contrasted with a pair of piercing blue eyes. "I suppose I have three options. Stay here but scavenge further afield, roam the countryside, or find somewhere for us to make a home and live off the land."

"What about the other groups along the motorway?"

"We've had a few minor skirmishes, but nothing we couldn't handle. The northern group worries me the most. They're by far the more aggressive of the two. We've heard gunfire further along as well, in both directions, so there are probably other groups further along. The future scares me. You don't fancy staying, do you?"

"We have to follow our own path for a while."

"And then?"

"Thought about it, like you, but haven't come to any conclusions."

"You could always come back here. I don't mean live in this mess, but join us in finding something more permanent."

Glen shocked himself by not immediately saying no. "I, well, we have a mission to fulfil before we make plans for ourselves."

"And that is?"

"Start with London, check out who's in charge."

"Wouldn't someone have been in contact by now?"

He sipped his coffee, avoiding the question. "Not bad."

"Thank you."

"Just look at where you're living. The rest of the country appears to be in a similar state, so far anyway."

"Someone will have to take control."

"Yes, but who? That's the million-dollar question."

Greg popped his head through the door. "Five-star accommodation, I see."

"What's the final count?"

Greg looked at Glen, asking the silent question. *Is it OK to say it in front of her?*

Glen nodded.

"Four wounded, two pretty clean, one has a shattered arm, and the fourth, well, he's in a bad way. But if looked after and given plenty of rest he could pull through. Three dead."

Judy sighed. "I should have stopped it."

Glen placed a hand on her hand that was resting on the table.

"You weren't to know someone would open fire."

"Everybody is so nervous of the other groups. I'm scared of the other groups, I just can't show it."

"Do you have a gun?"

"No, there's not enough to go round. I don't like them anyway."

Glen turned back to Greg. "We'll come and have a look. Give us a few minutes. Can you give Rolly a breather?"

"Sure, boss." Greg left to take over from Rolly and ensure the security of their vehicle and kit.

Glen unzipped his rucksack, fumbled around inside, and pulled out a small semi-automatic pistol. He placed it on the table, along with a magazine. He then pulled out a box of shells. "This is a Walther PPK. Keep this with you at all times."

She picked it up. "I've never fired one before."

"Then I'll have to teach you before we go."

"Are you married?"

Glen was shocked by the question. "Yes. No…I was."

"Was she killed by the bombs?"

"Yes, our married quarters were wiped out. What about you?"

"I had a man. He was in the army like you. Sent him and his tanks to Ukraine. His troop got hit by a Russian air strike, and Mathew's tank was destroyed."

"I'm sorry. How long ago was that?"

"It happened in the first week. Bloody Russians. Why couldn't they just settle for what they had? It's a big enough country."

"A lot of soldiers have died."

"A lot more since. Were you there?"

"Even before it all kicked off. We lost some good lads too."

A head popped through the door. "Ah, sorry to butt in, Judy, but George is asking after you in the hospital."

"OK, Adam, I'll be right there."

Adam left to pass on the news, and Judy stood up. "My break's over. I need to go and see if everyone is OK."

Glen stood up too. "If the lads are in agreement, we'll spend the night here."

Her smile was genuine, and Glen got his first glimmer of a youthful face through the tiredness. She had clearly suffered from her experiences, weighed down by the burden of responsibility that had been laid on her shoulders and the living hell they had all found themselves in.

CHAPTER 15

Sergeant Saunders drove slowly, trying to keep the partially contaminated dust down to an acceptable level, the Land Rover leading the rest of the convoy towards the small town of Chilmark. Captain Redfern looked back through the gap between the two alert armed soldiers in the rear of the vehicle. Behind were two MAN six-tonne trucks, followed by a three Dennis buses and two civilian HGVs, some of the few surviving vehicles in the region. The Region had two more buses, a JCB, five other Land Rovers, a Fox reconnaissance vehicle, and a Scimitar light tank. The remaining vehicles, those that hadn't been sucked into West Germany to feed the demands of the British Army fighting in Ukraine, had either been destroyed, damaged beyond repair, or made unserviceable as a consequence of the Electromagnetic Pulse, EMP, effects of the nuclear strikes. Alan felt sure that, once they could move further afield, other modes of transport, such as tractors, vans or industrial equipment, would be found.

They were now a kilometre from the town where the 400 labourers, being transported the seven kilometres from the camp, would start work. A workforce of 200 had also been dropped off at Fonthill Bishop to start work on clearing ground ready for planting some winter crops. Fifty had been tasked with tidying up the camp, and another fifty had been taken to a large farm south of the village to make repairs and get it ready to act as the agricultural base for the RGC and receive any animals they could find once scavenging started in earnest.

"There's the digger," indicated Sergeant Saunders.

A yellow JCB, with a large dozer at the front and bucket at the rear, was parked up on the outskirts of the village. It was being guarded by a security patrol of two soldiers and two police constables. The driver was sitting in the cab.

"Pull over alongside the JCB," Captain Redfern ordered.

The Land Rover stopped, and the convoy behind ground to

a halt. One of the soldiers by the JCB came over and saluted.

"Where do they want us then, Corporal Thompson?"

"A few hundred metres further up, sir. We've allocated a slot for the heavies to park up."

"Good, jump in the back and show us the way."

"Sir."

Corporal Thompson went around the back, indicated to the driver of his vehicle and the driver of the JCB to follow, then climbed over the tailgate and gave Captain Redfern directions. "There's a track up on the right, about one hundred metres, where the trees end. Turn down there, and you'll see an open field on the left."

"Right, let's go then."

Sergeant Saunders pulled away slowly, giving the convoy behind a chance to follow their lead. After about a hundred metres, they swung right and followed a hard-packed track for about half a kilometre until they reached an open piece of ground off to their left.

"There, sir," Corporal Thompson pointed to a large area of tarmac on the edge of a grassed field, "that's where we can lager the vehicles. I think it might have been a small warehouse or something."

"Good spot, well done."

Sergeant Saunders steered the Land Rover left, bumping across the grassed area in a large arc, the vehicle ending up facing the convoy, stopping, allowing Captain Redfern and Corporal Thompson to jump out and direct the convoy as it drew closer.

Corporal Thompson called out to a driver whose scarf-covered face was jutting out of the cab window. "Go forward 200 metres, then swing left and go to the far side of the tarmac area."

The civilian driver of the MAN nodded and accelerated away. Seconds later, the next vehicle in the convoy, driven by a soldier this time, came alongside.

"When the lead vehicle swings off to the left and parks up, pull up alongside it, this side of it, but allow a good twenty-metre gap."

"Corporal."

Then came the two buses and a second Land Rover, followed by two civilian trucks with the JCB as tail-end Charlie.

As the workforce debussed, the gang leaders, one for each group of thirty, shouted and cajoled them into some form of order. Alan's small force, six soldiers, four police constables and eight CPS officers, Civilian Police Support, also split up. The army unit would remain together as a quick reaction force (QRF) in case there should be any trouble amongst the workforce that the civilian security element couldn't handle. The QRF would also need to be prepared for any intrusion from an outside force: unknowns coming from outside the RGC's county boundary.

Once shovels, picks and plastic body bags had been offloaded, the gangs, led by one of Dylan Wright's men, headed north-west towards the outskirts of the town.

"Don't envy those poor bastards," said Corporal William Thompson. "Their first day on the job, and they've got the body-bag detail."

"Someone's got to do it, Will," responded Sergeant Saunders.

"I know, Sarge, but the smell! Makes you want to heave your guts up."

"They have surgical masks," Captain Redfern informed him.

"They'll help, but not much, sir."

"I'm going to take a stroll and check things out. Keep half the QRF here to watch the vehicles. Do you have somewhere we can use as a temp HQ?"

"Yes, sir," responded the corporal. "We've found a house with a roof that's not too bad. And no bodies."

"Whereabouts?"

"Frog Lane sir. We'll take our Land Rover up there now. Park it outside. That'll guide you."

"I'll join you for a brew in thirty."

"Do you want someone with you, sir?"

"No, Sar'nt, I have this." He held up his SA80. "Just send the Land Rover to find me if there's any trouble."

"Sir."

Captain Redfern adjusted his face mask, then headed towards the road where the tail end of a work gang was just disappearing in between two buildings before they turned left along the High Street. He followed on, hearing the Land Rover driving north across the field followed by Sergeant Saunders in his vehicle as they too headed towards the centre of the village, but by a different route.

Alan was soon amongst the houses on the high street, and by the time he got to Frog Lane, he could see the two Land Rovers manoeuvring in the drive of a requisitioned house, about 200 metres from the T-junction. He continued up the High Street. The work gangs were already getting to grips with the gruesome task assigned to them. He gagged slightly. Corporal Thompson had been correct:

the stench was pretty bad and getting stronger by the day as more and more bodies decomposed. The death toll was rising with individuals, succumbing to radiation sickness or their injuries on a daily basis. Many came to the town, perhaps to a house where they had lived, to lie down and die.

Four men, each holding a corner, carried a heavy black plastic body bag down the front path of one of the houses, unceremoniously dumping it on the edge of the road. He watched as another group of thirty men, interspersed with women, a gang leader who urged them on led them further down the road. The community that had survived the blast and the subsequent after-effects were moving into an era where responsibility meant recognition, and recognition meant guarantees for your family and the opportunity for perks if they ever arose. The group shuffled along the road, clouds of dust forming around their grubby footwear as they kicked up accumulated debris. Spades, shovels and pickaxes were resting on their shoulders, the new tools of their trade. Like Alan, they had scarves or other items of clothing wrapped around their heads to keep out the cold. Alan suspected that, by the end of their four-hour day, much of their outer clothing would be discarded as their bodies warmed up as a consequence of the physical work they were involved in. Due to there still being contaminants in the air, it had been decided to limit the work period to four hours for a couple of weeks, increasing it as the contamination levels dropped and more of the village was cleared of debris. It was not a healthy option being exposed for so long a period of time, but the choices of the regional government were limited if they were to survive. They needed to be ready for the winter, that was no doubt on its way, and to replace their diminishing supplies of food. Although just after seven in the morning, the sky was overcast and grey, but not just with clouds of moisture. The majority of the content was dust: millions of tons of it kicked up by the worldwide nuclear catastrophe. Everyone, without exception, caught Alan's eye as they shuffled past. The looks weren't hostile, but neither were they friendly. He and the army and police were unknown factors. The confrontations outside the RGC in the early days, crowds pleading for water, begging for food and medical aid, seemed to have been forgotten. There was a sense of a truce. How long that would last, Alan was unsure. But he certainly wasn't their enemy. On the contrary, his job was to protect them.

He walked further along the street where one gang, five labourers to a house, were removing bodies, bagging them up, and placing them alongside the road. They would eventually be picked up by one of the lorries and taken to site where they would be incinerated, preventing the spread of disease. Typhoid and cholera were a real threat to their new community and could wipe them out in a matter of weeks if the two diseases gained a foothold. A dog, sniffing around one of the bagged bodies, yowled and squealed as it was whacked with the flat of someone's shovel.

"Bloody pests. Been chewing at some poor bugger's leg," said the labourer who had delivered the blow. It must have been warm work as the man had already removed his headscarf and jacket. He had also pulled aside his face mask.

"What's your name?"

"Edward, Eddie, Captain."

"What's it like in there?"

"Shit, but to be expected with no roof, door or windows. Oi, if you've finished, move down six houses and check it out," he called to the five men allocated to this house who were now standing around leaning on their implements.

Eddie brushed his straggly hair out of his eyes and smiled through the four-week-old beard that, although bedraggled, looked clean. Alan took an instant like to this powerful-looking man in his early forties.

"Lazy sods. Need to keep on top of this lot or nothing will be done."

"What have you been tasked to do?"

"Bodies first. Then clear any houses still with a roof. Once the village has been sorted, houses will be allocated to families."

"That will be an improvement, won't it?"

"Too bloody right, Captain. You'll be glad to get out of that bunker as well, I'm sure."

Alan pulled his face mask down below his chin and laughed. "Yes, there's cosy and there's suffocating. Were you in the forces?"

"Yes, sir, REME. Ten years, came out about ten years back."

"Fancy a change in role?" Alan asked on the spur of the moment.

"What, put on a uniform again? Not bloody likely."

"Different ballgame now, Eddie. It's no longer just about soldiering. We're protectors, project managers, guides, engineers, taxis, you name it. We will fulfil whatever role is required to protect the community, those that are left, that is, and ensure our survival."

Eddie rubbed his chin.

"You don't have to give me an answer now, but think on it."

"I'll do that, Captain, but best be getting my lads moving or they'll be skiving and dropping me in it."

"If you change your mind, come and see me at the bunker."

"Will do." With that, the man swung his shovel onto his shoulder and bellowed at the nearest of his work parties, moving them on to their next task.

Alan turned round and headed back to their temporary HQ. He'd seen enough for now, and meeting Eddie had restored some of his faith in the remaining survivors of this region. As he made his way back down the street, he reflected on their current circumstances and the recent briefing by the senior members of the RGC. They were coping, but it was more than likely there were more stragglers out there somewhere. It was estimated that less than 10,000 people in the county of Wiltshire had survived the nuclear strike. Many of those would be sick or injured. Survivors had slowly drifted in from as far afield as Swindon and the much nearer town of Salisbury. Considering communications were almost non-existent, survivors had heard by word of mouth that government help could be sought from a centre near Chilmark. Alan felt sure that even more survivors would drift towards where it was believed help was on hand. With limited food available, there were tough times ahead.

He acknowledged one of the work teams as they shambled out of a house having cleared it of dead bodies, and he walked down the path of the front garden. He passed through the doorway, the door itself hanging on one hinge. It was fairly light inside with no windows or curtains to block out the light. A few of the houses had been turned into fortresses, their owners boarding up windows and building internal shelters for their families. But to no avail: the detonation had been too close, and the blast just ripped through the meagre defences, turning the town into a ghost town. He climbed the stairs and looked up at the tile-free roof, the trusses in place, but the roof tiles probably scattered for miles across the county. The intention was to repair as many of the houses as possible, rehouse the population, and get back to some form of order. It would be a big job. He headed back downstairs and exited the building.

Alan made his way back to the temporary headquarters where he found Corporal Thompson and Sergeant Saunders in the final stages of making a brew. After a hot cuppa and a chat with a few of his soldiers, whose morale seemed high, he, along with Sergeant Saunders, made a move.

"I'll leave you in charge, Corporal. I suggest you leave the police to oversee the town, and you complete a couple of patrols in the local area. Not too many. We always need to be conscious of our fuel state."

"Leave it with us, sir. Can we get some fags issued tonight, sir?"

"I'll check it out, but cigarettes are a commodity that will eventually run out."

"I'll give up in the new year," the corporal responded with a laugh.

Alan turned to the sergeant. "Let's go."

Both pulled their surgical masks back up over their mouths, pulled their netted scarves up around their necks, and headed outside into the cooler air.

Saunders shivered. "Is it me sir, or is it getting bloody colder?"

Alan buttoned the top of his jacket. "When we're on our own, call me Alan. We're in a different sort of world now, and everyone's future is much more closely linked. And, yes, the temperature is definitely dropping. Don't get excited, but you've been given your Warrant and Corporal Thompson will get your three stripes."

"Sergeant Major Scott Saunders…has a nice ring to it. And you, sir…Alan?"

"I now have the field rank of major and our beloved colonel is a brigadier."

"And the pay to go with it?" chuckled Scott.

"It will be in your bank account tomorrow."

"What's the sudden reason for this?"

"It seems that the rank of a brigadier is the authorised position for the head of the military in our new world order. Elliot is now the regional governor."

"Why the change?"

"Comms with other regional centres is non-existent, apart from the one further north, and they sound like they're in a sorry state. So, Elliot has the authority to take on the mantle of governor for this region and can form his own top table."

"We already have that, don't we? Seems a bit of a palaver."

"It does a bit, but it's about making a more permanent organisation, I suppose. Come on, I want to pay a visit to the camp."

They jumped into the Land Rover, and Scott steered the

vehicle along the track they had negotiated earlier. Turning left onto the road, they picked up speed, creating some dust, but it was behind them and away from any people. Passing Quarry Copse, the trees now nothing more than blackened stumps, they made their way south. They passed a farm on the right, the nuclear explosion having wreaked havoc to the buildings, literally shredding the farm buildings, leaving nothing but skeletal structures. RAF Chilmark was next on their left – an RAF base no more. Now, it was nothing more than a pile of rubble centred on a 100-metre crater.

On arrival at the camp, they drew up close to washing-up area, where another element of the newly formed labour force would be responsible for assisting with the food preparation, serving, then washing the cooking and eating utensils after the two main meals of the day. Another Land Rover was already there, parked in an area allocated for transport assigned to move supplies to and from the feeding centre. A soldier was sitting dozing in the front of the vehicle, his SA80 clutched in his arms, lying across his chest.

Alan and Scott, the sergeant major promising to speak to the soldier on their return, made their way down the line of workstations that made up a section of the feeding station. Alan was amazed how incredibly big and complex it was, particularly considering the devastation that had recently struck the country, and the disorganisation that followed. He took his hat off to the RGC administration that, once they'd been given the go-ahead by the regional governor, had got the facility up and running so quickly. On their far right, two large ovens were spewing out a steady stream of smoke, the cooks baking as many loaves of bread as they could. Bread would be a key part of the survivors' fare for the foreseeable future, so long as the ingredients kept coming, that is. The smell of freshly baked bread was somewhat comforting, reminding Alan of what had existed before. But he knew that circumstances were far from being on a par with what once was. On their immediate right, the two soldiers walked past a line of tables. These were being used to prepare the food. Initially Alan thought that the half-dozen labourers were busy peeling potatoes and vegetables but then he realised they were actually scrubbing them, not wanting to waste a precious commodity by throwing part of it in the bin. There were no pigs to feed, *not yet anyway*, he thought. The workforce appeared to be happy, chatting to each other across the tables as they got on with the task in hand, pleased to be away from the squalor of the encampment, the activity taking their mind temporarily off the predicament the survivors in the UK found themselves in. Experiencing a sense of organisation also gave them hope for the future. Planning and coordination constituted an element of the old Establishment that would protect them and take care of their needs for the foreseeable future. A few CPS officers wandered along the length of the preparation area, ensuring that food wasn't being stolen by the workforce preparing it. On Alan's left, a line of serveries were in the process of being cleaned, ready to serve the population under their control: a half pint of stew per person for their evening meal. The wind shifted slightly, and the smell of cooking wafted over from the boilers, set up not far from the bread ovens.

"Doesn't smell too bad, does it?"

"They'll be hungry enough by the time they're finished, they'll probably eat anything," replied Alan.

"I have to give them their due, having this set up in such a short space of time. Where have these supplies come from?"

"Some of it was stored in the main warehouse. The rest is from the government stores."

"Won't we need to start guarding that soon?"

"Not until we start to use it in earnest. Very few know of its existence, apart from half a dozen at the RGC. And me and you, of course. That's why we use our lads to collect what we need from there."

"How much is there?" asked Scott as he adjusted his scarf to keep the chill off the back of his neck.

"Not sure. But I believe there is at least a thousand six-pound tins of corned beef and the same again with 140-pound sacks of flour. Oh, and sugar and cooking oil."

"Bully beef, lovely."

"We'll be glad of it in times to come," responded Alan with a smile, acknowledging one of the CPS officers as she passed the two soldiers.

"Leave that until the civilian warehouse is emptied first?"

"That's the general idea."

"Makes sense."

As they arrived at the far end of the complex, two police constables, standing alongside a water tanker, guarding it and the food store, saluted Alan and greeted Scott.

Discipline is holding up well, thought Alan. Alan returned the salute. "All quiet, Constable?" he asked, casting his eye over the officer's uniform. What little light there was reflected off the silver chain of his whistle attached to the barely recognisable tunic beneath the warmer layers on top. His peaked cap was battered, and the black and white check was now more of a shade of grey. The only thing denoting that he was in fact an officer of the law was the grimy yellow fluorescent jacket with 'POLICE' in large letters across the back.

"Yes, sir, they're as good as gold."

"How many of you are here?"

"Just the two of us along with four CPSs."

"Will you be reinforced later?"

"So we're told," answered the second police officer. "A washing area has been set up over there." He pointed to a small stand of trees 200 metres from the feeding station. "Once the workers have had a chance to clean up a bit, the force from the village and the rest of the CPSs will join us here."

"Anticipate any trouble?"

"Not this time, sir. They'll just be pleased to have their first decent hot meal since the bombs. In weeks to come, when the working day is increased and the rations prove barely sufficient, there may be some bother."

"It's the non-labour force workers we have to worry about, sir," added Constable Bryant.

"Why's that?"

"Their rations are a lot lower, Sergeant. When they see that the workforce are getting more than them, they'll kick up a fuss."

"Good point," agreed Alan. He didn't bother to inform them of Scott's new rank. It wasn't important for the moment. "Something we'll need to keep our eye on."

Just then, Alison appeared from inside the food store. "Ah, Captain Redfern," she said with a beaming smile that could be identified even behind her face mask.

Alan excused himself from the two police constables and turned towards the sound of her voice.

"Hey, you're OK there, sir," whispered Scott.

"I can soon have you busted down to the rank of private, Sergeant Major," responded Alan. But without malice.

"Hello, Alison, you're away from your usual territory."

She pulled the surgical mask down, her smile still showing strong, a hint of pink lipstick adding to the attraction Alan felt in his

143

stomach. "Afraid you'll miss your tea and biscuits, Captain? No fear, I'm only helping out for a couple of hours."

"What job have you got?" Scott asked.

"Just giving them some tips on how best to organise getting the food from the preparation area to the cookers, then to the serving tables."

"Perhaps we should join the queue and test out the food," suggested Scott.

"It'll be a long wait, Sergeant. We'll have nearly 4,000 people queuing up here."

"It's Sergeant Major now, Alison, although I'm beginning to wonder if we've made a mistake promoting him."

"Likewise, sir. Should you really be made up to major?"

"My, my," interrupted Alison. "Does this mean I'm now chief cook and bottle washer?" She laughed.

Alan gulped, feeling a constriction across his chest as her laugh played with his senses. "How about head chef?" he offered, barely able to get the words out of his now dry mouth.

Scott looked on, keeping his grin to himself, knowing earlier what the major was only now coming to realise. *In this miserable world we now find ourselves in, some happiness can't be a bad thing,* he thought. The major had lost his wife to cancer over three years ago, and the officer had concentrated fully on his military career in an attempt to block out the pain he felt at her loss.

"Maajoor Redfern," she emphasised his rank, "you flatter me. The biscuits aren't home-made, just yet."

"Are the preparations going well?" asked Scott, taking some of the pressure off his flustered OC.

"Far better than anyone expected. The people are great, really wanting to make it a success."

"They have a vested interest," Alan reminded her.

"Ever the cynic?" She laughed out loud, and the two constables smiled as they looked over as did one of the CPSs. Things couldn't be too bad, thought all three of them.

"We'd best be checking the troops, sir," Scott reminded the Major, wanting to rescue his officer from any more blushing.

"Yes, Sar'nt Major. Well, Alison, we'll leave you to your task and catch up with you later at the RGC."

"I look forward to it," she said, beaming, recognising the effect she was having on him, and pleased about it.

The two men gave her a relaxed salute and walked back down the line. After a quick chat with Baxter, who was now wide awake after realising it was his commander's Land Rover close by, they returned to their vehicle to continue the rounds of their area of responsibility.

CHAPTER 16

Keelan crawled out of the upturned Commer van. A trickle of blood ran down the side of his face. His right eyebrow had split open as his head smacked into the window, shattering the glass. He finally eased his legs out and was able to move to a crouch, flashing lights in front of his eyes warning him not to stand up. He looked up at the bank the vehicle had rolled down, then back at the battered van, realising he was lucky to be alive. He heard cursing from the back of the van as Salt, stooped but uninjured, made his way round to where Keelan was situated.

He slumped down next to Keelan. "What the fuck happened?"

"Bloody Withers, that's what happened. Tried to dodge round a car, but was too thick to realise that he might need to slow down. And here we fucking are."

"What about the others?"

"Who gives a fuck?"

There was a sudden scream, one driven by immense pain.

"We should check it."

"Be my guest," responded Keelan. He rubbed a blackened hand across his forehead, leaving a dirty streak across his pale skin. "If I move, I'll pass out."

A second scream, followed by a third, echoed through the confines of the van, and Salt crawled around Keelan's legs, lowering his body to peer through the open driver's window. The sweaty face of Todd Withers looked back, his body suspended upside down, held in place by a length of the seatbelt that had wrapped itself securely around his leg. He was desperately trying to reach round with his right hand to release the belt, but every time he moved, excruciating pain travelled up his shattered left arm. Salt noticed the arm for the first time, bent at an impossible angle. He looked across towards the passenger seat, seeing Milo coming round, upside down, but securely strapped into his seat, his legs resting on the upside down dashboard.

"Milo, you OK," he called.

The only response was a groan.

"Right, Todd, I'm going to cut away the belt, so you need to be ready to break your fall."

"Can't you help?"

"I'll try my best."

"My arm's fucked, Doug. If I move it…it hurts like hell."

"I have no choice, you have no choice. We have to get you out of here."

"Can't Stan help?"

"He's injured as well. So, get ready."

Salt extracted a clasp knife from the pocket of his outer jacket, pulled it open, and started to slice through the webbing of the belt. "Get ready."

He continued to saw at the seatbelt, the fabric parting with each movement of the blade. "Any minute. Better brace yourself."

Todd used his good arm, pressing it against the roof of the van, ready to decelerate his fall and protect his damaged arm.

Milo groaned again, his eyes flickering open, sudden panic as he realised that he was suspended upside down, trapped.

"It's OK, Milo buddy. Once I've finished with Withers here, I'll come and give you a hand."

The blade sliced through the last few centimetres of the belt, the fabric suddenly parting, dumping Todd on the roof in a sprawl of arms and legs. Todd screamed again and again as his right arm did the job of buffering his fall, but it forced him over on his left side, onto his broken arm, two white pieces of jagged bone poking through his sleeve testament to the severity of the damage done. Under the current circumstances of no doctors or hospitals, his limb was broken beyond repair. Salt had no option but to drag the man out. Screams quickly followed. Todd lay on his back, moaning with pain, supporting his shattered arm.

"Stop bleating," complained Keelan.

Salt came over and whispered in Keelan's ear, "It's pretty bad. He ain't going to get that fixed easily."

"No bloody hospitals, that's for sure. Where's the nearest town anyhow?"

"Oxford, I reckon. Hospitals are out, Stan. They'll have been hit along with everything else. How you doing?"

"I'm OK."

"I need to go and give Milo a hand. He's strung up like a chicken."

Keelan laughed but quickly put his hands to his head as lights flashed before his eyes. Salt left him and went round to the other side of the van to help Milo.

After leaving the cottage in the early hours of the morning, Keelan insisting they made some headway and find a more permanent base, they had continued their journey south, keeping west of Leicester, Northampton and Milton Keynes, only approaching the M1 or M40 to get fuel. That had been a disaster, coming under fire the minute they got within 200 metres of the M1. So, they tried further down and were able to syphon enough fuel from a number of cars to continue their journey towards Oxford. Groups of survivors, moving north and south, had been passed during their travels. Many looked emaciated, and all looked ill, pale faces behind their scarves and mufflers. Keelan and Salt ensured that no contact was made. They only came across two patrols, both small-scale, a mix of police and army and no more than ten men, but had managed to avoid them at the last minute. Apart from the altercation during their first refuelling attempt, they had only been fired upon a second time when the four men approached a defended village. Anarchy appeared to be the order of the day. But the four men wouldn't be continuing the journey with their current transport.

Salt helped Milo out and, apart from being shaken up, like Salt, he was unhurt.

They moved away from the side of the stricken van, keeping a distance of about fifty metres, the smell of petrol fumes a worry. Being the only ones capable, Salt and Milo had volunteered to extract their food and water and other items they had collected since escaping from HMP Wakefield. It was now sitting in a pile in the middle of the circle of four men. Salt doled out some food while they debated what to do next.

Milo looked at his watch: the time was three twenty. "We need to get some shelter. It's bloody cold enough as it is now."

"We do," agreed Salt, handing Milo a bar of chocolate. "The question is where."

"And what about Todd?"

"If it wasn't for that twat's lousy driving, I wouldn't have this bloody lump on my head, and we wouldn't be in this position, would we?" exclaimed Keelan.

"What do we do about Todd?" asked a concerned Milo again.

Todd was drifting in and out of consciousness. There was little they could do for him beyond draping a blanket over him to keep him warm.

Keelan bit into his bar of chocolate. "We got some painkillers from the house in Wakefield. Soon as he wakes up, he can chomp on some of them."

"Yeah," agreed Milo. "It's a start, but how do we fix his arm?"

No one responded, engrossed in their task or their own circumstances.

Salt shuffled through their supplies and pulled out a tin of beans. He peeled the lid back and dug in with a spoon he always kept in his pocket. "We gotta move though." He slurped cold beans from his spoon, the smell triggering hunger in the other two who also grabbed a tin each. "We can't stay here. We need shelter before it gets dark." The sound of Salt's spoon clattering around the tin as he tried to scoop up the last few beans left. "How you doing, Stan?"

"Head throbs like shit. Where are those tabs?"

"Erm…the small rucksack, I think. I'll take a look." Salt rummaged around the pile in front of him, pulling out the rucksack where he had stored the first-aid kit taken from the first house. "Here you go." He chucked a pack of painkillers over to Keelan, along with a bottle of water. "So, it's quarter to four. We need to move, lads. Light's starting to go."

"I'll give it a go, Doug, but my head's still fucked up. Give us a hand."

Salt helped Keelan get up and, quickly examining the gash above his left eye. Finding a roll of bandages in the rucksack, he soon wrapped a dressing around the wound. "I'm no Florence Nightingale, but it'll do. I'll take a look at Withers."

Keelan swayed on his feet a little; then leant in closer to Salt. "If he don't come around, we can't carry him, and we can't stay here."

Salt nodded in agreement and walked over to Withers where he was joined by Milo.

"Come on, Todd, you lazy bastard. We need to get moving," Milo encouraged him.

Todd's eyes flickered open, the agony clear as he accidentally moved his shattered arm. He fainted again.

"We'll have to leave him."

"We can't leave him, Doug, it ain't right."

Salt grabbed Milo by his lapels. "Listen. There are no doctors, no hospitals, and no hope for him. He's not going to keep up with us, and with those bloody bones sticking through his flesh, it's bound to get contaminated." Salt let him go.

"Just don't seem right," complained Milo, but without conviction.

Salt turned back to Withers. "Todd, mate. We need to move. If we can find some wheels tonight or tomorrow morning, we'll come back for you. We'll leave you some water to keep you going, and an extra blanket should keep you warm."

There was no response.

Belongings were gathered and shared around, with Milo and Salt carrying the bulk until Keelan had a chance to recover. They took one last look at Withers before heading back up the slope the van had previously careered down. Once on the road, Salt took them left. It didn't really matter which direction they took: it was more important to find some cover and doss down for the night. By five thirty it was dark, and it was only thanks to Salt's height and good night vision that they spotted a barn close to a gated entrance to a field. It was a quarter full of mouldy-smelling bales of hay, but it was still a welcome refuge. Keelan was staggering by the time they got there. What blankets they had were shared out, and after nothing more than a swig of water and another tin of baked beans each, they crashed.

Salt lay awake for a few minutes longer than the other two, his thoughts on survival. *How the hell are we going to get through this?* he thought. One conclusion he had come to earlier on in the day was that they were not going to survive on their own. He would talk about his proposal to Keelan tomorrow.

CHAPTER 17

Tom woke up shivering, the sleeping bag having slipped off his shoulders during the night. The camp bed creaked slightly as he shuffled into a more comfortable position, pulling the sleeping bag further up his body, seeking warmth. He checked his watch: ten past three in the morning. Too soon to get up, so he lay there with his arms behind his head, the sleeping bag up to his chin. He could hear the gentle breathing of his wife, Lucy, on a camp bed next to his, and a slight wheeze coming from their daughter, Mary, on the other side of Lucy. This was their second morning in the farmhouse. They'd arrived in the early hours of the previous day after fleeing their burning home, escaping the psychopathic Reynolds family and their successful attempt at burning them out of their home.

He lay pondering their future, fighting back the panic that often welled up, threatening to engulf him. Even if they had been able to stay at the farm for a few more months, he knew it would have been just a very short-term option. If he and his family, and Andy, along with his wife and son, were to survive, they needed assured water and food supplies, access to medical treatment, shelter and security. He wasn't yet sure how that was going to happen. He was just a farmer. His skill was in arable farming as opposed to animal husbandry, although he did have a few sheep and cattle to keep his hand in. He believed there were two directions in which the future of the country, and even mankind, could evolve: Either an appointed administration would appear out of the ashes, take charge and lead the United Kingdom through what was undoubtedly going to be one of the darkest periods in the country's history or, worst-case scenario, the regional government structure, put in place for an event such as this, was decimated, along with the other RGCs across the country, and would fail to surface let alone lead the people of the UK toward a better future. Tom was sure that, without the support of a recognised administration, people would be left to fend for

151

themselves in a country that would quickly run out of food. He was certain a large percentage of the population was dying from the effects of radiation and other major injuries, and, no doubt, diseases such as cholera and typhoid would take hold only exacerbating the situation. *Then there's the cold*, he thought, shivering. Trawling the Internet for every scrap of information about the possible outcome should Russia and NATO push the button, Tom had been horrified at what he discovered: a climate with temperatures likely to descend so low that the suffering would only be increased and the capacity to survive severely reduced. There would eventually be no fuel, no vehicles, no power, no hospitals, no food, and no vaccinations against the old diseases such as measles, smallpox and polio. His mind raced, and he forced himself to snap out of it. His focus had to be on planning for the future and an assumption that their two families would be on their own. He pulled his arms back inside and, pulling the edge of the sleeping bag even higher, fell into a fitful sleep.

The four adults peered at the map laid out on the large farmhouse kitchen table while the two children, Mary and Patrick, lay on their camp beds, keeping out of the way and staying warm. A decision had to be made as to the next and, hopefully, final destination. Tom savoured his cup of hot coffee, feeling it warm his insides as the liquid slipped down his throat. Surprisingly, as it was at the epicentre of half a dozen nuclear strikes at Oxford, Gloucester, Worcester, Coventry, Milton Keynes and Northampton, the farm had most of its windows intact, but it was still cold. Tom had resisted the temptation to light a fire, the smoke and the smell identifying that the house was occupied. He didn't want to attract any unwanted guests. He felt certain that the Reynolds family wouldn't be able to pursue them. Any vehicles left at the other farm had been disabled, something he did every night before they locked down. Only their escape vehicle was ready for a quick getaway.

His wife caught his eye and smiled, pulling the blanket tighter round her shoulders. He smiled back, and then glanced at their other two friends, Andrew and Madeline. Although not as resilient and resourceful as his wife, Madeline was reliable, and as for Andrew, he had complete faith in him as a fellow survivor. Tom felt sure that the four of them, plus the two children, as an extended family unit, had every chance of surviving whatever adversity came their way. He focused his attention on the map again.

"Right, we're here." Tom tapped a point south of Chipping Norton. "About thirty kilometres north-west of Oxford."

"Glad you recced this place, Tom." Andrew sounded thankful. "It was always a possibility we'd need somewhere else, but I never thought it would be because someone chose to burn us out."

"Still, it was a good call."

"We're grateful to you, Tom," added Madeline.

"Where next though?" mused Tom.

"Why not stay here?" Lucy suggested.

"Tempting, but I think it's too close to Birmingham and Coventry. At some stage, any survivors will start to drift out from the cities as food and other supplies run out. I'd prefer to go south, probably more south-west."

"Where had you in mind?" asked Andrew.

Patrick came in from the sitting room opposite. "I'm still hungry, Dad."

"Not now, son," Andrew responded. "We'll have a bite to eat before we leave."

"Are we moving again?" Patrick grumbled.

"It's necessary. Now, please leave us to get on."

Shoulders slumped, Patrick left and went back to the other room, closely followed by Sam. Tom patted the collie as he trotted past.

Tom continued. "I was thinking of somewhere around Exmoor National Park. Not in it, but on the outskirts."

"Wouldn't we be better off heading north? Scotland, maybe?"

"I've considered that, Andy, but discounted it for a number of reasons. First, it's a long way, and we would be dependent on getting fuel on the way. What we have isn't enough, even with the jerry cans, to get us that far. Secondly, we'd be on the road for a long time, exposing ourselves to we don't know what. And I'm a bit worried about the weather. I'm sure it's going to get a lot colder than it is now, and going north would be inadvisable."

"How much colder?" asked Madeline.

"I'm not really sure, Maddie. What little reading I've done suggests that, with millions of tons of dust being shot up into the atmosphere, sunlight will be blocked for many years to come. Without the heat of the sun, it's going to get damn cold."

"Oh no," she groaned. "It's bad enough now."

"It'll get worse, but we'll find a way to keep us all warm, angel," Andrew consoled her.

"That's why I like the location chosen," added Tom. "Lots of woods and forests around there. Fuel for heating and cooking."

"We still need a farm though," suggested Andrew.

"Or something similar. But what we will need to do is gather the tools to help us grow food."

"We can still forage for food until then."

"We can, Maddie, but so will everyone else. Supplies are going to diminish, and it'll get tougher to find food. We need to start preparing to fend for ourselves."

"There's bound to be police and army out there. Didn't the Government always have emergency stocks of food for situations like this?"

Tom put his arm around Lucy, pulling her slim shoulders close into him. "Could well be. Our planning will be for nothing, and I'll be the first one to cheer," laughed Tom. "As we head south-west, we can suss it out. If we come across any administration, we can get an update. OK?"

She placed her head on his shoulder, reassured.

"Really hungry, Mum," whined Mary, her turn to pressure the parents for something to eat.

"I'll prepare us some food while you finish planning our journey."

"OK, love." Tom squeezed Lucy's shoulder again, and she got up to prepare a meal.

"Do you want a hand?" asked Maddie.

"No, you're OK, I'll manage. Patrick and Mary can help if I need it. Come on then, madam." She placed an arm around Mary's shoulder. "Let's get us all fed."

"So which way?" asked Andrew, wiping his thick beard with the back of his hand after taking a deep drink of his coffee.

"We go back across the A40, keeping west of Lechlade. Probably best to go via Bibury."

Andrew pointed to a point on the map. "West makes sense. We have to keep away from Brize Norton here."

"Probably still heavily contaminated," Tom agreed. "It's where next I'm unsure of. We have to avoid the Cleveland Lakes, but traversing right takes us too close to Cirencester, and left we would have to pass between Cricklade and Swindon."

"Do you think Swindon's been hit?"

"Bound to. We know there's some hi-tech industry there, and the Russians would have known that too."

"But not Cirencester, surely."

"Possibly. But Gloucester, Oxford and Bristol are bound to have been hit, and hard probably."

"We could swing west of Cirencester."

"But that'll take us closer to Gloucester and Cheltenham." Tom laughed. "Checkmate then."

"What are you worried about?" asked Lucy who came back into the room carrying foodstuffs to make some breakfast.

"Contamination, for one. The closer we go to where there's been a strike, the hotter the contamination will be."

"And undesirables," added Andrew. "We've seen what the Reynolds family are capable of. There could be far worse out there."

"Yes," agreed Tom. "There'll be people out there sick, injured and hungry. They'll probably stop at nothing to get what they need."

"What about the authorities?" exclaimed Madeline. "Law and order will be one of their priorities, surely."

"We've seen no evidence so far," Tom reminded her. "Both Andrew and I have been out on numerous occasions. When I did a reconnaissance of this place, I only came across a few stragglers, but no police or army."

"This is the only way we'll protect ourselves now," pitched in Andrew, patting the shotgun leaning up against his chair. "If I don't have that, then this will do," showing a clenched fist. Andrew was a big man, just short of six foot and with the physique of a heavy weight boxer, something he did a lot of in his younger days. It would be a brave person to take him on. Tom on the other hand, although still fit, spending many hours working his farm, was more slight and a few inches shorter, but would still put up a fight to protect his family.

"Andrew! Don't be ridiculous. We're not vigilantes!"

"Hey, hey, Maddie. I'm not advocating that we go out there and clean up the streets. We just need to make sure we protect our own families." He placed his arm around her shoulder, consoling her as best he could.

"Control will be returned eventually, Maddie," added Lucy as she placed some plated, sliced corned beef on the table along with some crackers and a tub of home-made butter. "Then we can all go back to our homes and rebuild."

"Don't be so sure, Luce. That's working on the assumption there's an organisation out there capable of regaining control."

155

"Something will happen. It has to, Andrew."

"Any more of that coffee, Lucy?" asked Tom. "We need to leave within the hour if we're to get to our next destination in daylight."

"There's some left. Pass your cups."

Lucy gathered up the cups and proceeded to spoon in instant coffee, the sound of bubbling water coming from the pan on the portable camping gas stove on the side.

"Kids joining us?" asked Tom.

"No, I've given them something they can eat in there. Best they stay warm for as long as possible."

Tom spooned an extra bit of coffee into his cup.

"Go easy with it." Lucy smiled at him. "It might need to last a lifetime."

Cups were topped up and powdered milk added. Tom pulled a face as he took a sip. "Yuk, can't stand this powdered stuff."

"Drink it black," teased Lucy. "Decided our route?"

The four buttered some crackers and added a slice of corned beef. Not the best of meals, but they needed to take care with their meagre supplies.

"So," asked Andrew, bringing the meeting back on track, "where do we head for?"

Tom, crunching on his cracker and meat feast, ran a pencil across the map. "Between the lakes and Cricklade?"

"Makes sense. Then Minety, Sherston, Marshfield—"

"That's what I was thinking," agreed Tom. "My worry is crossing the M4."

"We don't have any choice, Tom. It stretches from the River Severn across to London. Drive across it where we can find access?"

"No good. The barriers. We'll never crash through them."

"Of course not. Stupid of me." Andrew laughed. "They're crash barriers."

"There's bound to be an underpass somewhere. You know, crossing points built in for farmers like myself. I reckon the stretch between Chipping Sodbury and Chippenham will be the best option."

"I suggest we pick an overnight stop. Although we need to make progress, you never know what we might come up against."

"Good point, Andy. I want to try a few petrol stations on the way. Outlying villages would be preferable. We're OK for fuel, but it would be good to keep our tank topped up and eke out what we have in our cans for a bit longer."

"Sure. What about the stuff hidden at the farm?"

"We can go back for it sometime in the future, if and when we need it. The Reynolds family will never find them. Not forgetting the supplies hidden under your hotel."

"So long as the Reynolds Mafia don't find that either."

"They're too dumb," laughed Tom.

"Don't underestimate them, mate. They're a crafty bunch of buggers."

Tom returned his attention to the map. "I want to keep well west of Marshfield though. There's a small airstrip at Garston Farm and a small airfield at North Colerne. The farm may not have been hit, but a strike on the bigger airfield is likely. I suggest we stop over for a short break at West Littleton. It's in the middle of nowhere. Then make our overnight stop here, around Somerton."

"Why don't we just keep going? It'll only be a couple of hours' drive to our final destination from there."

"Better we approach that area in the early hours. Then spend a good part of the day searching the area."

"Yeah OK, makes sense," agreed Andrew.

"Finished?" asked Maddie, starting to clear away the plates.

Andrew picked the last crumb from his plate, savouring the thought of the great farmhouse breakfasts Lucy used to make. "I have, and thank you, Lucy, for that lovely fare."

"I'll treat us all to soup tonight," she laughed.

Everything was cleared, camping beds and bedding packed up, the Land Rover refuelled from some jerrycans, and the families said goodbye to their temporary home and continued their journey into the unknown.

CHAPTER 18

Bell woke with a start. Had he heard something, or was it just a dream? It didn't feel like he'd been dreaming. Sleeping on a hard tiled floor had hardly been conducive to a comfortable night's sleep. Then he heard it again: the crunch of debris, the sound of pressure being applied to the rubble that was strewn across the floor of the building where they had sought refuge. Reaching for his pistol just in case, he sat up to reach out to Captain Parry who was lying next to him, still asleep. *Best leave him sleep for as long as possible,* he thought. He pushed the sleeping bag off, then got up to a crouch and listened. He couldn't hear any more noise, but still did a tour of the rooms that adjoined the one they'd spent the night in. A dog, as startled as Bell was when he came across it, ran off, its tail between its legs.

Once the captain had come around, Bell helped him up and, with the use of the makeshift crutch to support Parry's crippled leg, they spent three hours searching for somewhere better to shelter, where they could set up for the next night, or even longer until Parry was fit to make a lengthier journey. Then they would have to make a decision: to go back to the sub or continue their journey to find civilisation. They eventually found an abandoned minibus that would serve their needs. All its windows were intact and there were no decomposing bodies within it. He had heard two gunshots earlier, probably a kilometre away at the time, he thought, so warned Commander Parry to be on the alert. He settled his captain on the back seat, and then went of to scavenge for some wood should they need to make a fire and drive away the cold that was starting to eat into his very bones. Then it would be time to discuss their options with the captain.

CHAPTER 19

Although they had sheltered in a barn, it had still proven to be a cold night, and Keelan, Salt and Gill had shivered through most of it. Before it was light, they chose to make a move, choosing warmth of physical effort over continuing with chattering teeth and discomfort. The three had traipsed back to where they had left the van, but there was no sign of Withers. They conducted a cursory search of the area but quickly gave it up. Salt then took them east. Although he was feeling much better, Keelan was happy for Salt to take the lead for the moment. They had discussed plans, and what Salt had suggested made sense. All they had to do now was get there.

After an hour of struggling with their individual loads, blankets, food, water and weapons, Keelan still maintaining control of their only shotgun, a small village came into view, a chance to search for transport, but also to take a breather. Out of the three cars they found, none would work. Milo cursed in frustration as he tried to coax them into life, but their electrics had been well and truly fried. But what they did discover were bicycles. After a few moments of erratic cycling, the three eventually got control of their new mode of transport, and, loaded down with personal effects and supplies, they headed south along the narrow lanes that would keep them away from the larger towns. As they crossed the M40, abandoned vehicles were searched but, to their disappointment, all those had been thoroughly ransacked. As they moved along the lanes, a gunshot aimed in their direction ensured they made a hasty exit, taking their bikes down the southern edge of the motorway, running for cover. Putting at least a kilometre between them and the motorway, they crouched together in a hedgerow, next to a field gate, set back from the lane they had been cycling down.

"Shit, that was close."

"Nearly crapped your pants, Milo," declared Keelan.

"I did as well," laughed Salt. He looked at the other two. The scarves and other protective clothing used to keep out the cold and the dust did little to hide their haggard looks. Both Keelan's and Milo's eyes looked red and swollen, their pallor sickly. Days of stubble looked ragged on their grime-covered faces. He pulled off a glove and looked at his hands: thick black dirt beneath the fingernails, his fingers and knuckles covered in a layer of God knows what. Salt prided himself on his cleanliness, and it distressed him to be in such a state. When they slept in the barn, amongst the rotting hay, he was still able to smell his own body odour.

He pulled the glove back on, the cold starting to nip, and spoke. "Stan buddy, and you Milo, we have to get some digs, get organised."

"Get a life, you mean," suggested Milo.

"What I mean, Gill," snapped Salt. "Is that we won't be alive let alone have a life unless we get our act together."

Keelan rubbed his throbbing forehead. "What you got in mind, Doug?" He was still happy to let Salt take the lead for the moment.

"I know Croydon. It's where I was brought up. We can make a start there, suss out the situation, find ourselves some permanent digs, and take it from there."

"What about finding a place around here?"

"Valid point, Milo mate, but there don't seem to be many people around here. You want entertainment, don't you?"

"Yeah, but we could look around."

"Have you felt the temperature lately? It's not getting any warmer, and winter's on the horizon. At least amongst the outskirts of the city there are bound to be some luxuries we can dig up."

"Won't it have been blown to shit?"

"Truth is, I don't know, Stan. North London, yes. Heathrow, Gatwick, mainline stations will all have been targets. But to the south or west? Who knows?"

"If none of us have a better idea, I'm a go on that, Douglas."

"We can give it a go at least. But if it don't work, we come back out to the country, right?"

"Sure, Milo." Salt leant forward, sharing his conspiracy. "With people around, we don't have to do all the work. We let them do it, and we take the rewards for ourselves."

Keelan shivered. "You've sold it. Now, I need to move. My arse is freezing."

The three men collected their laden down bikes and got back onto the lane. Salt led off, Keelan following with a slight wobble of the front wheel of his bike, and they cycled south. They were making good progress and Salt was even enjoying the freedom of cycling. At around four in the afternoon, Salt would keep his eyes peeled for somewhere to stop over. There was no way he wanted to travel through the approaches to London at night. It would be bad enough during daylight hours. He felt sure it wasn't an easy option he had chosen, but it was the right one. If they could pull a group together, a group they could control, people who would do their bidding, they could live like kings. *London is a huge city. There's bound to be places that have survived*, he thought. He could send out scavenging parties right across the city and, if there was any bother, Keelan as their security, their enforcer, would put things right. He chuckled to himself. *I've always wanted to be a king.*

CHAPTER 20

Tom changed down to a lower gear, slowing their vehicle down as they approached the outskirts of the large village of Sherston. He didn't particularly want to pass through the village, let alone stop there, the fuel tank was still over three quarters full, but he wanted to top up the jerrycans they had used. He was loath to dip into their reserves unless it was absolutely necessary, and wanted them kept topped up at all times. Over cautious maybe, but it helped him feel more at ease.

The map indicated a local petrol station at the far end of the village. The last one they stopped at had proven to be completely dry. Tom's fear was that this too would have been drained during the latter part of the period of panic that hit the country prior to the nuclear strikes. Another problem was that the petrol pumps would be unpowered, but Tom had crafted his own manual pump with a number of sections that could be pieced together for even the deepest of storage tanks. He had high hopes that they would find something at the bottom of at least one of the diesel tanks submerged beneath the forecourt of the petrol station ahead. They had come in on the B4040, passing a large farm on the left, surrounded by what were once green fields but were now lifeless: not only afflicted through the lack of rain, but also from the thin layer of ash and contamination that choked the air. The dust laden skies had suppressed any chance the grass or plants had of photosynthesising: producing the sugars they needed to grow.

Andrew, in the front passenger seat, silently pointed over to the right where he could see small mounds scattered across another open field. Some of the mounds were clustered together in small groups where the cattle, dehydrated, hungry and suffering from radiation sickness had gathered together rather than suffer a lingering death in isolation. What were once healthy dairy cows were now nothing more than rotting carcasses. They had also driven past a fox lying in the ditch that, having gorged himself on the carcasses available to feast on, had succumbed to the poisons that had coursed through his body.

It all seemed surreal. The hypnotic sound of the purring cross-country tyres of the Defender 110 long-wheel-based Land Rover on the tarmac gave rise to an almost dreamlike state, forcing Tom to shake his head, keep his eyes on the road, and his mind focused. Tiredness was also a contributing factor to his current mental state. It wasn't just about keeping the vehicle on the road, but maintaining a constant vigil: each house or village they passed, or person they came across, were a potential threat. The B4040 would take them right through the centre of the village, and Tom could see the outskirts about 200 metres ahead. He slowed down even further, a steady twenty as they approached the crossroads in front of them. Tom didn't intend to stop. They hadn't seen another vehicle since they left their farm so a collision was unlikely. In fact, the group had come across very few survivors during their journey. Those they did encounter were travelling along the roads on foot, laden down with bags of food and clothing. Some tried to wave them down, but Tom hardened his heart and sped past. The attack by the Reynolds family had frightened even him, and he was certainly not going to give strangers an opportunity to threaten him or his family again. As for sharing their foodstuffs and water, they would need every morsel of food and every drop of water they had if they themselves were to survive this purgatory, this living hell. Many of the individuals they had come across appeared to be suffering from major burns from both fire and ionising radiation. Some had sickly-looking faces; others gave the impression of having been to a tanning salon too often. However, theirs was a 'nuclear tan', far more deadly. One group appeared to be in a particularly dreadful state. Their exposed flesh, covered in wet ulcerated lesions, others with ulcerated necrotic dermatitis, their cells slowly dying, bits of flesh peeling off in patches, their faces too painful to be covered with face masks or scarves. But the two families, unable to tear their eyes off the pitiful sight, still found the fortitude to continue on with their journey.

Tom drove the Land Rover over the crossroads, automatically looking left and right, even though it wasn't necessary. He glanced left as he heard the clunk of Andrew's shotgun as his friend lifted it into a more comfortable position, ready to use if needed. When required, Andrew was ready to open the window and blast anyone who attempted to block their way. He too had been scarred by the near-death experience back at the farm and would also protect his family, no matter what. They passed some large houses off to their left, a large tennis court belonging to one of them visible. Opposite, the village church stood out, wearing its coating of grey dust like a shroud. Tom kept the Land Rover at a steady fifteen miles an hour, both men scanning ahead, their wives and the two children, perched on adjacent bench seats in the back, looking out of the glass-windowed sides, equally alert, knowing that this was a dangerous time for them all. A small open field appeared on their left, smaller humps distributed across it, the occasional black face visible through of the film of dust showing them to be sheep. They drove past larger and larger houses, an affluent village where many had moved from London for a more peaceful life, or were wealthy enough to have secured a second home out in the countryside. The road took them south as they got closer to the centre of the village, heading towards the High Street. Soon it would veer west again taking them to the less palatial part of the village, but first they would encounter the petrol station.

As they arrived on the High Street, the number of cars abandoned along the roadside increased. On both sides of the street, the odd dust-covered market stall was visible, tossed to the side by whatever hurricane force had passed through or over the village. The display tables were also strewn about the street, but had they survived, they would no doubt be bare of any items to sell, hoarding a priority.

"What's that ahead?" Andrew alerted Tom.

Tom applied the brakes, bringing the Land Rover to a slow crawl. "Where?"

"Ahead and to the left, next to the larger building. A Public building or something."

Lucy peered in between their heads. "They're bikes, aren't they?" she suggested, having better eyesight than both the men.

Tom brought the Land Rover to a halt. "I think you're right."

They surveyed the area ahead from the safety of the cab, counting about ten bicycles dropped to the ground in and around the entrance to what could have been a municipal building. Andrew pulled the binoculars from the glove compartment, brought them to his eyes, and zoomed in on the collection of bikes that had been left randomly on the footpath and part of the road, blocking their way. He still kept his shotgun close at hand. The bikes seemed to have bags strapped to their crossbars or on racks set above the mudguard over the rear wheel.

"What can you see?" quizzed Lucy.

"Just the bikes. I reckon they've been dropped there recently. Seem to be laden down with bags. Full of food and water, maybe?"

"Any movement?" asked Tom.

Andrew changed his focus to further down the High Street, then the foreground, before scanning the buildings either side of the road again. "Nothing. No movement, at least. I can see the petrol station, about three hundred yards further on."

"I'm scared, Mum," came a whimper from the back.

Andrew peered over his shoulder and made eye contact with Patrick. "We'll be alright, son. You just stay put."

"We could always backtrack and come at it from the other end of the village," suggested Maddie.

"If there's someone there, they'll still hear us whichever way we go, if they haven't already. We really need that fuel. We're burning it just sitting here, and we've a long journey ahead."

"Let's take a walk then," said Tom as he clicked open the door, swinging it back on its hinges as he stepped out, a shotgun, broken open, clutched in his right hand. Once out, he checked that the two shells fit snugly in the breach and locked it shut, the satisfying clunk boosting his confidence.

Andrew exited from the passenger side, and Tom leant back in the cab. "The four of you stay here. Andy and I will take a look first."

"The first sign of trouble and you get back here fast, you hear," pleaded Maddie.

Lucy, sitting opposite, patted Maddie's knee. "We'll be OK, Maddie. The doors will be shut, and I have this if we need it," she comforted her friend, holding up a single-barrelled shotgun.

Maddie nodded. The two children, who had been monitoring events, sidled up closer to their mothers.

Tom and Andrew closed the windows and pushed the driver and front passenger door closed, a satisfying click confirming they were secure. Lucy reached over and locked both doors from the inside, sitting quietly with her shotgun resting on the back of the driver's seat, ready if and when it was needed.

Tom moved across to the right of the road and Andrew to the left. Both had pulled up their face masks and covered most of their faces with a scarf. Each day appeared to feel colder, and the families were forced to wear numerous layers of clothing to keep the bitter cold out. The Land Rover, which didn't have the best heating system in the world, was proving to be a luxury when travelling.

Their shoes crunched on shards of glass, the shattered shop windows testament to the ferocity of the effects of the nuclear explosions in the surrounding areas. Although none had struck the village, the strikes on Bristol to the south-west, Corsham, the home of the old government emergency headquarters, to the south, would have been blown into oblivion by the Russians, ensuring that it couldn't function if the British Government had reinstated it, will have impacted on the village. Swindon to the east and Gloucester and Cheltenham to the north had all attracted attention from the Russian's nuclear bombs and missiles. Tom glanced through a shattered shop window that had once been a thriving greengrocer's but was now filled with splinters of glass and stripped of any item that could be eaten. He looked across at Andrew who nodded as he too peered through a shop window, which was a florist no more. The bikes were now about 200 metres ahead, and Tom gripped the barrel of the shotgun more tightly, raising it a few inches and pointing it in the direction of the dumped but seemingly not abandoned bikes. One hundred and fifty metres and he could clearly see that the bicycles had been used for carrying the trappings, bedding, clothing and the like, of whoever had ridden them.

The road widened slightly, and Tom went around the right-hand side of one of the spilled market stalls, the thick plastic sheeting, still pinned to the supports, blocking his view across the street, contact lost with Andrew across the road. He panicked slightly but was soon past the obstruction, and Andrew acknowledged him once they were both able to make eye contact again. One hundred metres from the bikes, and he looked back towards the Land Rover, the reflection off the windscreen making it difficult to see the occupants inside.

They'll be fine, he thought. Lucy was a smart cookie. She would watch over Maddie and the two children.

"Tom," Andrew hissed.

Tom looked back round and saw Andrew jerk his head in the direction of the bikes. Four men and two women had appeared from the town hall, the two women remaining on the steps. The four men moved toward the bikes and stood amongst them, watching Tom and Andrew as they approached. Broken glass crackled beneath Tom and Andrew's feet, breaking the silence, the disturbed dust forming a grey layer on their shoes.

Fifty metres away and Tom called out to the strangers. "Hello there. My name's Tom and this is Andrew. We were on our way to get fuel when we saw the bikes on the road." Tom scanned the faces as he talked. None wore any protective masks, but all had some form of scarf and headgear to protect them from the bitter cold. He would hazard a guess that the four by the bikes, all fairly slim, medium height, were in their early to late twenties. The two women on the steps perhaps older, bulkier, less confident, one shifting from foot to foot nervously. Tom felt the hair on the back of his neck stand up. He had a bad feeling about this.

"Er, Colin. My name's Colin. How come you have a vehicle?" responded the nearest of the group of four, a West Country accent apparent.

Andrew and Tom stopped walking. "It's my farm vehicle."

"Yeah, but how come it's working?"

"It's quite old. Seems some of the older vehicles are still drivable."

Tom and Andrew were now roughly six metres away from the nearest of the group, Colin.

Colin moved a little closer. "Are you carrying food and water?"

"We have some, enough for our families," replied Tom warily.

"That's a bit greedy, eh, lads?" Colin looked over his shoulder, and the three by the bikes moved forward, forming a semi-circle opposite Tom and Andrew.

"Look," said Tom, "we don't want any trouble. We just want to get some fuel then be on our way."

"We could always sell you some petrol."

"We need diesel. Is there some still in the garage's tanks?"

"Sure," responded Colin, "there's loads."

Tom and Andrew looked at each other, both knowing that he was lying. There would have been thousands of long vehicle queues right across the country and drivers taking their cars far and wide, desperate to get their vehicle tanks topped up. Tom felt the hairs on the back of his neck stiffen again, and he knew they had to get out of there, and quick.

"That's OK," Tom answered. "We'll leave the fuel to you and just leave the village."

Tom took a step back, Andrew following suit.

Colin took a step forward, the other three copying their leader. "Now, that's not very polite, is it, boys? We offer them some of our valuable fuel, and they just want to do a runner."

Tom heard sniggers and muffled laughter beneath their scarves, balaclavas and makeshift clothing. He looked across at Andrew and continued to back away, keeping the barrel of his gun pointed low, but aiming in the direction of the men blocking their way forward. Andrew also backed off, his shotgun mimicking Tom's.

"Wait!" called the man whom Tom had now classified as a thug and thought would fit in well with the Reynolds family. "We've not finished our discussion."

"We'll leave you in peace," responded Andrew. "And be on our way."

Both men took another few steps backwards.

"He speaks. You might want to reconsider. Take a look behind you."

Both Andrew and Tom spun round, fear gripping both of them when they saw their wives and children standing at the front of the Land Rover, guarded by four people. Tom wasn't sure but they appeared to be four males. Mary's desperate need for the toilet had been the chink in the armour, the vehicle door open long enough to allow the four men access to the Land Rover, seizing Lucy's shotgun, and taking Tom's and Andrew's families hostage.

Tom swung back round towards Colin, who he now felt sure was the leader of the group, or was it gang, and raised the barrels of the shotgun, aiming it directly at him.

"I wouldn't do anything foolish now. All we want is your food and water. Oh, and your vehicle, and you'll be free to go. Can't be fairer than that, can we, lads?"

The men with Colin grumbled their agreement.

"But we need that to survive," gasped Andrew.

"So do we," the gang leader hit back.

"We can't survive without food," pleaded Tom.

"We're not animals. We'll leave you something to get by on."

"And what if we don't give it up?" Andrew challenged him.

The man held up his arm and waved it in the direction of the Land Rover back up the road. Both Tom and Andrew quickly turned, seeing Maddie brought to her knees with an arm violently twisted up her back. A scream reached their ears.

"OK, OK, you've made your point. Tell them to stop."

A grin obvious beneath his scarf, Colin looked at Andrew, and he lifted his left arm this time and waved it. Maddie's arm was released, and she was allowed to stand again.

"Glad you've seen sense. Now, this is a bit of a stalemate. Yes, you've got the guns, but we have these," he waved a knife in front of Tom's face, "but more importantly we have your family at knifepoint. We could easily kill all of them before you could stop us. Yes, we could be killed as well, but I can guarantee you that your children won't survive."

There was silence for three or four seconds, Tom's mind racing, searching for a solution to get them out of this and keep his and Andrew's families safe.

The leader broke the silence, his voice menacing. "You're running out of time, Grandad. Do you want me to make your mind up for you?" He went to lift both arms up when Andrew shouted, "Stop!" Andrew then placed his shotgun on the floor and looked at Tom, the pain in his eyes clear. Tom knew he had to follow suit. The options that had raced through his mind moments earlier were now obsolete. He too bent down and lowered his gun to the tarmac road. He stood back up, his shoulders drooping, and turned to check his family were still there.

"Good, good. Now move back ten feet. We don't want you changing your mind just as things are going so swimmingly now, do we?"

Tom and Andrew shuffled back as commanded, defeat sapping their strength, leaching away any thought of action.

"Danno, Shifty. Get the guns, now."

One from the leader's left and one from his right, moved forward warily, still uncertain that Tom's and Andrew's capitulation would continue. Without taking their eyes off the two intruders, they crouched down and picked up the two shotguns. Only then did their demeanour relax, and jokes started to flow between them.

"Cut it," snapped Colin. "Let me have one."

Danno reluctantly passed him the shotgun he had in his possession. Colin then indicated for the rest of the gang to bring the men's families forward. The minute they arrived the two children attached themselves to their respective fathers' sides, seeking their protection. Their mothers joined them.

Tom knew they were in deep trouble the minute the leader spoke next. "Right, you two women get over here."

"Yeah," sniggered Danno, "fed up of fucking those two slags."

"Shut your fucking mouth," snapped the leader angrily.

"You said you wanted our food and Land Rover," responded Andrew, his voice shaky.

"We do," said the leader. "But we want some fun first. Then you can go on your way. Now, take your kids over to the steps leading up to the hall. Move it!"

Tom started to move towards the steps, Mary clutching his coat as her mother was prevented from joining them.

"You can't do this," growled Tom angrily, shaking Mary off and making a beeline for Lucy.

The butt of the shotgun hit him hard in the stomach, knocking the wind out of him, forcing Tom to drop to his knees.

Bang.

Colin fired a shot into the air and bellowed at Tom and Andrew, "You fuckers try anything again and I promise you that your kids'll suffer."

Bang.

Glen dropped his drink, the mug bouncing off the mudguard of the Land Rover, the contents splashing over his combat trousers. His HK weapon was immediately up and at the ready. "What the hell was that?"

Rolly had also reacted, dropping to a crouch, lifting his gun, and quickly scanning a 180-degree arc to his front. Greg and Plato, who had been adjusting the equipment in the back of the trailer attached at the rear of the Land Rover, also dropped to the ground, ready to react to any potential threat.

"Not far away," responded Rolly. "Shotgun, I think."

"Yeah," called Plato. "One o'clock from your position."

Bang.

"Definitely a shotgun," confirmed Greg. "It's bloody close as well, a hundred metres maybe. Do we investigate?"

Glen thought for a moment before he spoke. "I reckon. We need to know what's going on in this godforsaken world. Rolly, Plato, stay here and protect our stuff. Greg and me will take a look-see."

Glen placed his HK G36 on the bonnet of their vehicle, pulled on his personal load carrying equipment (PLCE), patted the extra magazines secured within it, and picked up his HK again. He also grabbed an MP5 and a radio out of the cab. "We'll take comms this time. If you need to move out, I'll give you a rendezvous point, and we can meet up there."

"Roger that." Both Rolly and Plato confirmed they understood.

"Let's go, before we miss the action," Greg said impatiently.

Glen grinned. "Come on then before you piss your pants."

He took the lead, running quickly through the trees in the large back garden of the house where they had set up for the night. Ahead, the elongated houses spread out in a hammerhead shape, the front of the houses and shops facing out onto the High Street. They clambered over a low fence, spotting a gap between the two buildings on the other side: a narrow passageway they were certain would lead them to the High Street. Glen slowed, looked back, and checked Greg was with him and ready. He indicated to Greg through hand signals that they would move to the end of the passageway, and then stop and observe before they went out onto the main road. Glen sidled along the left-hand wall and soon signalled to Greg that he had spotted something. Glen edged further along toward the end of the building, stopped, lowered himself to the prone position, poked his head around the corner, and scanned the street. Movement opposite in front of what could be a town hall caught his attention. But his full view was blocked by the metal frame of a market stall, blown over on its side and pushed up against a shop front, its plastic covering tattered and torn. Glen waved Greg forward and, once his friend was on the opposite side in position to cover him, he scooted across the footpath until he was up against the side of the plastic-sheeted stall. Now he was in position to provide cover for Greg as he moved forward and joined him. With Greg covering his six, Glen crept forward at a crouch, shuffling through the, until now, undisturbed dust, trying to keep the movement of it down to a minimum, thankful he was wearing a surgical face mask. He stopped and listened, then shifted position again, advancing along the right-hand side of the stall, more and more of the town hall coming into view the nearer he got to the front. The closer he got, the better the angle and greater the visibility of the activity that was materialising out to his half left.

Glen quickly assessed the situation, a skill he had learnt during his eleven years with the regiment, where a split-second decision was often necessary and could mean the difference between life and death. A man was on the ground, hands held up in front of his face defending himself as the person towering above kicked him repeatedly. A few metres away, a second man stood with his hands on his head, a shotgun barrel being waved threateningly in front of his face while, behind him, two young children, possibly a boy and a girl, clung to his coat. Glen looked slightly right as he heard sharp voices and saw two people being dragged up the steps of the municipal building. One shorter and possibly chubbier than the other was pleading with her captors and pointing in the direction of the two children, but her pleas fell on deaf ears and their custodians continued with their task of getting the two individuals to the top of the steps and into the building. Glen knew instinctively why the two women were being dragged into the bowels of the prominent building. His face reddened in anger and he keyed his handset.

"Golf, this is November. Go left. Three X-rays outside with four Yankees. Seven X-rays with two Yankees on steps."

"*Roger, on way.*"

"Romeo, this is November. Once contact made, move to location 100 metres west of High Street."

"*Roger,*" responded Rolly, the phonetic letter, Romeo, taken from the first letter of Rolly's name. As Greg and Glen had the same initial, the last letter, November, was used for Glen.

"*November, Golf. In position. Three X-rays still outside. Seven X-rays now in hall.*"

Glen focused back on the people out the front of the town hall, and slung his HK weapon over his shoulder, changing it for the silenced MP5.

"Golf. Go silent. X-ray with three Yankees left, and X-ray with single Yankee are yours. X-ray on steps is mine. RV top of steps."

"*Roger.*"

"In five…"

"*Counting.*"

"Four…three…"

Glen counted down to himself.

"Two…one…go!"

He thrust down with his thighs, launching his body up and forwards, appearing at the front of the collapsed market stall at the same time as Greg appeared out front to his left. Both shuffled forward in a gait that suited them, a stride that allowed them to keep their weapons steady and on target, yet enabled them to move quickly.

Phut. Greg fired a shot from his Welrod silenced pistol, the bullet taking X-ray one in the side of the chest, knocking him sideways. Mary, seeing the man who had been threatening her father violently knocked to the ground, cried out and clutched her father even tighter. The remaining two X-rays, alerted by Mary's wail, spun round to see what had caused the girl to cry out.

Phut. Greg's pistol jerked again in his two-handed grip as he fired at X-ray two, the person who had been standing threateningly over Andrew. The 9mm slug hit the man in the shoulder. Greg cocked the weapon again, and the second round smashed through the man's oesophagus, forcing him to the ground, his hands clutching at his throat as he fought for breath. Greg then turned back round, putting another bullet into X-ray one, before holstering the now nearly empty pistol and swinging his LMG up to the fore, the sling round his neck keeping it steady, his finger on the trigger ready to open up with the machine gun. In the meantime, Glen, who had the greater distance to cover, had run on ahead towards the town hall and fired a short three-round burst from his suppressed MP5, spinning X-ray three round before the man, or woman, fell prostrate to the ground, sprawled face down, sliding down the hard, blood-smeared steps. Glen accelerated, breaking into a run to get fully across the road, then taking the steps two at a time. Someone appeared at the entrance to the hall, perhaps sent to investigate the outburst from the young girl.

Phut…phut. Two shots from Glen, who was now less than ten metres from the top, killed the woman instantly as the first bullet scrambled her brain and the second one tore a hole through her heart. Glen reached the large double door, the right door open with a metre-wide gap providing access. It was darker inside as he stepped over the dead body and entered the large entrance hall, quickly moving along the closed left-hand door before swinging round, dropping to a crouch, the black inside of the town hall revealing nothing. Although the glassless windows allowed some light into the inner sanctum of the building, the overcast sky's blocked out the sun's rays, throwing a grey cloak over the country. He looked to his right as he saw Greg appear through the door. Glen moved further left, keeping his MP5 pointing in the direction of the wide staircase that was slowly appearing out of the gloom. He signalled Greg to join him.

As he peered into the dark, he could hear Greg shuffling across the floor before crouching down, ready to cover Glen when he made his next move. Glen's night vision was getting better, and he could pick out three doors to the left of the concourse, two leading to rooms on the left and one straight ahead. He assumed there would be a similar layout on the far side of the stairway. Glen cursed himself for not having his NVGs, and tucked away a reminder inside his head that he needed to remain switched on. They may not be conducting standard military operations, but some of the circumstances they were coming across were little different from some of those he had experienced in third world countries during his career in the regiment.

He heard someone cry out, possibly from behind the door straight ahead, to the left of the stairway. He could pick out Greg's silhouette quite clearly now, and he raised his hand, signalling Greg to go left, covering the left-hand wall of the building. In the meantime, he shuffled across the open space to the base of the stairs, his right shoulder up against the left-hand banister, a reception desk off to his right. The stairs, wide at the base and heavily carpeted, narrowed as they reached the next level, splitting into a wide landing, doubling back into two wide balconies either side. Glen couldn't see any movement or hear any activity above. The only sound he could pick out was from the far door directly ahead of him. He heard a crackle of broken glass and turned round to see the dark shadow of Greg moving behind him, past his position, closing in on the wall opposite. Glen pushed forward, his right shoulder touching the wall supporting the stairs. He tried to be as quiet as possible, but it seemed as though the entire country, inside and out, was carpeted in a layer of dust, ash and splinters of glass. He slowed his steps, placing each foot down carefully, but grit still popped beneath his boots.

He paused just outside the door and waited while Greg moved up to the first door on the far side. On arriving in position, Greg removed his helmet, placed his ear to the wood, and listened. Nothing resonated through the wooden door; the room was silent. He twisted the handle slowly. The unlocked door opened silently, the well-maintained hinges ensuring the opening would go undetected. What little light there was from the shattered windows was enough for Greg to confirm the room was clear.

Moving along the wall, Greg arrived at the second door and went through the same routine. Glen's head suddenly shot round from watching Greg as a clatter of what sounded like furniture crashing came from behind the door ahead of him, followed by the sounds of a woman protesting. He crept closer to the door, moving across at an angle, away from the stairs, until directly opposite, then moving straight towards it. Moving to the side, standing with his back to the wall, he was alongside the door. The sound of a loud slap was as clear as day and then what sounded like more furniture crashing across the room. The door would open to the left, and Glen took up a position on the right of it, his hand on the doorknob ready. He turned it slightly, checking its resistance, but didn't attempt to open the door. Greg moved opposite Glen's position and prepared himself on the left side of the door, pulling a flashbang from a pouch. Greg picked out Glen's shadowy face and watched his lips counting, his nodding head accentuating the countdown.

Three...two...one...go.

Glen twisted the knob all the way and, putting the weight of his shoulder behind the door, flung it open as far as he could. Then he pulled his body back out and Greg reacted instantly, tossing the flashbang through the opening. Both men turned their heads away, protecting their eyes from the flash that filled the high-ceilinged room. They crouched down, relaxing their bodies, focusing on the next steps, ignoring the violence of the explosion that erupted through the room. Then, standing up, Glen launched himself through the room, moving left, scanning the area, taking in the layout of any furniture, picking out X-rays from Yankees, looking for threats, conscious of Greg's position.

"What the fuck!" exclaimed Colin, looking back over his shoulder, a piece of Lucy's torn clothing in his hand. Still blinded by the bright light of the flashbang, his head and ears ringing, his scrambled thoughts struggled to assimilate what had happened.

Glen clocked the scene in less than a second. Colin was standing over Lucy, the woman spreadeagled on the floor. Two men had each been holding an ankle, and a third man had been gripping her wrists yanking them painfully above her head. But now she had been released as they knelt there shocked and dazed. To the left, a second woman was bent over a desk, where one man had been pulling on her arms, forcing the woman tight up against the edge of the desk as the last X-ray thrust into her from behind. Now, all three were standing there stupefied. More than 1 million candela and a loud 180-decibel bang had inflicted on all of them flash blindness, deafness, and complete disorientation. For Glen and Greg, who neither suffered from confusion nor loss of coordination, it was time to make themselves felt. Two shots from Glen's HKG shocked the occupants of the room out of their bewilderment, the flashes from the muzzle lighting up the room as Danno's startled facial expression was shattered by two 5.56mm rounds tearing through his face. Greg added to the cacophony of sound as he fired three-round burst after deafening three-round burst, the bullets punching into Colin's chest,

175

the second burst hitting Shifty just as he was about to dive for one of the shotguns. The force of the bullets knocked the young man off his feet, his body jerking in time to the strikes and flash from the barrel, creating a stroboscopic effect as his cartwheeling arms knocked the second woman of the group, Lizzy, over, saving her from the next burst fired by Greg. But, although not the best weapon for close-quarter fighting, the 100-round magazine meant he had plenty of ammunition left to finish the job, firing five rounds into her body as she crashed to the deck. To his left, Glen emptied his magazine into the last of the living X-rays, quickly replacing the empty magazine with a fresh one before taking stock. His chest heaved and his ears rang as a consequence of the din they had caused. He gagged slightly at the pervasive smell of fumes and burnt nitroglycerine mixed in with the stench of faeces as the dead evacuated their bowels.

The two surviving women whimpered as they clutched each other for comfort curled up on the floor. Glen and Greg check the bodies of the men and the woman. None had survived. Glen and Greg had come in with the intention of killing every single one of them. Once satisfied, they gathered up the weapons and were about to check on the two women when a body crashed into the room.

"Lucy, Lucy!" bellowed Tom, panic building up inside of him as the smell of death filled his nostrils. Another body, in the form of Andrew, stumbled through the open doorway, his cries for Maddie.

Both Glen and Greg swung round, weapons at the ready.

"Relax, Greg," said Glen, placing his hand on Greg's LMG, lowering the barrel, the heat felt even through his gloved hand. "It's just their husbands."

Both Tom and Andrew consoled their weeping wives, Maddie's cries becoming louder and more hysterical as what had happened to her clouded her thoughts.

"Get them both outside. They'll feel a lot better for it," suggested Glen.

"My wife's been raped!" snapped Andrew.

"Hey, hey," intervened Tom. "These men aren't to blame. They've helped us."

"I know, I know. I'm sorry," Andrew apologised. "Thank you. It's just—"

"Don't worry about it. Let's get the hell out of here. Then we can talk," Greg encouraged him.

Tom and Andrew helped their wives up and out of the room,

leaving the dead bodies behind. Greg pushed the dead woman away from the entrance to allow the women free passage. They stumbled down the steps, supported by Tom and Andrew, passing the dead X-ray near the bottom. A sudden squeal of delight let rip as Mary tore herself away from Patrick, left outside to look after Mary, and ran towards her mother. Patrick was not far behind her. Both women flung their arms around their respective children, and the sobbing started all over again.

While Lucy and Maddie were consoling their two children, and vice versa, Tom went up to Glen and held out his hand. Glen accepted the handshake, pulling down his mask and smiling.

"You've saved our wives from a fate worse than death, and probably all of our lives as well."

Before Glen could respond, Greg grabbed his attention, pointing towards the end of the High Street in the direction of the petrol station. A military Land Rover came into view, halted, and Rolly and Plato quickly debussed, skirmished away from the vehicle, and took up a defensive position either side of the road.

"Romeo, Papa, this is November. You can stop playing at soldiers and join us."

"*Roger that,*" responded Plato.

Both jumped back in and roared down the street to join the rest of the troop.

Grouped around the land Rover, fifty metres away from the building where they had rescued the two women, the lads soon had a brew going, and Plato put his culinary skills to good use warming up some tins of chilli con carne along with powdered mash.

"Not the most thrilling of meals," laughed Plato, "but it'll fill a gap."

"This is great. Better than my mum's cooking," piped up Patrick.

Andrew cuffed the lad playfully. "You never used to complain about her cottage pie coated in grated cheese, did you?"

"I suppose not." Patrick's face reddened.

"Where will you take your families to next?" asked Rolly.

Andrew and Tom looked at each other before Tom answered. "We'll continue with our plans."

"And they are?"

Tom looked at Andrew again, almost seeking approval to open up to these strangers. Seeing no objections, Tom continued.

"Exmoor National Park. There's fresh water, and trees we can use to build a home and for fuel when needed."

"What about the towns?" asked Plato.

"Potentially full of people like the ones we've just encountered. There'll be no food, no fuel for heating, and it's likely that disease will be rife."

"We have to protect our children from animals like those." Lucy indicated the bodies lined up along the kerbside, clothing draped over their faces so that the staring eyes weren't visible to the women and the two children.

"I'm sure there are some communities of a like mind out there. It's better you stick with larger groups. Better chance of survival," advised Glen as he got up out of a foldable director's chair and picked up the pan to spoon more chilli onto the children's clean plates.

"Where are you soldiers going? Do you have a commander?"

"Well, Tom," replied Glen, "we have no idea who's in charge. So, me and the lads are heading for London to see if we can find out."

"Go via Chilmark. There's supposed to be an RGC there," Rolly suggested to Tom.

"RGC?"

"Regional Government Centre, Tom. If it's survived, that is."

Mary yawned.

"We need to get the children set up for the night," Lucy advised the men.

"Yes, of course. Why don't you stay close to us for tonight?" counselled Glen. "You can get a decent night's kip, and we can go our separate ways in the morning."

"We'd appreciate that." Andrew thanked them. "Our wives and children in particular could do with a worry-free night."

"Right then, we'll finish our food, then follow us to the other side of the road. We'll go back to where we stopped overnight."

Food was finished, tea drank, and their stuff packed away. Plato helped the families top up their Land Rover from a small reservoir of diesel at the bottom of the large fuel tanks, topping their own up at the same time, impressed with Tom's makeshift pump.

Glen saw Maddie climb painfully into the back of their Land Rover, helped by her husband Andrew. Glen walked over to him and pulled him aside. "She OK? Stupid question, I know."

Although sadness was reflected in his eyes, Andrew's response was positive. "It's the world we live in now. She'll get over it. She has to. At least we're alive, thanks to you and your men. We need to be strong for our children. They're our future."

Glen nodded. "People are going to need each other much more than they realise. Not something I'd considered up until now."

"Come with us," a spur of the moment invitation from Andrew.

"No, but thanks for the offer. Our destiny lies elsewhere. No idea what or where, but..." Glen patted Andrew's shoulder. "Anyway, enough reflection. Let's go and get settled down for the night."

CHAPTER 21

The radio crackled just as they arrived at the Land Rover, and Sergeant Major Saunders grabbed the handset.

"*Two-Zero, this is Two-Zero-Delta. Over.*"

"This is Two-Zero-Alpha. Go ahead. Over."

Scott could hear the roar of the Land Rover in the background as Corporal Brodie responded. "*Tangoes. Approximately figures two-four, five klicks north of Two-Zero-Charlie's location.*"

"We've got company, sir." The CSM passed the handset to Major Redfern.

"Two-Zero-Delta, this is Two-Zero. What are the Tangoes doing? Over."

"*It looks like they're setting up camp. We came across a pickup truck doing a recce of the area. Over.*"

"Did they see you?"

"*Negative.*"

"Your location now?"

"*Found a piece of high ground to their south. Keeping watch. Over.*"

"Mix and weapons?"

"*A dozen adult males, seven females and a few kids. Weapons…I can see four or five shotguns. Wait…*"

The two men talked while they waited for Delta to continue.

"If they recce too far out, they're bound to come across the warehouse, sir."

"That's my worry too. Once Delta have finished with their update, we'll get over there."

"*Two-Zero. Their recce was a bit close then. Yes, five shotguns, probably two hunting rifles, and we've seen at least three SA80s. Nothing heavier. Over.*"

"Vehicles?"

"*Ah…Wrangler Jeep, two pickups, one on patrol, a couple of minibuses, Luton van and an old civvy Land Rover.*"

"Roger that. Maintain watch. We're moving to Charlie. Over."

"*Acknowledged.*"

"Out to you. Hello, Zero, this is Two-Zero. Over."

Silence.

"Come on, answer!" cursed Alan.

"Zero, this is Two-Zero. Over."

"*Go ahead. Over.*"

Alan recognised the colonel's, now brigadier's, voice.

"Two-Zero. We have armed Tangoes north of Two-Zero-Charlie. Over."

"*Hostile?*"

"Not so far, sir. We're heading that way shortly."

"*Numbers?*"

"Twenty-plus. Mix of males, females and children. Heavily armed."

"*Your recommendations?*"

"Withdraw our support from the town. The plods can handle that. But you'll need to warn the Superintendent. Then reinforce Charlie. Over."

"*What about the RGC and feeding station?*"

"Keep feeding station covered, but I'll take four men from the RGC. You need to lock down, sir."

"*Understood. I'll speak to Superintendent Collins and have four men on standby to support you. We're locking down now. Keep me posted. Out.*"

Alan updated the soldiers guarding the feeding station, warning them to be on their guard. "Let's go then."

"Sir."

"I'll contact the others on the way."

Scott turned the key, and the Land Rover roared into life. Dropping into gear, the vehicle pulled out of the car park and sped off west.

"RGC first?"

"Yes, we'll pick up reinforcements on our way." Major Redfern keyed the handset. "Hello, Two-Zero-Charlie, Two-Zero. Over."

"*Two-Zero-Charlie, go ahead. Over.*"

"Good lads, they've been monitoring the net," praised the CSM. "I gathered you heard? Over."

"*Yes, sir. We've locked down and brought all transports inside. Scimitar manned and ready and the boys are keeping watch.*"

"How many civilians with you?"

"About a dozen, sir. They're all being monitored."

"Good. Have call sign Golf-One get under cover, and assign two on foot to go with it."

"Roger that."

"Out to you. Hello, Two-Zero-Echo, you register that? Over."

Zero-Echo, based in the town, acknowledged. *"Where do you want us, sir?"*

"Move to Zero-Charlie's location. Come in from the south. The Tangoes are to the north of Charlie. But first let the civvy force know what's happening. They'll have no comms once you've left. Over."

"Understood. What if they get a bit flaky?"

"Tell them their boss is on his way to take command. Out."

The Land Rover headed down Chicksgrove Road, passed Place Farm, almost coming back on themselves just before the water outlet from Fonthill Lake, and headed west on Chilmark Road, a trail of dust left in their wake. Alan totted up numbers. "We'll have eight from Zero-Charlie, four from the town, and four from the RGC. And we have Delta."

"What about the Fox?"

"Good point." Alan contacted the patrol. "Two-Zero-Delta, move Golf-Two to Charlie's location and join Golf-One. Over."

"Roger that."

"And make it quiet."

"Understood."

"You're right there, sir. Thing makes a right racket, even with a Jag engine."

"Alan."

"Alan," Scott responded with a smile. "It's not as if we haven't been expecting it."

"I know, but I would have preferred us recceing further out and finding them before they came to us."

"You think they'll be a bother?"

"They're well armed and on the move. They're either looking for some form of authority or a group to join or—"

"Scavenging and not caring who or what," finished Scott.

The Land Rover swerved left as Scott nearly missed the turning into Mill Lane, the ground a lot rougher now. "Sorry about that."

"The plods don't have speeding tickets, but I do value my life," Alan laughed.

"So what do we do?"

"I've been thinking about that. Do we wait and see what they're up to, or pay them a visit?"

"They're bound to pay a trip to Chilmark."

"That's what bothers me. I can't see the PO wanting to keep the workforce inactive. He's set a precedent now and needs to maintain it."

"The lads are ready."

Ahead, as they approached the gated and fenced entrance to the RGC, Alan could see four of his soldiers hanging around a Land Rover near the entrance, talking to the brigadier. Scott pulled up alongside them, and Alan jumped out. He threw Brigadier Bannister a quick salute.

"I've got Zero-Echo coming from the town, six of us here, the recce group and the eight men from the warehouse."

"That should be enough," responded Bannister.

The radio crackled in both Land Rovers, and Scott leant in through one of the open windows and picked up the handset. "Go ahead. Over."

Alan and the brigadier joined him. They could hardly hear the voice at the other end.

"Who is it?" asked Alan.

"Two-Zero-Delta."

"*Have eyes on the Tangoes' encampment. Seem to be settling down, setting up a temporary encampment. At least another four vehicles have joined them. A bus, would you believe it, one HGV, a civvy one, and two people carriers. At least an additional one-zero males. Over.*"

Alan took the handset off Scott. "Just use the Prestel to respond, understood? Over."

"*Click…click.*"

"Are the new Tangoes armed?"

"*Click…click.*"

"Moving to Charlie. Will join you at your location soonest. Over."

"*Click…click.*"

"Two-Zero out."

Once joined by Zero-Echo, commanded by the newly promoted Sergeant Thompson, the convoy of vehicles headed off towards the warehouse, Bennet moving from Two-Zero-Echo, taking over the driving from Company Sergeant Major Saunders. Two soldiers from the RGC itself had also boarded the OCs Land Rover. There were two warehouses under the control of the RGC. One was deep underground, secured and well hidden from prying eyes, which held the stocks that had been built up by the National Emergency Committee, at least when they were in existence before the nuclear strikes hit. Primarily stocked with raw sugar, sacks of flour, tins of corned beef, drums of oil and fat, it was key to the survival of the RGC and the people under its auspices. The location of this particular storage site, although critical to them, was unguarded, but checked discreetly twice a day. The second warehouse, the one they were heading for now, had been a civilian warehouse before the start of the war, owned and run by a civilian logistics company. It too had been stocked up prior to the missile and bomb strikes. Taken over by the Government, it had been stockpiled with provisions, but of the more traditional type like tins of beans and tomatoes – anything the Government could commandeer and stash away for use in the unlikely event of a major nuclear strike hitting the United Kingdom.

The convoy sped along the A303, the cross-country tyres of the Land Rovers purring rhythmically, only interrupted when hitting the occasional rut in the road where vegetation, plant life that was able to grow under the austere conditions, had already started to force its way through tiny cracks in the less frequently used tarmac road. There were so few vehicles on the road now; it was inevitable that plants would quickly reclaim lost territory.

Bennet turned the wheel of the Land Rover, avoiding the slalom of abandoned vehicles. The road was a dual carriageway, and a line of vehicles had been abandoned either side of the road after their drivers' attempts to head west towards the M4 or M5 motorways had failed. Fortunately, two of the lanes, one in each direction, had been kept open for use by military and official vehicles during the short time before the first of the strikes hit. The entire network of major roads in the UK had become bogged down very quickly. Not only because of the sheer traffic congestion due to members of the public attempting to flee to somewhere they felt would be safer, or vehicles running out of fuel, but also because of the effects of the 300 nuclear strikes across the country. Most of the road networks in the United Kingdom went through or passed close to major cities and towns. These were natural targets of the Russian intercontinental ballistic missiles (ICBMs) and bombers. The hurricane-like blast wave, one of the deadly outcomes of a nuclear explosion, from the nuclear bombs and missiles striking the towns and cities, or airports and military installations, caused havoc on the arterial lifelines of the UK. And if any transport routes survived that then the effects of the super-nuclear electro magnetic pulse (super-NEMP) finished them off, the vehicles grinding to a halt. At least three of these weapons had been exploded 400 kilometres above the UK, burning out the electrics of motor vehicles, disrupting communications, and even affecting the military. Although the military throughout the world had done their best to harden their combat vehicles and communication equipment against the EMP threat, the truth was that, apart from in the early sixties, no real tests had been completed, for obvious reasons, to test the effectiveness of such measures. A few of the older vehicles, less reliant on the modern computer chips that controlled the majority of engine-management systems, were of a metallic construction providing added protection over their cousins made of non-metallic materials. Even though some vehicles were unaffected, the result was still one of the largest traffic jams in the world.

The driver of the Land Rover cursed as the front bumper clipped a large Range Rover, jarring the Land Rover's occupants.

"Take it easy, Bennet," ordered Scott sitting in the rear with Kothari and Baxter. "Best we get there in one piece, eh?"

"Yes, sir, just want to get there to support the lads."

"Me too," added Alan, looking across at the driver. "But there's no immediate threat."

The distance from the RGC to the warehouse was about thirty kilometres, and they soon approached Mere, the halfway point. This was the location of the RGC's reserve stocks, which had remained relatively untouched but also unguarded so far. The convoy climbed Chaddenwick Hill, dropping down towards the outskirts of the small town. The Mere bypass skirted the northern edge of the town, the treeline along the edge of the dual carriageway obscuring their view of the town itself. Alan had considered diverting one of his vehicles to do a drive-past, checking out that the warehouse was secure, but decided against it. Better to keep the convoy together until they knew what they were up against.

They raced through the southern edge of Nor Wood curving south between Zeals to the west and Wolverton to the east. The road then took them west, passing Bourton to the north. Most of the survivors of these communities, many suffering and dying from radiation sickness, starvation and dehydration, had been encouraged

185

to make their way to the RGC encampment where they would receive minimal medical treatment and, eventually, food and water.

"Five minutes out, sir."

"Keep your eyes peeled, lads," added Scott.

Weapons were held at the ready, Scott and Kothari covering out of the back of the canvas-topped Land Rover, the rear flap having been rolled up out of the way, even though it meant some dust made its way into the back. Alan slid back the front passenger window and he too prepared his weapon ready to repel an attack. They caught glimpses of Wincanton now as the convoy passed beneath Common Road. Bennet maintained a steady speed, having slowed down as they approached the built-up area. The vehicles crossed Moor Lane as they drew closer to the industrial estate off to the right.

"Junction coming up," warned the driver.

"Standby," added Alan.

Alan checked the wing mirror and could see Zero-Echo slowing down, increasing the gap between themselves and the lead vehicle should anything go wrong. Bennet swung the vehicle left onto the slip road, curving around until they climbed and crossed over the A303 they had just left. The road ahead was clear and, within seconds, they cut across the large roundabout, Morrison's supermarket off to the right. It had been stripped of whatever was left by the men of his unit and added to the RGC stocks in the warehouse they were about to visit. There hadn't been much left in the way of food and bottled liquids though as panic buying, setting in as the war went progressively from bad to worse, had depleted what stocks the supermarket chain and all the others, such as Tesco, Sainsbury's and Asda, had. A major industrial estate was further east, but the one they were heading for was ahead and off to the left.

They crawled down Dyke's Way, the crew scanning the road ahead and the buildings around them. Passing smaller industrial units either side, the main warehouse, significantly larger than anything else in the area, just under 10,000 square metres, came into view. Turning left down Murray Way, their access was blocked by a chicane of broken down vehicles, dragged there intentionally, which they negotiated until they arrived at the sandbagged entrance guarded by two soldiers. The gates were open, ready, and they drove straight through, the other vehicle not far behind. They parked up and Alan jumped down, weapon in hand ready.

A corporal came over and threw him a salute which he returned.

He was impressed with his unit, how discipline had been maintained, considering the circumstances and the break down in law and order elsewhere. What Redfern didn't know was that he and Scott were held in high regard by the soldiers, and they to a man, including two Women's Royal Army Corp (WRACs) soldiers, recognised that if they were to survive they needed to hold together and follow this man's leadership.

"Corporal West, what's the disposition of your men?"

"There's me and Laura watching the front, two round the back, and a two-man foot patrol poking around the perimeter. Two are off stag. Could be a long day, sir."

"I'll leave Echo and the RGC lads here. You come with us when we're ready to go and pay Delta a visit. Sar'nt Major, get Echo's vehicle hidden round the back, and then all to report upstairs."

"Inside the warehouse?"

"Yes, except ours. Park Echo and Charlie close to the back doors. If we need to move quickly, I don't want our transport blocked in. Leave two additional men to cover them. Sarn't Thompson, you take command of Charlie until we return."

"Doing a recce?"

"Yes."

The CSM went to instruct the men while the major and Corporal West headed inside. The NCO took the lead, holding the door open for his OC. They passed through a small reception area, a long leather sofa with a sleeping bag lain along it: somewhere for the lads on stag at night to grab a couple of hours' kip in the warm when it was their turn to stand down.

Before going upstairs, Alan poked his head through the door into the main warehouse, an open area lined with large battery chargers for the forklift trucks off to the right. He acknowledged the civilians sitting in a group at the far side, chatting and drinking tea. Work had been suspended while the emergency was on, and no supplies would be moved to the RGC or feeding centre until further notice. There were enough supplies to last the feeding centre for at least two days. Beyond that, a decision would need to be made about restarting the supply convoy. Across from Redfern, row upon row of steel racking towered twelve metres high, holding up to 6,000 pallets of food, water and other essential supplies needed to keep the population the RCG had assumed responsibility for alive. The warehouse, 10,000 square metres in size, could hold nearly 4,000 tons of supplies. Beyond the lines of racking at the far end were the loading bays where the supplies were loaded onto an HGV to take the food and supplies to the camp.

"Civvies OK?"

"Yeah," laughed the corporal. "Cushy number for them, sir. Sheltered, two good meals a day, beats pulling bodies out of houses or digging up fields."

"Sure," responded Alan, pulling his head back inside the reception area and moving towards the stairs that would take them up into the office area on the second level. Two flights of stairs found them at the entrance to a corridor, passing between two partitioned offices. At the end was a wide open space where over a dozen quad desk units had been pushed back against the walls. To their left, a long window section overlooked the upper levels of the warehouse, palletised goods clearly visible on the upper levels of racking.

The two soldiers turned right, passing other offices, the toilet area and kitchen, where one of the civilians cooked for the soldiers and the workers downstairs. The offices were now used as quarters for those soldiers off duty. Two of the men would be asleep somewhere now. In the corner was a larger office, now the small unit's HQ, with a double-aspect view, windows looking out over the front and sides of the entrance, and to the left, on the other side of two more partition offices, was a long conference room, their destination. Both entered, and Alan laid his SA80 on the long conference table and looked through the windows that ran the entire length of that end of the warehouse. Once the soldiers returned from their foot patrol, one would position themselves in the HQ where they would have an excellent view, north and east, and a second soldier would place himself in the conference room. Alan looked out onto the front car park where he spotted the foot patrol moving down the road out at the front. He looked further, beyond the small building across the road, his view out to the fields to the north-east and west.

The door clattered open behind them, and CSM Saunders, followed by Sergeant Thompson, made his way into the conference room. "All set, sir. Ready to go see?"

Alan moved away from the window, satisfied all was well within the warehouse, picked up his SA80, and headed for the door. "Yes, let's go and see what all the fuss is about. We'll leave Charlie in your capable hands."

"It'll be in one piece when you get back sir," responded Sergeant Thompson.

The three men headed downstairs, reunited with their Land Rover, and headed north to where Zero-Delta were holed up, observing the movements of the intruders. They arrived after a thirty-minute drive, taking it easy in case they came across one of their visitors scouring the area.

Corporal West guided the two men through the trees, leading them to a piece of high ground where a listening post had been set up and they connected with the NCO in command, Lance Corporal Brodie. West stayed with Jon Belmore, who was off stag, while Alan and Scott went forward for a recce. On a signal from Corporal Brodie, Alan and the CSM dropped down onto the ground, followed by an uncomfortable leopard crawl, their assault rifles resting in the crook of their arms, towards a point where they could get a good view of the interlopers.

Scott grunted. "I'm too old for this."

"Quiet," hissed Redfern.

They were soon alongside Jordan and Kirby who were on stag.

"Two on, two off?" the captain whispered to Corporal Brodie.

"Yes, sir. Don't know how long we'll be here for, so best they get some sleep."

They edged further over the ridge where they were met by a number of flickering lights below, out to about 200 metres, surrounded by vehicles on three sides.

"Looks like something out of a Western, circling of the wagons," hissed Scott, looking at the encampment cordoned off with at least half a dozen vehicles on three sides.

"Seems well organised," responded Alan. "What's their routine?" he asked Corporal Brodie.

"Pretty much just sitting around the camp fires in small groups. They have at least two doing a circuit of the camp, armed naturally."

"Constant?"

"Yes, sir. Always two, and they change every hour on the hour."

Alan laid his SA80 on the grass in front of him and extracted his binoculars from their case. It was still light enough that he could see the colour of the grass through the layer of ash that his elbows had disturbed. He readjusted his surgical face mask. A dank smell permeated his nostrils. He was immediately conscious that they were probably kicking up invisible particles that were more than likely still contaminated. They were all having to live with this new state of affairs. He held the binos up to his eyes and zoomed in to the camp. It was set up on the edge of a copse, with the vehicles forming a semi-circle around it, the treeline as the base. To the far right, he could see a blue civilian Land Rover parked across a hard-packed lane, guarding the entry and exit to the camp. Further east, the lane met up with a minor road, which in turn linked up to the main road. Two armed civilians, a man and a woman, both in their mid-thirties, stood guard. He watched as two more armed Tangoes came into view approaching the blue Land Rover, and stopping and conversing with the sentries before continuing the circuit of the camp, out to around a hundred metres. There was a car park area next to the entrance where the road sentries could keep watch over the rest of the group's vehicles. *Well organised*, thought Alan. There was the bus, a couple of campers and the Luton van. The rest of the assorted transport had been used to coral the groups sitting round their camp fires.

"Some tents going up."

Alan shifted his binos to where Scott was indicating. He could see at least two of the groups were erecting what looked like four to six-man tents.

"Looks like they're settling down for the night."

He moved his focus back to the perimeter, the vehicles about two metres apart. Zooming in to one of the camp fires, to a group of eight, he could see they were cooking some sort of food in a large pan bedded in the flames. One of the younger males was stirring it. There looked to be enough in the pot for the small group. A couple of bottles of what probably contained wine, or some other form of alcohol, were being passed around. Each person took a swig in turn before passing it on, faces lifted in laughter. He studied their attire. It was pretty ragtag: various layers of different types, and conflicting colours and style of clothing. All to keep out the chill of the rapidly cooling night.

Alan noticed movement close to the treeline and switched his gaze. It appeared to be a line of camp beds just inside the trees, with an awning strung out from the trees above them. What looked like a female was bending over one of the occupants of the camp beds, administering something.

"Looks like they've got some form of medical set-up," he informed no one in particular.

Scott zoomed in closer and studied the facility. "Yeah, that's what it looks like. Look at their faces. Some are pretty badly scarred. There are a couple not wearing hats, and you can see hair loss. Either third-degree burns or radiation sickness would be my guess."

A movement suddenly caught Alan's eye as he saw a man stride over to the group around the cooking pot. Alan shifted his elbows until he was more comfortable. The man bent down, tapped what looked like a young woman on the shoulder, and gestured that she should come with him.

"Check this out."

Scott took his cue and focused on where his OC was looking.

There was a minor altercation, the woman shaking her head. A slap across the girl's face appeared to end the argument. With no interference from the group, she was led away to one of the tents that was now fully erected and bundled inside, the man following behind her.

"Not so civilised after all," commented Scott.

"Have you done a full count?" Alan hissed to Corporal Brodie.

"Yes, sir." The NCO pulled out a small pocket notebook from his combat jacket and squinted at it in the rapidly diminishing light. "Twenty-two males aged between sixteen and fifty. That's approximate, sir."

"I don't want to know their birthdays." Alan smiled.

"Fifteen females and thirteen kids. Kids are five girls and eight boys. I'd say at least half the kids were under ten."

"What about the sick?"

"Seven, sir, but difficult to judge their sex or age."

"Weapons?"

Corporal Brodie consulted his notebook again. "Nine SA80, seven shotguns, five are double-barrelled, two, maybe three hunting rifles, a Gympy, and all seem to be carrying a sidearm. Including the women."

"Not too bad," suggested Scott.

"Still thirty-plus armed civilians who might not take too kindly to our intervention. Particularly taking orders from the Government and the military again."

"We need to keep an eye open for that Gympy. If someone knows how to use it—"

"Right, I've seen enough. Keep me posted on any new developments, Corporal Brodie."

"Will do, sir."

"I picked up some grub for you and your lads on my way out of the warehouse," added the CSM.

"Lads'll be pleased about that. They'd just started griping."

"Keep things tight," warned Alan. "We don't know what we're up against. I shall be paying them a visit tomorrow."

"Friendly visit, sir?" asked the corporal.

"Of course, we're not out to start a war. At least, not yet."

"We'll keep 'em covered, sir."

"As soon as I know the next steps, I'll inform you."

With that, the OC, CSM and section commander, Corporal Brodie, pulled back into the undergrowth and made their way quietly back to link up with West again. The Lance Corporal stayed with his men, and Alan, Scott and West made their way to the Land Rover. A twenty-minute drive brought them back to the warehouse, and they were soon in the ops room.

"What now, sir?" asked the CSM.

"I want the commanders of Bravo, Charlie, Echo and Kilo sections, along with the commanders of Golf-One and Golf-Two here in the next thirty minutes. In the meantime, I'll update the CO."

"You have a plan then, Alan?"

"It's forming, Scott, it's forming."

"I'll sort the lads out then."

Once orders had been issued, Alan took the handset off Scott and transmitted. "Hello Zero. This is Two-Zero. Over."

The radio crackled. Alan didn't have to wait long.

"This is Zero. Sitrep. Over."

Alan looked at Scott who said what Alan was thinking: "He sounds pissed with us."

CHAPTER 22

Commander Parry stumbled and Bell strengthened his grip, nearly dropping the weapon slung over his other shoulder as he did so. He supported Parry's right arm as the man struggled to move his badly broken leg over the rubble. Bell looked over his shoulder, the rattle of debris as the dog skipped and jumped across the carpet of rubble as he followed the two sailors. The dog, a mongrel, had been following them for the last five hours as the two men put all their efforts in getting back to the relative safety of the submarine and get away from the bitter cold. Bell turned his head again, hearing a much louder rattle of pieces of masonry cascading from one of the many piles of rubble that littered the ground around and in between the shattered buildings of Portsmouth. This time there was no dog. He stopped for a moment, restraining Parry, as he scanned the building remains behind them. The dog had gone, but the sound of movement had increased. A figure darted from behind a partially collapsed wall and Bell slipped his arm from around Parry.

"We've got visitors sir."

Bell dropped the weapon from his shoulder, placing it on the floor, then lowered the bags of supplies he was carrying, pulling the pistol from his pocket and checking the safety.

Parry wavered, unsteady on his legs, even with the crutch under his left arm, then staggered as he lowered himself to the ground, the crutch falling to the floor with a clatter. He pulled his pistol out of the holster with a shaky hand, not from fear, but as a consequence of the fever that was heating up inside of him. The open wound, although protected by a dressing, was clearly going septic and there was a real danger of septic shock setting in. He slumped as Bell crouched down next to him.

"You need to be ready sir, there's more than one," he warned as he saw two more people flit from building to building.

Parry lifted his head, held the shaking pistol at the ready as Bell reached over and released the safety. Looking up he could see half a dozen figures in the shadows and he shouted a warning, "clear off. We've nothing you want. Just leave us in peace and we'll be out of your area soonest."

There was no response and the figures appeared from their hiding places. He counted seven. He fired two shots, the sound shattering the silence, the intruders scattering wildly. He watched and waited, checked Commander Parry who was slumped forward, his injured leg at a funny angle, the pistol hanging loosely from his hand. More clatter of sound and he looked back to see the same figures lined up in a semi-circle about 200 metres away.

"Bugger off, the lot of you." He fired a shot, sparks flew from a piece of reinforced concrete and the two either side skipped away. In the meantime, the others had widened the half circle and moved closer. He fired two more shots, one missing the nearest person, the second singing of into the distance as it was deflected from a half shattered wall. Two more shots fired as they moved closer, both missing, but forcing the group to scatter, but not stopping their advance.

He grabbed for the assault rifle at the same moment he heard the crunch of gravel behind him, turning too late as the blade of a spade struck splitting his skull, his body sliding to the floor as a second blow finished him off. He didn't feel the pistol being prised from his fingers, or hear the two shots that killed Commander Parry.

The leader of the gang held the pistol aloft in victory, pulled the scarf down from his mouth and issued orders. "Strip 'em of everything, I want nothing left."

CHAPTER 23

Scott swung the Land Rover off the road and onto the track, the forest on their right, the encampment up ahead. The blue civilian Land Rover came into view, still parked across the track blocking their way forward.

"Two-Zero-Delta approaching sentries." Major Redfern informed the small force who had been watching the camp overnight, and who would now cover their backs.

"*Two-Zero-Delta. Roger.*"

"Here they come, Alan," warned Scott.

Two men came round to the side of the blue Land Rover, one with an SA80, the second with a single-barrelled shotgun. Although their weapons weren't held in a threatening manner, Alan suspected they were ready to move quickly should they need to.

The smaller of the two men waved them down, not that Scott could drive round the barrier without some difficulty. The men had chosen the spot, a choke point, well. Scott drove right up to the two men, only stopping when the smaller of the two men laid his hand on the bonnet of the army vehicle.

Alan didn't wait for them to come to the window. He was out of the vehicle quickly and confidently, his assault rifle left on his seat, but with his pistol still in a holster around his waist.

"Hello, Major, how can we be of assistance to you?"

Alan studied the man: fair hair, five nine, smooth-skinned, and in his early forties. *Ex-forces maybe*, thought Alan. The man had recognised his rank. Glancing over at the second man, who had held back slightly, Alan could see the glistening skin, just above the scarf around his mouth, indicative of a recent serious burn. He looked back at the man who had spoken to him, a surgical facemask pulled down beneath his chin, who looked healthy and well fed.

"It's more what we can do for you Mr..." Alan waited for the man to fill the gap.

"Ah…Dawson, James Dawson."

Alan reached out a hand, and Dawson reciprocated. "Major Redfern. My driver," Alan indicated back towards the driver's position, "is Sergeant Major Saunders."

Scott responded with a nod.

"And your colleague?"

"Jack. Jack Tomlinson."

"We're naturally aware of your presence and my brigadier, Brigadier Bannister, asked us to drop in on you and ascertain your intentions."

"Where's the rest of your army?"

"Army? Why do I need an army?"

"Well, I thought—"

"You have no hostile intentions towards a government representative, do you?"

The man started at the use of the term 'government'. "There's a government?"

"Naturally. Part of my task is to secure our area of responsibility. Are you in charge of this group?"

"Me in charge? No way. That's Mr Russell."

"Can we speak with him?"

"Er, sure. I don't see why not. You'll need to leave your vehicle and weapons here though."

"Vehicle yes, weapons no."

"Mr Russell won't be happy about that."

Alan indicated for Scott to join him. The CSM shouldered a man-pack radio, slung his SA80 over his shoulder, grabbed Alan's SA80, and came round the vehicle and handed it to his OC.

"I would remind you that we are government officials, and martial law still applies."

"Martial law?" The man spluttered a reply.

"Shall we go and see your boss then?" Alan indicated past the blue Land Rover.

"Sure, sure. Jack will watch over your vehicle for you."

"Good, just make sure he doesn't touch anything," warned Scott.

"Yeah, yeah, right." Dawson wandered over to his colleague, whispered in the man's ear, then indicated for Alan and Scott to follow.

As they walked down the track, Scott keyed the handset of his radio. "Hello, Two-Zero-Delta, Two-Zero-Alpha. Over."

The headset crackled as Scott held one of the earphones to his ear.

"*Roger that. We have you and your transport under surveillance. Over.*"

"Understood. Out."

"Some more of you out there?"

Alan smiled. "Yes, we have patrols out all the time."

"That's why we know you're here," added Scott.

The rest of the 200-metre walk was in silence. They passed the car park. A small fuel bowser had joined a bus, a couple of camper vans and a Luton van.

"Diesel?" asked Scott.

"Er, yeah. Keep this lot running." Dawson laughed uncomfortably. He was obviously concerned about answering the soldiers' questions.

They approached a gap in the wall of vehicles that encircled the camp. The three men passed in between a Ford Transit and a Mitsubishi 4x4 just as the radio crackled again.

"Go ahead," responded Scott.

"*Two-Zero-Delta. The bozo is taking an interest in your vehicle. Over.*"

"Roger that. Out. You need to talk to your buddy."

Dawson raised his eyebrows.

"Tell him our Land Rover is out of bounds."

"You have some guardian angels then."

"Yes, so inform him now." Alan reinforced his command.

"Peter," Dawson called over to a young boy close by, probably no more than ten years old.

"Yes, Mr Dawson?"

"Run over to the checkpoint," he indicated back towards the blue Land Rover and the parked army Land Rover, "and tell Jack to keep away from their Land Rover. Make it quick."

"Yes, Mr Dawson." With that, the boy ran off at sprint, eager to please.

They walked towards the tree line directly opposite the semi-circle of vehicles. Led by Dawson, the three men weaved around a mix of tents, some as small as two-man tents, others capable of homing a large family. One of the larger tents was set up on the treeline itself, a large brazier burning close to the entrance, a woman boiling water on it while a second woman was preparing some food. Both looked fairly healthy, perhaps a little skinny, but it was difficult to tell through the layers of clothing they were wearing to keep warm. Both were armed, pistols strapped around their waists. Next to the brazier was a collapsible camping table and half a dozen camping chairs. Beneath their feet, squares of rush matting had been laid over the ash and dust-covered grass. Alan wondered if the green of the English countryside would ever return.

"Sian, go tell Mr Russell that we have some visitors."

The nearest of the two women left her pot to boil and ran into the tent, calling after who Alan assumed was their leader. Moments later, she was back at the entrance indicating with a wave of her hand that Dawson should enter the tent. The man disappeared inside.

Alan took the opportunity to take in the layout of the camp. It seemed to be well organised, and small fires burned outside most of the larger tents. People went about their business. Preparing a midday meal seemed to be the task most were involved in.

The tent flap was pushed back and held open by Dawson as a man in his late forties passed through the entrance: short, quite stocky, dark hair, apart from a few wisps of grey at his temples, and a trimmed goatee beard. He wore a pair of black mock-combat trousers, with a disruptive-pattern combat jacket, the type worn during the eighties and nineties before the current multi-terrain pattern (MTP) style was introduced. A 9mm Browning pistol was strapped around his waist.

He held out his hand. "Major. My apologies, but my colleague failed to remember your name."

"Redfern. And your name is Russell."

"It is. Excellent. Major Redfern and Sergeant Major...?"

"Saunders," responded Scott.

"Please, take a seat. Where are my manners?" He turned to one of the women. "Sian," he called across to the woman who had originally gone in to fetch him, "tea for these officers. You will join me?" He indicated to the camping chairs. "Take a seat."

Alan sat on the nearest, resting his SA80 across his lap. Scott sat next to him after placing the radio on the floor in between their seats.

"You have working radios, I see." Russell pulled a chair up opposite the two soldiers. "We had a couple working for a while, but keeping them working and the batteries charged was proving more trouble than they're worth."

"These, along with the rest of our kit, were well protected. We also have sufficient vehicles and power to keep the batteries fully charged," responded Alan, confidently.

The man leant forward, his interest piqued. "You have generators?"

"Yes, at our headquarters."

"Dawson tells me you represent the government. I didn't think any meaningful administration had survived."

"Where have you and your group come from?" asked Alan.

"We came down from Birmingham, travelling through Oxfordshire and Swindon. Is it a regional or national centre you're from?"

The two way probing had started, thought Alan.

"We have an appointed regional governor, Principal Officer Elliot, and he is in turn supported by a large admin group and Brigadier Bannister. We're also in contact with the national government," Alan lied.

"Dawson here tells me the area is under martial law. Is that so?"

"The United Kingdom in its entirety is still under martial law. That was initiated prior to the nuclear strikes hitting the country and has not yet been revoked."

The man scratched his beard, his brown eyes searching Alan's face. *This has all the makings of a poker game*, thought Alan.

"I do remember. But since then, most of the country as we knew it has been obliterated, along with the bureaucratic chain of command."

"That's as maybe," replied Alan, "but a regional structure was initiated to run the country after an event of this kind."

"There's nothing to govern, Major."

"We have 4,000 people in this local area alone that need feeding, medical attention, shelter—"

"My people also need shelter and food." Russell waved his arm in a circle indicating the encampment they were in. "I have provided them with that without any government assistance or interference."

"What happens when food and supplies can no longer be scavenged?"

"Sergeant Major Saunders, isn't it?"

"Yes."

"I have my thoughts."

"Share them with us?" asked Alan.

"They're not fully formed yet, so there would be little point. Four thousand people, you say? You'll need a lot of supplies to feed that many people."

"You and your group are more than welcome to join us, Mr Russell."

"Providing we abide by your rules."

"Every society has rules, Mr Russell. It's how communities survive living together."

"But the price they have to pay for that food? Slogging their guts out clearing dead bodies from towns and digging up contaminated farmland?"

"Stocks of food will eventually run out. It has to be replaced. What alternative is there?" asked Alan. Feel the cold air about you. The predictions are that the drop in temperature will continue for some time to come. Families will need homes and shelter."

Russell scratched his beard again. Although listening to Alan's arguments, he was slowly becoming impatient. He had his own plans and didn't particularly want to share them with the army or any form of government for that matter. Further conversation for the moment was interrupted as Sian handed Russell, Scott and Alan a white bone china cup of Earl Grey tea.

Alan and Scott thanked her.

Alan took a sip. "Fresh milk?"

Russell hesitated. "We have a few cattle."

"Won't the milk be contaminated?"

"Sure it will. The grass available to the cattle is bound to be contaminated, and that will have been passed on to the milk."

"That doesn't worry you?"

"Of course. But we can't afford to waste anything, you know that, Major."

"I've not seen any cattle."

Russell's eyes blinked quickly, and his response was delayed momentarily. "They're further afield. I have a couple of people watching over them. Best they're kept away from the camp."

"So, how many additional people do you have?"

"Half a dozen."

"How many in your group in total?"

"You ask a lot of questions, Major Redfern."

"It's important that we know what's occurring in our region, Mr Russell, that's all. What are your short-term plans?"

"Let my people have a few days' rest, then move on."

"For the number of people I've seen in your camp so far, there's no evidence of a large stock of supplies."

Russell knew he was being backed into a corner. He didn't like it and and his patience was now wearing very thin. "We have adequate supplies, Major. Let me worry about providing for my people."

"I'd like to talk to your group."

"Talk to them?!" exclaimed Russell, standing up and knocking his chair back and over as he did so.

Alan noticed Dawson's hand slide towards the trigger guard of his assault rifle, but remained calm himself. He was pleased to see that Scott had made no sudden move either. *The poker game continues,* he thought.

Alan stayed seated. "They have a right to hear what their local government representative has to say and what the plans are being made to ensure their future survival, don't you think?"

"They don't need a bureaucracy to ensure their survival, Major. We're more than capable of taking care of ourselves. I think this meeting is over."

Alan stood up, Scott following his lead.

"I'll report back to my brigadier and the regional governor."

"And that means?"

"What happens next is down to the regional governor but, in the meantime, I would appreciate it if you and your group remained in the vicinity of your camp and leave all property and goods in the area alone."

"A mobile prison, then?"

"Not at all, Mr Russell. Providing you leave the region, you're free to leave at any time."

"And that area is?"

"Our region consists of Gloucestershire Wiltshire and part of Dorset and Hampshire."

"Nothing more to be said then, Major. Good day to you." With that, Russell turned on his heel and stormed back into his tent.

"Thank you for the tea," Alan called after him.

"If you gentlemen will come with me, I'll see you safely off the camp," offered Dawson.

"You're fine," Scott snapped back. "We know the way."

Scott hoisted the radio onto his shoulder, but kept the SA80 in his hand and headed for their Land Rover, Alan walking alongside him. Dawson followed them, about five metres back, uncertain what to do.

As they arrived at the Land Rover, the other guard watched them menacingly. The two soldiers climbed into the cab, and Scott started the engine. He reversed the vehicle down the track, backing into the treeline when he saw a gap, enabling him to turn the vehicle and face the direction of travel. Shortly, they pulled out onto the road, leaving the track behind.

Scott spoke. "Stinks."

Alan looked at him quizzically.

"He's up to no good."

Before Alan could comment, the radio crackled.

"*Two-Zero, this is Two-Zero-Delta. Over.*"

"Two-Zero. Go ahead. Over," Alan responded.

"*Motorcycle just left your previous location, headed into treeline. Over.*"

"Roger that. Any other activity? Over."

"*Negative.*"

"Understood. Returning to Zero-Charlie. Out."

"Off to warn their buddies?"

"Seems so. I'll let the RGC know. I don't like the look of this, Scott."

"Me neither."

Alan picked up the handset again. "Hello, Zero, this is Two-Zero. Over."

There was a ten-second delay before the brigadier responded.

"*Zero. Go ahead. Over.*"

"Not good, sir. Our suspicions are correct. Scavengers on a large scale. Additional Tangoes off-site. Threat imminent. Over."

"*What are your next steps, Alan?*"

"They're too big a force to take on in the open. Send recce out, confirm their strength, then deal with them."

"*Your plan? Over.*"

As Alan explained briefly what he had in mind, a smile formed across Scott's face.

"*I like it. Brief me on the details when you return to Zero-Charlie. Out.*"

"Shrewd bastard, sir."

"You can't mean me, Sar'nt Major."

"That's exactly who I mean."

CHAPTER 24

Tom and Andrew brought in the last of the wood from outside and added the logs to those piled up next to the burning fire. Maddie and Lucy were in the kitchen, preparing food for the evening meal on the Aga which Tom had managed to bring back to life. They couldn't believe their luck. After leaving the soldiers in the early hours of the morning, they had weaved their way further south, crossing the vehicle-encumbered M5, bypassing Bridgwater and Taunton until they arrived on the outskirts of Exmoor National Park. Two days had been spent scouting the area, looking for somewhere to settle in the short-term, but hopefully somewhere that would serve their needs for the longer term. Tom had taken them deeper and deeper into the park, eventually coming across an abandoned farm between Culverwell Wood to the north-west and Langridge Wood to the south. It seemed ideal, and the families were surprised that it had been abandoned – that is, until they found the two bodies in the main bedroom. The couple, lying side by side, had probably made a pact to die together rather than face the future that lay ahead of them. Two empty pill bottles were testament to their choice of suicide.

The two men acted quickly, removing the part decomposed bodies and burying them at the back of the farm. The smell was foul and permeated throughout the farmhouse but, removing all the remains and contaminated bedding, and using a liberal amount of disinfectant to wash everything down, it soon cleared. A few windows were broken, but nothing major, and the roof was intact. The ground was still covered with the customary layer of ash and dust. Strikes would have hit Bristol to the north-east, Cardiff on the other side of the Bristol Channel, Exeter, and, of course, Dartmouth and Plymouth. The Washford River ran close by, so water wouldn't be a problem. Tom's only concern was that they were close to a road, albeit a very minor one.

This was their third day here now, and various foods had been discovered, including potatoes, which they put to good use by eating, or storing away for the future. They had all agreed the next steps: to search the area for other signs of life, not necessarily to make contact, but just to know who was about; to find out if any neighbours were a threat; and also to scavenge for anything they could put to use. A diesel tank, well hidden, had also been found on the farm with just under 3,000 litres left in it.

Lucy called them around the large kitchen table where, assisted by Maddie, she served up hot braised steak, from tins, along with mashed potato and a few shrivelled carrots. But, to the two families, it seemed like a feast. Tom looked at their faces. Andrew was tucking into his food, hungry like Tom, after spending most of the day chopping wood. The kids were over their ordeal and were chatting happily, Lucy taking them to task for eating their food too quickly. She seemed OK, but Maddie still appeared to be in a state of shock. She could never be left on her own and jumped at any sharp sound that caught her by surprise. However, Tom felt secure for the first time since they had left the farm and felt sure that Maddie would come through the ordeal eventually.

"Pass the spuds, Andy, before this lot eat them all," laughed Tom.

CHAPTER 25

PURGATORY | GROUND ZERO D +28 DAYS
NEAR STOKE COMMON

To say Keelan was pissed off was an understatement. He'd held a knife to Milo's throat just because the man had taken an extra share of food, and even Salt had been on the receiving end of the giant's wrath. They'd spent an uncomfortable night in an abandoned house near Stoke Common, where they had finished off the best part of their food and water. An attempt to light a fire had ended up with them being smoked out. The chimney, damaged from one of the blast waves, was blocked, and smoke had billowed back down and quickly filled the lounge with fumes. Resorting to using the damp bedding found in the upstairs of the windowless house, a further uncomfortable night had been spent. Waking up in the early hours shivering, they had agreed to make another early start.

The three men, still with their bicycles, rode through the centre of Stoke Poges, followed by Stoke Green and the eastern outskirts of Slough. Coming across an increasing number of people, around fifty in the area of Slough, all in a sorry state, both Salt and Milo became worried about their personal security. Keelan laughed it off, waving his shotgun and promising to deal with anyone that became a threat. Salt was not so much scared of a fight but more concerned with the competition for resources. At least one of the shops they had rifled turned up trumps however. Although it had been ransacked and half of the building had caved in, Milo's rat-like nose had sniffed out a full box of cans of lager, hidden beneath the rubble. It wasn't food, but it quenched their thirst and made the onward journey much more pleasurable.

Salt continued to encourage them to press on, conscious that they were dirty, Keelan still had a head wound, it was getting colder, and their food had all but run out. They crossed the M4, passing Windsor Castle. No flags were flying, and it certainly hadn't fared well from the nuclear missile that had targeted Heathrow Airport. Salt took them south-east down to Cobham, then east, following the A3 as far as Claygate. Although they'd discussed searching for a car amongst the thousands abandoned along the A3, enabling them to travel the rest of the journey in style, seeing a mobile police patrol changed their minds. At least with the bikes they could be more discreet, and Keelan was finally getting the hang of it and had stopped complaining.

The last nine kilometres were all through built-up areas, and Salt switched from elation at being closer to home ground to depression at the devastation that had been brought down on the city. Groups of survivors were picking their way through the rubble, gutted shops, blocks of flats that were partially standing and any house that looked like it might hold a secret supply of sustenance. All looked ragged, underfed and ill. As they approached Beddington, Salt took them north through Beddington Park, then east, bypassing the sewerage farm and heading to where a new Asda store had once existed. Unsurprisingly, the bulk of the store was badly damaged, but some sections were accessible. Each man took an aisle but found nothing. They all agreed, although pressure from Keelan overruled any objections, to spend the night in the supermarket and strike out for the centre of Croydon the next day. Then, Salt felt sure, they could get organised.

CHAPTER 26

PURGATORY | GROUND ZERO +28 DAYS
REGIONAL GOVERNMENT CENTRE, CHILMARK

SIERRA-ONE

Sergeant William Thompson shifted position as he scanned the rear of the main warehouse with his NVGs. It was clear and quiet, as was Murray Road below him. To his right, two of the soldiers in his section, Bennet and Marsh, the lower half of their bodies in sleeping bags, checked their weapons for the tenth time. Over to the left, Haynes, the third soldier in the section, covered their flank and rear. It was cold on top of the warehouse roof, and when Marsh took over in thirty minutes' time, he could shuffle deeper into his maggot and warm his ice-cold upper limbs. Bennet and Marsh were nervous, as was he. But, along with the rest of his section, and the entire unit for that matter, he had confidence in their OC and the CSM. It was a good plan, one that deserved to work. He just hoped the hostiles out there would take the bait.

Sergeant Thompson moved slightly deeper into his sleeping bag, feeling the cold creeping up his body. They were located on the other side of the road that ran alongside the main warehouse, sited opposite the open loading bay area at the rear. From this position, he and his men could cover a large access gate, originally for use by the emergency services should there be a fire or other emergency. With his and Marsh's SA80s and Bennet's LMG, any attackers would be cut down the minute they approached the building round by the loading bay and loading dock area. He checked his watch and gave Marsh a nudge. It was time for Marsh to call in and for the two soldiers to swap duties. Thirty minutes on stag, and sixty minutes zipped up in the sleeping bags.

"Charlie-One, this is Sierra-One. Radio check. Over."

"*Charlie-One. Five-five.*"

"Sierra-One. All quiet."

"*Roger. Out.*"

SIERRA-TWO

Lance Corporal Bryant cursed as a rivet dug into his knee, and he shuffled further across the fragile roof, ensuring he maintained a position above one of the spans that supported the roof. He leant against one of the roof skylights of the warehouse that was their location for the evening. This was the second night his section had been on top of the warehouse roof, this one situated opposite the entrance to the front gate of the main storage warehouse. Along with his gun group, who manned the general-purpose machine gun (GPMG) loaded and ready, and capable of firing over 600 rounds per minute, he had a perfect view of the main entrance to Warehouse they were tasked with protecting, where a single soldier, as planned, guarded the barrier and mesh gate that controlled access to the front of the main building. From this position, his small section of three men plus himself could also cover Murray Road that ran along side the warehouse as well as the junction with Dykes Way. He looked to his right as he heard one of his men change position. After two nights on top of the composite roof, their arm and leg muscles were starting to feel the strain, especially during daylight hours, what little there was of it, when keeping low and movement to a minimum was necessary.

"Charlie-One, this is Sierra-Two. Radio check. Over."

"*Charlie-One. Loud and clear. Over.*"

"Roger that. All quiet this sector. Your guardian angels are watching over you."

"*Focus on the task, Sierra-Two. Out.*"

SIERRA-THREE

Chris Burns unscrewed the cap off his thermos flask, pouring the contents into a mug until it was half full. Hot tea, with a dash of whisky, was what was needed to keep them both warm and awake. Chris took a sip, savouring its taste and warmth before passing it to his mucker, who shivered as his shoulders left the warmth of his sleeping bag.

"Fucking cold," Billy hissed.

"Yeah, good of the OC to let us have this prime position."

"What are we doing here? They ain't coming this way, surely?"

"OC's a smart cookie, Billy. Yeah, it's a gamble, but he's seen us right so far."

"Bloody civvies have got a cheek, wanting to nick our stuff."

"Just hungry, mate."

"Work for it like the rest of us do."

"Time to call in."

Chris eased himself forward slightly, his elbows on the cold ground, a twig from the hedge scraping against his helmet as he shifted his position in the observation post at the back of the warehouse until he could sit up. They were both well concealed, strips of scrim netting suspended from the shrubs, small trees and hedgerow ensuring their position was shielded from prying eyes. A person would have to get very close to their position before they spotted the two soldiers, who were also well camouflaged. Their biggest risk had been disturbing too much of the dust on both the ground and the hedgerow while setting up.

Before calling in, Chris checked the field and track, the track that could take a vehicle from the minor road to the east to the rear of the warehouse unseen.

"Charlie-One. This is Sierra-Three. Radio check. Over."

"*Charlie-One. Clear. All quiet your location? Over.*"

"All quiet my location. We still on? Over."

"*Patience. Out.*"

Chris picked up his binos again. He was on stag for another thirty minutes. Two hours on, two hours off during night-time hours, and four on, four off during daylight.

SIERRA-FOUR

Corporal West checked the clackers for the Claymore Mines for the umpteenth time, making sure all four were ready available. He looked across at Mark Grant as he adjusted his posture and changed the position of the butt of the light machine gun until it was more comfortable. This was the second night of waiting and muscles were now starting to protest. Paul would have a chat with them all later, and keep them alert. This was just the time when all hell could break loose, when they least expected an attack and were at their most tired and weakest. He peered over the gunner's shoulder. Both were hidden from the road by the two layers of scrim netting that were suspended from the top of the window frame in the wall of the building. There was no moon, as usual these days, and it was almost pitch-black outside. Paul checked the switches for the flares that lined each side of Dyke's Way. He hoped to God that if it was going to kick off, it would be soon. The waiting was starting to do his head in, and it was becoming difficult to maintain a cool composure in front of his men. But he would. If or when the shit hit the fan, their lives would depend on their response being deliberate and professional.

He heard the click of a Prestel as Lance Corporal Danny Carr whispered into the handset and called in a radio check.

"Charlie-One, this is Sierra-Four. Radio check. Over."

"*Charlie-One. Four-four.*"

"Roger. Out."

"OK?"

"Yes, Paul. Buggers aren't coming, are they?"

"There's still time, Danny." He looked at his watch: 0230. If they were coming, it had to be soon.

GOLF-ONE

Corporal Butler lifted himself up and out of the turret of the Scimitar, the scrim net catching on his helmet. He cursed inwardly, his limbs aching like they hadn't for a long, long time. His vehicle, Golf-One, along with Golf-Two, the Fox, had been hidden in a small copse that bordered the large roundabout that led into Dyke's Way, the direction of the warehouse a few hundred metres away. In the building opposite, he knew Sierra-Four were in position. The two Golf call signs were dependent on Sierra-Four fulfilling their mission if the armoured unit was to succeed with theirs. Sierra-Four's Claymores and firepower were needed to stop the enemy in its tracks if they chose to approach the warehouse along Dykes Way.

CHARLIE-ONE

Major Alan Redfern paced up and down the ops room, previously a civilian conference room, before 'the death', on the upper floor of the warehouse, the windows looking out to the north and east. 'The death' was becoming a common way of referring to the event that had put life in the precarious position it now found itself in. Only time would tell if they would come out the other side.

"QRF ready?" he asked the CSM.

"Yes, the reaction force is ready. Chill, boss, that's the fourth time you've asked me in the last thirty minutes. There's nothing else we can do now but wait."

"Easier said than done."

"Having doubts?"

Alan thought for a moment before shaking his head. "No. What options do they have? Move on? We know they're still here. Stay where they are, knowing we'll eventually be forced to act? Or go for the main prize: fill their boots, then get out of the area while it's in chaos?"

"Big risk they'll be taking."

"They'll come. Russell will come. His ego is big enough to take that chance."

"Brew, sir?" Kothari offered his OC a mug of coffee.

"Thank you, Kothari. God knows what we'll do when this stuff runs out." Alan lifted his mug in the air.

"I'll make sure we get dibs on the last of the supplies, don't you worry about that, sir," laughed Scott.

Shielding his red filtered torch, Alan peered at the map on the conference table for the umpteenth time that night. He knew he was taking a gamble, and it worried him. Once he had briefed the brigadier and principal officer on the status of the group to the north and his men's observation of the group's activity so far, he felt certain the Intruders would take a stab at stealing some of the RGC's stocks of food. One thing was for sure: they didn't appear to be making plans to move on. In fact, they had been sending out foraging parties north of Wincanton and the surrounding area. It could only be a matter of time before there was a clash. Alan had ordered all his units to continue with low-profile patrols, but under no circumstances were they to come into contact with the potentially hostile group. One of Alan's observation posts had spotted three individuals, with binoculars, watching the warehouse entrance. He had forbidden the unit from interfering as a plan was already forming in his mind.

The brigadier, supported by the PO, wanted Alan to take a much larger force and order the group to either surrender their weapons and come under the control of the RGC or to disperse and leave the area. Alan stood his ground, adamant that there was a real risk that his unit could end up being ambushed and potentially wiped out, requiring the QRF to go in and support them, putting them at risk. Russell didn't come across as a stupid man. Although Alan had a total force of at least twenty-plus, and the intruders had, as far as he knew, in the region of thirty-plus, he felt that the risk was too great to take them head on.

Eventually, both the brigadier and the PO relented when he briefed them on his proposal. Rather than go to the enemy, his plan was to encourage them, through lack of activity on his and his men's part, to come to them, believing that the RGC force was impotent and much weaker than Alan had portrayed at their initial meeting.

Well, thought Alan as he studied the map, this was the second night, and he felt embarrassment was going to be his companion if the enemy didn't turn up. All the roads had been blocked off, so the only route vehicles could take was straight down Dyke's Way. He guessed that they would want the warehouse, with all the supplies they required in one easy hit.

He picked up the radio again, knowing that he was letting his troops know that he was frustrated. *Not good, but what the hell*, he thought.

"All call signs. Only respond if positive. Any signs of activity. Over."

Silence.

"Damn!" he uttered to no one in particular.

"If it's not tonight then it'll be tomorrow," encouraged the CSM.

"We can't keep sitting here like victims waiting. If it's not tonight, against my better judgement we have to take the fight to them." Alan slumped in a chair and picked up his mug. Realising it was empty, he slammed it back down onto the table causing Kothari to jump.

Suddenly, the radio crackled. *"Charlie-One. Golf-One. Two unidentified, blacked out vehicles just crossed Uniform, heading south along Bravo-three-zero-eight-one to Victor. Over."*

Alan's hand shot out for the radio, beating Scott to it. "Roger that. All call signs, we have movement. Standby."

"Golf-One. Packet crossed Victor, on route to Whiskey. Over."

Roger Golf-One. All call signs, packet moving towards Sierra-Three." He looked at the map. The vehicles had crossed the two roundabouts opposite Dykes Way and were now headed south along the A371 to the third one, close to where one of his OPs was watching the back door. "Sierra-Three. Target with you in approximately figures five. Acknowledge. Over."

"Sierra-Three. Roger that."

Alan saw the CSM's white teeth gleaming in the darkness and felt the excitement welling up inside as the adrenalin started pumping. Maybe he hadn't got it wrong after all. Russell's greed and ego were working for them. It seemed like ages, but was only a matter of minutes before the intruders were next sighted.

"Charlie-One, Sierra-Three. We have target in sight. Looks like five-up in first, four-up in second."

"Charlie-One. Roger. Keep me posted."

"One X-ray gone Foxtrot." Chris Burns's voice was barely audible. "Recceing on foot. Looks like they've taken the bait."

"Let's hope so, Sar'nt Major."

"They're opening the gate now. Over," whispered the OP commander dug into the hedgerow less than 300 metres from the rear of the warehouse.

"Roger."

"Through the gate. One Foxtrot leading. Vehicles, one Range Rover, one Wrangler Jeep following down track. Over."

"Roger. Sierra-One. Standby."

"Sierra-One. Roger."

SIERRA-ONE

Sergeant Thompson stirred his men quietly, and the section prepared themselves to go into action. He checked the magazine on his SA80 was secure and that his assault rifle was loaded and ready. Bennet pulled the stock of his LMG into his shoulder with Laura Marsh alongside him acting as his security. She was a good shot and he was pleased it was she alongside of him. Off to the left, Haynes slid out of his sleeping bag and crawled across the roof, keeping low. His task was to make sure that, while the rest of the section went into action, they weren't taken by surprise with an attack from behind. Sierra-One was ready.

CHARLIE-ONE

"Sierra-Three. Targets now stationary. All decamped. Fifty metres south of Sierra-One."

"Charlie-One, Roger. Sierra-One standby, standby. X-rays approaching your location."

"Sierra-One, Roger."

"Charlie-One, Golf-One. Unknown number unidentified vehicles crossing Uniform and Victor.

"Occupants? Over."

"Wait. Over."

"Roger."

"Golf-One. Can't tell at the moment. Wait. Pulled up on Dykes Way. Possibly five, minimum four. Over."

Alan looked at his watch: 0320. The black chess pieces were on the move. He just hoped that his white pieces were in the right place to counter them. He gripped the handset.

"Golf-One, Golf-One. Charlie-One. Stay in situ."

"*Roger.*"

"All call signs, this is Charlie-One. Estimate kick-off at 0330. Standby, standby."

"Waiting for their buddies to get ready at the back of the warehouse."

"Seems so. Have the QRF mount up," he ordered Scott.

The CSM quickly contacted the quick reaction force, and they confirmed they were ready.

"I'm joining the QRF," Alan informed the CSM, "so I'll leave you to oversee the ops room."

"Keep your head down. I reckon these could be tricky buggers," responded Scott.

Alan picked up his SA80, checked his magazine was secure, patted his other ammo pouches, and made his way out and down to the main body of the warehouse. He made his way through the lines of racking and jumped into one of the two Land Rovers. He slid into the passenger seat next to Baxter. Ellis was in the back. The second Land Rover contained Lance Corporal Cole, along with Sutton and Lane.

"Anything?"

"Nothing new, sir," answered Baxter.

"All call signs, this is Charlie-One. Mobile with Quebec, Romeo, Foxtrot. Out."

"*Charlie-One, Sierra-One. Movement west of my location. At least three X-rays are watching the back door. Over,*" whispered Sergeant Thompson from the top of the warehouse roof opposite.

Alan responded, talking quietly. "Understood. Hold your fire. Out."

"*Charlie-One, Golf-One. Vehicles on the move. Now see figures six. Moving slowly, coming on to Dyke's Way. Standby for count of occupants. Over.*"

"Charlie-One. Go ahead."

"*Victor-One, four up...Victor-Two, five up, Victor-Three, three up. Last three Victors, four up in each.*"

"Sierra-Four. Talk to me. Over."

"*Sierra-Four, nothing yet. Over.*"

"Shall I start the engine?" asked Baxter.

"Not yet," responded his OC. "We don't want to spook those outside just yet."

"*Sierra-Four. Lead vehicle just coming into view. Orders. Over.*"

"Wait. Out to you. Hello, Sierra-Two. Sitrep. Over."

"Front gate clear, no sign of lead vehicle yet. Over."

"Understood. Sierra-Four. Act on triggers. Out. Sierra-One. Sitrep. Over."

"Can see nine Tangoes now. South of warehouse. Not crossed the line yet. They're clearly waiting for something. Over."

"Roger. The minute you hear gunfire, they're likely to move. Once in the open, light them up and open fire. Acknowledge."

"On sound of gunfire, light up area and make contact."

"Good luck. Out."

Alan looked at Baxter. All they could do now was wait.

They wouldn't have to wait for long.

"Sierra-Four. Lead vehicle crossed Trigger-One."

"Roger. All call signs. Standby...standby."

Nothing more would be said now. They say that once the first shot is fired, the planning is over and it is in the lap of the gods, along with the training kicking in and a steady hand.

SIERRA-FOUR

Corporal West watched the first vehicle, a Mitsubishi 4x4 with four people inside. All the windows were down, and the shimmering green figures inside, seen through his NVG goggles, had weapons held at port-arms, ready to leap out and complete whatever task they had set themselves. The Mitsubishi crawled along Dyke's Way and was closely followed by a second, this one an old Volvo. This too had its windows down and was also making its way down Dyke's Way carefully.

"Get ready," West hissed to his men. "Lead vehicle approaching Trigger-Two. Sierra-Two, this is Sierra-Four. Do you have visual? Over."

"Sierra-Two. Roger. Just coming into view."

"All call signs, this is Sierra-Four. Trigger-Two, Trigger-Two. Out."

The entire company now knew that the lead vehicle had passed Sierra-Four and was in sight of Sierra-Two, close to the warehouse entrance. The convoy snaked down Dyke Way, the NCO counting the vehicles as they passed until the last one, a Toyota, was directly opposite.

"Steady, steady, steady. Now!" yelled Corporal West.

He smacked at the clackers, one after the other, and Mark Grant triggered the line of flares set up along the road. The 700 steel balls from each of the Claymore mines bracketed the last four vehicles in the convoy. Some were deflected by the vehicle chassis or engines; others flew over the roofs or passed through the gaps in between each car. But hundreds found their mark.

Those furthest away from the swathe of steel balls clambered out of their seats, throwing themselves to the ground, blinded and silhouetted by the flares that lined that side of the road. They left half a dozen of their comrades behind, either dead or wounded. Those that had received some military training immediately positioned themselves behind some form of protection, preferably using the engine block as a barrier against the incoming fire, West's men having now opened up from inside the warehouse as well as from the roof. Those less experienced simply hugged the ground, hoping that the incoming fire would cease and they could get in a better position to return fire.

The flares continued to burn, lighting up the column of vehicles. Kirby stepped out from where Golf-One and Two were hidden, onto the road and, as planned, levelled an anti-tank missile at the rearmost vehicle. Locking on, the operator triggered the launch, and the missile, once leaving the launch tube, rocketed towards its mark. Missing its intended target, the rearmost car, it shot by, streaking past the face of one of the intruders kneeling behind the rear wheel, about to take a pot shot at the soldiers across the road. Without connecting with the man's head, the sheer heat and velocity of the passing missile literally peeled back the man's face from his left ear to his right, taking his lower jaw with it, leaving behind his upper molars and a gaping mass of destroyed tissue. Thrown sideways, the man struck the tarmac road, unconscious, oblivious to the pain and his imminent death. Cursing, the soldier who had missed the target allocated to him ran across to the far side of the road as he heard the roar of the Scimitar tank, Golf-One pulling alongside him.

Thump, thump, thump, thump, thump. Five 30mm rounds fired from the Scimitar's RARDEN cannon struck the immobilised convoy, shattering windscreens, tearing into metal, ripping apart the vehicle bodies that had been providing the attackers with some form of cover. Five more rounds smashed into the wreckage, devastation becoming more and more apparent. Powell raised a second Javelin anti-tank weapon, and another missile flew towards its target, hitting the side of the lead vehicle which erupted in a ball of flame, torn apart, flipping up and over, and landing on its roof some twenty metres from its original position. The second vehicle in the line was forced over onto its side. A woman and a man, previously given some protection behind the vehicles that had just been wiped out, were now partially exposed to the fire coming from the soldiers in warehouse. Both shocked by the violence of the explosion, panicked and ran from the Volvo, darting for the buildings behind them, seeking safety amongst the walls.

Perched on top of the warehouse, the gunner, one of the men in Sierra-Four, opened fire on the two fleeing attackers, sparks flying around their feet as high-velocity rounds tore into the road. Using tracer rounds to guide him onto his target, a five-round burst soon struck the two fleeing enemy. The woman took a 7.62mm round in her lower back, shattering her spine, and a second in her left shoulder, spinning her around and forcing her sprawling body to the ground where her wide eyes flickered left and right as she struggled to move her paralysed body. Her comrade, who was in fact her beau, was equally unfortunate. The single round that punched through the back of his neck, taking the majority of the man's oesophagus with it, left him gagging and gasping for breath, bubbles of pink froth exuding from the mangled mess that was once his neck. He dropped to his knees, clutching his bloodied throat with both hands, his face alive with panic as he sucked phlegm, gore and spittle into his lungs. A second bullet hit him in the back, throwing him to the ground, his heart ruptured and silent, his life extinguished seconds later.

The flares died down, the area suddenly in darkness, silence, a break in the firing, only broken by the groans of the wounded. Sergeant Dunn fired two flares, lighting up the area again as the Scimitar, now with the Fox covering its back, moved further down the line of vehicles, its turret swung over to the right. Two soldiers walked behind the rear of the reconnaissance tank, protecting it and its crew from any attack. Corporal West, accompanied by Mark Grant, left the warehouse they were in, to provide additional cover. They now needed to finish the enemy off, or to at least flush them out and clear them from the local area. In the middle of the convoy, the survivors of the Claymore mines, after throwing themselves out of the peppered vehicles, moved west, congregating at the front of the convoy as the tank ground towards them, 30mm shells whittling away their protective cover. Sierra-Two, taking advantage of the confusion, fired round after round into the cowering cluster of attackers, bullets tearing through flesh and bone, the massed bodies proving to be a perfect target. Out of the seven, two, one clutching a shattered arm, managed to drag themselves into cover off the road. Lance Corporal Bryant ordered a ceasefire, coinciding with the Scimitar also ceasing its pummelling of the convoy. There was near silence again; just a steady drone from his ears, the after effects of the heavy gunfire, the distant sound of a fire fight at the back of the warehouse and the groans and cries from the wounded. Apart from Grant, who had a gash in his leg from a ricocheting splinter, the soldiers of Sierra-Two and Four along with Golf-One and Two were unharmed.

SIERRA-ONE

Whoosh…whoosh. Two ground-based flares lit up the area, followed by the louder thumps of four Claymore mines that swept the concrete apron, normally used by HGVs and other vehicles to deposit or collect goods from the rear of the warehouse, with a lethal hail of hundreds of steel balls. Five of the intruders crumpled as the balls peppered their fragile bodies, causing horrific wounds to their faces and bodies. The nine men who had been waiting for the cacophony of sound to come from the front of the warehouse, indicative of the main attack being launched, had run across the open ground, mistakenly secure in the knowledge that all focus would be at the front gate of the warehouse.

Haynes, his L115A3 sniper rifle tucked in close to his body, his cheek snug against the butt, had already zoned in with his telescopic sight, and he now breathed out, holding his breath halfway, and squeezed the trigger. Almost instantaneously, the figure in the scope's lens jerked as the 8.59mm slug knocked him sideways. The scope moved. Haynes was already changing targets. The four still alive, one dragging a shredded leg behind him, were soon picked off. Haynes accounted for another one, the LMG and Sergeant Thompson the rest. It hadn't been a fair fight. Marsh, crouching next to Bennet, spotting for him on the LMG, cried out as a heavy round from a hunting rifle, fired by one of the wounded lying on the concrete apron, smacked into her chest. As she was thrown backward, she immediately began struggling to breathe, pink froth forming around her mouth, the wound to her ribcage preventing her lungs from expanding.

"Man down! Man down!" yelled Bennet.

"Bennet, Haynes, watch our front." Thompson ran at a crouch across the roof towards Marsh while the other two provided cover.

Zip. A bullet whipped past his head, Haynes's response audible as the bullet from his sniper rifle took the man down.

Thompson threw himself down alongside the gasping soldier. He acted quickly, pulling out a knife to cut away at Marsh's uniform. He sawed at the soldier's clothing, four layers making it difficult to get to the wound. Eventually the small hole was exposed, a small pool of blood welling up, the sound of the sucking wound as Marsh fought for breath.

"Hang in there, Laura, hang in there. I'll get you fixed up." Thompson pulled out the dressing he knew was needed if he was to keep his soldier alive: a triple-layered bandage, a square of plastic sandwiched between the two gauze layers, was pressed onto the wound, immediately creating a seal. Howard drew in a deep breath, taking in badly needed oxygen. Now Thompson needed to bind it tightly, sealing the gap, allowing Howard's lungs to fill out and function as best they could even with a hole in one of them. Thompson sighed with relief. If he could get her to the RGC, there was a very good chance she would come through this.

A soldier pulled on the rattling chain faster and faster as the loading bay roller shutter door clattered upwards and open. Then he guarded the back door as the two Land Rovers sped out. The lead one weaved around the bodies on the apron, turned left, and continued down the road that ran alongside the warehouse, and towards the main entrance. The second swung right, came to a halt, and the soldiers decamped and searched and disarmed the dead and wounded.

CHARLIE-ONE

Alan, in the lead Land Rover, communicated with his unit. "All call signs, QRF mobile. Sitrep. Over."

"*Sierra-One. Area appears secure. Can see QRF call sign down on the apron. Man down. Over.*"

"Roger that. Who and how bad? Over."

"*Marsh sir. She's stable, but need RGC soonest.*"

"Soon as site secure, we'll collect. Out."

"*Sierra-Two. On ground. One man topside providing cover. Checking enemy casualties. Probably two or three fled north-west. Over.*"

"Roger. Hold your position, Do not pursue, I repeat, do not pursue."

"*Understood. Out.*"

"*Sierra-Three. All quiet our location. Orders. Over.*"

"Remain in situ. Corporal West will collect when area secure. Out."

"*Sierra-Four. With Golf-One and Two. Sweeping west. Disarming wounded. We agree with Sierra-Two's estimate of two to three hostiles fled north-west.*"

"Continue sweep. Leave Golf call signs to secure area. Link up with Sierra-One and continue sweep. But do not pursue."

"*Will do. Out.*"

The CSM reported in from Ops. "*Two-Zero-Alpha. Charlie secure. They got more than they bargained for.*"

"Definitely. Could still be hostiles in area so keep the lads on the alert. Handing command of area over to you. We'll pick up Marsh. Then move to RGC."

"*Roger. Keep you posted. Out to you. All call signs, this is Two-Zero-Alpha. I have control. Out.*"

Alan ordered the driver to turn back, acknowledging Corporal Bryant with a wave. He turned to Baxter, his driver. "Let's go and pick up Marsh and get her some medical attention."

"We done good, eh, sir?"

"Yes, Baxter, we done good. A lot of wasted lives, though."

CHAPTER 27

PURGATORY | GROUND ZERO +28 DAYS
NLA OFFICE BLOCK, CROYDON

They lay their bicycles on the ground amongst the blackened trees just off what used to be Dinghall Avenue. They spread canvas sheets over the frames, hoping to keep them hidden from any scavengers that could be in the area, or, worst case, from one of the roaming gangs that recently had attempted to assert control on the entire remains of the London Borough of Croydon. Losing the bikes would be a problem, but the biggest risk was the finders knowing that half a dozen scavengers were on their patch. But Bill had no choice. The scavenging patrols had to push further afield if his own community were to survive. His roaming teams were already bringing in bags of earth, along with sacks of fertiliser, to spread over the roof in an attempt to grow additional food for the occupants beneath it. At this very moment, one team was out looking for packets of seeds; carrots, peas, parsnips and tomatoes. The penultimate floor had also been cleared and put aside to function as a garden nursery. Bill remembered chuckling to himself at the time, never thinking he would be responsible for opening up a garden nursery. He looked about him, seeing that the other five had finished their tasks, and the bikes no longer stood out as tempting targets for anyone who was passing by.

It was a grey morning, but then it was only four thirty, and generally all mornings were grey these days. Even by mid-morning, there would be little improvement. Bill tightened the scarf around his face and mouth, and cast an eye in the direction of the route they would be taking. He signalled his team to follow, and led them towards what used to be Meridian House, now windowless, with half of its roof missing. He led them up the steps of the main entrance, his shotgun following the direction of his eye line. Jake followed him, a crowbar in his right hand, then Curtis, Vincent and Aleck each carrying a slender but hard oak table leg that could be used as a club. Following up at the rear was Terry, with the second of the shotguns the group had as their main weapons.

Getting in was easy: the doors and window frames were either blown or burnt out, allowing easy access. Once inside, Bill waited a couple of minutes to allow his eyes to adjust to the darker interior. "Tread carefully through here. There's lots of rubble underfoot. We can't afford to have any one injured, so take it easy."

Satisfied they had all heard, Bill picked his way across the ground floor of the building. Leaving the reception area, the group arrived in the main ground floor offices. Pieces of burnt-out office furniture were scattered across the floor; globules of melted plastic, from personal computers and other office equipment, were splattered across the ash-covered floor that was once an opulent carpet. In the corner of the room, rats were scurrying around what appeared to be a burnt, blackened corpse, the white bone showing where they had stripped the putrid flesh.

The men crossed to the other side safely, exiting out of a door less fire exit, bringing them back out into the grey light of dawn, directly in front of the southern edge of the Whitgift Shopping Centre. Bill led them down a narrow passageway, the rear walls of numerous damaged shops either side. There was a significant amount of wreckage in between the battered buildings, and at one point, the group had to physically climb over a large corner section of wall that had collapsed across the path they needed to take, helping each other to cross. Bill didn't mind though. If it was difficult for them, it would deter others from using this route. The course curved around to the right, eventually bringing them out onto North End Mall. Now they were moving into dangerous territory, as no doubt other scavengers could also be picking through the remains of what was once a major shopping precinct.

"We listen for a few minutes, so keep it quiet," instructed Bill.

They nodded their understanding.

Opposite left was the burnt-out Debenhams store and even further left Primark. To the right: a branch of the Britannia Building Society, a Pizza Hut and other small but now useless shops.

Bill planned on taking the group left, down the centre of the plaza, and keeping left, moving amongst the burnt trunks of what were once green and healthy trees that lined the mall. "Keep in amongst the trees, guys, and keep it quiet. We're in bandit country now."

To a man, they gripped their shotguns and makeshift weapons tightly, now very alert, knowing that their lives were at stake here. Bill took point again, leading them amongst the trees, which although blackened and without foliage, provided them with some cover. The alternative was to stick close to the shop fronts, but the plaza was littered with broken glass that would, if stood on, crackle loudly, advertising both their presence and location. They trudged through a layer of ash, the damp of the early morning keeping the dust down. As they came to the end of the line of trees, Bill found the shop he was looking for: an optician's. An abandoned car outside was pressed up against the shop front.

"Curtis, Vincent and Terry, you three keep watch out here. The rest of us will take a look inside."

"What do you want us to go for?" asked Jake.

"Any complete specs, or even just frames. And any lenses, but they have to have been made up. It's no good us going for any of their fresh stock. We could never cut or grind them down to size or shape. Right, let's go."

Bill led the way again, passing the front desk, flicking on a torch as they moved deeper into the darker interior. They stepped carefully, the crackle of broken glass and debris setting their nerves on edge. The three men searched the shop from top to bottom, even the offices in the back. The second floor didn't exist, having collapsed inside as a consequence of the fire, making it difficult for them to move around. They rifled through the remnants of the shattered and burnt display cases, their initial bout of ferreting disappointing. After about thirty minutes, Bill called a halt. Although not as successful as he had hoped, they had found six pairs of glasses still in their toughened cases, prescriptions waiting for customers who were never able to collect them. The cases were brittle, but the spectacles inside seemed intact. Dependent on the prescription, who would benefit from them would only be known on their return to their home, their Tower Block, the Threepenny-Bit.

"Not too bad, eh, lads? Next port of call, yeah?"

"The Pony and Trap next?" asked Jake as he stored the spectacle cases in the rucksack on his back.

"Yes, I don't think all of the pubs will have been picked bone clean yet, but it's only a matter of time. Let's just hope whoever paid it a visit missed something. Come on."

They headed back outside, picked up their three companions, and continued south, crossing over to where another line of bared tree trunks would provide them with some cover. The line of trees eventually ran out, and the group were forced to move in closer to the walls as they passed Primark, disturbing a pack of dogs rooting around a half-dozen bodies interspersed amongst the remains. The dogs ran off at the sight of Bill and his men. Bill didn't bother with the burnt-out clothes store, fairly certain that the fire would have destroyed most of the garments and anything left would have been picked up by numerous survivors. At the end of the street, a wide crossroads, the junction of Church Street, High Street and North End Mall, was silent and unoccupied.

He called the group to him. "Me and Jake will cross first, check out the other side of the road, and if it's clear, we'll wave you over. Understood?"

They all acknowledged the order.

"Stay back in a shop doorway and keep your bloody eyes peeled."

Bill and Jake crossed over. Finding the other side clear, they quickly gave the rest of the group the all-clear, and they crossed the road to join them.

Bang!

"Move it, move it," yelled Bill to the rest of the group as they ambled across the road in a staggered line.

Bang...bang.

"Come on," he screamed at them this time, pulling them into cover, shoving them roughly into doorways. "Get down!"

"Was that gunfire?" Vincent asked nervously.

Before Bill could respond, a van careered around the corner from Frith Road, racing down Church Street. A jet of black smoke ejected from the exhaust as it backfired again. It sped past them. The driver and front passenger, wearing what looked like paint spray masks, were focused on the road ahead, clearly off somewhere in a hurry. A red flame shot out from the pipe again, surrounded by a black cloud of smoke as the engine struggled to cope with the dirty fuel being used, the last supplies the scavengers had dug up from an underground diesel tank at a petrol station on the outskirts of the city.

"Christ, that made me jump."

"Me too," responded Bill to Terry, the second man carrying a shotgun. "We need to be bloody careful. Let's get the hell out of here. Come on, you lot, we need to get this done quickly."

Leaving the shop doorways, they quickly found their way through the gaps in the buildings, across Surrey Street, the home of the Saturday market but now an ash-covered street lined with burnt-out buildings. Again, Bill thanked their lucky stars that the railway line to the west of his tower block had acted as a firebreak, and the fires had burnt themselves out to the east, the Threepenny-Bit surviving almost intact apart from blast damage to most of the windows.

The six men scoured the Pony and Trap from top to bottom, finding four large catering packs of beans tucked away in the corner of the collapsed beer cellar. Although the pub had been practically stripped bare, the main target had been alcohol. And, of that, there wasn't a drop to be found. Bill slumped on a chair. Although blackened, there was still enough integrity in the wood to hold his weight. He cursed. They needed to find some more alcohol soon. Not just for recreational reasons, but also for use as a sedative should someone urgently need dental treatment or to be treated medically. It was about the nearest they were going to get to having an anaesthetic. Once their foraging was completed, the four large tins of beans were allocated to individuals to be carried, and they pressed on with their search of the precinct. An optician's around the corner yielded two bent frames, but no lenses. They crossed Church Street again, passing the gutted Holiday Inn Express, and Bill led them down Frith Road, the direction the van had come from, so he warned everyone to be on the alert. They soon came across the iconic House of Fraser building, the high-value products it used to sell now nothing more that melted metal and plastic, its ornate windows blasted out, and the roof collapsed inwards, crashing through all five floors. They passed an Argos store, completely destroyed, and a local supermarket, burnt out but probably stripped of food before even the bombs struck. But Bill did stop when they came across a chemist shop.

"Won't get anything from here, Bill," offered Jake. "Well and truly gutted, there'll be nothing in there."

Bill was not so sure, and issued instructions for three, including Terry with the shotgun, to remain outside on guard while he and the remaining two, Vincent and Curtis, scouted around inside. Jake was right: the place was a mess. The fire had done significant damage. Part of the back wall and the rear of the roof had collapsed, and all the shelving, cabinets and serving counters were smashed or covered in a grey mash of debris and ash.

"Be careful, but check any gaps beneath where stuff may be hidden," instructed Bill.

Their perseverance paid off, Curtis finding a bulk packet of paracetamol, a major find. His face beamed from Bill's praise. They gathered outside, ready to push on with their search when the sound of a vehicle drew their attention.

The white van flew around the corner, this time no warning from a backfiring engine. It screeched to a halt directly in front of the group, the back doors swung open, and three men exited. The driver and passenger also clambered out. The driver swung his shotgun towards Bill who was much faster and responded with a blast from a single barrel of his side by side shotgun straight into the man's chest. A pistol cracked, and Curtis clutched his chest, a red bloom already forming on his clothing. Before the pistol bearer could line up on someone else, Jake's crowbar connected with the man's skull, the crack almost as audible as the second pistol shot from the passenger of the van who, panicking, missed, but felt the full force of Bill's second shotgun barrel. The man was flung back into the middle of the street. As Bill charged around the front of the van, then down the other side, he heard a single gunshot and hoped to God it was Terry firing, and not one of his own lads going down. Once at the rear of the van, he quickly assessed the situation. He saw Jake, the crowbar dropping from his hand as a knife dug deep into his gut. But Jake's attacker now had a bloodied back from the spread of shot pellets fired from Terry's single-barrelled Remington. The one assailant left ran at Bill, whose shotgun was now empty. Bill brought the butt of his shotgun round and down on the side of the man's head. A wet thump was heard as the butt connected, the man dropping to the ground, unconscious, possibly dead.

Bill looked about him, breaking open the shotgun; the used shells ejected, and frantically reloaded his shotgun not taking his eyes off the immediate vicinity.

"Grab their bloody weapons," he yelled to his stunned group as he ran over to Jake, who was on lying on the road, groaning as he clutched his stomach. Having seen the long-bladed knife, Bill didn't hold out much chance of Jake surviving. They had some medical supplies back at the tower and two highly qualified nurses, but getting him back there would be another matter. His ears pricked up as he heard an explosion off in the distance, coming from the east, followed by the sounds of gunfire.

"What the hell is that?" called Terry.

"Buggered if I know, but I don't like the sound of it. Vincent, Aleck, get Jake in the back of the van now. Have you got their weapons?"

"Yes," responded Aleck. "I've searched them for ammo as well. A nice little haul."

"Great job, Aleck, but we need to get a move on before any of their friends decide to turn up. How's Curtis?"

"He's a goner, Bill," called Terry.

"Grab his stuff and get it into the van."

"We leaving him?"

"Yes, but we'll come back if we get the chance."

Bill went over to the one of the survivors who had attacked them. He was sitting up with his head resting between his hands.

"Why?" Bill asked him.

The man looked up, blood running down his face from the deep wound where the butt of Bill's shotgun had connected with his head. "This is…our patch."

"So you decided to kill us, is that it?"

The man lowered his eyes, and Bill struck again with the butt of the shotgun, this time on top of the attacker's head, jarring Bill's powerful arms such was the force of the blow that split the man's skull. "Let's get the fuck out of here."

"But what about Curtis?"

"Leave him, Terry. We can't take him back, can we? Think about it. Get in."

They piled into the van, Vincent and Aleck in the back with Jake, his midriff now soaked in blood. Aleck, using scarves, stuffed as much material as possible over the wound in an attempt to staunch the flow of blood. They were losing the battle: the knife had been thrust deep into Jake's stomach, the blade tearing an even bigger hole as the assailant had collapsed from the blast of pellets that struck him from behind, dragging the knife down, tearing more flesh. The van jerked and Jake groaned.

In the driving seat, Bill ground the gears, quickly double-clutching in order to get the van moving. The vehicle kangarooed slightly until the labouring engine found the revs to power the wreck forward.

"Keep a watch," he warned Terry in the passenger seat.

"Do you think there'll be more?"

"Who knows?"

Bill wound down the window as he accelerated along Frith Road, the van leaning over dangerously as he swerved left down Church Street, a black cloud of smoke ejected from the exhaust as it backfired, the engine straining as Bill took the vehicle up and down the gears. Above the noise of the engine, both heard two more shots to the east, in their direction of travel, possibly coming from the location of the tower. The engine screamed as the van powered down Church Street, Bill's eyes flicking left and right, conscious that something was amiss. The scavengers, or one of the gangs, were likely on the prowl. The gears grated again as he changed down, swinging the van left onto the wide four-lane Wellesley Road and left again, skidding to a halt in Dinwall Avenue.

"Why are we stopping?"

"The bikes, we need the bloody bikes."

Bill was out in a second, leaving the engine running. He pulled both back doors open and yelled at the men inside. "Get the bikes in."

"There won't be enough room," responded Vincent.

"Fucking make room. Come on, move, now."

Vincent and Aleck jumped down from the back and, along with Bill, collected the six bikes from their hiding place while Terry watched over them. Bill knelt on the back step of the van. "How you doing, buddy?"

Jake's eyes flickered, the whites showing for a moment. "Feel like shit, Bill. Get me back, yeah?"

"Don't worry, we're minutes away now."

A clatter of bikes interrupted the conversation, and Jake was pushed over to the side to make way for the bikes that were to be stowed in the back, the last one lying flat on top of the five others. It was crammed in the back, one of the bikes lying across Jake at an angle.

"We can't shut the left-hand door, Bill," exclaimed Vincent.

"Don't worry about it, just hang on to the bloody thing. Get your weapons ready. Something stinks."

Bill returned to the driver's seat, aware that the engine was barely ticking over. He revved it before it completely gave up the ghost, coaxing it back to life.

"Load this." Bill handed Terry a pistol. "Do you know how to use it?"

"I think so."

"Give it here."

Terry handed Bill the pistol, the one he had taken off one of the attackers, and Bill took off the magazine, and tested the spring. Three or four rounds, he estimated. He pulled back the working parts, ejecting a live round. He clipped the bullet into the magazine, reattached it to the pistol, and cocked the weapon again; ensuring one was now up the spout. He ensured the safety was off.

"You've got about five rounds and the safety's off, so watch where you bloody well point it. Just aim and shoot at anyone that gets in our way."

Bill slammed his door shut, put the van into reverse gear, left hand down and completed a one-eighty turn, back out onto Wellesley Road, straight across all lanes and the tramlines, and headed down George Street, past the burnt-out McDonald's and Waitrose on the left. They crossed the bridge over the railway line, Croydon's railway station down below on the left, the barrier that had prevented the firestorm on the western side from reaching the tower block.

Bill could see their home now. A flood of relief washed over him and a hint of sadness that the battered tower in the distance was in fact now his home. "Standby, Terry."

His spirits lifted when he saw two sentries outside the front door of the tower, only to drop when he realised that neither of them were from his group. The nearest man, holding up what looked like an SA80, held up his hand in acknowledgement of the van, believing it to be reinforcements. Although the fight was going well, and they were already on the fourth floor, they had taken some casualties. The shock on the man's face was palpable as he realised that it wasn't Frank and Joseph in the front of the van. Shock and fear gripped him, rooting his feet to the ground as it suddenly dawned on him that the van was heading directly for him and clearly had no intention of stopping.

Bill lowered his head and, through gritted teeth, warned Terry to brace for impact. The enemy, because that's who the man was, threw himself sideways at the last minute, the front left wing of the van clipping his legs, shattering both the man's shins, screaming as he hit the ground hard. The second sentry took the full impact as he turned, alarmed at the yell from his friend. His head hit the windscreen, the glass shattering into hundreds of fragments, bathing Bill and Terry in a shower of glass and blood. The sentry, tossed sideways after the initial impact, crumpled beneath the nearside rear wheel, his legs broken. But it didn't really matter: the fractured skull and crushing chest injury had ensured his death.

Bill slammed on the brakes, throwing Terry forward violently, only the seatbelt preventing him from any injury. Bill grabbed his loaded shotgun, flung the door open, and jumped out at the ready. He ran back to the first man he had hit, banging on the side of the van as he did so, yelling, "Get out, get out." He reached the injured person who was crawling away from the scene, pulling his battered body along with his elbows. He struck the man twice with the butt of his gun, leaving him unconscious or dead while he looked for the man's SA80.

Having found the gun, Bill gathered his group together outside the entrance to the tower block. Jake had been left in the back of the van for now. The shattered door lay just inside the entrance, the blackened frame around it evidence that explosives had been used to blast a way in. Graham and Vic's bodies could be seen crumpled on the paving slabs outside, a pool of blood having congealed beneath and around each one, verification of a brutal death.

"Bastards," exclaimed Bill. "Time we sorted these buggers out."

Two shots were heard from somewhere inside the building. Bill checked their weapons. He had a fully loaded double-barrelled shotgun draped over his neck and shoulder, a piece of thick cord used as a sling. In his hand, he held the SA80, with two magazines he had taken from the attacker stuffed in his pocket. Aleck and Terry had a shotgun each. Terry had swapped with Aleck and now had the double-barrelled shotgun along with a pistol. Aleck was unfamiliar with weapons but knew the basics of how to fire it, and Bill was glad he'd had the TA lads give all of them some instruction on firearms. He just hoped he pointed the Remington in the right direction. Vincent now had a shotgun that had been taken off the attackers.

"Right with me, but keep your weapons pointed downwards until you have a target. I don't want a hole in my backside."

They laughed nervously, sheens of sweat on their faces, visible in the now grey dawn light.

Bill went in first, through the wrecked entrance way, the large reception area empty, the attackers satisfied that the two they had left, plus the occupants of the van, would be sufficient to cover their backs. Ahead was a long central reception desk with a bank of unused lifts behind it, and to the right, where Bill was headed, a wide set of stairs that would take them up the twenty-four storeys of the tower. Bill placed a boot on the first step. The torch, with his fingers over the torch face restricting the glow, showed him the way. The assault rifle, slung around his neck, the grip clutched in his right hand, pointed upwards as he slowly ascended. Terry was on his right, the rest close behind. At the top, the stairs bore left, doubling back on themselves, and Bill peeped around the corner, checking it was clear before climbing the next set of steps. At the top was a short landing, another set of steps off to the left that led up to the second floor, and a door on the right that would take them into the first-floor area. Originally offices, they were now used as a makeshift guards' room, the first barrier to protect the tower block from attack such as this. Another shot resounded above them. Bill pushed the door open slowly, keeping his body back from the door, two bullet holes in it and a number of chips in the wall evidence that there having been a firefight in this area. He shoved the door all the way open, crouching and scanning the area ahead. With what little light there was coming through cracks in the boarded-up windows, he could see one body and recognised from the clothing that it was Howard. No sign of movement, and no one else could be seen.

"Vincent, you wait here and cover our backs. Don't let anyone get past."

"I'll hold it, Bill. Just sort those buggers out," Vincent encouraged.

Bill, Terry still on his right, Aleck not far behind, ascended two more flights of stairs as they zigzagged to the second floor. This floor, normally sealed off, had its door kicked in, but no one was to be seen. Halfway up the next flight of steps, three more shots were heard in quick succession, and the higher up they got the more bullet strikes and holes were evident. Three more floors were cleared, but now, just below the seventh floor, the fight definitely sounded closer. The invaders must have pushed Bill's group back to the eighth floor.

Bill held his hand up, signalling they moved slowly and quietly, then turned off his torch. Just before he got to the corner, he heard voices. When he peered around the corner, dark shadows were lined up along the stairway. A flash of light from a gunshot further up the stairway took away any night vision he may had momentarily. He cursed silently. Pulling Terry and Aleck close in, he whispered instructions, and the three of them moved into position. There was enough noise ahead to disguise any sound they made.

Bill knelt down, just at the base of the steps, on the left, with Terry standing to his right, both barrels of his shotgun pointed at the shadows above. With his shotgun, Aleck also got ready to play his part. *We're as ready as we'll ever be,* thought Bill. He nudged Terry.

One of the shadows, sensing something, turned and looked over his shoulder. He was met by a blinding flash of light and 250 pellets of the number 5 shot that disintegrated his face, turning it into mass of churned-up flesh, bone and blood. As the badly wounded man fell down the steps landing at Terry's feet and nearly knocking him over, and before the other intruders could react, Terry raised the barrels of his gun again and, with a crash of fire, emptied the second load into the two shapes he could see further up. His weapon empty, barrels smoking, the smell of burning gases filling the air and having done what Bill had asked of him, he stepped back to be replaced by Aleck with his shotgun aimed at the attackers above. The attackers now found themselves in the position of being defenders. In the meantime, Bill got up from his crouch and fired round after 5.56mm round into the group above. Not aiming at a specific individual but just wherever he could see a shadow, the shocked faces of the enemy lit up every time he fired a round. The smell of blood and death filled the air. Three more crashed or slithered down the stairs. Five of the eight men who earlier had been waiting for the seven ahead of them to launch an attack were either dead or seriously wounded. The survivors panicked, escaping, charging up the stairs and around the curve, seeking protection from the walls around the corner. They collided with their colleagues causing even more panic and confusion.

Bill didn't bother to check how many rounds he had left but just replaced the magazine and charged up the stairs. The sound of a gunfight higher up the building filtered down. Just before he could turn the corner to follow the fleeing men, the carpeted surface was torn and the concrete beneath chipped as half a dozen rounds ripped into the floor ahead of him. Bill threw himself back against the wall, glad he hadn't turned the corner.

A swathe of fire continued to splatter the small landing, flakes of concrete and masonry ricocheting around the walls and Bill, causing him to bend his head and duck. A sudden racket of shots and crashing footsteps on the stairs could be heard higher up. The firing stopped. Bill took the opportunity to sprint around the corner, firing wild round after wild round into the melee above him, the intruders now trapped between Bill's men at the bottom of the stairway and the counter-attack falling on them from above. Terry came alongside Bill, the shotgun kicking in his shoulder as he fired the first then the second barrel in the direction of the screaming men above.

"Stop, stop!" yelled a voice from the top of the stairs.

"We give in!" screamed another, the sound of weapons clattering to the floor.

"Hold your fire, hold your fire!" bellowed Bill, his ears throbbing from the earlier cacophony of sound and the shotgun cracking in his ear. He had to stop the wild-eyed Terry from continuing, a hand placed on the man's wrist. The people from Bill's group, further up inside the block, must have heard Bill's call as they too ceased firing down into the men below them. Keeping the assault rifle aimed upstairs, Bill flicked on his torch and shone it over the carnage that it exposed. A mass of bloody bodies and limbs, glistening with blood and viscera along with faeces and urine from the evacuated bowels and bladders of the men who had just died.

"Make sure you've dropped all of your weapons and move down the steps one at a time," Bill called to the group. "You, nearest me. Come down first."

Bill looked back around the corner to instruct Aleck to provide additional cover, but the beam of his torch lit up the man's crumpled body draped head first down the stairs.

The survivors of the group that had attacked Bill's tower, Bill's home, came sluggishly down the stairs one at a time, heads lowered, ensuring they didn't have to make eye contact with the men who had just routed them. Ordered to sit on the steps, at least two steps between each man, and instructed not to talk, with Terry watching them from the bottom, Bill called to his group higher up. Robbie, Bill's number two, was the first to appear, his blackened face and wide eyes witness to the ferocity of the fight they had been through.

"Thank God it's you, Bill. I thought we were for the chop there. But we gotta move now."

Bill suddenly smelt something: an acrid smell coming from higher up in the building.

"The bloody place is on fire. These idiots set fire to a door to get into floor seven, and it's caught. The furniture in there is adding to it." Just as Robbie had said that, a cloud of grey smoke drifted down the stairs, stirred up as his people started to evacuate the building. Trevor joined them as Sally, Owen, Mathew, Kelly and others started to make their way down the now smoke-filled stairway.

"Get them to pick up food and water, as much as they can carry," Bill called after Owen,

"OK," Owen called back.

Bill started to cough, the smoke and fumes getting thicker.

"Trevor, take Terry with you, and get these bloody prisoners out of the way. But watch the devious bastards."

"Don't you worry. The first one that makes a move will get a bullet."

Terry and Trevor started to usher the prisoners down the stairs while Bill ascended, giving encouragement to the people evacuating, telling them to pick up as much food, water and supplies as they could on the way down. On the way up, he met a spluttering Simon, the last one to leave the upper floors, pushing the last of the occupants in front of him.

"God, am I glad to see you, Bill."

Both shook hands but quickly got to the point.

"How bad's the fire?"

"It's spreading, and quickly."

"Will we be able to put it out?"

"Not a chance, mate. The entire room is aflame, and it's starting to move upwards. Can you feel the draught?"

Bill felt a sucking breeze pulling at his trousers. "Yes."

"Well, that's feeding it."

"That does it then. In less than an hour, the entire upper levels will be ablaze. We need to evacuate, and fast."

"There's no one behind me."

"Let's go then."

CHAPTER 28

Alan ordered Baxter and Ellis to fire a couple of rounds above the heads of a stream of people entering and leaving the concrete bunker. The ones leaving were clutching the spoils they had managed to acquire, such as blankets, food, water, and even crockery was considered valuable enough to steal. The half-dozen shots fired over their heads caused some to scatter, but a group of thirty to forty who were about to enter, or even re-enter, decided to take on the soldiers. They gathered in a semi-circle, slowly edging round, trying to join up the edges, encircle the men that were going to interfere with their pillaging. The crowd slowly swelled, more coming from the feeding centre, the town and the camp. Once news spread that the defences of the Regional Government Centre had been breached and there were no soldiers, only a few lightly armed policemen, the CPSs choosing cowardice in preference to confrontation to protect it, the mobs moved in.

"Stop where you are!" shouted Alan. "I will personally shoot the next person that moves towards me or my men, or the bunker. You are achieving nothing by continuing this behaviour."

"What you mean is bloody slavery," called a woman from the back of the crowd. Those at the rear pushed those at the front forward, the line edging closer to Alan and his two men, the ones closest to the soldiers' guns spreading their arms to try and hold them back, conscious that they were the ones that risked injury or death.

"All we want is food, not the miserable rations you give us while you live like kings," yelled another.

"You're worse than the bloody commies who bombed us," shouted someone else.

"You know we have to make this food last. If it runs out before we have crops and vegetables ready and proper accommodation for us all with fuel for heating, we will die."

"We're dying now."

"If control is lost now, I promise you, we will all die."

235

The crowd seemed to relax slightly, and Alan felt he was making progress until an empty glass bottle flew over the heads of the mob and struck one of his soldiers. The soldier was unhurt, but it was a trigger for others to throw objects, deemed worth losing, at his small force. The crowd started to surge forward again, and Alan genuinely feared for his and his men's lives.

"Ready!" he ordered.

The soldiers levelled their SA80s, the barrels pointing at the crowd. This time, Alan felt sure his men would open fire. Their blood was up, and adrenalin was still pumping. What made the soldiers angrier was the fact that they had put their lives at risk defending the food and supplies for the very people that now saw them as the enemy. One of their comrades had been badly wounded and needed urgent attention, and their lives were under threat, so they were in no mood for what they deemed an ungrateful population.

"Don't make us open fire. I will give the order." Alan now wished he'd brought more men with him, but he had not anticipated this. He hadn't imagined that the very people he and his soldiers were putting their lives on the line for had would have turned on them. But he'd had to leave the bulk of his force with CSM Saunders to protect the warehouse. They'd won the first bout, but until he and his men could ensure that the enemy had been well and truly been routed and weren't preparing for another assault, it was his only option.

"Sir," whispered Baxter, "they're cutting us off."

As Alan had been talking to the crowd, almost pleading with them to stop the looting, some of the smarter individuals had been leading the edges of the crowd further round, to meet up with each other's side, forming a complete circle and trapping the soldiers.

Alan was about to give the order to open fire when a shotgun was fired by someone near the front of the crowd, the pellets peppering Alan's left arm and shoulder, knocking him back, causing him to stumble over the soldier behind him. As he dropped to the ground, his hand clutching his arm, the warm blood wet on his fingers, a sudden burst of fire, an LMG by the sound of it, shattered the shocked crowd, silenced after seeing the officer get hit and go down. A long burst was sprayed over the heads of the mob, and double taps from other assault rifles added to the crescendo. The crowd panicked, broke and ran, heading away from the bunker as quickly as they were able, stumbling in their weakened state, even dropping some of their contraband in their eagerness to get away.

Baxter helped Alan to his feet as he struggled to get up with his injured arm. "You OK, sir?"

Alan, still dazed, didn't respond immediately. Before he could answer, a tall, lean soldier that he had not seen before brushed the younger soldier aside and stood next to Alan. "Just plant yourself back down again, sir. I need to take a look at that injury."

"Who are you?"

"Name's Rolly, sir. Let's get your kit out of the way. Give us a hand here."

One of Alan's soldiers helped him remove his officer's kit as they sat him back down, Rolly peeling off the officer's shredded combat jacket. A pair of scissors appeared, and Rolly was soon cutting away at Alan's jumper and shirt.

"How's it looking?"

"Lady Luck's on your side today, sir. Range was too great. Messed up your arm and shoulder a bit, but give it a week and you'll be as right as rain. Need to patch you up though. Then get some antibiotics down you."

Another soldier appeared, along with Ellis. Alan ignored the other soldier. "Ellis, sitrep please."

"The crowd has dispersed, sir. Area pretty secure, thanks to the 7th Cavalry here."

"Glad we could assist," responded Glen who had arrived with Ellis. "Seems you've a bit of a situation here, sir."

"It does that…"

"Glen, sir."

"You're unit?"

Rolly continued to patch Alan's wound, wrapping a dressing around the major part of the injury, bathing the rest with an antiseptic cream.

"We're a spec ops unit under independent command."

"Well, Glen, we're certainly glad you came along when you did."

Glen immediately liked this officer. He wasn't like the one they came across on their way from Hereford. This one seemed switched on, but also down to earth.

"There you go, Major. Not the prettiest job but, in the circumstances, it'll hold up until we can get you to a medical centre. You do have one, I take it?" asked Rolly.

Alan got up as quickly as he was able, wavering a little, steadied by Rolly on one side and Baxter on the other.

"You need to take it easy for a bit, sir," advised Rolly. "You're in a state of mild shock, no doubt."

"The RGC?" asked Alan.

"We're about to go in sir," responded Baxter. "Just making sure the bulk of the mob have moved on."

"Pass me my weapon."

Picking the SA80 up, Glen passed it to Alan. "We can help your men. You need to sit this one out."

Alan winced a little as he clutched his gun in his right hand, knowing it would be extremely difficult and a little painful to support the stock with his left. Nevertheless, he slung the weapon over his left shoulder, trying to ignore the pain, but at least he was able to draw his pistol from its holster. "We need to check out the bunker."

"You sure?" asked Glen.

"Definitely. There were, are," Alan corrected, "over sixty people inside it."

"Rolly and me will come with you. The rest of my team can cover us out here. You expecting anything?"

"We've held off an attack from a group of outsiders on a warehouse we have and, as a consequence, things have got out of hand here. How many are you?"

"Just four, but we can manage."

"That's good. I have a small force further west. I'll call in some additional support from them. Ellis, get onto Two-Zero-Alpha. Send a section of four to the RGC."

"Sir."

Alan adjusted his SA-80, "ready?"

"Hang on a sec. Golf, Papa. November and Romeo supporting local forces in bunker. Watch our back. Possibility of external armed hostiles."

"*Roger that,*" responded Greg. "*Plato is with me. Out.*"

Glen turned back to Alan. "Let's make a move then. Lead on, sir."

Alan checked his pistol and then ordered Baxter and Ellis to remain outside to cover their backs until reinforcements arrived from the warehouse. He was relieved that two additional Special Forces soldiers would be supporting his two men. They were far from being in the clear yet.

The three soldiers moved up the right-hand ramp – the left-hand ramp that descended into the depths of the bunker, giving the occupants access to the air plant and control gear. Both ramps were situated, side by side, at the northern end of the bunker complex. The group arrived at the right-hand dog-leg which took them through the blast door. Once inside, steps took them down to the upper level of the two storey bunker. It was dark: the generators had probably been switched off to make it harder for the looters to see items to steal once in the inner depths of the bunker. The air plant was on their left. To the right, the fifty-metre long corridor stretched out in front of them, the odd flickering light from a torch carried by a survivor or looter could be seen at the far end.

Alan turned right. The common room and sickbay were on their left. They could hear the sound of crashes and movement up ahead – perhaps looters scavenging for more stuff, or, hopefully, survivors of the RGC. The common room and sickbay were empty. Alan's torch beam lit up scattered medical supplies strewn all over the floor – obviously not what the intruders had been looking for. The double doors of the canteen, next on the right, were shut and, after being tested by Alan, thought to be locked from the inside. After a quick debate between Alan and Glen, Glen and Rolly put their shoulders into the centre of the double doors, splintering the privacy lock and lock recesses. They flew open easily, and Rolly ended up sprawled on the floor.

"Take another step, and I'll slit your fucking throats," growled a voice from the darkened room.

Alan shone his torch in the direction of the voice: a scowling face, a clear message on it: *Don't fuck with me.*

"It's OK. It's me, Major Redfern."

"Alan?" came a distressed voice from somewhere behind the powerful man facing them.

Alan lowered his pistol. "Just let the hostages out. Then you're free to leave. No harm will come to you."

The female voice piped up again as a head popped around the side of the man holding the knife. "Alan? Is that you?"

"Alison? Are you OK? Has this man hurt you?"

Alison stepped out in front, between Alan and the man they thought was her jailer. She ran towards Alan, ignoring the pistol, and flung her arms around his neck. Alan groaned but continued to allow her to hold him tight, placing his left hand on her back, ignoring his pain but keeping his pistol aimed at the unknown figure. Despite the situation, he actually enjoyed the feeling of being needed by someone and the sensation of her trembling body close to his.

"It's OK, it's OK. I'm here now with some help. We can soon get things cleared up." He prised their bodies apart, wincing again as the pain lanced through his left shoulder.

She recognised something was wrong. "You're hurt," she gasped.

"It's nothing serious. A guardian angel has patched me up."

"Who's that with you?" asked Alison.

"Just some badly needed help. Are there others here with you?"

"Yes, Anjali and Jill. We were all in the kitchen when the place was just swamped with people. They stripped the place of food and just about everything. Then a couple of men decided we would provide them with some entertainment. It was then that our rescuer arrived."

"Do you know him?"

"No, Alan, but if it hadn't been for him I dread to think what might have happened."

"Step forward," ordered Glen, the beam of the torch attached to the end of his HKG lighting up the man's face. "And don't do anything stupid."

The large man moved forward, covering his eyes to protect them from the glare of Glen's torch. The dark, straggly, shoulder-length hair, with a hint of grey but with a well-trimmed goatee beard looked somehow familiar to Alan. He racked his brain to put a name and location to the face.

As the man brushed some dishevelled hairs from the front of his eyes, a picture was immediately dragged from the depths of Alan's memory. "Eddie?"

"Captain."

When they had last met, the man leading a labour group helping to clear the houses of Chilmark of bodies, Alan had held the rank of captain, "decided to rejoin then?"

"Looks like it."

Alan slid his SA80 off his shoulder, not without some discomfort, and handed it to Eddie. "Can you handle one of these?"

"Bit rusty, but I'm sure it'll come back pretty quickly in the circumstances."

"Best look after the women here then and watch our backs." Alan turned to Glen. "You can lower that. He's one of us."

"Must say, I like your recruiting technique, Major," responded Glen as he lowered the HK, the beam of light striking the floor and no longer blinding Eddie.

"Eddie is ex-REME, but would love to serve his country again."

Alan smiled. "Anjali, Jill, you can come out now. You're safe."

Two middle-aged women appeared from a dark recess, tears in their eyes and a little fear still etched on their faces.

"Sorry to butt in with your reunion, Major, but we could do with clearing out this nest of thieves."

"OK. Alison, I'll leave you, Anjali and Jill in Eddie's capable hands. Just keep out of sight until we've made the bunker safe again. Eddie, let anyone out, but no one back in. But watch out for my lads. They'll be a bit trigger-happy. Just give them plenty of warning and tell them you're under the authority of Two-Zero."

"Gotcha, Major."

"We need to move on, sir," Glen reminded him. "OK out there, Rolly?"

"Got it covered."

Half a dozen figures rushed down the corridor, heading out, Rolly moving inside the canteen to allow them to pass. "Rats are leaving," he warned.

With that, Alan, followed by Glen, with Rolly as tail-end Charlie, turned right and headed deeper into the complex. They cleared the four male and two female dormitories, ordering out anyone that couldn't prove they were part of the RGC. Two dead bodies were found in one male dormitory, Alan recognising them as staff belonging to the RGC. The rooms had been stripped of bedding, and even some of the mattresses had been dragged out. The store holding supplies for the bunker had also been cleared out. They emptied the upper level of intruders, shooting two who chose to attack rather than succumb to the soldiers' orders. The section allocated for government departments revealed a third dead body, stabbed to death, a dozen wounds to his face and body.

"We need to go to the lower level. Bottom of the steps and we turn left. The first room is for more government types," Alan informed them.

"You're not short on bureaucracy," suggested Glen.

"I know where you're coming from, but the system was working. Well, up to now, at least."

Alan led them down the concrete steps, his torch providing enough light for them to get to the bottom safely. Glen was close behind, and Rolly was still covering their back. Alan nearly stumbled as his foot caught on the legs of a body prostrate at the bottom of the steps.

"Watch your step," he whispered.

He placed a foot on the concrete floor, and peered around the corner, his flashlight showing the corridor was clear. The government room on the right had two doors, and the strong room was on the right. Alan moved left, keeping central in the narrow corridor. He could hear Glen behind him, the soldier's torch beam shining past Alan's shoulder, moving in line with the gun it was attached to.

Alan stopped. The solid steel door of the strong room was still closed and secure, but the door to the department opposite was wide open. He could hear movement, but no lights were visible. Alan looked round and pointed at the door, indicating he would enter the first doorway and Glen was to watch the second one further down. Both led to the regional Government offices.

Alan moved quickly. The door had already been pushed aside, and he slipped through the gap as he heard Glen move past the entrance, Rolly moving up to watch their backs. Alan's torch lit up three figures at the other end, a flickering match enabling the intruders to rifle through the desks and cupboards in their search for anything that would aid their survival or prove valuable enough to trade. He held his right arm out straight, his pistol steady, the torch wavering slightly as he held it with his wounded shoulder, but the beam fully on the three looters.

"Army. Stop what you're doing and put your hands on your head."

Before there was a verbal response from the looters, or before Alan could take any further action, a blinding flash of light lit up the long room, his eardrums pounded by the blast of the shotgun as pellets rattled overhead, peppering the ceiling. Alan threw himself to the floor as the gunman, one of three intruders, fled out of the farthest door, knocking Glen aside in his haste to escape.

Bang...bang. A double tap from Glen took out one of the two men left. Two further shots from Rolly took out the second intruder, the third managing to escape, fleeing down the main fifty-metre long corridor.

Glen called out. "You with us, Major?"

"Y-yes. He pulled high." Alan pulled himself up, using one of the desks for support, and joined Glen and Rolly at the far entrance.

"You're a lucky guy, Major. Nine lives, eh?"

"Rolly, isn't it?"

"Yes, sir."

"I hope so. I've just used two up in the last couple of hours."

"Sorry to push you, Major. Time's not on our side. I'll take point, Rolly backing me, and you can have tail-end Charlie."

Alan looked at Glen and nodded. "Before we turn the corner, a quick outline of the corridor. Around fifty metres long, similar layout to upstairs. On the left, six rooms, civilian radio, room comms, equipment, HQ radio, the boffins' room, and the military. On the right, conference room, accommodation, secretariat, toilets, our radio shack, and more government areas."

"What's at the end?"

"Oil tanks, generators, control gear, and our water supply."

"Let's get this place cleared then," pushed Rolly.

Glen led the way, looters running from them as they cleared the lower bunker room by room. There were no more incidents. The earlier gunfire had sent a clear message to the remaining looters that order was being enforced again. They did come across a further three dead bodies: two from the government services, the last one a scientist. They regrouped at the main entrance where they were joined by CSM Saunders and a section from the warehouse, and a perimeter was set up. They scouted the immediate area, rounding up as many of the RGC staff they could find and, within two hours, the generator was running again, and, aided by Anjali and Jill, Alison was tasked with providing the soldiers and the survivors of the RGC with a hot drink along with a bowl of soup each. Major Redfern called a meeting which was held in the canteen.

Alison, still shaken up by her recent experience, placed a bowl of hot leek soup in front of Alan, Scott, Glen and Rolly. Jill provided Greg, Plato, Baxter and Ellis with the same. They had pulled chairs around a couple of tables in the canteen and chatted while they tucked in to the first hot meal for twenty-four hours.

"First, Scott, can you update us on the security state?"

"Sure, sir. The standard unit structure has been reinstated. Zero-Charlie have the warehouse, although they're pretty knackered, so we're keeping ops to a minimum."

"Have they scouted the enemy camp again?"

"Yes, sir. Delta have done a recce, nothing. They've scarpered by the looks of it."

"And their wounded?"

"They've been brought into the warehouse, under guard. Saying that, they're in no condition to do anything. There are now fourteen wounded, and two have died in the last hour. We've placed the dead in one of the buildings on the other side of Dyke's Way. Thirteen in total."

"How far out have you patrolled, Sar'nt Major?" asked Glen.

Scott looked at Alan who nodded. "For the country areas, we've scouted out from Wincanton to about five miles. Major routes we've gone as far as twenty miles to the west and back this way as far as Chilmark. North and south, as far as Shepton Mallet and Stalbridge. No sign of them."

"It sounds like you've kicked their arses for them," Greg put forward.

"We've paid the price though," responded Alan. "The RGC staff are scattered to the four winds, and we potentially have up to 4,000 hostile people out there."

"Zero-Bravo have the RGC secured," continued the CSM. "Zero-Echo have done a tour of the town, trying to locate any of the police officers."

"Delta?"

"Once they completed an area search of Wincanton, I had them return to Charlie and remain on standby as the QRF. The lads need a breather, sir."

"I understand, but we're not out of the woods yet. Leave the CVR(T) and Fox at the warehouse, but send a low-key patrol to have a look at the camp and feeding station."

"If it's OK with you, sir, I'll go myself and take a couple of the lads with me."

"Me and Rolly'll come with you," volunteered Greg.

"That OK with you, Major?" asked Glen.

"Yes. Watch yourself, Scott. The locals may still be hostile."

"Will do."

Scott gathered his kit and, along with the two SF soldiers, left to complete a patrol of the area. Alison gave the soldiers half a dozen biscuits each to take with them. The looters hadn't managed to find all of the food in the RGC, she'd added gleefully.

"What are your plans next then, Major?"

"The name's Alan."

Glen nodded. "Alan."

"Look, the survival of those people out there, and us, is dependent on being prepared for the coming winter and beyond."

"Don't you have stocks of food in the warehouse you were defending?"

"Yes, and we have government stocks hidden elsewhere. But

it's not going to last when we need to feed over 4,000 people. And anymore that join us."

"You can just start growing some food as soon as the season is right, can't you?"

They were interrupted as Alison placed piping hot cups of tea in front of the three men, the interruption immediately followed by a second one as Eddie knocked on the door.

"Sorry to butt in, Major."

"What is it, Eddie?"

"A couple have just wandered in, claiming they're from the RGC. Do you want to check them out?"

"Let them in, but keep them secure on the lower level."

"Sort things out later?"

"Yes. Treat them well. We'll get some hot food and drink sorted out soonest."

"Some supplies on their way then?" asked Alison.

"Yes. Could you knock up another urn of soup and one of tea or coffee?"

"Gladly. It'll be good to get back to reality."

"I'll let them know, sir."

"Thanks, Eddie."

Eddie flicked Alan a casual salute and left.

"He one of yours?"

"Plato, is it?"

"Yes, some dumb name these guys dreamed up for me."

"No, he's not. Ex-REME, but was considering taking the Queen's shilling again," laughed Alan.

"Who's in charge here then? You?" asked Glen.

"No, no. We have a principal officer, Mr Elliot. He was a director for the local authority until this was thrust upon him."

"He done a runner?"

"I'm hoping he, along with other members of the Centre, will turn up somewhere, alive."

"He been doing a good job then?" asked Plato.

"As good as you could expect under the circumstances."

"When me and Rolly turned up, the mob were rebuking you for slavery," suggested Glen.

"As I was saying earlier, we need to get ready for when the food runs out. We need to start farming."

"Can't you ask for volunteers?"

Alan took a sip of his tea, placed the cup back down, and leant towards Glen. "We have no tractors, no seed, very little know-how, contaminated land and a workforce that is not in the best of health. But they're the only labour force we have, and the only way to get them working is with the promise of food." He leant back in his seat. "Just look outside, look at the sky. The boffins are telling us that we might not see the sun again for years."

"Hence the cold."

"And it'll get even colder. More importantly, without sunlight, we'll struggle to grow crops, and there'll be too little food for livestock. But anything we can grow will help, no matter how little."

"If you're trying to scare me, Major – Alan, you're doing a pretty good job."

"The Major's right, Glen," agreed Plato. "This is the honeymoon period. When the processed food we have runs out, we need to be able to fend for ourselves. Have you heard from any other RGCs? Or other military or government departments?"

"We were in touch with two RGCs further north. We know at least one was overrun. We haven't heard from the other for nearly a week now, but that could just be communication problems."

"All in all, up until now at least, it seems you've been doing a pretty good job here," acknowledged Glen.

Alan lowered his head. "Not sure how things lie now. Anyway, what are your plans?"

Glen looked across at Plato. "Well, we had all agreed to head for London. See if Pindar is up and running."

"London will have got hit pretty hard."

"That's our worry. But we have to tick that box."

"Why don't you stay here? We could do with all the support as we can find."

"Not sure it's us, Alan, but me and the lads will have a chat about our next move, I'm sure."

Before the conversation could continue, a clattering of boots could be heard coming down the corridor, and Scott, Greg and Rolly came through the door into the canteen. Scott's face told Alan all was not well.

"It's the governor. We've found him."

"And...?"

"He's dead, sir, along with a few other of the senior staff. Superintendent Collins was found with them."

Alan placed his head in his hands, hiding the despair on his face. Alison started to sob by the kitchen door.

There was another clatter of boots as two more soldiers came in with a couple of boxes of supplies, smiles on their faces after surviving the fight with the intruders during the night.

"There you go, sir," trumpeted Sergeant Thompson. "Enough to feed the 5,000."

CHAPTER 29

Bill, Robbie, Trevor, Owen and Simon, grouped in a huddle in a battered shop doorway, discussed the final plans. Looking back, Bill could see the line of people from his group, laden down with food and water, and anything else that was deemed necessary for their survival. Half a dozen of the men stood around in strategic positions, put there by Simon to guard the vulnerable group. The light from the burning tower, the upper storeys now engulfed in an inferno of licking flames and curling smoke, flickered over the huddled group. To him, they looked like wartime refugees: to keep warm, wrapped up in anything they could find on their way out; laden down with their worldly goods; afraid. Bill knew that they were looking to him to keep them safe. But, at the moment, they were exposed and in danger. One gang had already approached them, but they'd quickly backed off when confronted with the array of weapons that Bill and his security team now had in their possession. They were certainly stronger now, but would not be able to survive out in the desolation of the city for long. With thousands of rotting corpses left after the bombs and fires, and rats and dogs having free rein of the city, Weil's disease, typhoid, typhus, dysentery, tuberculosis and even an outbreak of cholera amongst the survivors were serious risks. Bill knew he had to act, and act quickly.

The other four men looked at Bill, wanting answers, needing answers to the plight they had found themselves in.

"Do we try and find another tower, Bill?" asked Robbie.

"If they're any good, they'll be too well defended," suggested Trevor.

"We can fight our way in. Take one over for ourselves," proclaimed Simon.

"No, not an option," Bill finally answered. "We need somewhere we can protect, somewhere where we can defend ourselves and, equally as important, somewhere we can keep warm. The temperature's dropping every day, and winter's not even upon us yet."

"Where then, Bill?" challenged Robbie, starting to feel a little exasperated by Bill's calm exterior.

"The Underground, the Tube stations."

"Shit," exclaimed Trevor. "Why the fuck didn't I think of that?"

"Of course," added Simon.

"Won't they have been used as bomb shelters?" asked Simon.

"Could still be occupied."

"It's a possibility," agreed Bill, "but there's nothing down there, so most people will probably have left after the all-clear. Anyway, there was some scaremongering, if you remember. People were afraid of being trapped down there when the bombs hit."

"It's worth a try."

"It is, Robbie. So, let's get this show on the road. Let's get everyone moving. I'll take a dozen on ahead to scout the area, and we'll take it from there. Agreed?"

All four agreed, to a man.

"Let's go then."

For more information about Harvey Black, his works and background information, including maps and photos, visit his website at www.harveyblackauthor.org.

Lightning Source UK Ltd.
Milton Keynes UK
UKOW04f1940250315

248537UK00004B/239/P